THE AURORA ANTIDOTE

THE AURORA ANTIDOTE

Book I of the Aurora Anthology

By Ela Hugh

The Aurora Antidote

Copyright © 2023 by Ela Hugh

First edition, 2023

Published by Fox-on Fiction

All rights reserved.

www.foxonfiction.com

This book is a work of fiction. Any references to real people, places or events are used fictitiously. Other names, characters, places and incidents are the product of the author's imagination, and any resemblance to actual persons, living or dead, events or locales is entirely coincidental.

Library and Archives Canada Cataloguing in Publication information available upon request.

ISBN 978-1-9994232-0-9 (paperback)

Also available in electronic form.

Edited by Kim Graff

Cover artwork by Nikkie Stinchcombe

Cover lettering by Teresa Bonaddio

*For Sean and Stephanie,
my sassy and spirited,
yet always supportive siblings.*

CHAPTER ONE

KIT'S KINGDOM

"Refill?"

Kit shifted his dark, maroon coloured eyes towards the bartender for only a moment, and nodded. He swiftly slid his glass over to the sturdy looking barkeep, without once turning his head to face him.

"Another ginger ale?" asked the bartender, clearly annoyed with his sullen patron's choice of drink. But Kit did not answer him.

"Alright," said the bartender, as he seized the glass with his large left hand, and reluctantly refilled its contents with a bottle that he pulled from beneath the bar. His eyes remained fixed upon his customer. It was not often that he served men like this in his grungy Old Las Vegas pub.

Most of the men coming in and out of *The Rose* were large, brawny, and often had ugly and coarse faces. Kit, on the other hand, appeared to be the embodiment of all that was sleek and smooth. The clean, black hood fitted over his head could not hide the beauty concealed beneath it. His was a face which could have been described as 'perfection'. This boy belonged in a cheesy cologne television advertisement – not in *The Rose*. The bartender wondered how long it would be before one of his regulars picked a fight with him, and how many blows it would take to bring the boy to his knees. The thought brought a crooked smile to his fat lips, and he sniggered quietly.

The sound caught Kit's attention, and he quickly turned and stared into the barkeep's eyes. His eyes squinted, but the rest of his face remained completely still. He nimbly snatched the freshly poured drink from the startled bartender's hand, and in an instant, twisted his body back into place. With his back turned towards the bar, he sipped at the fizzy beverage and silently resumed his surveillance of the dimly lit, cigarette smoke-filled pub.

Kit's quiet confidence confused the burly barkeep. His demeanour betrayed no unrest, no nervousness, no fear. It was past midnight, and *The Rose* had a full house. Shady, beady-eyed, drunken roughnecks from all corners of Old Vegas populated the room. Any other man, when faced with such a crowd, would at the very least have experienced some form of anxiety. Yet, Kit sat on the small barstool there in silence, gazing over the rest of the pub like a King seated on his throne overseeing his realm and his subjects. His calm and assured composure was unsettling, and caused feelings of unease to stir in the pit of the otherwise unflinching bartender's stomach.

It had been nearly two and a half hours. Kit had consumed three drinks in that time, and had not once shown any signs of fatigue, impatience or boredom. He only sat – constantly scanning his obscure surroundings, as if patiently waiting for something, or someone.

"C'mon, Freddy! One more game!"

The sudden exclamation had come from the small back room set in the corner of *The Rose* farthest from the bar. Frederick Jones stood under the frame of the room's large, wooden door. He kept it ajar with one hand and waved at his opponents, who were still seated at *The Rose*'s back room poker table.

"Nah! I'm outta here!" cried Freddy, belligerently. "I'll see you ladies on Sunday! For another whopping!" He turned and let the door shut behind him and on his card companions, who continued to hurl loud insults at him from within.

There was silence in *The Rose* now, as all eyes, including Kit's, fixed themselves upon Freddy, as he leisurely strut his way between tables, towards the bar. He wore crisp, dark jeans, a clean white shirt and a caramel coloured leather jacket. His attire looked expensive and brand new, as though he had just walked out of a designer clothing store, adorned with his purchases. His skin was darker than most men in *The Rose* that night, and although his head was shaved, one could clearly see the roots of his hair were jet black. His dark, almond-shaped eyes and the large, black tribal tattoo decorating the right side of his neck betrayed his Native American heritage.

He smiled to himself. It seemed the cards had been good to him. Stepping up to the bar, he called to the bartender by name.

"Jimmy! Your best whisky on the rocks!"

Jim Rose appeared all too happy to oblige. He was glad to be serving something other than ginger ale, and was grateful for the distraction from the awkward exchanges he'd been made to endure with the strange hooded pretty-boy, still seated at the other end of the bar. He worked fast, throwing ice cubes into a clean glass, and pouring the golden fluid over top.

"Good night?" he asked casually, as he handed the drink to Freddy.

"Ohhh yeah!" Freddy replied. He quickly tilted his head back and downed the entire drink in one swig. Slamming the empty glass back onto the bar, he exhaled loudly. "In fact, I think I'll head on up to the Strip and find myself some action. I'm on a winning streak these days, Jimbo!" He smiled, revealing yellowish and slightly crowded teeth, before reaching into his jacket pocket and pulling from it a fifty-dollar bill. He tucked the bill into the bartender's front shirt pocket and gently tapped his chest, letting the barkeep know he could keep the change. With a nod of his head and an arrogant wink of his eye, he turned his back on the bar and headed for the exit.

Some of the men around the room watched him go, their eyes full of envy and resentment.

Meanwhile, Kit had continued to observe Freddy's boisterous antics from his own seat at the bar. Unlike the rest of the men in *The Rose* who watched, his attentions had not been drawn by Freddy's drunken cries of victory. In fact, Kit had targeted the poker room's door the very moment it had first creaked open.

It had taken Kit months to track down this particular Las Vegas punk, and he had spent the last few weeks learning everything there was to know about him.

Freddy's life, it seemed, had been unremarkable. One could even have described it as unfortunate. His childhood had been spent on an American Indian reservation in western Arizona. From what Kit could tell, Freddy's father had been an alcoholic, and had physically abused both Freddy and his mother. At the age of seventeen, Freddy had left the reservation and come to Las Vegas. Being uneducated and altogether inexperienced, he had quickly fallen in with the wrong crowd. Kit had found evidence of multiple arrests by the police for suspected robberies and assaults.

Like so many before him, Freddy had developed a gambling addiction that had slowly destroyed what little life he'd had left. He had accumulated sizeable debt, and had inadvertently sold his soul to a number of especially dangerous Las Vegas loan sharks. A few months ago, Freddy had hit rock bottom when he was beaten to within an inch of his life – most likely for failing to make yet another payment on one of his illegal loans. But then... everything had changed for Freddy. There was a silver lining to his story, after all.

After Freddy had recovered from the attack, he had somehow come into a large fortune. He had paid off all of his debts – plus interest. Suddenly, he'd had enough cash to put himself up in the penthouse of one of the Las Vegas Strip's most exclusive hotels. He'd purchased a number of expensive sports cars, dozens of glamorous toys and lavish accessories. He'd reinvented himself, and almost overnight, gone from scruffy to flashy.

Kit had spent the last few weeks attempting to learn the source of

Freddy's unexpected affluence. Freddy himself had gone about town claiming to have received a grand inheritance from a distant relative. But Kit knew this to be a lie. He'd investigated Freddy's family tree in great detail, and it was there that he'd discovered what made Freddy so very special. It wasn't some *rich cousin* who'd 'hit the jackpot' and uncovered a gold vein in South Dakota, as Freddy had reported. It was so much more than that…

Kit's thoughts were interrupted then, by the sound of Freddy slamming the front door of *The Rose* behind him on his way out. And mere seconds later, he was on his feet. Pulling a silver money clip from his back pocket, Kit carefully removed a few bills from his stash and deposited them onto the bar. He took one last glance at the large bartender, before he too, made his way out of *The Rose*.

Jim Rose watched as the strange boy left his sight. He mumbled "good riddance" under his breath, as he saw him disappear with the closing of the pub's large, glass panelled door. *There was something different about that boy*, he thought, *something in his eyes*. He couldn't quite tell what it was, only a peculiar sense that he didn't belong. Jimmy was pleasantly surprised by the large tip Kit had left behind. But still, he silently hoped it was the last he should ever see of him.

◆

It was a clear and cool night. *The Rose* was located on an unusually quiet cul-de-sac in Old Vegas, and so there was not another person in sight when Kit stepped out of the pub. All was silent, which made it easier for him to hear the sound of Freddy's stomping footsteps, only a few meters ahead of him, around the corner to his left. He turned to face the direction from which the sound had originated, and nimbly took his first steps to follow.

Freddy was a fast walker, and he had a head start on him. Kit considered upping his speed to a slow jog to catch up, but decided against it. He was confident he would not lose his mark.

Agile as a cat, Kit moved silently between buildings – all the time, never losing track of Freddy's clatter. It was clear the man was intoxicated, as Kit could clearly hear him singing to himself, as he happily and aimlessly strolled through the dark streets.

Kit sighed as he envisioned the long night ahead of him. He did not relish the thought of stalking this drunk. The man was undoubtedly lost. But Kit knew he had to press on, as long as there was even a *slight* possibility tonight was the night Freddy would lead him to where he wanted to go.

And so, Kit continued on in his pursuit, taking one step after another for what felt like ages – his feet guided by the sound of Freddy's awful song and heavy footfalls. The tediousness of his task soon took its toll, and his thoughts wandered towards the star-filled sky…

Kit had always taken comfort in the night sky. He had no *real* home or family – not for a very long time. Wherever he went, though, the moon and stars were forever the same. *Constant.* No matter where he laid his head down to sleep at night, the familiar lights were always there with him. Unchanged by time and space.

Lost in thought, Kit failed to register the faint shift in the air around him. His mind snapped back to attention. He could no longer hear Freddy's off-tune singing. It had been replaced with the *almost*-silence of his surroundings.

Kit stopped and stood perfectly still, alert. *An 'almost' silence,* he thought to himself. The sound had come from behind him. A very faint rustling. Kit turned on the spot, his body pulling a complete 180-degree spin. He'd made his way into a tight alley, which on first inspection appeared deserted.

Taking two steps forward, Kit carefully scanned the darkness. There was no fear in his heart, only a nagging curiosity. In all his years, he thought, *no one* had ever managed to track him. And so, he took another step, examining the alley one last time.

But for a few scraps of trash littering the pavement, the alley was definitely empty. Even *he* must have flights of imagination at times, he supposed.

Dismissing his momentary alarm, Kit turned on his heels to resume his hunt, only to find himself doubled over and in extreme pain. There was a sharp sting in his abdomen. It was cold. His eyes began to water, and his vision blurred.

Kit managed to lift his head, and was able to discern the shape of a man standing in front of him. The man was close. He clasped Kit's shoulder with his left hand and twisted what must have been a blade, plunged deep into Kit's stomach. Kit felt it violently ripping deeper into his flesh. He moaned softly and fell to his knees. The man knelt and followed him down. Kit could see into his eyes now. Hard, black eyes. He also glimpsed what appeared to be a large scar, running across the man's lower jaw. The man's teeth were clenched, but his face was otherwise calm. Kit felt his heart pounding in every inch of his body. His breathing became quick and laboured, his mouth dry. The feeling was foreign to him. Was he… afraid?

Confused, Kit wondered how this man had managed to sneak up on him. *Where did he come from?* he thought, *Does it even matter?* Kit had lost, and the thought occurred to him that he might not survive. Gently, he closed his eyes, desperately longing for the home he had once known.

All he had been thinking before then left his mind. And all that remained now was the image of a beautiful garden, bathed in white light and crowned by a large tree adorned with thousands of tiny, white blossoms. Their sweet cherry scent filled his nostrils, and he felt his body instinctually being pulled away from his dark surroundings, towards the paradise in his thoughts. The blade in his belly turned scorching hot then. It felt like he was roasting from the inside out. Kit lost feeling in his legs – as though the life force within them had been sucked into the blade lodged in his core. His eyelids fluttered momentarily, and he glimpsed the knife protruding from his gut. He thought he saw it glowing ever so slightly, and there was darkness once again, as his eyes slammed shut.

The pain was throbbing now. Kit drew in a breath of air, summoned his strength and grabbed at his attacker's chest. His hand caught the man's clothing, and he clenched his fingers around the fabric tightly. His head began to spin, and as his last breath left his lungs, he was ripped away from the alley.

Kit gasped for air and sunk down onto his heels. He was still on his knees, but his entire body was loose and slumped over. His hand found his abdomen. The knife was gone, and he felt the warmth of his blood running down his belly now, and over the palm of his hand. He opened his eyes, but all he could see were blinding lights. He could sense a commotion around him, the sound of moving cars, shoes on pavement and falling water. The image of the garden was gone. Panic gripped Kit's heart.

Where am I? he thought.

The sweet scent of the cherry blossoms had disappeared also. All he smelled now was his own blood. Something collided with him. He was knocked over onto his side, his blood spilling onto the ground and flooding his mouth. There was a shrill cry – a woman shrieking, drawing more commotion. There were whispers coming from every direction, and then, there was nothing.

-- CHAPTER TWO --

DYLAN IN THE DARK

Dylan Dubois lay sleeping uncomfortably in her room. She groaned quietly and rolled over, causing the sweat-soaked sheets of her bed to wrap tightly around her thin body. Her eyes shifted rapidly from side to side beneath her eyelids.

She stood in a field. The grass surrounding her was thick and tall. Slowly, she moved forward through the brush. The long blades on either side of her were parted, allowing her to glimpse a large rock formation almost twenty yards ahead. Running through the center of the cliffside was a narrow opening. In gazing at the gap in the stone, Dylan felt her heart skip a beat. She drew in a sharp breath of air and rushed forward, reaching it in a mere bound.

The sound of flowing water tingled in her ears. It seemed to be resonating from somewhere within the hollow. Drawn onwards by the echoes, Dylan pushed against the opening – again, and again. Yet try as she did, she could not reach their source. Her muscles ached from attempting to push her body past the rock. She clawed at the stone as hard as she could, but it did not give.

Bruised and tattered, Dylan peered through the crevice in a last desperate attempt to see what it was within the cave, which called her forth. All was dark, but for a faint glow coming from deep within. There, masked by the light, was the outline of her mysterious prize. It called to her, yet again. And so Dylan resumed her efforts to move past the mouth of the cave. Summoning all of her strength, she threw her body against the gap. Pain shot through her shoulder and deep into her sides, as she collided with the stone. She cried out. Yet the sound of her voice did not reach her ears. Only a low rumble from deep within her chest.

Gasping for air and freeing her arms from her bed sheets cocoon, Dylan jumped and woke from yet another restless sleep. Her eyes wide, she sat there, her body shaking gently. Perspiration ran down from her forehead and onto her cheek. Dylan cupped her face in her hands and slowly ran them upwards through the roots of her long, wavy hair. Her face, which under normal circumstances was soft and gentle, appeared strained and worn. It had been weeks since she'd had a good night's sleep.

"Not again," she mumbled under her breath.

Supporting her weight with her arms, Dylan slowly swung her legs off the edge of her bed and placed her bare feet firmly upon the wooden floor of her room. Though still shaking slightly, she managed to stand and proceeded to take a step towards the door, clumsily stumbling over an old backpack left lying in her path.

"Damn it," she swore without thinking.

Dylan immediately clasped her hand over her mouth. Her roommate and best friend, Holly, was sound asleep in the next room. She did not wish to rouse her.

Quietly, she made her way past the small living room to the kitchen, and poured herself a glass of water. Her mouth was dry. She had most likely been breathing heavily and talking in her sleep again. Raising the glass to her lips, she swallowed thirstily. Her heart rate had slowed significantly since leaving her bedroom, and Dylan could feel the shakiness leaving her limbs now. After lightly placing the glass on the counter, she made her way back towards the living room and plumped herself down on the sofa nearest the window.

She peered out onto the night lit streets of downtown Montreal.

It was a rainy night. Raindrops upon the window made it difficult to see anything below her second floor apartment. Nevertheless, Dylan sat staring through the foggy window and watching the occasional car go by – its bright headlights illuminating the road. Her delicate eyebrows furrowed uncharacteristically, as her mind turned back to the nightmare she'd been having.

Why is it I can never remember what's in that cave? she thought. *It's important. I know it is.*

A chill passed over Dylan then, causing goose bumps to form all along her long, bare legs. The fever she had suffered due to the dream was now wearing off; and the loose-fitting plaid blouse she wore was not enough to keep her warm on this cool October night.

Shivering, Dylan reached for the woollen blanket that sat on the other end of her couch, perfectly folded. As she removed it from its resting place, she glimpsed what had been hidden beneath it – her old family photo album. Dylan's father had brought it over the night he had visited with her sister. They had come over to celebrate Dylan's twenty-first birthday.

That must have been over a month ago now, she thought to herself, a sudden sadness falling over her features.

Holding the album tightly in her hands, Dylan sat back down and stared intently at the dark cover. She shifted her body uncomfortably, so as to reach the lamp on the small stand behind her, switched on the light, and was momentarily stunned. Gently, she reopened her big, green eyes as they adjusted to the light and fixed themselves once more upon the photo album. Throwing the blanket over her legs, she proceeded to open the album carefully, as if it may disintegrate if her movements were too sudden.

The first page of the album featured only one large photo. A family photograph, like any other. Dylan's father was smiling widely in it. His body was bent forward, and he held his wife (Dylan's mother) by the shoulder with his left hand. He was a jolly looking man, white skinned with rosy cheeks and bright green eyes. Dylan's mother was darker and had short, straight, black hair. Any man would have described her as beautiful. She smiled as though it was the happiest day of her life, her arms wrapped tightly around the necks of two children. Two girls. One was taller than the other – Dylan looked as though she was less than ten years old in the photograph. But she was unmistakable. Her hair was as long as ever, dark brown and wavy. She had the same gleaming green eyes as her father, but the rest of her facial features were fragile and feminine looking like her mother's. The other girl in the picture looked as though she were only five or six years old. Her hair was nearly blonde, and her skin paler than her mother's. She was laughing and gazing adoringly at her elder sister.

"Dani," Dylan whispered, tears welling up in her eyes.

Dylan felt her throat tighten, as she attempted to hold back the sudden swell of emotions within her. The photograph had reminded her of a happier time in her life, a time when her family had been complete, a time when she had not felt so alone. The picture had been taken over ten years ago, before her mother's passing.

Although Dylan had never really missed her mother, she'd always wished she'd had a chance to know her better. She had died so suddenly… For the longest time, Dylan's only family had been her father and sister, and that had been enough. They had lived cheerfully and without incident. That is, until nearly three weeks prior.

Warm tears rushed down Dylan's cheeks now. Hastily, she wiped them away with the soft sleeve of her blouse. She grabbed a tissue from the coffee table in front of her and blew her nose, gently crumpling the tissue in her hand as she finished. Drawing her long legs in close to her chest, she rested her head on her knees. Her face was turned towards the window, and she wept quietly, as she watched heavy raindrops fall upon the glass.

-- CHAPTER THREE --

HOUSE AND HOLLY

"Pickle, wake up! I made breakfast."

Dylan creased her nose and slowly squeezed her already closed eyelids, so as to delay re-joining the waking world.

"Don't call me that," she mumbled, as she pulled the tiny blanket covering her body tighter over her shoulders. "It's too early."

'*Pickle*', as it turns out, was an unfortunate nickname Dylan had picked up as a child. Growing up, her friends had shortened her name to '*Dyl*', and from there, the name had naturally evolved into '*Dill Pickle*', and then to simply: '*Pickle*'. The teasing she'd received had never been particularly malicious or wicked. Nonetheless, Dylan still disliked the reminder. And so, obviously, her best friend had taken to calling her by the name fairly regularly.

"Pickle? I can't hear you. You'll have to speak up."

The sound of Holly's voice was unmistakable. It was deep for a woman's, but also warm and soft. The pitch of her voice was counter-productive in this one instance though, as the comfort flowing from her tone only encouraged Dylan's slumber.

Dylan drew her legs in closer to her body, and buried her face even deeper into her pillow.

"Dylan!"

Holly's voice had turned now. Patience had never been one of her strong suits.

"It's getting cold. Wake up! I'm not telling you again."

Dylan discerned the clinking sound of a plate being placed on a table's surface, somewhere very near to her face. The smell of fresh bacon and eggs reached her nostrils, and she cautiously allowed one of her eyelids to open, so as to assess the scene. Only then did she realize she was still in her living room. She'd fallen asleep on the sofa, flipping the pages of her father's photo album.

"My album!" she cried, suddenly springing to her feet.

"I've got it," Holly reassured her. She held the volume up in her hand, and carefully placed it upon the wooden coffee table, next to Dylan's cooling breakfast. "Now would you eat something, please?"

Dylan let out a sigh of relief, before deciding to obey her friend. She sat back down, reached for the plate and leaned back to consume her breakfast. "You know you don't always need to feed me, right?"

Holly was bent over, picking up Dylan's used tissues from the floor. "Oh yeah?" she teased. "Cause you've been doing *such* a good job of that yourself these past few weeks."

Sensing the sarcasm in her voice, Dylan smiled. She knew her friend had a point. She'd been so pre-occupied of late; she hadn't been the best at looking after herself…

Apparently recognising the look of gratitude washing over her friend's face, Holly gave her a gentle smile. She shuffled past Dylan's lap and sat down on the couch beside her.

Dylan watched her move, all the while, shoving large spoonfuls of scrambled eggs into her mouth. The food, although lukewarm, was oddly satisfying. Dylan supposed she hadn't appreciated just *how* hungry she'd truly been. Holly had once again predicted and seen to her needs, before she'd even had an inkling of them herself. Her friend's efficacy in this was both commendable and… slightly irritating, all at the same time. Dylan grimaced at the thought, but quickly wiped the expression from her face, when she saw Holly turn to face her.

The look on her friend's face too, it seemed, had shifted. Holly's bright blue eyes, now overflowing with sincere concern, bore into hers like a drill. Dylan swallowed a big bite of bacon and felt a lump forming in her throat.

"Dyl," Holly started, "we need to talk about these dreams." Dylan opened her mouth, about to protest, but Holly interrupted her: "I know what you're going to say. That I shouldn't worry, that you're fine. But Pickle, I really think you should talk to someone. I heard you last night. This *isn't* normal. You've been having this same dream for weeks now."

"It's not *always* the same," Dylan clarified hesitantly.

Holly flashed her a look of exasperation. "Dylan, stop. You know what I'm saying. It's the same 'brand' of dream, then. Every night." She sighed and slumped her shoulders.

Holly Andersen was the same age as Dylan – twenty-one. She had a 'girl next door' look that never failed to charm those around her. Her hair was a gorgeous blonde, and her cheeks... usually had a beautiful pink glow to them. There was no red in Holly's cheeks today, however. All of the colour had gone from her face. Dylan saw the dark circles under her eyes. She saw her friend's tired skin, and realized how the last few weeks might have taken its toll on her as well.

Holly turned to face her. "I just worry about you."

"I know," Dylan replied, "but I'm going to be fine. You'll see." A thoughtful expression came upon Dylan's features, and she added: "Besides, they don't *feel* bad. The dreams, I mean. I don't know how to explain it. I just know. They're more like... " She struggled to express herself, and then sighed before adding: "I just feel like... they're something I have to figure out on my own, you know?"

Dylan smiled hesitantly, as if seeking permission from her

concerned friend.

Holly gave her a blank look. "You know you're crazy, right?" she asked, a familiar smile forming on her lips.

Dylan laughed, and they both sat there quietly a moment, gazing at each other affectionately.

Holly rose from her seat, taking Dylan's empty plate from her as she went. She crossed the tiny living room and entered the kitchen, where she quickly washed the dish and placed it to dry on a rack next to the sink. Drying her hands, she turned back to face her friend, adding in a defeated tone: "I guess I'll just have to leave you to it then. But I'm not letting this go, Dyl. And you have to promise me: If it gets out of hand, you'll see a doctor." Holly waved her hands about casually, some of the flush returning to her cheeks. Her eyes wandered so as to avoid Dylan's gaze, and she finished: "You know… a shrink?"

Upon hearing Holly's words, Dylan frowned and rose from her seat. There were *a lot* of things she needed at the moment. On that, she could agree. But a *'shrink'*, she thought… was not one of them!

Deliberately ignoring her friend's comment, Dylan retreated to her room and began rummaging through her wardrobe.

"Alright!" Holly hollered back at her from the other room. "You're right. I shouldn't have said it."

Dylan heard footsteps and turned to find her friend standing in her doorway. Holly was leaning against the doorframe, watching her sift through a pile of laundry on the floor.

"I'm sorry, Pickle."

"Forget it, Holly. It's fine. But… you know how I feel about 'psychologists'." Dylan rolled her eyes as she uttered the dirty word. *Psychologists! What a waste of time,* she thought. She resumed her search for clothing and went on, never turning to face her friend:

"Dad made me see one when Mom died, and… I hated every

minute of it. So let's just drop it, OK?"

"Sure," Holly replied, her eyes glued to her feet.

Too busy tossing about different articles of clothing, Dylan failed to notice her friend's repentant manner. She stood up straight and searched about the messy room, only to have her attentions further diverted to the desk on the far side by the window.

Sitting there, atop a dusty stack of books, was a gorgeous bouquet of bright yellow flowers. Quietly, Dylan made her way across the room to it. Up close, she saw the bouquet consisted of exactly eight stems of a very distinctive species of flower. Dylan recognized it immediately. A single yellow petal wrapped-up upon itself around a lone filament of pollen. Like a cone – wrapped tightly around a glistening treasure…

Mom's flower, she thought to herself smiling.

Her mother had called them: *'Serradas'* – a very rare species of Calla Lily, which resembled upside-down, golden yellow bells.

She couldn't help herself. Dylan reached for the bouquet, and slowly picked a single stem from the bunch. She turned to face her friend, a dozen questions shining in her eyes.

"Don't look at me," said Holly, holding her hands up preemptively. "Someone dropped them off for you this morning."

Although Holly refrained from telling her *who* had made the special delivery, Dylan knew almost immediately.

Michael, she thought. *It had to be Michael.*

"He remembered…" she said to herself softly, a gentleness falling over her features.

Dylan had only ever told her ex-boyfriend of her mother's flower once. But of course, he'd remembered. *He always remembered.*

"He asked how you were," said Holly then, tentatively.

But the unexpected gentleness had already retreated from

Dylan's face.

"Oh yeah?" she asked, feigning indifference and grabbing an old pair of jeans from atop her bed. "Why?"

Dylan pulled a white T-shirt over her head, and Holly answered:

"Well… because he cares about you, Pickle. I know you said you don't want to see him. But… he's stopped by a few times now. Maybe you should give him another chance? I mean, you two *were* together for nearly a year."

At this, Dylan threw her friend a tired look.

While Michael had been (for all intents and purposes) her boyfriend of nearly a year, the relationship had found its natural end, she thought. *Long* before all of the tragic events of late.

The recent fire at Dylan's family home had forced Dylan to re-evaluate many facets of her life. Losing a father had a way of… putting things into perspective. And it was time to face facts. Michael just… hadn't made the cut.

Since the accident, Dylan knew Michael had been trying to reach out to her. He'd called, left her voicemails, and even showed up at their apartment a few times. Unmoved by his efforts, however, Dylan had yet to reciprocate his advances. *He feels bad. I get it.* But alleviating Michael's guilt just… wasn't on her list of priorities at the moment.

Having finished dressing herself, Dylan grabbed her backpack from the cluttered floor and quickly filled it with items that she picked from various corners of her room. A wallet, a green cardigan, her cell phone, a bundle of keys and a thick envelope, which had been resting atop a large pile of official-looking documents beneath her desk.

"I'm sorry, Holly," she said. "I know you've always liked Michael. But… I just can't, OK? He and I… we're just done."

Holly merely nodded supportively in reply. She followed Dylan out of her room, and watched her slip into her leather boots at their front entrance.

"I'll see you at the hospital?" she asked. "We have Dani's appointment today."

"Yeah, I remember. 3:00 o'clock."

Holly was quiet thereafter, but Dylan saw the solemnness return to her friend's clear blue eyes. With difficulty, she forced herself to ignore it and stepped out of their apartment. She closed the door behind her, and after taking a few steps down the hall, stopped herself at the edge of their building's stairwell.

In her left hand, Dylan still held the single stem she'd picked from the bouquet of Serradas back in her room.

Carefully, she glanced back behind her. Judging herself sufficiently alone, she held the stem up in front of her and fixed her eyes intently upon the flower's bright yellow center. A softness settled back into her features, and gently, she closed her eyes. Holding the blossom up to her nose, Dylan slowly inhaled its sweet fragrance. A moment of quiet contemplation was all she allowed herself, before exhaling a deep and dispirited sigh.

And so, with a heavy heart, Dylan resumed her journey down the stairwell, out of the apartment building.

-- CHAPTER FOUR --

THIEF

"I told you he was handsome."

Susan Hill, an Emergency Room nurse at Sunrise Hospital and Medical Center in Las Vegas, had been caring for Kit and tending to his wounds for almost a week now.

"Dr. Chandler and I call him," she paused a moment and lowered her voice before going on, chuckling: "'*Sleeping Beau*'."

Susan spoke to her colleague, Margaret Miller, one of the newer additions to the ER team at Sunrise.

Margaret smiled shyly back at her supervisor. She agreed with Susan's overall assessment of their patient. He did have a particular glow about him. The man, whom she estimated to be in his mid or early twenties, had been knifed less than a week ago. And yet, he was lying in the hospital bed looking more like he'd just rolled out of a weeklong spa treatment. His face was radiant. He had striking features that were soft, yet still masculine. Locks of his hair were swept over his forehead untidily. The hue of his hair made him all the more special. Margaret had never seen hair like his before. It was very peculiar – a sort of strawberry blonde, only with a deeper reddish tint to it. A beautiful shade, she wondered if it was natural.

"Pass me the fluids, Margie."

Susan's request interrupted Margaret's thoughts. She had been staring at Kit almost dreamily. "I wonder what colour his eyes are," she blurted out stupidly without thinking, as she passed the clear bag of IV fluids over Kit's unconscious body, to her boss. Her cheeks turned pink as the words escaped her mouth.

Susan chuckled heartily, her large bosom jumping up and down. "We'll know soon enough," she said. "Doctor says he should have been up yesterday. I reckon we'll be seeing those eyes open any minute now."

She quickly replaced Kit's IV bag, and was proficiently adjusting his antibiotic drip. "I'm more anxious to hear his story. You know they found him right outside the Bellagio? Right by the fountains. Can you believe it? And no one saw nothing!"

"Really? That *is* strange," Margaret replied, as she watched Susan's skilful hands lift the sheets from Kit's slumbering body.

"Will you help me with his bandages, darling?"

Margaret nodded to her supervisor, as she leaned over to help Susan lift Kit's hospital gown over his chest.

With the bed sheets removed, Margaret got a better view of Kit's physique. It was lean, yet still strong and muscular. His skin, she saw, was both soft and fair. Try as she did, she couldn't stop herself from blushing.

"Honey! He won't be the last looker you see come through here. Pull yourself together, will ya?" said Susan, her southern accent coming through clearer than before.

"Yes, ma'am," answered Margaret sheepishly.

The two nurses slowly removed the bandages from Kit's abdomen and replaced them with fresh ones.

"Almost no blood, and his incision looks good," Susan commented. "He's healing up real nice."

"Yes," Margaret agreed, as she applied fresh tape to his belly.

She had only just finished applying the last piece, when Kit's body made a sudden movement.

Margaret barely had time to look up at Susan, before Kit's hand had instinctually darted from the bed and to her wrist. He held her arm tightly in his hand now, his eyes open wide, staring at her.

"Sir, it's alright. You're in the hospital," she told him.

"I'll get Dr. Chandler," Susan assured her, as she ran from the room.

Kit had sprung into a seated position, and his eyes hungrily searched around. He was dazed, confused. His thoughts chaotic. He squeezed Margaret's tiny arm reflexively, as he tried to make sense of his situation.

He'd been in an alley following Freddy. And now, he was where exactly? A hospital? *Yes, definitely a hospital.* The scent of putrefaction and disinfectants filled his nostrils. He had to hold his breath to keep from gagging. Kit had always loathed hospitals. The taste of death and disease… *Disgusting*, he thought. *But why am I here? Surely, there was no need for this.*

There came a slight aching pain in his belly then. Kit's face became perturbed as he looked down and caught sight of his bandages for the first time. His memories came tumbling back. He'd been stabbed. A man had followed him. In the alley. *The knife…*

Margaret's whimpering disturbed his thoughts. Kit turned his gaze to examine her. He hadn't realized he'd been gripping her so tightly. She stared at him, wordlessly pleading with him to release her. Carefully, Kit loosened his hold of her arm, and she pulled it back in towards her. She was quivering. He'd frightened her.

Margaret cradled her throbbing arm and looked deep into Kit's eyes. The eyes she had imagined would be a gorgeous green or blue were, rather, a strange crimson-brown – as if his pupils were floating in a soup of mud and blood. His gaze was intense and pierced right through her. Unable to stand his presence even an instant longer,

Margaret chose instead to retreat and quickly fled from the room.

Kit was relieved to see her go.

Alone at last, he thought.

Swiftly, he liberated his legs from the hospital bed sheets and hopped off of the bunk – with *far* too much ease (considering his injuries). He took a step forward and felt an uncomfortable tugging coming from his right arm. There was a catheter taped there, feeding a clear fluid into his veins. Horrified by the sight of it, Kit tore it off without hesitation and threw it aside. He felt a chill down his backside, and turned his head to see that the gown he wore only covered the front of his person.

This is ridiculous, he thought. *Why do people even bother with these places?*

He glanced around quickly, hoping to find something suitable to change into. But his clothes were nowhere in sight. Most likely, those butchers (who called themselves 'doctors') had torn his favourite shirt to shreds when they'd examined him without his consent. Kit began rummaging through some of the cabinets in the room in search of the elusive, dark hooded top. Alas, all he found was an assortment of various plastic and metal tools – a lot of needles of different sizes and colours.

Kit wondered why so many flocked to these so-called 'hospitals', to be poked and prodded like animals. Of course, he'd never experienced illness before. *But what could possibly be so bad*, he thought, *to let yourself be subjected to such torture?*

Coming up empty handed, Kit abandoned his search. He was wasting time. The look, smell and feel of the hospital room were beginning to drive him mad.

He stopped and calmed himself. Taking a deep breath and closing his eyes, he conjured up an image of familiar surroundings in his mind. He waited a moment more, and then re-opened his eyes, suddenly.

Something's wrong, he thought to himself. *This can't be right.*

Kit stood straight as a board, taking in his surroundings, with utter panic now shining in his eyes.

How could this be? Why am I here? What's happening?

The knife.

He remembered the searing pain, the faint glow.

It's not possible. There's no way.

Kit could not accept the notion that the man who'd attacked him could have bested him in this way. He shut his eyes again tightly, desperately longing to be wrong.

Anywhere but here, he thought.

His head felt as if it were about to explode. Images flashed in his mind, one after another, faster and faster…

"Hello?"

The voice had come from behind him. Startled, Kit turned abruptly to face the direction from which it had come. He was terrified, and it must have shown on his face, because the woman who stood in front of him offered him reassurances.

"It's alright. You're safe here."

Dr. Beth Chandler wore a white lab coat and a stethoscope around her neck. She stood at about five-foot-six (only five inches shorter than Kit). She had straight, chocolate brown hair, and wore a pair of thick, dark-rimmed glasses that made her look more the part of a lawyer, than a doctor. She had a calm and peaceful air about her, which immediately had a positive effect on Kit. He relaxed almost immediately. His heart rate slowed, and his breathing became more even.

I've been dealt bad hands before, he told himself, *and still came out the winner. This time will be no different. I'll find him, and take back what's mine. I'll find him. And I'll make him pay for what he did to me…*

Beth Chandler could tell her patient was tense. She reached her arm out in the direction of two sofa chairs, and asked carefully:

"Would you care to sit with me? So we can talk?"

Kit was wary, but accepted nonetheless. Where else was he to go? It seemed he was trapped there for the moment. He figured he might as well gather as much information from this doctor as possible. He would need it, if he hoped to escape the hospital undetected.

Beth Chandler began by introducing herself and the hospital.

"And can you tell me *your* name?" she asked.

Kit thought for a second before answering: "Chris. Chris Cook", which was an alias he'd used on many occasions before. (It was easy to remember.)

"It's nice to meet you. You're a very lucky young man, Mr. Cook. Can I call you Chris?"

Kit nodded his ascent, and Dr. Chandler continued:

"As I was saying, Chris, you're lucky we got to you when we did. In fact, you're lucky to be alive. I won't bore you with all of the details. But you suffered a very serious laceration to your abdomen. There was some damage to your liver, and you'd lost a lot of blood by the time you arrived at the ER. The doctors gave you a transfusion whilst they operated. I'm happy to say that the surgery was a success, and we believe that we've repaired any internal injuries you may have had. We expect you'll make a complete recovery."

She smiled as she finished, apparently awaiting Kit's thanks.

The gratitude Dr. Chandler had expected to receive never came, however. Kit simply continued to watch her, a concerned look in his eyes. He'd listened to Beth Chandler's speech intently, but *not* because he wished to know the extent or status of his injuries. Kit's 'miraculous' recovery was unsurprising to him, in fact. Now that he was thinking clearly, Kit managed to recall *a few* times in past-lives where he'd recovered from similar injuries – even without surgical interference.

Rather, Kit had listened to the doctor's ramblings, because he worried about what was to come next. He worried what the doctors may have spotted in their illicit examinations of him. What might the doctors have noticed was *different* about him, he wondered. Would Dr. Chandler believe whatever outlandish cover story he could come up with on the fly? Or would he need to silence her, after all…?

Apparently coming to terms with her patient's unappreciative nature, Beth Chandler simply went on:

"We'd like to keep you for observation another day or so, in order to make sure no infections set in. But your vitals have been stable, and you're not running a fever. The nurses tell me your incision looks perfect. You really *are* a miracle patient. When this is all over, you'll have to tell me your secret."

She laughed. Kit didn't, however. His lack of any sort of emotional reaction made her feel a bit uncomfortable. Kit may have been the healthiest and most resilient patient Beth Chandler had ever had the privilege of treating. But his medical resistance and vigour came at the expense of a personality, she thought.

What a drag he was.

"Whenever you're ready, we'd like you to sign off on some tests we'd like to run. Just some routine blood and urine checks. I'm sure they'll come up clean. It's just standard procedure. We can even take the samples and send you home, if you like?"

Kit broke his silence then for the first time.

"Wait," he said, "you haven't done any tests?"

It was barely distinguishable, but there was elation in his words.

Finally, some good news.

Interpreting Kit's question as an echo of concern for his wellbeing, Beth Chandler offered him more reassurances:

"When you were first brought in, the doctors had to operate immediately, and so there was no time for tests. The blood we gave you during surgery was O-negative – universal-donor type. And the medications we gave you are standard for all knife victims. Sadly, we get more stab wounds coming through this ER than we'd like to admit…" She looked down at Kit's medical chart, and began flipping pages. "Seeing as you weren't displaying any signs of post-op complications, we held off on further tests until we could get your signature on the paperwork. Like I said, you're doing *extremely* well, and so, I don't expect the blood work will flag up anything concerning. It's just an extra precaution."

Kit smiled slyly upon hearing her words. A large burden had been lifted from his shoulders. "Thank you, doctor," he answered. It was best he played the appreciative patient, now that he was confident there was no *real* evidence of his stay at Sunrise.

Pleased by her patient's sudden show of gratitude, Dr. Chandler continued: "Well, whenever you're ready, one of our nurses will come in and walk you through the paperwork. There's a phone on the bedside table there, if you need to call someone. We'll need to see some identification and your insurance details, OK?"

"Of course. I'll call my mother. She'll sort everything out," Kit lied. "Thank you, Dr. Chandler." He smiled brightly up at the good doctor. He certainly knew how to charm a lady, when he wanted to…

Beth Chandler rose from her chair to exit the room, but stopped before she'd reached the door. She turned back to face Kit, who was still seated in the small hospital room's sofa chair.

"Oh wait," she said. "I nearly forgot. The police."

Kit's body stiffened at the mention of law enforcement, but he waited for her to finish.

"I'm afraid they have no leads on who attacked you. They'll likely want to question you, when you're feeling up to it. I've managed to keep them at bay whilst you were unconscious. But now that you're awake, I imagine you'd like to speak to them?" She didn't wait for his answer, and added: "When you're through with the paperwork, you can ask Margaret to call them for you. I'm sure you have a lot of questions."

Kit did not respond, and merely nodded his head.

Yes – he did have many questions. But he was also sure the police would be able to answer none of them.

Dr. Chandler smiled sweetly at Kit before reaching her hand deep into a pocket of her white lab coat.

"There's just one last thing," she said. "The doctors found this – it was clenched in one of your hands when you were brought in."

She pulled what looked to be a long chain necklace from her coat, and dropped it into Kit's now outstretched and open palm. His mouth opened, as he felt the delicate metal land in his hand.

"We kept it from the police," Beth Chandler told him, her eyes hanging low, searching the ground at her feet. Evidently, she was slightly ashamed of her and her colleagues' actions. "We figured you'd have wanted it back. It was the only thing that thief hadn't managed to take from you, after all…"

Thinking she'd managed to return a priceless, sentimental possession to an anguished patient, she added: "It's very beautiful. Now… try and get some rest."

At this, Beth Chandler turned and left the room.

Kit sat, staring down at the object resting in his hand.

What a strike of luck! He figured he must have ripped it from his attacker's chest, right before he'd left the alley.

The doctor had called the man from the alley a 'thief' – and a *thief* he was, Kit thought. If only she knew what he'd taken from him – it wasn't cash or credit cards.

In fact, Kit was fairly certain someone *else* had stolen his cash – after the alley – maybe someone at the hospital? He wondered if Dr. Chandler knew there was a pickpocket in her midst, stealing from patients. The thought made him snicker involuntarily, as he began his inspection of the necklace nested in his palm.

The chain on the necklace was an ordinary chain – silver, most likely. Although, it appeared to have been broken. It was unremarkable, and so Kit dismissed it almost immediately, turning his attention to the pendant to which it was attached.

The matching silver coloured pendant was oval in shape – roughly the size of a quarter. It looked vintage, and was decorated with a beautiful vine-like pattern. The carvings looked to have been done by hand – they were so intricate.

A piece like this *had* to be one-of-a-kind – which would make its origins easier to track. Kit smiled widely as he contemplated the retribution he planned to take on the man who'd owned it. There would be punishments in store once Kit recovered what had been taken from him.

He turned the pendant over in his hand, searching for further clues that would help him in his quest to find his attacker. He fiddled with the necklace, digging his fingers into any and all of its miniscule gaps and cracks, when finally, he found what he had hoped for.

A locket – it was a locket! Kit couldn't believe his good fortune. *This is too easy*, he thought. He could almost hear the pleas coming from the writhing man within his grasp already. That thief was as good as his.

Inside the locket were two tiny photographs. Both looked old and faded. Kit wondered if they had originally been printed in sepia tones, or whether the colour had drained from them with the passage of time. The photo in the left half of the locket was of a young boy, and the photo in the other half, a girl. *Siblings* – was Kit's first thought. The two just had a similar look about them. Neither was smiling, each posed elegantly for what must have been a formal occasion. The style of their clothing suggested the mid-1970s, early 1980s. Whoever these children were, they would have to be over forty or fifty years old now.

Kit shut his eyes and summoned his recollections of the man from the alley: mid-sized frame, a scar running down his face, black eyes. It had been dark, but Kit was fairly certain his attacker had not been a *'young'* man.

Kit dropped his gaze back down to the locket lying open in his palm. He slowly raised his free hand, and began digging at the edges of the photographs it held with his fingernails. Within a few moments, he'd managed to remove the rightmost picture – the one that featured the girl. There was an engraving hidden behind it. Kit quickly repeated the action with the photo on the left, and also managed to dislocate it from the locket. Another engraving was revealed, very similar to the other.

Together they read: *'L.L. 1966'*, the boy, and *'L.L. 1967'*, the girl.

Kit closed his fingers tightly around the locket and exhaled proudly. He lifted the precious locket to his lips and kissed it forcefully. His mouth opened and twisted into a large smile.

He laughed.

"I've got you now, L," he whispered.

There was a gleam in his eye, a lift in his spirits.

CHAPTER FIVE

THE BANK BOX

A cold breeze blew by Dylan as she stepped out of the black truck and slammed its door closed behind her. The large vehicle had belonged to her father, and Dylan had been unable to part with it since his passing. The interior still smelled of his favourite brand of old cigars. It was much too big and clumsy for driving in the small streets of downtown Montreal, and had been much better suited to the potholed dirt roads it had enjoyed back home.

Dylan had grown up on a farm in the countryside, just outside of the city. Although her father had retired from farming years ago, he had refused to move Dylan's sister, Danielle, and he out of their family home. Dylan fondly recalled how he used to rant about the dangers in the city, and how he had begged her to move back home. "We'll get you a brand new truck, and you can drive to school," he had pleaded, "any colour you want…"

The memory brought a smile to Dylan's lips. At the time, she'd been so desperate to strike out on her own, and to experience the glittering, trendy streets of the city. Not even the promise of a brand new sports car would have swayed her. How she regretted that decision now. Perhaps if she'd been home, things would have turned out differently…

Dylan pushed against the wind, as she continued to make her way down the street. Falling yellow and orange leaves flew past her.

Trees lined each side of the street, their branches bursting with the brightly coloured foliage. But for her general state of melancholy, Dylan would have probably stopped a moment to admire them. Autumn had always been her favourite season.

Every year growing up, before the first snowfall, Dylan's father had made she and her sister rake up all of the leaves around their house. "Make sure you get them all, girls! Or else the grass will die," he had bellowed at them from their front porch. Dylan remembered how strenuous the task had been. Hers and Dani's hands had always been full of blisters by day's end.   But it hadn't mattered, as afterwards, their father had always allowed them to enjoy the spoils of their labours. The piles of freshly raked leaves were sometimes taller than even little Dani. Dylan and her sister had spent hours jumping around in the multi-coloured heaps. Dylan recalled the crisp crunching sound of the leaves crackling under her shoes, the smell of the fresh air, and the sight of her little sister's smile. The memory warmed her heart for a moment, before the sound of a honking car driving past cruelly hauled her mind back to her miserable present.

Dylan had arrived at her destination, the main branch of the Montreal Bank. As she made her way towards the entrance, she caught her reflection in the building's glass windows and was taken aback.

Her features appeared tired and her long, dark hair was in a complete disarray. Dylan barely recognized herself in the image before her. The girl in the glass appeared far too thin and haggard. *What a mess*, she thought. She realized then that she hadn't even brushed her teeth that morning. Raising her right hand to her mouth, she gently exhaled onto the inside of her wrist and took it to her nose, grimacing at the smell. Her mouth tasted horrible. She stood still and silent before the glass, slowly taking in her state of debacle. A month ago, Dylan would have died before allowing herself to be seen publicly as she was now. But lately, simple tasks, such as combing her hair or washing her face… seemed almost pointless.

Squinting her eyes, Dylan cautiously peered through the paneled glass. The men and women inside the bank, she saw, all wore business attire. She frowned as she re-examined her own appearance in the window. Though admittedly a bit 'rough around the edges', the situation wasn't hopeless. After all, Dylan had always considered herself to be somewhat 'pretty'.

Determined to transform her facade, she reached deep into her coat pockets and found an old rubber band, along with a single stick of chewing gum. Swiftly, she popped the gum into her mouth and combed her fingers through her hair, gently pulling it back into a high ponytail. By this time, Dylan could taste the mint flavour of the chewing gum slowly spreading through her mouth. She took a step back, turned her head from side to side and nodded towards her reflection.

"That'll do," she said to herself. An old woman walking past her overheard her, and gave her an inquisitive look. "Ignore me," Dylan told her, slightly embarrassed.

Now feeling more at ease, Dylan took her first steps through the front doors of the bank and into its large, high-ceilinged entrance hall. Slowly, she made her way across the grand marble floor, past some impressive potted plants and two leather sofas, and walked straight up to the customer service desk. It was the middle of the day, and so there were relatively few customers around.

"Bonjour! Comment puis-je vous aider?"

The man who addressed her in French looked to be in his early forties. He was tall and lanky, and had dark hair that was gelled back in a sort-of sideways fashion. A thin moustache decorated his upper lip. Dylan had seen men coiffed in this way before. Though, it had never really appealed to her – much too 'slippery' for her tastes.

Before answering, she scanned François – his name, clearly written on the nametag pinned to his grey blazer – and considered whether she should address him in his chosen tongue. This was the beauty of living in a bilingual city, she thought, having to choose a language to converse in every time one approached, or was approached, by a salesperson (or, in this case, a bank employee).

Dylan's father, Jean-Pierre, had hailed from a French Canadian community, and so both Dylan and her sister had been raised bilingual. The truth was that Dylan had always preferred conversing in English. It had reminded her of her mother, Lenora. Although Dylan had few memories of her mother, she knew when Lenora had been about, her family had only spoken English, so as not to exclude her.

"Hi. I was hoping you could help me? I need to access my parents' safe deposit box."

François looked back at Dylan blankly. He was clearly disappointed she hadn't responded to him in French. A common reaction amongst people from Quebec, and so Dylan was accustomed to the disapproving glare. She continued on with her inquiry, all the while reaching into her knapsack to pull out the envelope she'd placed within it earlier.

"I think I'm one of the signatories on record?"

"Very well, *Madame*," François responded absent-mindedly. "I will need to see a piece of identification, and you will also need the box key."

"Of course."

Dylan pulled her wallet from her backpack, and flipped through the plastic cards held within.

"Here it is," she said, pulling out and placing a turquoise coloured driver's license onto the marble desk. "And I have the key as well," she added, dexterously removing the small, silver-coloured key from her keychain. "I think it's box number eighty-eight."

Meanwhile, François had been examining her driver's license. His demeanour had changed somewhat since laying eyes on the small plastic card, and he grinned now, turning his attention to his computer.

"Dubois," he said aloud, as he typed. "Dylan Dubois." He paused before going on, clearly holding back a small laugh: "*Signataire* to box *numéro quatre-vingt-huit.*"

It was clear François was having trouble maintaining his composure. He took a deep breath and added with as much seriousness as he could muster: "I'm sorry, *Madame*. But, you will need one of the owners with you. It is the bank policy."

Having succeeded in suppressing his laughter, François now stood very straight, staring Dylan down with an authoritative air. He appeared quite happy with himself. Dylan half expected him to pat himself on the back for a job well done.

She paused a moment, and then quietly slid the envelope she'd been holding over the counter towards him. "I know," she said, "that's why I have *these* – my parents' death certificates." She made sure to emphasize her last words.

Dylan watched in silence as François' face fell. There was a look of alarm in his eyes, as he removed the death certificates from their envelope to examine them.

"Jean-Pierre and Lenora Dubois. *Boîte quatre-vingt-huit.* Yes. Well…"

The man appeared to be at a loss for words. It seemed he hadn't appreciated he'd been speaking to an orphan, and was now ashamed at the way he had treated her. He cleared his throat before adding, in his thick French Canadian accent: "I am so sorry for your loss, *Madame*. I didn't realize. I was completely inappropriate. *Pardon*. It's just… your name…" He hesitated before finishing: "It is a little bit funny, *non*? 'Dylan'?"

François held the two death certificates in his hands, folding and unfolding them nervously, as he waited for her to respond. His apologetic manner caused Dylan to take pity on him, and so she chose to forgo embarrassing him any further.

"That's alright," she reassured him. "My name *is* a little unusual.

My parents named me before I was born. I think my mother thought I was going to be a boy…" Dylan smiled at the thought.

Out of respect, François remained quiet a moment more before answering.

"Thank you, *Madame*," he said. "*Et bien.* Everything is in order. I will take you to your box." Grabbing the small key from the marble counter, he motioned for Dylan to follow him through the door located at the very end of the long desk.

Dylan followed François through the door, down a narrow corridor and a long flight of stairs. At the foot of the stairs, he turned right and led her around a corner, past an armed security guard. The guard glanced at François and nodded, before turning his attention back to his dozens of security footage monitors.

François stopped and asked Dylan to remove her jacket and bag, and to leave them in a tray on the table next to the guard. Once satisfied she wasn't concealing anything dangerous, he smiled and invited her to continue following him past a very large and impressive metal vault door. The doorway led into a large, low-ceilinged room, which contained what must have been hundreds of smaller safety deposit boxes, all arranged into rows.

Dylan walked closely in behind François, and as they moved forward through the vault, she peered down each row, glimpsing all of the many rectangular safes embedded in the walls. The boxes in the first two or three rows they passed were small – the size of tissue boxes – but these seemed to grow bigger with every passing row, until finally, François stopped.

"Please wait here," he said, as he turned down one of the narrow hallways and approached a specific box located in the far wall.

Dylan watched impatiently as he inserted both her key and his own bank key (which he pulled from his blazer's breast pocket) into the locked safe. He turned both keys, one after another, and then pulled a large metal strongbox from the wall, carrying it back towards her.

The box was much bigger than Dylan had imagined it would be. It was wider than François' shoulders, yet shallow, and looked as though it was made to hold a very large World Atlas (or some other great tome, or volume). Upon seeing it, Dylan drew in a sharp breath of excitement.

"Follow me, *s'il vous-plaît*," said François, as he awkwardly carried the large box to the far end of the vault, and down a narrow hallway. He led Dylan into a very small, yet comfortable-looking room, which contained a velvet upholstered chair and a large, sturdy, mahogany desk. Gently, he placed the large strongbox onto the desk, and invited Dylan to sit in the chair with a polite motion of his hand. Dylan accepted the seat, and François proceeded to insert her key into the lid of the box. He turned the key and slid the lid ever so slightly, so as to demonstrate the proper method by which it could be lifted. His eyes met with Dylan's, and she nodded her head to let him know she understood.

"Very well. I shall be right outside." François withdrew silently from the room then, and pulled a luxurious red velvet curtain behind him as he went.

Following his departure, Dylan remained very still. Her mind raced as she sat staring down at the box, quietly imagining what priceless treasures her parents may have left for her within. Perhaps some of her mother's jewellery was hidden inside? Dylan recalled her mother had always worn a beautiful, white jade bangle around her wrist. *It would make a lovely memento*, she thought. Perhaps the box would contain handwritten letters, addressed specifically to Dylan and her sister? Or better yet, maybe her mother or father had kept a journal?

Most people, preparing to open a safe, the contents of which unknown, would have wished for gold, jewels, or other riches. Dylan, however, longed only for family heirlooms. Anything that would bring her closer to the ones she'd lost, anything that would bring her some sort of comfort and peace.

She took a deep breath and turned the key in the lock. Carefully, she slid and lifted the metal lid off of the box, placing it gently on the floor beside her, and gazed down at the contents of her parents' safe.

There were multiple stacks of paper within, and a number of smaller boxes of various shapes and colours. After a brief moment of unrest, Dylan reached out a shaky hand. Slowly, she lifted a small, blue fabric box out from the very edge of the tray, and proceeded to pop it open. It creaked open to reveal a beautiful, solitaire diamond ring.

Mom's engagement ring, she thought, smiling. *It must be.*

Dylan gently grazed the tip of her finger over the surface of the rock and silver coloured band. Her heart beat hard in her chest, and she felt her throat begin to tighten. This was the closest she'd been to any of her mother's possessions in years. Her father had not kept any of his late wife's belongings in their home, as he'd always considered them to be painful reminders of her death. The ring sparkled as Dylan tilted the box back and forth in the light. Mesmerized by its beauty, she barely found the strength to put it back.

Having returned her mother's ring to the box, Dylan resumed examining the rest of the contents before her. She happily opened a number of other jewellery boxes, and found many beautiful pieces, each bringing her more joy than the last: a pair of emerald earrings, a string of white pearls, a large, luxurious looking watch, a diamond wristlet. When at last, she found what she had hoped for – her mother's jade bracelet, tucked away in the very last box she opened.

Eyes wide, Dylan quickly removed the bangle from its wrappings and slipped it over her hand and onto her wrist. It fit perfectly. She held her forearm up, so as to get a better look at it. The bangle was just as she remembered. Carved from solid jade which was white as snow, and sanded down into a perfectly smooth, rounded finish, Dylan slowly shifted and rotated it around her wrist, carefully examining its every surface, gleaming and glowing. She smiled.

Having fulfilled her desire for family heirlooms, Dylan's mind snapped back to the task at hand. Her father's lawyer had asked her to look for insurance documents. As lovely as the jewellery within the safe deposit box was, it was not going to help Dylan pay her rent (or Dani's medical expenses). Money. She needed money.

The cost of the funeral, alone, had nearly depleted their family's bank accounts. But Dylan was certain her father would not have left them with nothing. He had loved his girls, and his sole purpose in life had been to provide for them. No. Dylan knew her father. She was confident he would have made provisions.

All business now, Dylan lifted the first stack of papers from the tray, and began flipping pages. The first document she found was a copy of her father's 'Last Will and Testament'. Dylan scanned it quickly, and found her father's signature at the bottom, witnessed and dated two years ago. Yes. This was the same will she had received a few weeks prior.

Jean-Pierre Dubois had left his entire estate, everything he had owned, to his two daughters – Dylan and Danielle Dubois. Dylan felt a chill crawl its way up her spine now, as she remembered the day their lawyer had read this document aloud to her for the first time. She could still feel Holly's hand tightly gripping her own. She recalled the numbness she had felt in her heart, and in her soul. At the time, she'd felt like a ghost hovering overhead, observing a scene from afar – a scene that couldn't *possibly* have been real. It was as if she'd been trapped in a nightmare, unable to wake. *This isn't happening*, is what she had thought to herself, over and over. Their lawyer's voice had sounded so far away... muffled, by her own denial.

Dylan shut the memory out and dismissed the document. She disliked dwelling on unpleasant thoughts, preferring instead to distract herself from such things.

Further examination of the papers within the safe deposit box yielded her parents' marriage license, old mortgage and lease papers, birth certificates for both she and her sister, and finally, her father's life insurance policy, along with several different types of home and car insurance policies. Each of the insurance deeds consisted of twenty-thirty odd pages, and seeing as Dylan was not well-versed in legal jargon, she dispensed with any attempts at deciphering them.

The precious papers in hand, Dylan reached down to the floor for her backpack, only to realize she'd left it with the security guard outside the vault. She frowned and lifted her head back up, so as to take a quick gander at her surroundings. Thankfully, the bank had thought to provide disposable bags to its customers. Dylan happily grabbed one of these from the neatly folded pile in the corner of the room, and proceeded to slip the insurance papers within.

Longingly, she turned her attention back to the tray of treasures.

I still have some time, she thought to herself.

Under the stack of legal documents she'd been rummaging through was a mass of old black and white photographs. Dylan turned now to these timeworn prints, hoping against all odds to find *some* clues as to her parents' pasts. She relished the thought of possibly learning more of their lives before they'd met, before they'd had children, even.

At first glance, Dylan didn't recognize any of the people in the images before her. She lifted the topmost photo from the pile and held it close to her nose, so as to better make out the faces.

The photo was small, perhaps three inches squared, and looked as though it could have been over thirty years old. Time had given it a pale yellowish tint. It featured two faces, that of a young girl and a young boy. The two children, who looked as though they could have been anywhere between eleven and fourteen years old, had their arms around each other's shoulders, and appeared to be holding each other very tightly.

The boy had a crooked sort of smile, the type of smile one would have expected to see on a trickster who'd just managed to pull off a really great prank. The girl, on the other hand, had a large, toothy and almost angelic looking grin. It required a little imagination on her part, but after a short while, Dylan recognized her. She turned the photo delicately over in her hand and read the inscription on the back:

Luca & Lenora, 1979

This was a photo of her mother as a child. Dylan's mouth broke into a large smile, albeit a short lived one. It was her mother, yes. But who was the boy? A friend? A neighbour, perhaps?

A look of confusion painted Dylan's face now. The two children looked to be comparable heights, and wore similar style clothing. The boy's hair looked to be a shade akin to her mother's, and although their smiles were different, the likeness of their facial features seemed to suggest a familial link. Was he maybe a cousin? Dylan wondered.

She put the photo aside a moment, and began sifting through the rest of the photos sprawled out in the box. There were many faces in the photographs she couldn't identify. However, Dylan soon found another that, again, featured both her mother and the mysterious boy. In this photo, the two looked to be about the same age as they'd been in the last. Dylan's mother was seated in a chair with Luca, the boy, standing at her side, her hand tightly clasped in his. Who was he?

Creases appeared on Dylan's forehead as she painstakingly tried to answer her own burning question.   The two children looked as though they had been inseparable. And so, why was it that she could not fathom who he was? She hurriedly inspected another dozen or so photographs, and amongst these, found at least four more featuring the enigmatic Luca – some alongside Dylan's mother, and others by himself.

Determined to solve the mystery, yet conscious of the fact that she could not delay any longer, Dylan gathered up all of the photographs from the box and swiftly threw them into her bag. It took a number of handfuls to transfer all of the dozens of pictures from the safe deposit box to her carrier bag, but Dylan managed to do so fast enough. As she lifted the last bundle of photos from the tray, she glimpsed one final item, resting at the very bottom of her parents' strongbox. She'd almost missed it, seeing as it blended almost perfectly with the black rubber bottom of the tray.

"What's this?" she whispered, without thinking.

The large, thick and ragged leather envelope looked ancient. If the photographs were thirty years old, she thought, then this sachet *had* to be at least a few hundred. Dylan would not have been able to guess at its contents if her life had depended on it. It seemed so very out of place…

Curious, Dylan carefully removed the envelope from the tray and saw it was sealed shut by a long and thin cord, which had been wrapped repeatedly around it. The string appeared to be made of the same delicate leather from which the envelope itself had been constructed. Dylan made a few enthusiastic attempts to unfasten it, but was unsuccessful. She tugged at the skinny leather strips to no avail, and exhaled heavily. Mindful of the fact that she was out of time, Dylan resigned herself and shoved the unidentified envelope into her bag.

Yet another mystery that'll have to wait, she thought.

She called out to François, whom she knew patiently awaited her on the other side of the curtain. "Do you have the time, François?"

"*Oui*. It is 2:30, *Madame*. Do you require something further?"

"No thanks. I'm done here," she answered, as she replaced the lid over the box and turned the key, locking it once more.

François drew the curtain and re-entered the room.

"Did you find everything you needed, *Madame*?"

Feeling rather fulfilled and excited by the prospects of her recent discoveries, Dylan chose to respond to him in his mother tongue.

"*Oui, François. Tout ce que je voulais, et plus.*"

François was startled by her sudden change, but his surprise quickly melted away. He beamed back at her and replied: "*C'est bien, Madame. Très bien.*"

He bowed politely and indicated the door.

"*Après vous?*"

Her overflowing bag in hand, Dylan exited the room, nodding to François as she went.

Following her departure, François nimbly lifted the metal box from the mahogany table, and carried it out of the room after her.

-- CHAPTER SIX --

A PAINFUL PROGNOSIS

Holly sat in the surprisingly spacious hospital room, staring up at the shiny, round clock that hung on the white wall opposite Dani's hospital bed.

3:18pm, she thought, disheartened. *Late again. Why am I not surprised?*

Holly recalled a time when her best friend had been the most reliable person in her life. Punctual, prepared and in control, Dylan had been an extremely bright student and athlete. She'd excelled in all her classes in her first years of university, despite any distractions that had come her way. She'd had an adventurous spirit, and most importantly, she'd been the best friend Holly could ever have asked for. Supportive. Caring. Loyal. But lately, Holly barely recognized her anymore. Since the night of the fire, Dylan had been distracted, disorganized, and depressed.

Night after night, it was the same routine. Holly would wake in the middle of the night, to the sound of Dylan's cries.

Night terrors.

The dreams had started almost immediately following Dani's admittance to the hospital, and had only become more aggravated as time passed. Dylan insisted the nightmares were nothing to worry about. But Holly knew better. Dylan had always been a terrible liar.

She barely slept anymore, and spent most of her days wasting away at Dani's bedside in a dream-like state.

Over the last few weeks, Holly had had the privilege of witnessing her best friend come apart. Slowly, piece-by-piece, she could feel Dylan slipping away from her. She was circling the drain and Holly knew, at any moment, she could lose her for good. And there was nothing she could do to stop it.

At first, Holly had tried to assuage her friend's suffering by giving her constant and unfaltering support. She'd offered encouraging and hopeful words. She'd sat by Dylan's side and held her hand for hours in silence. She'd been present at each and every one of Dani's doctor's appointments. But there was only so much she could do. At some point, Dylan would have to help herself.

The past few weeks had been vicious and disparaging – not only for Dylan, but on Holly as well. Dylan and Dani were like sisters to her, after all. They had all grown up together. Being forced to watch helplessly from the sidelines as *both* of her sisters gradually vanished from her life was, quite plainly, destroying Holly. So far, she'd managed to maintain a brave face. But underneath, she felt herself a bubbling pool of grief and strain.

The hospital room was quiet. Holly was aware of the general hustle and bustle going on outside. But with the door closed, she could barely hear the doctors and nurses running around. She gently placed her right hand over Dani's unmoving arm and surveyed her face.

Dani looked very much like her sister. They had the same youthful cheek bones, the same straight-edged, yet soft noses. And although Dani's eyes were closed now, Holly knew that beneath those delicate eyelids were the same gorgeous green eyes she'd come to know and love.

"Please wake up," Holly pleaded. She extended her left hand and lightly brushed her fingertips across Dani's forehead as she spoke, parting the sleeping girl's caramel coloured fringe. She ran her fingers down through the long, honey coloured hair, past Dani's shoulders, and finally found her other hand, still resting over Dani's slumbering arm. Holly squeezed it imploringly. Her features grew grave.

"Dylan needs you, Dani," she whispered. "*I* need you."

But for the small tube that fed into her left nostril, Dani appeared quite normal. The burns she had suffered to her arms and legs were healing nicely, and her features were peaceful and calm. She could have been sleeping, Holly thought, dreaming beautiful dreams of clouds and rainbows.

Sunlight poured into the hospital room through an open window, and shone over Dani's frozen face. The white light, in combination with the assortment of flowers decorating her bedside table, created an illusion of harmony and tranquility. Holly couldn't help but smile, as an old memory sprung into her mind.

Every Saturday morning, whilst other children were sat in front of the television watching cartoons, she, Dylan and Dani had taken to visiting the meadows on Dylan's father's farm. They'd enjoyed sitting amongst the wildflowers, and playing tag with the horses. Some days, when the weather had been particularly beautiful, they hadn't even bothered changing out of their pyjamas. Holly fondly recalled those mornings when they'd quietly rolled out of their beds, slipped on their rubber boots, and sneaked out to the orchard, leaving behind Dylan's snoring father. Dani, being the youngest, had always been the most thrilled and invigorated on those mornings, overjoyed at being included in her elder sisters' shenanigans.

On one such morning, Dani had climbed one of the apple trees nearest to the barn. Laughing, she'd made it all the way up to the first branch. Holly remembered how Dylan and she had watched, unsuspecting, as their little sister had reached out to grab her first apple, missed her step, and tumbled out of the tree, feet first. Horror stricken, they'd rushed to her side, their hearts beating and pumping fear through their veins. Dani's eyes had been closed at first, but had sprung open in no time. The fall hadn't been so bad after all, and Dani had only suffered a few bumps and bruises to her shins. After hosing away the dirt from Dani's tiny hands and legs, the three of them had made a pact not to tell Dylan's father about the incident, for they were all afraid they would be punished for their wanderings.

Staring down at Dani's illuminated face now, Holly was transported back to that morning by the Dubois family barn. Dani's eyes would spring open any moment now, she thought, just like before. And all of this… will have just been another bad dream.

The hospital room's door creaked open then, startling Holly out of her hopeful daydream. She jumped slightly at the sound and exclaimed: "Geez! You scared me."

"Sorry. I'm late. I know."

Dylan carefully shut the door behind her and took a seat opposite Holly, on the other side of Dani's comatose body.

"It's OK. Dr. Green came by, but I told him you'd be a few more minutes."

"OK. Thanks, Hol," Dylan replied. She leaned in close to her little sister and kissed her on the cheek, before whispering into her ear: "Good news, Dani. I brought you something."

In her hand, Dylan held the yellow Calla Lily she'd received that morning from Michael. She smiled widely.

"Mom's flower. You remember, right? It's a Serrada."

Despite her sister's comatose state, Dylan had a tendency of speaking to her as though she may actually answer at any moment. Holly had witnessed this troubling behaviour from her before. The doctors had told them that comatose patients could sometimes hear their friends and family speaking to them. But Holly felt that Dylan took the whole idea a little too far. She feared that Dylan's way of speaking to Dani, as though she were already awake, prevented her from accepting truth – that Dani may never wake up. Holly dreaded the day that realization would come crashing down on her. Would

Dylan be able to cope? Though worried, Holly remained tight-lipped and kept her concerns to herself.

She watched in silence, as Dylan delicately lifted her sister's hands and carefully crossed them over her abdomen, one on top of the other, sticking the yellow Serrada in-between. A look of concern washed over Holly's face as she contemplated her friend's motions.

Dylan was manipulating Dani's fingers now, adjusting the lily to be perfectly aligned with the unmoving torso. She ran her hands over the white hospital bed sheets, erasing any wrinkles and pleats that may have existed there. The movements, Holly thought, were slow and thoughtful – the product of a slightly neurotic mind. When she'd finished massaging the sheets, Dylan shuffled her chair over so as to be closer to her sister's head. She leaned in closer to Dani's face and caressed her forehead. Keeping completely still, she stared intently at her sister's resting features, as if patiently waiting for her to wake.

A chill ran up Holly's spine as she observed the scene before her. The way in which Dylan had adjusted Dani's body was reminiscent of that of a corpse lain in an open coffin, with dead, rigid hands clasped tightly around a bouquet of burial flowers. A sudden sinking feeling enveloped Holly, as visions of people crying and dressed in black, surrounded by tombstones and white roses came to mind. *Dani's funeral*, she thought. She didn't want to admit it to herself, but it was inevitable. Dani wasn't coming back. Deep down, she knew this. She and Dylan would have to let her go.

Tears welled up in Holly's eyes then and blurred her vision. She blinked hard, managing to swallow her sadness for the time being. She had to remain composed, for Dylan's sake. She sniffled and sat back in her chair, trying to remain as silent as possible. These final moments with Dani were precious, she thought. It was important that Dylan be allowed to cherish them without interruptions.

Just then, the hospital room's door opened once more, and Dani's doctor stepped in. Dr. Simon Green was a tall and slim man. He had an unassuming look, brown eyes, white skin, small, round glasses and a receding hairline. He was dressed in light green scrubs, and wore a pair of clean white sneakers.

"Dylan, Holly," he said, nodding to the two girls. "How are you today?" The question was rhetorical, and neither Holly nor Dylan answered.

Dylan didn't even turn to acknowledge the doctor's entrance. Her gaze remained fixed upon Dani. Her back was turned, and it looked as though she was holding her breath. These appointments had never failed to disappoint her. There was always *some* bad news to be had. Holly knew that Dylan found these moments with Dani's doctor difficult, and so she spoke in her stead.

"You said you needed to speak with us, Dr. Green?"

Dr. Green gave Holly a forced smile. He rolled a small stool out from the far side of the room, over to the foot of Dani's bed, and sat down. Although Holly had been the one to address him, when he spoke, he directed his speech at Dylan. She was, in fact, Dani's only 'official' family. And although she wasn't looking at him, he knew she was listening.

"Miss Dubois," he started, "we need to talk about your sister's condition." He took a deep breath before continuing, and Holly knew from his hesitation that it was as she had feared. The moment she'd been shirking had finally come.

"Your sister's been comatose for a month now, and so I think it's important we go over some of your options. If you want to keep her on life support systems, then I think you should consider moving her to a special care facility. I can recommend a few homes that can provide her with the fulltime care she needs. However, I have to warn you that these types of facilities can often be quite costly, and there's a good chance you'd only be prolonging Danielle's suffering by choosing to admit her."

Upon hearing Dr. Green's words, Dylan turned her head to face him. Her expression appeared cold and detached, her mouth hard.

"What are you saying exactly?" she asked, displaying no emotions whatsoever.

Dr. Green paused before answering.

"What I'm trying to say," he began gently, "is that there was no way of knowing how extensive the damage to your sister's brain was when she was first brought to the hospital that night. There was no way of knowing how long she'd been deprived of oxygen. So we waited. But we've waited long enough now, and I can tell you with confidence that the probability she'll ever regain consciousness is… almost negligible. And even if she did wake up, there's a good chance she'd be severely disabled."

Tears welled up in Dylan's eyes as she listened to the doctor's words. Her breathing became quick and agitated. A single drop fell from her eye, streamed down her face and fell from beneath her chin, as she struggled to speak.

"I don't understand," she managed to say. "She came off of the ventilator." Dylan appeared to be pleading with him, begging him to change his prognosis.

"I'm sorry, Dylan," Dr. Green answered, clearly pained. "It's true. We thought it was a good sign when your sister was able to breathe on her own. But the brain is the most complicated organ in the human body, and while that motor area of your sister's brain (the one that controls her breathing reflex) recovered, she still hasn't regained consciousness, nor has she shown any signs of movement. She doesn't respond to stimuli, and her EEG isn't good. Meanwhile, her physical condition is deteriorating. Soon, her muscles will begin to atrophy, and seeing as she's not able to eat solid food, her weight will continue to drop at an escalating rate."

Dylan couldn't speak. She turned her head down and hid her face, crying softly. Holly stood and made her way around the bed, over to Dylan's side. She rested her hand on her friend's shoulder, and Dylan grabbed at it immediately. She squeezed Holly's hand, as if desperately seeking relief from her agony.

Holly managed to remain calm in the face of Dylan's anguish. She turned to Dr. Green and asked: "What's next, doctor? What do we do?"

"That's your decision. Like I said, we can move Danielle to a long-term care facility. Or…" Dr. Green stopped for a moment. He braced himself before making his next suggestion. "Or, we can make her comfortable, and let her pass peacefully."

Dylan's weeping stopped then, as she lifted her head up again to face the doctor. Her facial expression had changed. In a split second, it seemed all but one of the feelings she'd been experiencing had left her. Only anger remained now, burning in her eyes.

"Get out," she snarled through clenched teeth.

When Dr. Green did not immediately rise to leave at her words, Dylan stood upright and shouted at him, violently.

"Get out!" she screamed. "You're wrong!" she cried. "You're wrong…"

Startled and shaken by her sudden outburst, Dr. Green nearly fell off of his stool. He stumbled to his feet and stood there, stunned.

"I think you'd better go," Holly told him apologetically. She had her hands on Dylan's arm, and was desperately trying to calm her.

His head hung, chagrined, Dr. Green took two steps towards the hospital room's door.

"I'm so sorry," he said sympathetically, before exiting.

Dylan watched him retreat and then turned to face Holly. Tears were overflowing from her eyes, and her mouth was turned upside down in a wretched sort of scowl.

"He's lying, Holly," she muttered miserably. "Dani's going to wake up. She's *going* to be fine."

Her words were staggered and almost incomprehensible. Her entire body was shaking, and she collapsed then, her knees giving out from beneath her.

Holly caught her and eased her back into the hospital chair. She knelt next to her and looked up into her best friend's puffy and blood shot eyes.

"Listen to me, Pickle."

Her tone was serious, her gaze determined. She placed her hands on either side of Dylan's head, and looked her straight in the eye.

"You listen to me, OK? I don't know what's going to happen. But what I do know for *sure* is that we're going to get through it. We are. No matter what, you have me, you hear?"

Dylan had ceased crying. Her eyes were swollen, words caught in her throat, but she managed to rustle up a smile for her friend. She reached her arms around Holly's neck and hugged her.

Holly held her trembling friend in her arms. Her eyes were wet too. She wiped her tears away with her sleeve – so Dylan wouldn't see. Unlike Dylan, Holly had prepared herself for the doctor's news. Nevertheless, the truths he had conveyed were difficult to accept. Holly struggled to contain her sorrow. Life without Dani would be difficult, she thought, but she and Dylan would get through it – together. Forcing a smile, Holly withdrew from her friend's embrace.

Standing, she reached over, gently picking the yellow Serrada from Dani's grasp. Holding the blossom up, she tickled the tip of Dylan's nose with its petal.

Dylan squinted, wrinkled her nose, and smiled sadly in response.

"So what's with this flower, anyways?" Holly asked her, hoping to provide a pleasant distraction. "You keep saying it's your Mom's flower. But in all the years I've known you, I've *never* heard you say anything about any *special* Lenora-flower. How could you tell Michael, and not me?!" she teased.

The distraction seemed to be working. Dylan's hysteria appeared to be behind them. Her tears had dried, and her breathing was growing more regular.

Dylan exhaled and gave a small laugh. She blew her nose with an old tissue she pulled from her pocket, and answered: "It's nothing really, just a story mom used to tell us when we were sick. Somehow… it always made us feel better."

"Well," Holly said smiling, "what are you waiting for? Tell me."

She pulled her chair up and sat down. Reaching her hand out, she gently placed it over Dani's arm and said: "Tell *us.*"

-- CHAPTER SEVEN --

"L" IS FOR LUCA

And so, his name was: Luca Lynch.

Kit's eyes were fixed intently upon the single sheet of paper he held in his hand. The document was the last written record he'd been able to find for the man he believed was his Las Vegas assailant.

Over the last few weeks, Kit had begun referring to him as simply: 'L'. However, he now had a full name to put to the obscured face from his memories of the attack in that dark alley.

Who are you, Luca? Kit thought to himself, still gazing down at the paper in his hand.

The document was a photocopy of an adoption record dated 1978, for a set of siblings named 'Luca' and 'Lenora' by a Mr. John Lynch, living in the northern city of Quebec, Canada.

After weeks of searching, Kit had managed to track the origins of the silver locket he'd pulled from L in the alleyway to a small vintage jewellery shop, located in the provincial Canadian town. Following this discovery, it had not been difficult to unearth the names of the finite number of historical Quebec residents with initials 'L.L.', and to narrow these down based on age and familial ties. Luca and Lenora Lynch were the only pair that had fit Kit's profile to a tee.

Kit had scoured the city's local archives for further records of the two children, but had come up empty handed. It seemed Luca and Lenora Lynch had never even been born. Their adoption papers were incomplete and missing vital pieces of information, such as their birthplaces and the names of their birth parents. According to the paperwork, the pair had simply appeared out of thin air, as if by magic.

Kit suspected the adoption had not been completely legitimate. Apparently, Mr. Lynch had been a very wealthy and well connected man. Kit presumed that it would have been child's play for him to push through an illicit adoption.

The so-called 'John Lynch' had also been careful, for Kit had found no trace of him post-1980. His paper trail had gone cold following the liquidation of the entirety of his Canadian assets. He certainly was an interesting and enticing puzzle. But Kit was not in the least side-tracked from his immediate goal – locating Mr. Lynch's alleged adopted son, Luca (or rather, 'L').

Creases appeared on Kit's forehead as he wracked his brain, trying to come up with answers to the dozens of L-themed riddles that plagued his mind. Who was Luca Lynch? Where had he come from? What were his motives? Where was he now? Kit set down the sheet of paper he held in his hand, and began shuffling through the dozens of notes, prints, and newspaper cut-outs sprawled out on the table's surface in front of him.

An older man, sitting in the booth across the way, sneezed loudly and broke his concentration momentarily. Kit's eyes darted sideways, and he gave the man a disapproving glare. He was not accustomed to working in such pitiable surroundings. The ambiance of the little Montreal deli in which he sat was definitely *not* an ideal research setting. But Kit was starving, and this particular restaurant happened to offer the perfect vantage point for his surveillance of the residential building across the street.

Kit's stomach growled loudly, as he turned his attention away from his mess of papers. He gazed out of the dirty diner's glass windows, and at the four-story apartment building across the way. *Patience*, he thought to himself, *it won't be long now.*

The last few weeks had been tougher on Kit than he would care to admit, and he was growing impatient. It had been difficult for him to get on day to day in his crippled state. He'd been cut off from his resources, marooned, forced to survive in what he considered to be barbaric circumstances.

Since embarking on his search for L, Kit had journeyed cross-country, sleeping in one dirty motel room after another. Stained carpets, unwashed sheets, and rock hard mattresses were becoming a way of life for him now. And some nights, he hadn't even been able to afford himself *these* luxuries.

One particularly cold Chicago night came to mind.

After spending a full twenty-four hours, desperately searching the Windy City for smuggling services, Kit had failed to secure passage across the Canadian border. The setback had been unexpected, and Kit had been unable to obtain shelter before nightfall. He shuddered now, as he vividly recalled sitting on a Lincoln Park bench, shivering, his arms clasped tightly around his core, trying to keep warm. He remembered struggling against his heavy eyelids, fighting to remain awake, and finally giving in to his exhaustion. Ashamed, he'd allowed his primal instincts to take hold. He remembered crawling in behind a large patch of bushes, away from the main path, and curling up on the damp grass under the branches of a towering tree... like some, common animal.

More than a week had passed since that night, and Kit could still feel the humiliation crawling under his skin. He'd attempted to cleanse himself, to wash away his indignity with hot showers. But nothing could erase the degrading experience from his recollections. He would not forget – not for a long time. No matter. Since in a way, all Kit *ever* had... was time.

Kit's thoughts snapped back to his present. His stomach was still rumbling. Yet another of his basic instincts, prodding and prevailing over him. It had been almost two days since Kit had eaten a proper meal. He was like a machine running on fumes. Since his discovery of the Lynch adoption papers, Kit had not stopped for even a moment. He'd been in and out of public libraries and Internet cafes, relentlessly following lead after lead, until he'd landed here… in Montreal.

Kit was so close now. All of his L-facts were falling into place, lining up like dominos. He took a deep breath, reached out his right hand, and plucked a small, rectangular scrap of newspaper from the dozens of papers before him. Now holding the newspaper article with both his hands, he scanned the title with his eyes.

DEADLY FIRE CLAIMS FATHER OF TWO AND LEAVES DAUGHTER IN COMA

Luca Lynch may have essentially disappeared from the face of the planet. But his sister, Lenora, had been a very 'good' girl. She'd grown up, married, changed her name and then died (relatively young) in a car accident. Upon first discovering the news reports of Lenora's demise, Kit had feared his search for L had met its end. No Lenora meant no L, right? *Wrong.*

Kit's body jumped suddenly then. In the corner of his eye, he'd caught sight of movement across the street from the diner. He was alert now, waiting, watching. Two figures, two young women (or girls, really…), climbed the steps leading up to the front door of the red-bricked apartment building. One was blonde. The other had long, dark hair. Kit squinted his eyes and focused them upon the latter. She looked upset, anxious, and seemed to be crying. Kit watched indifferently as the girl wiped tears from her cheeks with the sleeve of her jacket. Her blonde companion, having successfully unlocked the front door, put her arm around her and delicately guided her into the building.

A large weight was lifted from Kit's shoulders, as he watched the two girls disappear from his sight. He sighed and smiled to himself.

His muscles relaxed, and he slumped down into the plastic cushioned booth. He'd found her – Dylan Dubois, Lenora Lynch's only remaining daughter and L's last surviving blood relative. L wouldn't be far now, he thought. People never strayed too far from their families…

"Votre sandwich, Monsieur?"

Kit had been so distracted by the events taking place on the other side of the street. He hadn't even noticed the little, black haired waitress standing at the foot of his booth. In her left hand, she held a large plate of red meat on rye bread, smothered in mustard. The aroma from the hot Montreal-style smoked meat floated up from the plate, and into Kit's nostrils. His mouth watered at the scent.

"Vous-en avez des papiers, eh!" the waitress exclaimed in French, gawking at the papers that covered nearly every inch of the diner table's surface. She raised her eyebrows, as if seeking permission to set down the plate over top.

"Ah… oui, un moment s'il vous plaît," Kit told her, as he quickly ran his fingers back and forth across the table's surface, collecting all of his research into one thick pile, and setting it down on the bench beside him.

The girl smiled at him. He wasn't from around there, she realized. He spoke the language. But his accent sounded far too Parisian, to be Canadian. She set down the plate of food in front of him.

"C'est onze quarante-cinq en tout," she told him.

"Eleven dollars, forty-five cents," Kit translated to himself. He turned his back on her and began rummaging through the old leather satchel resting on the seat beside him.

There were about six or seven men's wallets rolling around inside of Kit's bag (all stolen, of course). It was lucky Kit was a skilled pickpocket, or else he'd have been in *real* trouble after his encounter with L. Careful not to let the waitress see over his shoulder, he opened one wallet after another, looking for cash. The first two wallets contained only American money, but Kit soon found a Canadian five and ten dollar bill, tucked away in the third wallet he opened. He slipped the blue and purple bills from their case, closed his bag, and handed the money to the girl as payment. She opened her mouth to speak, but Kit merely shook his head and waved his hand at her, shooing her away.

Content with her fairly large tip, the little waitress turned and left Kit to his food. Slowly, he picked up the thick meat sandwich and bit into it happily. He turned his head back towards the window, and allowed his eyes to, once again, target Dylan Dubois' apartment building.

Kit could barely contain his delight. *She* was the key, he thought, and he'd found her. Soon, he would find L too, and everything would be as it had been before…

His mouth full with delicious smoked meat, Kit continued his observation of the building across the street. The juice, seeping from the meat, rolled down his throat and into his all-too empty stomach. He swallowed, and felt the food land in his belly. Ravaged, he took another bite, and another.

Kit did not move from his seat when he'd finished consuming his food. He simply sat and carried on with his stakeout.

The sun set, evening fell. And when the little, black haired waitress began wiping down tables and mopping up the floor before closing, Kit finally took his leave. He gathered his things and stepped out into the moonlit streets of downtown Montreal.

-- CHAPTER EIGHT --

DREAM DELUSIONS

The air was crisp and cool. Dylan could barely catch her breath. Her limbs ached from her countless attempts at clearing the rock blocking her path. And yet the cave before her remained closed.

The wind was blowing, carrying sounds of running water on the air and swaying the tall grasses of the field behind her. But Dylan ignored these flurries, instead remaining focused on her task. She shifted her body from side to side and peered through the dark opening, until she glimpsed it again – that same faint glow, coming from the furthest reaches of the cavern. Frenzy ignited within her, as her eyes locked onto the light. For Dylan knew it was there, upon that ledge. The object which she craved so desperately.

Her impatience growing, she resumed her efforts to widen the mouth of the cave. Carefully, she inserted her arm through the crevice and ran her hand roughly along its interior. Her hand met with a jagged piece of rubble, and there came a sharp sting in the palm of her hand. Reflexively, Dylan withdrew her arm from the opening and clenched at her wrist. The pain was unexpected. She lost her balance, and fell to the ground.

The gash in her hand felt deep and burned. Dylan winced, as she tried wiggling her fingers back and forth. She watched silently, as blood oozed from the open wound and pooled in her palm. The little puddle grew bigger, and soon, blood began trickling down Dylan's forearm and onto the ground. She tried pressing her now throbbing hand down onto her thigh, but the bleeding only worsened. Time seemed to slow, and with every passing moment, the pain became more excruciating. There was blood everywhere, staining her clothes and sticking to her skin. Dylan cradled her wounded hand in close to her body, as her eyes turned glassy with un-cried tears.

The sun suddenly grew brighter. All that surrounded her became blurred and whitish in colour. Eyes squinting, Dylan gazed out at the scene. There were patches of blood splattered all around – like remnants of a bloodstained battle. The raw stench of blood now hung in the air.

Overcome with an overwhelming urge to flee, Dylan attempted to push herself up to stand, but tripped, and found herself instead face down in the grass. A sudden pang ran its way up her arm. Paralyzed with pain, and with her cheek pressed to the ground, she watched helplessly as blood flowed freely from her open wound and into the grass beneath it. She saw her blood travel across the landscape inexplicably (as though with a life of its own), quickly enveloping each strand of grass in its path. The thick red liquid then seemed to penetrate the grasses' pores, as if defying the very laws of nature. In mere moments, every last drop of her spilled blood had vanished from sight. Disappeared. Somewhere in the depths of the blades before her.

Dylan watched in awe, the spectacle far from over. Somehow, her blood appeared to be precipitating a sort of change in the plants before her. It was quick, but Dylan saw it clearly: the shift in the pigment of each absorbing strand. The grasses, which at first had appeared almost devoid of colour, now took on a pale-reddish hue.

It was a cheerful colour, she thought. Like fresh watermelon, or pink champagne…

A calmness seemed to come over Dylan then. In witnessing the meadow's metamorphosis, the ache in her hand vanished entirely. Fear turned to serenity. Pain turned to joy. And gently, Dylan lifted herself up from the ground to look out at the field around her. With tranquillity in her heart, she watched, as the remaining splotches of blood scattered all about gradually drained away into the undergrowth – each one triggering an identical change of colour in the surrounding grasses. The pale red tinge spread from the grasses' roots, all the way up to the tips of each and every blade, until the entire field was transformed.

A wind blew past her. Dylan's deep brown locks were blown upwards into her face, tickling her cheeks and forehead. She, however, remained as she was – quietly sat on her knees, admiring the beauty of the now-strawberry blonde meadow before her.

There was something... magical – in the transformation she'd witnessed. This change that, somehow, had been borne from her blood. She couldn't explain it – nor did she want to. Prior to the shift, there had been pain, fear, confusion even. But these sensations had since been replaced. All felt peaceful now. All was clear.

Dylan closed her eyes and lifted her chin towards the sky. The sun still shone brightly. She felt its rays warming the skin of her face, spreading through her body and into her limbs. She took a deep breath, as all of the strain in her shoulders, and in her neck, drained away into nothingness. The terrible pain in her hand was but a distant memory now...

Dylan's eyes sprung open, and her gaze dropped. Her right hand, she saw, rested facedown in her lap. She eyed it suspiciously. Not a single trace of blood was left there. The skin of her arm, and of her hand, looked clean and bright under the sun. Yet something still nagged at her. A weak prickling sensation, hidden under her fingers, somewhere in the very center of her palm.

Gently, Dylan willed her hand to open. Her fingers loosened, and her bare palm was revealed. All appeared normal at first glance. Her flesh looked healthy and unbroken. But when Dylan focused her gaze and peered more closely at her skin's surface, she found it had changed somehow. The lines in her open palm appeared different, warped.

Together, they made up an arrangement of shapes: two circles, interlocked and superimposed over one another. Both circles looked to be of roughly the same size, with each of their edges placed precisely within the other's center. The arrangement would have been symmetrical, but for the presence of one final, unbalancing element: a single straight line, piercing the outer edge of the rightmost-circle.

The three shapes, altogether, were small, barely the size of a dime. Dylan had to raise her palm to within mere inches of her nose, in order to even perceive them properly. Nonetheless, she now had a clear appreciation for the mark at the center of her hand. While she did not know its meaning, she recognized it nonetheless.

The mark was a part of her now. Somehow, she knew this to be true.

No sooner had Dylan accepted her new mark, that there came a loud roar, thundering all around her. The noise shook Dylan to her very core, reverberating through her head and chest. She should have been afraid. Undoubtedly, the clamour had originated from some ungodly creature... yet Dylan remained calm and composed as she listened. Though the rumblings persisted after the initial explosive uproar, these remnant echoes were fewer, more subdued, and less threatening than the original cry. Dylan climbed to her feet and managed to follow the menacing growls to their source.

The cave.

As she turned herself about to once again face the ominous rockface that had taunted her so, she finally saw it. Instead of a barred cavern, Dylan now found herself staring at a large gaping hole in the center of the cliffside. The mouth of the cave had opened. The stone, which for so long had blocked her entry, had vanished from her path.

Dylan now stared yearningly into the blackness before her. Drawing in a sharp breath, she took her first steps into the hollow, and towards the grumblings coming from within. All at once, she was overtaken by obscurity. The darkness of the cave captured her, and all light was extinguished.

"Dylan?"

Someone was speaking to her, calling her name. Dylan was drawn to their voice. She opened her eyes to find herself in warm and familiar surroundings. Her heart was beating at an alarming rate, and she was drenched in sweat.

"Dylan, are you OK?"

It took a moment for Dylan to collect herself. She felt disoriented, but soon recovered enough to return to reality.

She'd been dreaming, she realized. Not just dreaming, but also… sleepwalking.

She stood now in the living room of her apartment. It was dark outside. But she had no sense of time. How long had she been standing there, she wondered.

Holly was sitting upright on the living room's sofa, staring up at her with an inquisitive and surprised look on her face. She'd been up watching television. There was a late night talk show program blaring in the background.

"What are you doing?" Holly asked. "It's nearly one o'clock in the morning."

Dylan did not answer her friend's question. Her mind was still racing, thinking back on the dream she'd just been living. It had felt so real – so right. Dylan's heart now ached to be back in that dark cave. Something inside of her told her that the answers to all of her questions, and to her prayers, were there – that she needed only claim them.

She was having trouble catching her breath. Perspiration ran down her cheeks and neck. Dylan lifted her right hand up to wipe the sweat from her face, but stopped as she caught sight of her open palm. Gently, she held it up in front of her.

It's gone, she thought. *Where is it?*

For some reason, Dylan had expected the mysterious double-ringed mark to be real. But the palm, which in her dream had been so remarkable – so special – now looked all too ordinary.

Mesmerized, Dylan couldn't tear her gaze away from her hand. Maybe, if she stared long and hard enough, the mark would reappear to her? Without it, she felt directionless and incomplete.

"Dylan, you're burning up!"

Holly was now standing at Dylan's side. Her right hand was resting upon Dylan's forearm, and she reached her other hand up to Dylan's forehead to feel her temperature. There was a deep look of concern in her face as she guided Dylan towards the sofa, and gently encouraged her to sit.

"Here," she said, "let me get you a glass of water."

Holly was only gone a minute or two. When she reappeared, she was holding a tall glass, filled to the brim. "Drink this, Pickle," she said.

"Thanks," Dylan managed to mutter, as she accepted the drink.

Holly watched quietly, as her friend swallowed the entire glass of water. She did not say a word, until Dylan had finished and placed the empty glass on the coffee table in front of her.

"You had another dream, didn't you?" Holly asked.

Dylan was still feeling slightly feverish. Her thoughts were a bit muddled, but slowly, she regained her clarity. Raising her hand to her head, she brushed some of the sweat-soaked hair from her forehead.

"Holly, please. I'm fine," she answered.

Her features looked strained and worn. She couldn't have sounded more unconvincing if she had tried.

"You're not fine. You're trembling," Holly replied with force. "What's going on? Tell me."

The talk show was still bellowing in the background, and so Holly reached for the television's remote and pointed it towards the flat screen mounted on the wall. She fiddled with some of the buttons, and the sound coming from the speakers ceased.

"I don't want to talk," Dylan answered. "Please, can we just leave it?"

She shivered as she spoke. Her fever subsiding, she reached for the folded blanket that lay on the couch beside her, and wrapped it around her trembling body.

Holly frowned, as she took a seat next to her friend. Quietly, she reached over and tucked the blanket in under Dylan's legs. Though not particularly happy with her, she respected her friend's wishes and refrained from asking her further questions about the dream.

Dylan smiled, as though thanking her for her restraint. She leaned her head upon Holly's shoulder.

Holly took a deep breath and allowed her eyes to close. After taking a moment to compose herself, she reached her hand towards the coffee table, and once again, picked up the television's remote. Pressing a single button upon the handheld controller, she heard the sound of the talk show program return in full force.

A man in a snazzy baby blue suit sat behind a large, modern-looking desk. He was interviewing some celebrity, which neither Dylan nor Holly recognized. His hair was black, and gelled into a funny sort-of upwards flip. He had a comical looking face, and was cracking jokes left, right and center. The crowd was laughing with him, and so was the handsome, blonde celebrity that sat next to him on the stage.

Dylan giggled softly upon hearing one of his jokes, and Holly twisted her head around uncomfortably to look down at her, still leaning up against her shoulder. Though she couldn't see her face,

Holly smiled anyways. In recent times, the sound of her best friend's laughter was a rare gift.

"Dani always loved *The Donald Dusk Show*," Holly remarked tentatively.

"Yeah. She did," Dylan replied.

Neither of them really spoke again after the exchange. They watched the remainder of the television program in silence, each content with the other's company. There were a few more laughs and playful jests, but no talk of doctors, dreams or death. The silence between them, in combination with the droning laughter and applause from Donald Dusk's audience, was strangely… rejuvenating.

Donald Dusk was now shaking his celebrity guest's hand and waving energetically towards the spectators, taking in their applause, as the show's credits began to roll.

"You should get some sleep, Pickle," Holly told Dylan, as she mechanically made a move to shut the television off.

Dylan nodded, and the two girls stood up from the sofa.

Dylan stepped away from Holly then, and slowly made her way across the living room. Before disappearing into her bedroom, she turned and smiled sleepily at her friend.

"Goodnight," she said.

Holly smiled to herself, as she saw her friend leave the room. Picking up Dylan's empty glass, she made her way quietly towards the kitchen. Gently, she placed the glass in the sink, too tired to bother washing it then. She walked past the kitchen island, bound for her own bedroom, but stopped, after only a few steps. Something had caught her eye – there, upon the kitchen island – and curiosity got the best of her.

Backtracking to the granite counter, Holly peered over at the stack of photographs that had lured her there.

Dylan's family album was lying open on the kitchen island, and there was a mass of loose black and white photographs sprawled out over top. At the very top of the pile was a large sepia-toned picture of a young man who couldn't have been more than fourteen or fifteen years old. It was *this* particular photo that had stopped Holly in her tracks. The boy was… familiar to her somehow. He had dark hair, dark eyes, and a whimsical looking smile.

Holly managed to tear her eyes away from the photograph, long enough to quickly examine the rest of the photos scattered about over top of the album.

The timeworn, yellowing photographs were new to her. *Dylan must have just brought them home*, she thought – souvenirs from her trip to the safe deposit box.

But who was this boy? Holly felt she had met him somewhere before. *But where? When?*

Without thinking, Holly reached for the photograph and lifted it from the stack. Her eyes remained fixed on the face in the photo. She squinted as she glared at it, searching her memories for the smiling boy's identity.

"I know you," Holly whispered to herself.

She wondered if her imagination was playing tricks on her. How could she possibly recognize this boy? Judging by the apparent age of the photograph, he'd have to be old enough to be her father now. Still, his face haunted her. She was absolutely certain she'd met this boy before, not so long ago either…

Holly stood staring at the old photograph, much annoyed with herself for her lapse of memory. Soon, she felt the heaviness of her eyelids, and thus resigned herself to sleep. Though intending to return the photo to the top of the pile, Holly couldn't quite bring herself to part with it yet.

Dylan won't mind if I keep it a little while longer, she assured herself.

And so, with the photo of the smiling boy still in hand, Holly left the kitchen, turning the lights off as she went. She crossed the now dark apartment's little living room, and entered her own bedroom, shutting the door behind her.

-- CHAPTER NINE --

CAUTIONARY CLOUD

"Once upon a time, deep in the woods of the Far East, there lived a lovely, young maiden and her mother. Now, this maiden was very different from other girls in the land, for the Gods had given her a very special and rare gift. She was a healer, and with a single touch, could cure any ailment, injury, or disease.

"Being kind-hearted and generally inexperienced in the ways of the World, the young maiden was not able to appreciate the true value of her gift. But her mother was the wiser, and it was for this reason that she hid her daughter away, deep in the Eastern Wood, far from those who would seek to exploit her. There they had lived, undisturbed, happy, until one fateful day when a mysterious stranger wandered into their domain.

"The man, who was a messenger from a neighbouring realm, had heard whispers of the young maiden's powers, and had travelled a great distance to seek her aid. His beloved Emperor had fallen deathly ill, and traditional medicines had failed to restore his health. The man begged the young maiden to travel back with him, and to save his master's life, for he was a good Emperor, and the people had prospered under his rule.

"Moved by the Emperor's story, and by his people's plight, the young maiden resolved herself to answer the man's pleas. She left her home in the Eastern Wood, despite her mother's warnings, and against her wishes.   Together, she and the Emperor's messenger travelled west, back towards the Emperor's palace.   The two faced many dangers along the way, and the young maiden proved herself to be very brave and steadfast on the long and perilous road.

"When they finally reached the Emperor, he was but moments from his end. He lay in his imperial bedchamber, surrounded by his subjects, unable to eat or speak, gasping for breath. The young maiden, still exhausted from her quest, wasted no time, and knelt by the Emperor's side. She laid her hands upon his flesh, and within moments, the Emperor's vitality was returned to him, and the illness drained from his body.

"The transformation was remarkable, and the Emperor's subjects were in awe of the young maiden's talents. The realm rejoiced, and as thanks, the Emperor gifted the young maiden with a thousand of his most treasured and prized golden blossoms – the majestic *Serrada*."

Dylan sighed and quietly pulled her chair in closer to her sister's hospital bed. Gently, she took Dani's hand in hers and squeezed it softly as she gazed down upon her resting features. The yellow Serrada she'd laid upon her sister's bust the preceding day had not been moved in the night. Dylan reached her free hand over to the flower now, and slowly ran her fingertips along its bell-shaped rim. Her mind lost in thought.

"I always loved that story."

The deep resounding voice startled Dylan out of her reverie. She'd been so focused, she hadn't noticed the man standing in the hospital room's doorframe. Her attention now captured, however, she lifted her gaze from her sister's bed, so as to ascertain the identity of her visitor.

When her eyes met with his, Michael Evans' thin lips curled into a brilliant white smile.

"I never did understand the ending, though," he mused. "It always seemed to me a bit… unfinished."

Dylan hesitated at first. Blankly, she stared up at Michael, and did not speak. The silence caused him to shift uneasily.

"I mean, what happened after the Emperor recovered? Did they live happily ever after?" He laughed nervously.

Dylan finally snapped out of her stupor.

"I suppose saving the day and being celebrated by an entire kingdom isn't a *happy* ending to you?" she asked sarcastically, smiling slyly up at Michael.

"Touché," he answered. "But don't these fairy tales normally end with a grand, royal wedding? Doesn't the hero normally get the girl, or the boy, in this case?"

Dylan laughed. "Come on, Michael. It's not that kind of story. My mother wasn't the romantic type."

"Yes, and she only told *magic* stories," he teased.

Dylan's eyes grew wide, and her mouth twisted in protest.

"You said it helped you!" she exclaimed, half-laughing, half-complaining.

"I had a broken arm, Dylan! No 'magical' story was ever going to fix that."

"Well, I probably just don't tell it right…"

Dylan paused a moment, before going on.

"Hey Michael," she added, "thanks… for the flowers, I mean. I should've called, but…"

He interrupted her, before she could finish.

"No problem. Really. It was my pleasure."

They both smiled at each other then, like two friends reunited over old memories. Dylan was surprised at herself. She'd been dreading her next, unexpected visit from Michael. But after the events of yesterday, she actually found herself welcoming his intrusion. His presence felt familiar, comforting.

Neither of them spoke again for a moment or two, and so Dylan took the opportunity to scan Michael up and down. He'd snuck up on her, and she hadn't had the chance to take him in properly.

There he stood, leaning against the doorpost, arms folded. Dylan wondered if he was on duty, for he was wearing his black sergeant's uniform. Michael was a police officer with the Quebec Provincial Police force, and very much looked the part. He was about six foot, two inches tall, had a square-ish jaw, and a set of arms and shoulders that had always reminded Dylan of an American football player. He really was an impressive male specimen, with hazel eyes and soft, curly, brown hair. On this particular day, he looked in well and fit form, much like on the day Dylan had first met him.

Nearly two years had passed since their chance encounter in the Montreal Metro. But Dylan still recalled how Michael had swept into her life, like a knight in shining armour, saving her from the two delinquent teens that had tried to rob her in the dark corner of that subway station.

So much time had passed, yet here he was again. Still trying to save the day… The difference being that Dylan no longer felt herself a 'damsel in distress' in need of rescuing. She wondered if Michael was actually here for *her*, or whether his recent approaches had just been further manifestations of his eccentric hero complex. Would he disappear again, when he felt she no longer needed him? When his prowess could be put to better use elsewhere?

Michael was a good man, but one who was married to duty and honour. He was a soldier at heart, forever searching for the next battle. Never able to settle in times of peace. It was for this reason that their relationship had dwindled in the first place, Dylan reminded herself.

Her heart sank slightly at the thought, and her smile faded.

Sensing her sudden recoil from him, Michael stiffened, unfolded his arms, and lifted his weight from the doorframe.

"May I come in?" he asked politely.

"Of course," she answered, "I'm being rude. Please."

Dylan loosened her grip on her sister's hand and motioned for him to enter.

As Michael took his first step into the hospital room, there came an unexpected rustling from outside. Dylan's eyes were immediately drawn by the sound. Her eyebrows creased with confusion, and she stared, for she could have sworn she'd spied movement from in behind Michael's legs.

It was only after he'd taken his second step into the room, that Michael's furry companion finally revealed himself to her.

"Ah!" Dylan exclaimed, as she spotted the young shepherd, timidly poking his head out from in behind his master's legs. He'd been hiding in Michael's shadow the entire time.

Michael gave a small laugh at Dylan's reaction. "I knew you'd like him," he remarked. "Dylan, I'd like you to meet Cloud."

The dog, who couldn't have been much more than a year old, came tumbling clumsily into the room ahead of his trainer. Having finally been given permission to enter the premises, Cloud immediately began investigating his surroundings. His nose pressed to the ground, he wandered about the room, sniffing curiously.

Whatever melancholy Dylan had been experiencing vanished entirely with Cloud's appearance. Her eyes followed him around the room, and she couldn't help but allow herself to smile again. He really was a magnificent animal.

Years spent on a farm had made Dylan an excellent judge of all sorts of domestic animals. It was obvious to her, at once, that Cloud was both strong and healthy, and of excellent breeding. His thick, brown and black fur was rich and full. He had a long and handsome snout and large paws, which told her he still had much growth ahead of him.

"I see you finally made the K-9 unit," Dylan noted aloud.

Her eyes did not break contact from Cloud, whilst she patiently awaited Michael's reply.

When the dog had finished examining every last inch of the hospital room's floor, he began inspecting the furniture in the room. His nostrils flared as he ran his wet, black nose along the hospital bed's railing. He found the stem of the yellow-gold Serrada, which hung loosely from atop Dani's chest.

Evidently intrigued by the flower, Cloud began nipping at it with his sharp teeth. The lily became dislodged and fell to the ground, causing Cloud to start suddenly. His surprise passed quickly, though, and when he re-examined the fallen flower, he lost interest in it almost immediately. Boredom seemed to overcome him then, and he tucked his hindquarters in and sat down on the floor. He stared up into the air at his master, with his tongue hanging out of his mouth, and his tail wagging fervently.

With Cloud having calmed himself, Michael bent down and gently picked the lily up from the ground. Supporting himself on his knee, he slowly handed the flower back to Dylan.

"I did make the unit," he answered her, as he held the lily out towards her. "A couple months ago. They had me training for a while, and Cloud was assigned to me a few weeks ago."

He smiled as he spoke, his eyes shining with obvious affection.

Dylan shook her head from side to side, as she accepted the lily.

"Always the gentleman, I see," she answered, clearly a bit annoyed.

While Michael's manner appeared lovely on the surface, Dylan had never enjoyed being wooed in this fashion – at least, not by him. To her, Michael's romantic way had always felt a bit... unnatural – almost like he was trying too hard.

Embarrassed at her reaction, Michael's cheeks became flushed. He gave a small, nervous laugh, and slowly raised himself off of the ground, taking a seat in the vacant chair across from Dylan. Cloud watched him move, and then quickly repositioned himself to be closer to his master, playfully knocking his head into Michael's side and licking his hand.

Michael seemed only interested in Dylan, though. Dismissing Cloud, he rested his forearm on the hospital bed and leaned forward, so as to be closer to her.

"How are you, Dyl?" he asked, the sincerity in his voice ringing truly.

"I'm fine," she lied. "I know you spoke to Holly, but… you know how she exaggerates…"

Michael didn't push her further on the subject.

"And Dani?" he diverted, his eyes darting quickly to and from the slender body resting motionless under the hospital bed's sheets.

Dylan only shook and bowed her head in answer.

"Oh," Michael added sheepishly. "I'm sorry."

A lump formed in Dylan's throat, and she waved her hand up at him dismissively.

"Don't worry about it," she said, all the while, fighting to maintain her composure.

The back of her eyes began to sting, as all of the doctor's warnings of the preceding day came flying back into her mind.

Swallowing her distress, Dylan turned from Michael and reached down to grab her knapsack from the floor. She lifted it from its resting place, plopped it into her lap, and began rummaging through it in search of a distraction.

"Are you alright?" Michael asked her empathetically. "If you need me to leave…"

"No," Dylan interrupted abruptly. "No, it's fine. I'm fine."

She didn't meet Michael's eye when she spoke, but carried on shifting items around in her bag. Loose scraps of paper, a pair of sunglasses she'd forgotten she owned, old tubes of lip-gloss that she hadn't used in months. Dylan collected some of these garbage articles now, and swiftly chucked them into the trash bin at the foot of her sister's bed.

Captivated by her actions, Cloud watched eagerly from his spot on the floor. His head swayed back and forth, his gaze locked upon the items as they sailed through the air, landing in the basket, one piece at a time. The dog seemed to be growing increasingly agitated with each and every shot.

"Down boy," ordered Michael, "shush." Cloud had begun squirming and whimpering loudly.

His whines did not reach Dylan's ears, however, for her focus had been deflected by something deep in the pit of her bag. Gently, Dylan reached her hand into the pack and lifted out the ragged object she'd uncovered.

"What is that?" Michael asked, he too, intrigued by the mysterious package.

After the horrible chat with her sister's doctor, Dylan had forgotten *all* about the old leather envelope she'd collected from her parents' deposit box. It had remained buried in her bag, beneath a layer of debris. But in lifting it out of her bag now, the same sense of urgency Dylan had felt the first time she'd laid eyes upon it came rushing back. And so, she resumed her efforts to unfasten the thin leather cord, which was wrapped tightly around the parcel.

"Whatever it is, it looks ancient," Michael observed.

Cloud had lost interest in Dylan the moment she'd stopped emptying the contents of her sack. He'd ceased his whines, and now stretched his front paws across the floor and allowed his belly to drop to the ground. He rested his head down upon the floor, but kept his eyes fixed upon his master, patiently awaiting his next instructions.

Meanwhile, Dylan continued yanking at the different bits of leather string, which were tied tightly around the ancient envelope. She was making no progress in untying the knots. Tired of watching her fail, Michael pulled a small Swiss Army knife from his pocket and leaned over to her from his chair.

"Here," he said, as he flipped a small blade out from the handle, "let me."

Carefully removing her fingers from the black leather package, Dylan allowed Michael to make a single swift incision into one of its many cross-sections of rope. The sharp blade cut through the cord like butter. Michael then retracted the knife, sat back in his chair, and re-pocketed the tool.

Dylan barely uttered a "thank you", before ripping into the envelope spiritedly. She untied the thin straps from around the package, threw them aside, and then proceeded to unfold the thin pleats of ragged leather coverings.

There were four flaps of this delicate cloth, each folded over, one on top of the other. Dylan quickly lifted them, one at a time, but did so carefully. Whatever treasure was hidden inside, she was certain it must have belonged to her mother – that its safekeeping was paramount.

Dylan lifted the last flap of leather and revealed the contents of the parcel. She drew in a sharp breath as she gazed down upon what could only be some sort of antique manuscript, or journal. Its forty-odd pages were old and yellowing – yet thick like parchment. They were bound together by a single thin section of dark leather, which covered both the back and front of the book, and which was wrapped tightly around its edge. The binding was old, but still in good condition – each page appeared to have been sown in place by hand. It was clear much care had been taken in fabricating the document.

The book felt heavy in Dylan's grasp. Somehow, its importance was weighing on her. Slowly, she opened it right down the middle, only to discover that the writing within it was illegible…

The characters scrawled upon the pages were written in an undecipherable language. Dylan guessed, perhaps ancient Chinese or Japanese? In any case, it wasn't an alphabet that she recognized, and she was wholly disappointed upon realizing she wouldn't be able to read it.

If that wasn't strange enough, the whole manuscript also appeared to be backwards. What looked like the title page had been sown into place at the very back of the book, and each sentence had been written in reverse order, from top-down and right to left. Dylan had to browse through the journal from what (in her point of view) seemed like back-to-front. She turned the pages from left to right, instead of from right to left.

There were a few hand-sketched illustrations scattered here and there on some of the pages. But these were small, and only depicted what appeared to be random plants, stones, or tools – none of which had any meaning for Dylan.

"Dylan, are you OK?"

Michael was vying for Dylan's attention. She'd been quiet for some time now.

"Yeah," Dylan replied haphazardly.

She did not heed Michael's words, and only carried on flipping the pages of her mother's journal.

Dylan may not have been fluent in whatever language the book was printed in, but she still felt connected to it in some way. It was a part of her history, she was certain, of her heritage. She turned each page, one at a time, staring down at the mass of characters – all so alien to her. The last few pages of parchment (which, in a regular western volume would have been the first few pages) had been left blank. But she turned and examined each of them, nonetheless.

Dylan turned the last page and shut the manuscript. Feeling somewhat unfulfilled, she took a deep breath, exhaled, and turned her attention back to Michael. She didn't utter a single syllable, however, and only looked at him. Her big, green eyes having lost their usual sparkle.

"Not what you were expecting?" Michael guessed.

"No, not really," Dylan answered.

She ran the palms of her hands over the leather cover of her book, quietly collecting her thoughts. The material felt soft and worn.

"I don't know *what* I was expecting," she chanced. "I guess I got my hopes up."

Michael didn't answer her and only stared, a confused expression on his face.

"It belonged to my parents," Dylan explained. "I guess I thought it might give me some answers."

Dylan shrugged her shoulders sadly. Cloud, recognizing the shift in her mood, sat back up and yelped at her sympathetically.

"I'm sure you could find someone to translate it for you," Michael suggested positively. "If it means that much to you?"

He was being helpful, and Dylan recognized his efforts.

"You're right," she answered. "I may still be able to salvage something of these pages."

Dylan smiled at Michael, and once again, flipped the manuscript open. Her eyes dropped back down to the elegant, inked script, and her smile vanished entirely. Her breath escaped her, and for a second in time, her heart seemed to stop.

There, hidden amongst the runes in the center of the page, was the mark she'd seen in her dreams. Dylan shut her eyes forcefully and reopened them once more, expecting the symbol to disappear. She was certain she was hallucinating.

But there it was again, clear as day, the same two overlapping rings, the same piercing stroke. She'd glazed over it in the first place, as the mark blended-in so perfectly with the other characters surrounding it on the page.

Dylan quickly flipped to the next page and ran her finger down each column of text, one at a time, searching. She found the mark once more, this time, nestled in between some of the characters in the bottom left-hand corner of the page. She flipped to the next page, and again, there it was on the right-hand side. She found the mark again and again, page after page, and with every sighting, her heart leapt in her chest. The colour drained from her face, but her eyes grew brighter and brighter with intrigue.

"Dylan?" Michael ventured. "What is it? You look like you've seen a ghost or something."

Completely bewildered and struggling to make sense of her discovery, all Dylan could do was sit, dazed and shocked. She looked up at Michael, then over to Cloud, then back down again at the sacred manuscript in her lap.

"Michael," she finally mustered. "I'm sorry. But... I have to go."

Dylan was up on her feet a moment later; and without another word, determinedly exited the room. Michael stared after her, slightly flabbergasted. Cloud too, tilted his head to one side, confused by her unexpected departure.

◆

Dylan marched her way along the busy hospital corridors, not even noticing the dozens of people brushing past her. She'd long forgotten about Michael and Cloud. All she could think of was getting to the bottom of this plot. Everything else could wait.

A million questions whizzed around her head. What was that obscured symbol? What was its meaning? How was it possible that she could dream of it, before ever even seeing it? Were her dreams somehow connected to her mother? Could this *all* just be a coincidence? Or was she losing her mind?

Dylan's heart beat quicker, and her body seemed to be entering a sort of fervour. She'd reached the hospital's main entrance, and hurriedly pushed her way through its glass doors, and into the fresh outside.

The sun was shining brightly. There was a cool breeze in the air. Dylan pressed forward, maintaining her fast walking pace, still preoccupied by the countless questions plaguing her mind.

She made her way blindly – for the only image she saw was that of the cryptic twin-ringed symbol. Dylan recalled that, in her dream, it had appeared to her in the center of her hand.

She raised and examined her palm now, as she crossed the hospital's giant front lawn. With her head tucked and her eyes fixed intently upon her open hand, she was *all-too* oblivious to the world around her. And it was at this moment, that she entered into a full-on collision with a stranger – a kindred spirit *also* lost in thought, or so she presumed.

They crashed into one another. Hard. Dylan lost her balance and fell to the ground.

After shaking off her surprise, she found that some of the pages of her precious manuscript had been ripped from the binding in the fall. Distraught, she hastily crawled over to, and began collecting the pages, checking each of them for signs of any irreparable damage.

"Let me help you," said the stranger.

His voice rang warm and invitingly in her ear. But Dylan did not respond. She was far too absorbed in the task of preserving her treasured heirloom.

Without being asked, the stranger squatted down in front of her, and he too began collecting pages from the grass.

"Please don't," Dylan said, flustered and waving her arms around, attempting to shoo the stranger away. Her efforts to ward him off were in vain, however. The stranger had already collected a number of pages, and he was staring at them curiously.

Dylan faced him now, but was unable to get a good look at him just yet. The sun was shining directly into her eyes, and everything seemed a blur. A gust of wind blew by them, and a single sheet of stray parchment launched up into the air.

Dylan jumped, but the stranger was faster than she was. His reflexes were superb, for he had caught the flying page before she'd even made it to her feet. The wind had also blown some clouds into the sun's path, and Dylan could now see the stranger clearly in front of her.

He looked young. She guessed her age, perhaps a bit older. He was lean, not skinny – tall, but not lanky – and he had bright reddish-blonde hair, which actually managed to dazzle Dylan for a moment. Something about its atypical scarlet lustre caused her pause: there was something strangely familiar in it, she thought. For a second, Dylan forgot all about her mission.

Since picking up the loose papers, the stranger had not made eye contact with her. Not once. His gaze was locked upon the sheets of fallen manuscript, which he held in his hands, and his lips quivered faintly. When Dylan finally came to her senses, she recognized that he was, in fact, reading to himself.

"Excuse me," she protested, thinking the stranger quite rude. He was, in her opinion, without manners, trespassing upon her private documents.

He, however, was not fazed by her retort, and only kept scanning the papers avidly. Having finished with the first page clutched in his hand, he roughly stuffed it to the back of the pile, and began scanning the second, his eyes growing wider with every passing second.

"Excuse me!" Dylan exclaimed, more forcefully this time.

Her complaint finally produced the desired effect, and the stranger abruptly halted his offensive conduct. He looked at her straight in the eye. His gaze was penetrating and intense. Dylan felt like he was searching her with his eyes. His look caused her to flinch involuntarily, and she instinctively took one small step backwards and away from him.

He offered her no reassurances, and in response, only took an even larger step forward, closing the gap between them. His face was inches from hers now, and she could feel his breath upon her skin. His features were striking, his eyes strange – like staring into irises of blood-infused chocolate. Dylan wasn't sure whether she should be afraid or entranced by him. He was both beautiful and terrifying, all at once. She couldn't breathe, and only waited for him to make the next move.

It was some time before the boy spoke. The seconds spent trapped in his gaze felt more like hours. His aura was unlike any Dylan had ever experienced before. Being close to him was intoxicating – the way he stared through her, like he was determined to learn all there was to know about her, like she was important.

"Aurora?" he whispered finally.

His voice was scratchy and trembling. His posture remained still and in control. But in speaking, the veil concealing his true state of mind had been pierced. He swallowed anxiously, and his face twisted into a look of what could only be concern, perhaps even fear.

Dylan remained frozen at first, paralyzed and staring up into his dark maroon eyes. But her body loosened upon sensing the stranger's unease, and she managed to pull herself together.

Grabbing her prized, missing papers from his grasp, Dylan took yet another step back, giving herself room to breathe again. She mustered all the power she could, lifted her chin, and glared up at the strange boy.

His face softened when confronted as such. But again, he asked, as if he were desperately trying to verify some burning theory: "Aurora? It is you, isn't it?"

His eyes squinted as he spoke this time, and he pursed his lips apprehensively when he'd finished.

"I don't know what you're talking about," Dylan answered, frowning. But her words were drowned out by the sounds of a barking dog.

The howling had come from in behind her. Startled, Dylan turned automatically to check on the source of the disruption.

Cloud came thundering towards her at full speed, barking at the top of his lungs. He'd made it to her side in two seconds flat, and was now growling menacingly, his lips curled back and his teeth bared.

Dylan wasn't afraid. She'd grown up around dogs, and so she knew at once that Cloud's growls weren't directed at her. His behaviour was protective, not aggressive.

"Down boy," she told him. "It's OK."

Cloud immediately settled down at Dylan's order, and she rewarded him with a gentle pat upon his crown.

"Don't be frightened," she said aloud. "He's a good dog. He belongs to a friend of mine."

She turned back to face the stranger whom she'd addressed. But there was not a trace of him left anywhere. Dylan turned upon her heels and looked out in every direction. But the boy was nowhere to be seen.

"I'm so sorry, Dyl."

Michael had finally reached her. He'd been running, but wasn't in the least out of breath.

"I don't know what happened," Michael continued as he took up Cloud's leash in his hands. "We were leaving the hospital, and Cloud went mental all of a sudden. He got away from me. I heard him barking. Is everything OK? I swear he's never done this before."

"Yeah, everything's fine," Dylan answered, a bit rattled.

She was still confused, searching the distance for the shadowy figure of her mysterious stranger. Her heart was a flutter from her bizarre encounter with him, and she was not paying Michael much attention.

"Well," Michael told her, "you forgot your coat and your bag."

He held the items out to her, and Dylan seized them from him absent-mindedly. She took one last look around, cautiously hoping she'd spot the stranger once more. But when satisfied that he'd disappeared for good, she banished him from her thoughts.

Packing her mother's journal into her bag and swinging it over her shoulder, Dylan resumed her march, this time with Michael and Cloud traipsing after her.

◆

Kit had hidden himself in the shadow of a parked vehicle, not ten meters away from where Dylan had stood confused and looking for him. He now watched in silence, as she slowly disappeared from his sight, the cop and man's best friend close on her heels.

"Stupid mutt," he muttered to himself, irritated.

Kit sighed and carefully rose from his hiding place, his eyes never straying from the direction in which his mark had disappeared on the horizon. He was not his usual, confident self.

This simple manhunt was proving to be much more complex than he had originally foreseen. This girl – L's niece – was more than a mere girl, it seemed. He would have to proceed with extra caution. His instincts told him there was something *not quite right* about this family… something dangerous, perhaps even sinister.

-- CHAPTER TEN --

JACKPOT JONES

"What have we got?"

Dr. Beth Chandler came charging into Sunrise Hospital's operating room, dressed in her peach coloured surgical scrubs. She held her freshly scrubbed hands up in the air, still dripping wet. Her chocolate brown hair was tied back in a tight bun behind her neck, and her mouth and nose were hidden under a surgical mask. Her hazelnut eyes were focused, framed by her dark rimmed glasses.

From the moment she walked in, she commanded an air of respect and reverence from those already present in the room. They all stared up at her with a mix of hope and relief in their hearts. The patient lying on the operating table in the center of the room was in critical condition, and there was an air of chaos hanging over the operating team surrounding him. They all looked to Dr. Chandler now, for guidance and instructions.

Outside the operating room, Dr. Chandler was renowned for her extraordinary bedside manner. She brought a certain gentleness to post-operative care. But first and foremost, she was known to be an absolute *shark* in the operating room. Put a surgical scalpel in her hand, and she was like… 'magic'.

The residents and nurses at Sunrise all held Dr. Chandler in the highest esteem. There was always a waiting list to make it onto to one of her surgical rosters. She was currently on the fifteenth hour of her eighteen-hour shift, but still as sound as a bell. There was no better trauma surgeon than she in the city of Las Vegas, no one better suited to take on this particularly difficult surgical case.

"Male. Mid-to-late twenties. Stab wound to the left abdomen. Dr. Bernstein's prepping for an exploratory laparotomy. Massive transfusion protocol already in effect."

Susan, Dr. Chandler's favourite surgical nurse spoke fast, updating her boss on the patient's condition as she hurriedly dried her hands with a clean white towel, and helped her into her surgical gloves.

"Alright. Let's do it," Dr. Chandler announced, as her trusty nurse finished tightening up the strings of her surgical gown and fitting her surgical cap over her head.

Now fully dressed for the task ahead, Dr. Chandler stepped up to the surgical table in the center of the room. She quickly took in her patient. His abdomen was distended, and there was blood spouting from a slit wound, located two inches from his belly button. He was bleeding internally, and had been for some time.

Dr. Chandler knew in an instant that her patient's chances of survival were low. Nevertheless, she remained calm and collected in the face of these low odds of success. She'd saved patients in worse situations than these before, and with a little luck, she was confident she could do so again.

"OK. We need to get in there. Now!"

Dr. Chandler commanded her team as she hastily took up a scalpel from the assortment of surgical instruments on the tray to her right.

"Where is Sam?" she asked.

"I'm here! I'm here!"

Dr. Samuel Wilson, a relatively young senior resident at Sunrise, had just come bursting through the operating room's doors. He was out of breath, and his shaggy blonde hair was all awry atop his comical-looking head.

Sam's presentation could not have been said to be worthy of the title 'doctor' – let alone 'surgeon'. He looked more like a California surfer bum who'd just come from the beach. Regardless, he was Dr. Chandler's favourite surgical apprentice. What she saw in him, her colleagues at Sunrise could only guess.

As soon as Sam entered, Susan and the other surgical nurse in the room immediately accosted him. Together, with speedy and practiced hands, they carefully popped a surgical cap over his unruly hairdo, and quickly covered him with proper surgical attire. He stepped away from the two nurses looking quite unrecognizable, transformed, and ready for work.

"Dr. Wilson."

Dr. Chandler addressed her prized student with a stern voice.

"Next time we receive a trauma page, I expect you to be here *before* I arrive. Are we clear?"

"Yes Ma'am," Sam replied, as he took his place next to his teacher. "Whoa!" he said, as he looked down at their patient and absorbed the seriousness of his injury. "Awesome," he beamed, excited by the prospects of the complicated surgery ahead.

Despite her disagreement with Dr. Wilson's inappropriate remark, Dr. Chandler couldn't help but smile beneath her surgical mask. She was glad her resident was displaying such zest for his job.

Though his demeanour needed some work, Dr. Chandler had no doubt that Sam had a natural talent for surgery. She'd chosen him because he was quick with his hands, and had a general gift for making fast yet correct decisions under pressure.

Besides his sometimes-unprofessional disposition, Dr. Wilson's only shortfall was a tendency for tardiness, which in certain circumstances (such as these) *could* realistically translate to fatalities.

The patient before them required urgent care. Every second that passed was a second wasted.

There was not a moment to lose. Dr. Bernstein, the thirty-five year old surgical fellow, standing on the opposite side of the surgical table from Sam and Dr. Chandler, had already begun making his incision into the patient's belly. With speed, he cut through the patient's flesh and exposed his innards. Blood began oozing and overflowing from the exposed cavity. Dr. Chandler and Sam immediately went to work, as Dr. Bernstein pulled back the patient's skin and muscle, clearing the way so his colleagues could have a full view of the trauma site.

Sam sprayed sterile water into the abdomen, washing away much of the blood so that his teacher could hunt for the source of the bleed. He reached for the suction tool and checked the patient's vitals.

"His blood pressure's real bad, doc," he warned his teacher.

"Dr. Wilson," Beth Chandler began, "I really need you to concentrate on clearing. I can't see anything in this mess."

Her words were polite, but her tone was urgent. One look at her patient's entrails, and she knew his prognosis was even worse than she'd first suspected. He was spiralling. She estimated she had less than a few minutes to locate and repair his wounds before he went into cardiac arrest.

"I know this guy," Sam said, in far too jovial a tone.

"What?" Dr. Chandler answered, irritated by the lightness of his words.

"I know him." Sam laughed now, still suctioning blood from inside of his patient. "It's Jackpot Jones!"

"Jackpot what?"

Dr. Bernstein intervened, while Dr. Chandler continued to search the surfaces of her patient's abdominal organs. She had no time for her student's crazy antics.

"Jackpot Jones," Sam repeated again, his smile hidden under his surgical mask. "This guy is like Las Vegas' Native American hero! He's a crazy high roller. Been hitting up all the major casinos in the last couple months. I think his name's Freddy. But everyone calls him 'Jackpot'. You know? Cause he hit the *Jackpot* a few months ago, and he's totally loaded now!"

Dr. Bernstein stared Sam down with harsh and judging eyes as he maintained pressure on either sides of their patient's cavity. He truly couldn't believe how insensitive Dr. Wilson was – telling stories and laughing, as his patient's life was slowing right before them... No matter his disapproval, however, Dr. Bernstein knew that Sam would never be punished. The kid was just... *gifted*, he thought. Even in jest, Sam was able to outperform most of his peers in the operating room. In the few moments Dr. Bernstein had taken to respond to the surgical resident's jokes, for instance, Sam had already managed to clear their patient's abdomen.

"Thanks, Sam. I've got it," said Dr. Chandler then.

Upon hearing her remark, Sam straightened his back and smiled to himself proudly. Dr. Bernstein only grimaced under his surgical mask, thinking him an arrogant pest.

"Damn! It's his spleen," cried Dr. Chandler. "Pass me the suturing kit. Hurry!"

She held her hand out in the air, impatiently awaiting the life-saving tools she required.

Susan placed the suturing implements into Dr. Chandler's hand, just as the patient's monitor sent out an alarm, alerting them to his heart failure.

"He's crashing!" cried Dr. Bernstein urgently, as Dr. Chandler hastily grabbed the needle from her nurse.

"Push epinephrine," Sam told the surgical nurses, as he reached up over his patient and began chest compressions.

Dr. Chandler left all of the aggressive resuscitation actions to her student, and on her side, merely continued to suture the wound in her patient's spleen. She expertly weaved the suture needle through the injured organ, and in less than a minute, saw a marked difference in blood spillage. Throwing herself into the repairs, she lost all sense of time. The needle dived in and out, in and out, and slowly, she saw her patient's injury becoming less and less. She had nearly finished closing the perforation to her patient's spleen, when she was startled out of her work.

"Dr. Chandler."

Dr. Bernstein interjected, pulling her out of her feverish labour.

"I think he's gone. He's been down too long."

Beth Chandler paused her sewing, looked up at her colleagues, and then over at the display on her patient's monitor. Her breathing was heavy, and she signalled Sam to halt chest compressions. As soon as he lifted his hands from the patient's chest, the machine let out a shrill flat-lining tone. It appeared his efforts in restarting their patient's heart had been unsuccessful.

"Damn it!" Dr. Chandler swore, as she withdrew her hands from her patient's open abdomen.

She ripped her gloves off and tore her surgical mask from her face, as she looked up at the time on the digital clock in the corner of the operating room.

"Time of death," she called out, "1:08 AM."

The flippant light-heartedness drained from Sam's face, as he stared down at his deceased patient, at his tanned skin, shaved head, and at the beautiful tattoo art decorating his neck and jaw.

"I can't believe it," he said in a solemn, disbelieving tone, "Freddy 'Jackpot' Jones… dead… in our OR…"

Beth Chandler gently placed her hand over her resident's shoulder and gripped it tightly.

"Don't be too hard on yourself, Sam," she told him. "We did everything we could."

"Yeah," Sam replied quietly, "I guess his luck just… ran out."

"Close him up for his family," Dr. Chandler told her young pupil, as she exited the room with Dr. Bernstein, "then meet me for rounds."

She left Sam alone with the nurses to clean up the body of their fallen patient, and to contemplate the lessons learned from his unfortunate case.

CHAPTER ELEVEN

SCARLET SPECTERS

"Dear Ms. Dubois."

Dylan's lips quivered softly as she quietly and eagerly read from her open laptop's screen. Her eyes squinted as she whispered the words of the email message aloud to herself, her eyebrows wrinkled with concentration. She'd patiently awaited this message for over a week now, and was positively buzzing with anticipation.

With the tip of her finger, and using the small touch pad on her computer, Dylan impatiently scrolled to the body of the email and continued. The pupils of her eyes darted from left to right, as she read the remainder of the message from her inbox.

Dear Ms. Dubois,

Apologies for the delay in my response. I was away at a conference upon reading your email, and have only just had the chance to examine the scans of your mother's book.

As you are no doubt aware, I have devoted my career to deciphering ancient scriptures. Based on my experience, I think that I would agree with my colleague, Dr. Cao, and I am delighted that he referred you to me. The extracts you sent me appear to contain characters that strongly resemble previously uncovered samples of old East Asian script.

With your permission, I would like the opportunity to study the original text in its entirety. At first glance, I would guess that the samples of scripture you sent me all herald from different eras.

Some of the text bears striking similarities to writings dating as far back as the Shang Dynasty, while others appear much more recent. It is truly rare to find a compilation, such as this, containing what promises to be dozens of examples of scripture, all varying in age.

It would do me a great honour if you would visit me in DC. If your mother's journal is as you describe it, I am certain that my colleagues at the Smithsonian Museum will also wish to share in its inspection. Given enough time, I am certain that we can uncover the messages it contains.

I will instruct my secretary, Ms. Forrester (copied), to make arrangements for your travel and stay in Washington. Please contact her at your earliest convenience.

I look forward to meeting you in person.

Kind regards,

Dr. Will Gallagher

Dylan re-read the email twice more, her frustration increasing each time. A month ago, when she had set out to find an expert to help her translate her mother's journal, she had not anticipated encountering such difficulty. Since then, she'd corresponded with three different specialists, including Dr. Jason Cao, a professor of archaeology at the local University of McGill, who had finally referred her to Dr. Gallagher. Dr. Cao, who had collaborated with Dr. Gallagher before, had assured Dylan that the Smithsonian linguist was the best in his field.

Research into Dr. Gallagher's credentials had left Dylan thoroughly impressed. He had over thirty years of experience in dealing with ancient languages, and had, in the last decade, devoted himself exclusively to the study of antique East Asian scriptures. He'd received numerous awards in the fields of anthropology and archaeology over the years, and had even been granted honours by the government of Vietnam for his services in recovering a priceless historical artefact (which had previously been thought to be long lost).

His skills in translating ancient texts were meant to be unparalleled. So why was it that the 'talented' Dr. Gallagher required a *team* of Smithsonian doctorates to help him in deciphering her mother's journal? How long would it take him, Dylan wondered. How many weeks or months would he expect her to wait, whilst his team trawled through the pages of her family's private property?

It was a violation, Dylan thought – one she knew her mother would *never* have approved of. Lenora Dubois was likely turning over in her grave, at this very moment. Surely, there were other ways of translating her mother's book…

Dylan's impatience boiled up inside of her. Visions of the bright haired stranger from the hospital now flashed into her mind.

Aurora?

More than a month had passed since her encounter with him on the front lawn of the Montreal General, and yet his voice still resonated clearly in her head.

The stranger had laid eyes on but a few scraps of her mother's journal, and within moments, he had understood something. The clarity that shined in his eyes then, the recognition – Dylan still had visions of it. What was it that he'd seen there in those pages? And who was he? What made *him* different from the rest? Was there no one else who could help her understand?

Nothing made sense. That boy with the disconcerting look in his eyes and the scarlet-blonde hair… he couldn't have been more than twenty-three or twenty-four years old. What would someone of *his* age know of ancient Asian runes that a sixty-five year old world-renowned specialist did not?

Dylan's jaw tensed in irritation, and her hands darted up to her skull. She held her forehead up against the palm of her hand, and ran her fingers through the roots of her hair, massaging her scalp. Her head ached. Sleep had continued to elude her. Her dreams had grown more intense with each passing night. These days, she was lucky to catch even an hour or two of shuteye at a time. Meanwhile, her waking hours had become hazy, uncertain, and riddled with sporadic hallucinations.

Everywhere Dylan turned, he haunted her – that red-haired stranger. She was certain she'd seen him watching her, at first from the park by the hospital, then from the bus stop down the road, and even from the café across the way from her apartment building.

Time and time again, he would appear to her, but then be gone again, before she could even blink. These recurring apparitions had caused Dylan to seriously question her sanity on more than one occasion. But the more she ran things over in her mind, the more convinced she became that they were real.

Aurora?

At the hospital, he'd asked her repeatedly – *"Aurora?"*

The word, literally translated, meant "the dawn" – that red-orange masterpiece that paints the sky each morning, signalling the start of a new day with the rising of the sun.

It was ironic. That blaze of burning colours seemed to swirl around inside of her, each time she thought she'd found him.

Somehow, in her muddled and sleep-deprived mind, Dylan had convinced herself that *he* was her salvation. That boy with the unusual coloured hair was the *only one* who could show her the way. If she could only find him, he would explain everything – the dreams, her mother… that cryptic book. They were all connected, and Dylan was certain that *he* knew how.

Taking a deep breath, Dylan took up the mug of hot coffee that sat on the table in front of her, next to her computer. Slowly, with jittery hands, she lifted the rim to her lips and sipped at the warm beverage. She closed her eyes and inhaled, as the delicious, earthy fragrance soothed her throbbing head.

In the past few weeks, Dylan had come to rely far too heavily on her daily doses of caffeine. This particular coffee shop had become one of her most frequent haunts. Its coffee was the only thing that seemed to offer her any form of relief, albeit temporarily. Come nighttime, the dreams always came.

Holly had repeatedly implored that Dylan obtain herself sleep-aid medications, but Dylan refused every time. Her friend called her stubborn, but Dylan preferred: 'determined'. "I'm not a pill-popper, Holly," she would say.

Things weren't so bad. They would get better. Dylan had faith that her situation would improve. It had to.

Loud vibrations suddenly erupted from the table's surface, and nearly startled Dylan right out of her seat. Her phone, which she'd left lying on the table switched to silent, was screaming for her attention. The sound caught Dylan off-guard, and caused her to spill some of the coffee she'd been drinking down her chin and into her lap. The liquid burned into her skin and through her jeans.

Wincing, Dylan hurriedly put the mug down and reached for a napkin. She wiped her mouth clean, and with shaky hands, began dabbing at the mess in her lap. Multi-tasking, she reached a free hand out to her phone and carefully pressed her finger against its screen, which immediately lit up at her touch.

"That will be Holly," she said to herself, as the words 'Missed call Holly Andersen' flashed up on the cell phone's display. Speak of the Devil checking in on her.

Dylan sighed, and upon contemplating the stains on her jeans, decided it was time she be heading home. Dr. Gallagher's disappointing offer had managed to sap what little energy she'd had left. With a heavy heart, she pocketed her phone and gently shut the screen of her laptop computer. Lifting her bag from the seat next to her, she stuffed the laptop within, and threw a single strap over her shoulder.

Having collected all of her belongings, Dylan stepped out of the coffee shop, and into the busy street. It was a cold and overcast day. The sky was littered with dark grey ominous-looking clouds, and the air was heavy and humid. The wind felt freezing against her coffee-soaked legs.

It was a short walk to her apartment building, and so Dylan pressed on, taking comfort in the thought that she would soon be able to change into fresh clothing. Her steps were quick. She expertly weaved her way through the maze of slower Montrealites she encountered strolling along the sidewalk.

It wasn't long before Dylan was dandily hopping up the front steps of her apartment building. Standing before the large entrance, she fiddled with her keys. She was breathing hard after her stint of speed walking and was anxious to enter her home. In her haste, she fumbled and accidentally lost grip of her keychain. The keys bounced from her hand, as she tried in vain to catch them before they hit the ground. The inevitable clinking sound resonated then, as they landed on the cement stairs behind her.

Dylan let out a large sigh, and allowed her head to fall backwards in exasperation. *What a klutz I am*, she thought to herself.

Setting her bag down, she stepped her way down a few stairs, before grabbing the staircase's railing and gingerly lowering herself down to her mislaid keys. The tips of her fingers met with the tiny, metal pieces, and her eyes wandered. Something caught her eye in the distance.

From her strange angle on the stairs, Dylan was just able to make out the far end of her apartment building. And it was there that she saw him – a man, standing with his back propped up against the building's far wall.

The man's head popped out from in-behind the corner, and immediately, Dylan recognized his sunset-red hair. He looked to have it covered under a sort of cap, but it remained unmistakeable.

Dylan did not hesitate. She rapidly took up her keys, stood up straight and launched herself into the air. She landed at the foot of the stairs, and without a second thought, sprinted as fast as she could towards the end of the building and towards the man concealing himself there.

The stranger. He wasn't a figment of her imagination, or a ghost. He was real. And he was right here. He wouldn't get away from her this time. *Not again*, Dylan decided.

The stranger must have seen her coming. For he'd already gone by the time Dylan had reached his lurking spot on the corner of the building. But she had him on the run. He was still in her sights, only a few meters ahead of her, dashing down the sidewalk.

"Wait! Stop!" she screamed. But the stranger did not heed her.

Dylan followed on his heels, moving in grand strides across the pavement. Her eyes watered as the cold wind met with her corneas, but she did not blink, for fear that she may lose him.

The stranger was fast… unbelievably so.

Despite her somewhat weakened state, Dylan ran with the strength and resolve that only one as desperate as she could muster. She was like a starved predator, chasing after the first meal to cross her path in days, or like a frantic hunter, pursuing the most rare and elusive of prey. Her heart beat fast and resilient, spreading adrenaline through her body and chemically pushing her forward. In her current state, Dylan felt that not even Cloud, Michael's trusty, young pup, could have outrun her. But her efforts were futile nonetheless. Simply put, the boy was faster than she. He was better.

Over the next few minutes, the distance between them steadily grew, and the figure of the stranger in Dylan's sights shrunk into the distance. She saw him slyly dodging pedestrians ahead of her with ease, and nimbly bounding from one street to the next, never losing momentum. She was incredulous at how skilled he was.

Even in the face of his obvious talent for flight, however, Dylan did not waiver. She continued to push against the pains in her legs and the cramp that had manifested in her abdomen. She drew in one long breath after another, trying desperately to oxygenate the blood feeding the muscles on which she relied so urgently now. Every impact with the cement under her feet sent vibrations up through her shins. She could feel the aches beginning to spread to her bones, but still, she did not quit.

Her fleeing target was nearly out of sight, when Dylan saw him commit a lethal mistake. He was stealthy. But Dylan caught him, regardless, ducking in-behind a newsstand a few streets up, and into the alley hidden behind it.

As a long-time resident of these parts, Dylan knew that this particular Montreal backstreet would offer him no means of escape. It was a dead-end in disguise. A sudden bout of cheer overcame her, when she realized she'd been dealt a lucky break.

You're trapped, Dylan thought to herself, a smirk forming on her lips.

She drew in a sharp breath of excitement, as a second wave of energy washed over her and caused her to pick up speed again. She had only to persevere a few moments longer. She was nearly there. A few more minutes, and she would have him cornered.

Dylan wasn't afraid – not in the least. The thought never even occurred to her that her stalker might be dangerous. He'd been following her, but she was certain he would not hurt her. She trusted her instincts in this completely. Holly would have called her 'naïve'. But Dylan knew that this boy carried the keys to the many mysteries that had plagued her. She *needed* him. If she could only speak with him, she knew she could discover the secrets that he sheltered, and expose the truth, which until now, had remained shrouded from her.

She'd reached the newsstand. With surprising agility, Dylan planted her foot into the pavement and managed to pivot herself in a fraction of a second. She braced herself momentarily, and then took off once more, taking the same path she'd seen the stranger take. She ducked her head and hopped through the narrow opening, which led into the back alley.

The vendor manning the newsstand shot her a dirty look as she brushed passed him.

"Sorry!" Dylan called out, as she ran past.

The alleyway behind the newsstand was dark. What little sunlight there had been out in the streets, shining through the clouds, did not penetrate this passage. The buildings on either side of the alley were tall, and blocked out most of the sky.

Dylan ran through the narrow path, her feet kicking up dust that had settled upon the ground. The alley was empty and silent. The sound of Dylan's footfalls echoed against the cold brick walls on either side of her. The stranger would hear her coming. She had no doubt. But it didn't matter. He had nowhere to go.

There was a sharp bend in the alley just ahead of her. *The end of the line*, Dylan thought. The stranger would be waiting for her there. The alley had been boarded off years ago, when one of the adjacent buildings had undergone construction. The wooden planks, which had been used to block the path, spanned nearly an entire storey. *He'll be there*, she thought, *trapped like a mouse in a maze.*

Dylan reached the bend now, and abruptly, came to a complete stop. She threw herself sideways and landed, legs spread, with her hand gripping her thigh and her head slunk. She gasped and gave a slight cough, as the stale air hit her lungs like a suffocating puff of smoke. She was sweating. Her skin flushed. But it was over. She'd made it.

Slowly, Dylan lifted her head and stood up straight, allowing her muscles to loosen, and her limbs to relax. Her vision was a bit hazy. It took a moment for her to adjust to her dank surroundings.

When her eyes finally adjusted and took in the scene before her, Dylan's thumping heart came to an outright halt. The alley, she saw, was absolutely empty. It was otherwise just as she remembered: a dead end with brick walls on either side, and a wooden barrier, nearly fifteen feet tall – directly ahead. But nothing else.

"What? Where is he?"

Dylan stepped up to the wooden wall, panic taking hold of her. She placed her hand firmly on the surface of the old wood, as though testing it. But there was no trick. The wall was sturdy. She spun herself around, her back now against the wood, and painstakingly searched the alley again.

As far as she could see, there were no doors or cracks in the walls. There were no objects of any kind, anywhere – no way under, or over, the wooden blockade.

Distressed, Dylan began walking the lengths of the brick walls on either side of the barricade. She ran both her hands roughly along their surfaces, testing the stones here and there, unsure of what she was looking for. She half-expected one of the bricks to give way, and for the wall to suddenly open onto a secret entrance that would lead her to her prize. No such luck, however. The closed off alley was just... a closed off alley. Plain and simple.

Dylan felt like she was going mad. She stood alone in the center of the alleyway, and spun herself in circles, wildly eyeing every wall surrounding her. Soon, she was overwhelmed with dizziness, and her head began to spin.

Somehow managing to keep her balance, Dylan held her arms up and took her head into her hands. She held it tightly, trying desperately to calm her tempestuous thoughts.

He was here. I know he was here, she thought to herself loudly. *I didn't imagine it,* she repeated to herself, over and over.

But no matter what she told herself, reality remained unchanged. Even if he *was* real, the bright haired boy had gone. He'd blown away with the wind, and taken Dylan's last shred of hope with him.

-- CHAPTER TWELVE --

DATE WITH DESTINY

The wind howled and the skies above her growled as though they had a life of their own. The atmosphere over the field surrounding the now open cavern had grown dark and turbulent in past weeks – the storm brewing overhead incidentally mirroring Dylan's dwindling strength and resolve.

Following the inexplicable disappearance of the wall of rock that had so long blocked her entry to the cave, Dylan had rejoiced. She recalled how triumphant she had felt, having surmounted her obstacle. Only feelings of courage and confidence had coursed through her then. Her glorious spirit had been premature however; for weeks had passed now, and Dylan was still no closer to grasping the glowing artefact housed within the cave.

The yearning she felt for the yet unidentified object had also grown more intense with time. The restlessness it awakened within her was difficult to bear, especially when coupled with the countless aches and pains growing throughout her body. Her muscles burned, her bones throbbed, and her joints cried out for relief. Both her physical and mental resources had been nearly depleted in what felt like the thousands of attempts she'd made of crossing the dark threshold that stood between her and her goal.

Dylan's mouth was hard, her face expressionless, as she stared now into the blackness before her. Lightning flashed across the sky, momentarily illuminating the gloomy red grasses on either side of her. And all was dark once more. Mere seconds passed, and thunder echoed throughout the field.

The sound ignited something within the cave. Deep, almost animal grumblings and aggressive snarls began emanating from within, as if warding off intruders. Dylan was unfazed by the menacing sounds, however, having heard them many times before.

Squinting her tired eyes, she continued to stare into the gaping black hole until she found the one glimmer of light there, still shining in the deep. Hope was not lost yet, she thought to herself with difficulty. She would try again, one more time...

Dylan took a deep breath, sucking cold, damp air into her lungs. She planted her back foot into the ground and pushed herself forward with all the strength she could muster. She sprinted, running as fast as she could into the abyss, towards that tiny light which continued to call to her.

Blackness enveloped her as she left the crimson field and entered the shadows of the cave. She felt the ground beneath her feet harden with every bound, and soon, every connection she made with the earth was brusque and hard. The stone floors of the cavern sent violent jolts up through her legs as she ran, the soles of her feet repeatedly striking its solid and unyielding surface. And despite the agony it caused her already-tender body, Dylan continued to run blindly in the dark.

Her breathing quickened, and her skin began to warm and perspire. Still, she pushed forward, never letting her gaze stray from the little light ahead of her. She planted one foot in front of the other, pushing herself closer and closer – or so she thought.

Dylan ran towards the flicker of light, but no matter how long, or how hard she ran, it was never any nearer. The twinkle in the dark remained... merely a twinkle. She was as far from her goal as she had been upon first entering the cave.

Soon, she could run no more. Her body faltered. Dylan slackened her pace and finally came to a stop. Panting, she stood in utter obscurity, searching her surroundings.

Her ears, like her eyes, were of little use to her here – all the sounds in the cave drowned out by the vicious growls bouncing about her. The deeper she ran, the louder they rung, rendering it almost impossible to hear anything else.

Dylan's heart raced in her chest as self-doubt crept back into her thoughts. It was no use. Unable to hear. Unable to see. How was she to reach the light at the end of this tunnel? It was too far, she thought. And she was so weak.

The cave had defeated her. Without aid, Dylan knew she could go no further.

In an attempt to swallow her anguish, she drew in a deep breath. The air in the cave was colder than it had been out in the field. The frosty draft struck her like a blade of ice. Coughing, she let her eyes settle once more upon the light, still glowing softly from deep within the cave.

She felt a familiar tingle in the palm of her hand. Startled, Dylan looked down to find the mysterious symbol there, also glowing. The light in her hand was dim at first, like the light in the cave. But as she stared at it, it intensified. Dylan's eyes sparkled as reflections of light danced upon their surfaces, and soon, she was blinded.

The pitch black of the cave was replaced by burning white spectra. Dylan slammed her eyes shut, but her eyelids offered her no protection from the whiteout, which burned all around her. It shined and overwhelmed her – consuming both her and everything else it touched.

Dylan's eyes sprung open. She cried out, as she woke from the latest iteration of her nightmare. Her mouth spread wide as she drew in large gaping breaths. Her eyes moistened in her panic, and she struggled to breathe. Slowly, oxygen travelled from her lungs back into her blood. Her head cleared, and her awareness grew.

There was both darkness and light around her. The light was shining from directly above, but everywhere else was black as night. Dylan shivered. She was cold and wet. The bare skin of her arms and legs felt numb and were covered in goose bumps. Her teeth chattered. The thin nightdress she wore was soaked all the way through. Her long, dark hair was drenched and hung heavily over her shoulders. The sound of falling rain filled her ears.

Dylan raised and crossed both of her arms over her chest in attempts to seal in her body heat. She turned herself about, straining her eyes for a better look around.

She blinked her eyelids once, twice, three times. For her eyelashes too, were full of water. There were raindrops sprinkled all over her body. Cold water ran down her face and dripped down from under her chin. The bottoms of her bare feet were frozen, and rested upon the cold hard asphalt of the street.

Startled by the realization of her surroundings, Dylan jumped to her feet. She took a step forward and landed in a shallow puddle of rainwater. Her body retorted in shock, and she shuddered, as she stepped backwards again, retreating into her original stance. Dread crawled its way up her spine, as she took in her predicament. Somehow, she'd sleepwalked herself out into the cold, rainy streets of the city.

It was the middle of the night. All was quiet. The only light was that of a street lamp towering above her head. There were no stars. In fact, Dylan couldn't even see the sky through the deluge of rain falling around her.

Terror shined in her eyes. She whipped her head from side to side, painstakingly trying to identify the buildings in front of her. Where was she? She couldn't be too far from home, she told herself, attempting to soothe her fears.

Alas, the street was unfamiliar to her. One side was lined with abandoned buildings, their windows and doors covered with planks of wood. The other side of the street bordered what must have been a park of some sort. A short metal railing was all that separated the sidewalk on which Dylan stood from the dozens of large trees which grew there.

Standing in the secluded street, cold and dripping wet, Dylan knew that she'd hit rock bottom. She'd been in denial. The dreams were not something she could handle on her own, she realized. She needed help. She wished then, that she'd listened to Holly when she'd had the chance. Perhaps she could've avoided this mess.

For a time, Dylan failed to move even an inch. Panic kept her paralyzed – rigid and unmoving in the rain. Where was she to go? Right? Left? Not knowing which way would lead her home, she chose at random, and hoped for the best.

"Well I can't stay here," she whispered to herself.

Slowly, Dylan forced her bare foot off of the ground and placed it flat in the unavoidable puddle before her. Water splashed at her ankle. She barely felt it though, her skin still numb from the cold. Without further hesitation, she broke into a brisk walk. Her legs, at first, felt a bit gangly and awkward, but they soon adapted to her hurried strides.

Dylan walked fervently down the deserted street, desperately searching for familiar crossings or signs. But minutes upon minutes passed, and no luck.

Heavy raindrops continued to fall relentlessly from the sky, obstructing Dylan's view and chilling her to her core. There was another street lamp, not too far from her, and so she quickly made her way towards it, hoping it would help illuminate the way.

She'd nearly reached the light of the second overhanging lamp, when her foot met with a dip in the sidewalk. Tripping, she stumbled forward, her toes dragging and scraping against cement. Though she fell, Dylan managed to save herself from colliding with the asphalt, catching herself instead on the lamppost. Wincing, she leaned back against the metal post, and gently lifted her foot from the ground to inspect it.

A sharp rock had lodged itself in the ball of her foot, and the remaining surface of her skin was scratched and scathed. Grimacing, Dylan extracted the foreign body from her flesh, watching as blood oozed from the wound and mixed with the rain dripping off of her foot. The blood streamed down to the pavement below, spreading with the rainwater flowing over the sidewalk.

Dylan breathed in deeply through her nostrils and placed her injured foot back onto the pavement. She held her breath as she gently attempted to stand, but fell back again upon sensing the burning sensation from under her foot.

Dylan flinched, silently scolding herself for her misstep. She re-examined the wound. *It's not so bad*, she lied to herself, *it'll be fine*. Limping, she took two steps forwards, but immediately doubled back to her spotlight under the lamp.

Shivering, she stood under the white light, her wounded foot perched upon the base of the metal post. She held her hand up to her forehead and shielded her eyes from the rain, looking out in every direction. The street around her looked the same as it had when she'd first awoken. She'd made near to no progress. Having expended what little strength she'd had, she suddenly felt herself in no shape to continue.

Accepting her fate, Dylan leaned back against the lamppost once more, and gently lowered herself down to the ground. She was so tired. The cold had worked its way into her bones. There was barely any feeling left in her extremities, and the rest of her body was on its way. Her one piece of wet clothes stuck to her chest and belly like glue. Dylan felt the soaked nightgown weighing down on her, draining away all of her remaining energy.

All she wanted was to sleep, to return to the forever cave in her dreams, to lose herself in that blaring white light once and for all. Gently, she allowed her eyes to close and exhaled her last breath of warm air. Fading fast, she felt herself on the verge of unconsciousness, when something roused her once more.

There was a sudden sound from the woods – the crackling of branches from under someone's feet. At first, Dylan thought that she'd imagined it – just a false echo in the dark. But the sound came again, louder this time, and it was enough to keep her from sleep.

Dylan's eyelids fluttered open and closed. In her haze, she was able to just barely glimpse the figure of a hooded stranger, emerging from the trees in the park. Her sluggishness, combined with the curtain of rain blocking her view, caused her vision to cloud. But as the stranger grew closer, he also grew clearer.

Soon, Dylan saw him stepping over the metal railing and onto the sidewalk in front of her. He was taller than she remembered, but Dylan was certain it was him – the strange boy from the hospital, the one she'd sensed was watching her all these weeks. He'd followed her here and had finally decided to reveal himself to her.

Dylan's heart leapt when she saw him. *He* would save her, she thought. He had to. Why else would he show himself now? Why else would he be here? In her delirium, Dylan had re-invented her mysterious pursuer into a skulking hero. He was her champion. All this time, he'd watched over her, waiting for this very moment to present himself, and to rescue her from her demons.

Dylan dug deep into her strength reserves and opened her mouth. She struggled to speak, her vocal chords frozen in place like the rest of her body. Nevertheless, she managed to cough out a few words.

"Help me," she said bleakly. "Please."

Kit remained planted in place in the rain, staring down at her, evidently debating with himself at what action to take.

Dylan, too weak to do anything but beg for his help, only continued to stare up at him, hope shining in her emerald eyes. Her lips had turned blue, and her body was trembling. The rainwater that ran down her cheeks looked more like warm tears of grief.

"I know its you," she attempted again, this time more clearly so she would be heard over the clamour of the rain. "Please help me."

Her innocent pleas dug their way into Kit's idle heart and tore down its barricades. He could no longer stand by and do nothing. He had never wished for any harm to come to her, after all. But he also had not envisioned initiating any contact with her. Events were not unfolding according to his original design. He'd never meant to interfere, to inject himself so deliberately into this girl's life. But his options were limited. She would die if left alone now.

It had been some time since Kit had lent aid to another living being. His was a solitary life, and he had preferred it that way. All these years, he had survived by minding his own business, and by keeping to himself. But looking down at her then, Kit felt compelled by her pleas.

Growing weaker with every passing second, Dylan shut her eyes once more. There was no time to lose. Kit threw the hood of his jacket off of his head, exposing his fiery mess of red hair to the rain. He quickly unzipped the front of his coat and withdrew his arms from the sleeves. He knelt down next to Dylan and carefully helped her into the warm jacket. Dylan mumbled something incomprehensible. And he realized then, she was delirious.

He held his hand out and gently pressed his fingers into her neck. Her pulse was weak, but not dangerously so. She would be able to walk.

"Dylan." He addressed her loudly. "I'm going to take you home."

In hearing her name so plainly, Dylan briefly came to her senses.

"You know my name?" she said to him softly, her eyes squinted with a mix of fatigue and confusion.

Kit did not answer her. He reached his arm behind her back and took her by the waist. Dylan did not protest and only continued to watch him with a muddled and weary expression on her face.

Slowly, he helped her to her feet, supporting her weight with his arm wrapped around her. Still shaking, Dylan had trouble steadying herself on her one good leg. But Kit waited patiently as she found her bearings. He squeezed her in closer towards him and helped her steady herself. Neither of them spoke whilst they adjusted to each other's stances, and when Dylan seemed ready, Kit helped her take her first steps out from under the street lamp.

Together they began their journey down the deserted street, and towards home.

-- CHAPTER THIRTEEN --

ANSWERS FOR AURORA

The whistling of a boiling kettle pierced the silence in the small Montreal apartment. The shrieking sound stirred Dylan from her hazy, near-death slumber. Slowly, she came to, and found herself wrapped in layers upon layers of warm blankets. She felt warm, safely tucked-in on the sofa of her living room. Her head was foggy, but she remembered being outside, cold and alone.

There was movement in the kitchen behind her. Someone was there, making use of the stove.

Dylan shifted her body and tried peering over her shoulder, but the blankets prevented her turning. They'd been wrapped tightly around her entire body. She felt like she'd been strapped into a straight jacket.

"Holly?" Dylan called out instinctively, without thinking, as she began digging her way out of the nest of blankets that held her.

The sounds coming from the kitchen stopped after she spoke, and footsteps could be heard upon the wooden floor coming towards her.

Dylan halted her tunnelling efforts and stiffened. The steps she heard were definitely *not* Holly's. They were different. She didn't have much time to contemplate their origin, however, for their owner appeared before her then, holding a mug of hot cocoa in his hand.

Dylan's face turned white, and her big, green eyes grew even bigger when they met with Kit's.

Here he was, in her apartment – her 'stalker', so to speak. The one she'd so urgently chased after in the street mere days ago, the one with all the answers she'd been searching for, the one with the key to unlocking all the mysteries that had plagued her life of late...

"You're awake. That's good."

He spoke. His voice was shaky. He too, it seemed, felt a bit uneasy.

"You went kind of limp near the end. I had to carry you up the stairs."

Kit sat down on the coffee table in front of her. His movements were slow, deliberate, and he never broke eye contact with her.

He seemed to be watching her reactions, checking her for signs of alarm or aggression. But Dylan didn't react, nor did she speak. Her mind was working overtime, processing the extraordinary events of the evening. All at once, her memories came tumbling back to her, hitting her like wildfire.

She'd almost died. She remembered being alone in the dark, freezing in the rain. He'd saved her... brought her home. And now, he was here, and she could talk to him, ask him anything she wanted. It was all just... too much. What was she to ask first? There was so much she wanted to say.

"No one was home when we got here," Kit continued. "You'd left the front door wide open. Do you do that often? Leave your apartment in the middle of the night? In rainstorms? With no shoes... or proper clothing?"

Kit was grasping at straws. He'd never been very good at small talk, and sitting here with Dylan was proving to be much more difficult than he'd anticipated. She wasn't saying anything. Her silence felt suffocating to him. He had to get out. He'd done his bit. She was alive and safe. It was time that he left.

Carefully, Kit placed the warm cup of hot chocolate on the table next to him, and rose to his feet.

"Drink that," he told her. "The sugar will help."

He leaned over to grab his jacket, which was resting on the couch, and threw it over his back. In an instant, he had his arms in both sleeves and was adjusting his hood, getting ready to flip it over his damp, shaggy, red hair, when Dylan jumped from her stupor.

"Wait!" She exclaimed suddenly, startling Kit and staggering him to a standstill.

She was up a second later, carefully balancing herself on her one uninjured foot.

She faced him, hobbling slightly, as her blankets began to unravel. A few layers fell to the floor, exposing patches of her bare skin. Her cheeks turned bright red, as she recognized her state of undress. Embarrassed, Dylan clutched at the last of her coverings tightly, and held them in place against her thin body. She was at a loss for words, and looked back up at Kit, blushing.

Kit held both of his hands up in front of him defensively, as if preparing himself for an onslaught.

"I'm sorry. Your clothes were soaked," he explained, his face contorted with apologies. "I had to remove them."

Dylan imagined she should have been angry, standing in front of this stranger who'd so blatantly disrobed her without her consent. But all she felt was gratitude. She was glad that Kit had been there to help her, when no one else had. She was glad that, despite his own agenda (which still remained a mystery to her), he'd intervened when he had. She was glad to be alive.

Sure. She would have preferred to express her appreciation in a more suitable manner. But this would have to do.

"Please," she said. She hesitated before continuing, gathering her blankets tighter around her and biting her lip. "Please. Don't go."

She took a step forward and held her hand out towards him.

"I'm Dylan," she said, introducing herself properly.

Kit was puzzled by her apparent kindness. He was guarded at first, looking Dylan up and down with distrustful eyes, but he soon took her at her word. Carefully, he took Dylan's hand in his and squeezed it gently. She smiled at him, and he couldn't help but feel some affection for her then.

"Kit," he answered.

He'd used his real name, and was surprised at himself. He wasn't normally so forthcoming with newcomers.

"Well, Kit," she said smiling, "thank you. For saving me."

There was warmth in her words. They were both honest and true, qualities that Kit found were all too often lacking in people of the day. Her nature, he thought, was humbling. And so he did as she asked. He didn't go, and rather, stayed. There. In her presence, just a tad longer.

The two stood in silence, shaking hands. Until Dylan, sensing the moment was over, withdrew, her cheeks still flushed in embarrassment.

"Here," said Kit, recognizing her discomfort. He turned, took up a piece of clothing from the sofa, and offered it to her. "I found this T-shirt hanging over one of the benches in the kitchen," he told her. "It was dry, so I left it for you."

It was one of Holly's sleep-shirts. "Thank you," Dylan said, taking the shirt from him. "It's actually my roommate's. She must have forgotten it. She's visiting her parents. Would you mind?"

She hinted to him with her eyes that she desired some privacy.

"Of course." Kit nodded and then politely turned himself away, averting his gaze from her as she slipped into the over-sized garment.

When she'd finished, Dylan repositioned herself on the couch and began sipping on the hot chocolate Kit had prepared for her.

"It's good," she noted aloud.

Kit turned back to face her and sat down on the coffee table once more. He was calm, the calmest he'd been in months. There was *something* about her. She evoked something in him. He couldn't quite pinpoint what it was, but it made him stay. He had no desire to leave her just yet. All of his long, thought-out plans and schemes left his mind then.

"I'm not always like this," Dylan told him, "sleepwalking myself into harms way. This is a first for me."

Kit's attention was piqued at her mention of sleepwalking. Earlier that night, he'd watched Dylan wander out into the street and been confused by her actions. He hadn't appreciated she'd done so inadvertently – until now.

"There was an accident," Dylan continued, "my house, it caught fire. It was horrible. I lost my father. And my sister, she..." Her throat tightened, but she went on. "My sister's been hospitalized ever since and... I've been having these... *intense* dreams."

Kit's back straightened upon hearing Dylan speak of the hospital. He prepared himself for what was to come next.

"In fact," Dylan said, "we've met before. I saw you there, at the hospital. That was you, wasn't it? On the front lawn? You bumped me, and I dropped some of my papers on the ground...?"

Kit looked at her, his maroon eyes boring into hers. He wasn't sure what to tell her. He couldn't possibly reveal his reasons for being there that day. And so he diverted her instead.

"How long have you been experiencing the calls?" he asked, with legitimate interest.

"What do you mean, 'the calls'?" she responded.

Kit was thrown by her question, and so he repeated himself, this time, enunciating.

"The *calls*," he said.

Dylan only squinted her eyes, confused.

It dawned on Kit then. Suddenly, everything made sense to him: Dylan's inexplicable goodwill in the face of his obvious intrusions into her life, her multiple attempts to catch and talk to him… This girl had *no clue* what was happening to her. She'd never been prepared. *He* was her first (and only) contact with her new world.

Kit finally saw Dylan for what she really was: a child, in need of teaching. The realization softened him, for he remembered a time when he, himself, had been in her place. Lost, without anyone to guide him. Even *he* would not have made it on his own, he realized. And she wouldn't either… without help.

Kit was uncertain what he could really do for her. But he resolved himself to try anyways.

"The dreams," he clarified, "they're calling you, and you're not answering. That must be why they've become so intense."

"Calling me to what?" Dylan asked in earnest.

"The Aurora?" he ventured hesitantly. "You are the Aurora, aren't you?"

"Yes!" Dylan answered, excitedly. "You said that before. At the hospital. But, what is…" she wavered, "'Aurora'?"

Kit was dumbfounded. How was it possible that she knew so little?

"You really don't know?" he asked disbelievingly. "None of your family ever told you?"

"No." Dylan answered. His incredulousness was unsettling. She almost felt ashamed of her ignorance.

Kit reassured her, "It's OK," he said. "It's just that… I don't really know where to start. You might not even believe me when I tell you."

But Dylan was ready to accept almost anything at this point. Anything that would tie together the dozens of undecipherable clues bouncing about her head.

"I'll keep an open mind," she told him with fortitude, placing her hands on either side of her and leaning forward, eagerly.

Kit couldn't help but smirk at seeing her so enthusiastic. His lip curled upwards, exposing his very white and unexpectedly sharp teeth. Dylan especially noted his incisors, beautifully pointed and sparkling. Though she was not deterred. She reserved any comments she had regarding his unusual fangs, or his wonderfully bright red-blonde hair. These could wait, she thought. Her answers could not.

"Well," he began, "I've never met one of you personally. I've only ever heard stories, borne from myth. But, it's said that only *one* in your family, one Aurora, is active at any one time. And that the Aurora's gift is passed in secret from generation to generation, from mother to daughter, and then to *her* daughter, and… so on, always."

"And… this gift?" Dylan asked, captivated by Kit's tale. "What exactly is it?"

"I'm not sure," Kit answered, "considering I've never met an Aurora before. All I know is…" He took a deep breath and exhaled deeply before finishing. "They say that to be with *Aurora* is to never know illness or injury, to never feel pain… that she is *life* itself, eternal and… undying."

Having expressed all he knew, Kit grew quiet, and Dylan considered his story for some time. He sat in silence, watching the wheels of her mind turning round and round. When finally, she spoke.

"So," she said, "it's some kind of… fountain of youth?"

"Not quite," he replied, "Aurora is meant to be a *gift*, a treasure. Eternal youth, on the other hand. That's… more of a curse."

Dylan followed Kit's suggestion to conclusion.

"That must mean she just... keeps people healthy, then?"

"Yeah," Kit said. "That sounds more like it."

Dylan leaned back into the sofa, still pondering all she had just heard, meditating over its many implications. She spoke aloud as she thought.

"So my mother was an Aurora," she said.

"If you're the Aurora," Kit said, "then yes. She would have come first, before you."

Dylan's eyes shined with glee, and she smiled to herself softly. For the first time in months, she felt at peace. A large weight had been lifted from her shoulders. It was as though the clouds had parted, and sunshine had finally made it's way back into her life.

"When Dani and I were kids," Dylan recalled, "we were never sick. It wasn't until *after* she died..." Dylan paused, as memories of her mother came flooding in. "She used to tell us this story. It was a 'magic' story, she told us... to make us feel better when we were ill. I still remember it. I tell it to Dani sometimes, at the hospital. And... all this time, it wasn't the story at all. It was *her*."

Kit was pleasantly surprised at how willing Dylan seemed to accept his suggestions as fact. In his experience, 'regular' people generally rejected any notion of the supernatural. Dylan, however, accepted the legend of the Aurora as her own, without any pushing. It was as though she'd known all along, and had only needed him to illuminate the way.

"But mom died years ago," Dylan snapped suddenly. "What's changed?"

Kit did not answer, and Dylan only kept going, travelling down her trail of thought. Her excitement was growing with every passing moment.

"If I can learn what my mother knew, then I can save Dani! My sister, Kit, I could save her!"

Dylan's eyes had grown wide. She stared at Kit expectantly, her mouth wide and smiling. It was as though all of her prayers had finally been answered. The universe had sent her an angel, in the form of this beautiful stranger, to help her accomplish the impossible.

Kit could see Dylan's hopes burgeoning inside of her, which only caused him to shrink in response. She was taking things a bit too far, he thought, throwing him into the deep end.

"In theory," Kit responded, "the Aurora *could* help your sister. But, you'd have to answer the calls first, and…. I don't know how you do that."

"But, you said my dreams were the calls?" Dylan answered. Her tone shifted from excitement to concern. "So I thought you knew?"

"Everyone knows that dreams are your subconscious' way of communicating with you," Kit continued. "In your case, it's a way of alerting you to the Aurora. But, answering that call is a *whole* different story. That's the secret that should have been passed to you – a rite that only members of the Aurora's family are privy to."

What he said made sense. But Dylan was not so easily discouraged.

She wracked her brains, and it hit her – her mother's journal! Quickly, she sprung to her feet and hopped across the room to the kitchen counter, where she'd left the ancient leather-bound book. She grabbed it from its resting place and hurried her way back to the living room, pushing through the pain in her throbbing foot.

"Maybe I should look at that?" Kit asked, pointing to Dylan's awkwardly hanging foot.

It was clearly hurting her, but Dylan ignored his offer. She had no time for weakness, not now, not when she was *this* close to a breakthrough.

Collapsing back onto the squishy sofa, Dylan threw open the old leather manuscript in front of Kit. Eagerly, she smashed her open hand down onto its delicate pages and cried: "This! These are the instructions, right? This will lead me to where I need to go?"

Dylan was so proud of her genius. She'd figured it out. There, right in front of her, was the key. The ancient text would fill in *all* of the missing pieces. She was certain. But Kit only looked down at the book with disinterested eyes.

"What is it?" Dylan asked. "What's wrong?"

Kit sighed. "Sure," he started, "that book *might* tell you how to answer the calls. But you'd have to be able to read it first."

"What do you mean?" Dylan expressed incredulously. "I saw *you* read it! At the hospital."

"I didn't read it," Kit told her indifferently.

His short, unhelpful answers were starting to annoy her.

"Yes," she reiterated, "you did. I *saw* you. Right before you called me 'Aurora'."

"No," Kit told her again, more forcefully this time. "You misunderstood. I saw the crest of Aurora in its pages. That's all."

"The crest?" Dylan said. "You mean this?"

She was pointing to the pierced double-ringed symbol on the pages of her mother's manuscript.

Kit nodded, and Dylan continued with her eyes now hanging low.

"I see this symbol in my dreams, too."

Kit could sense Dylan's sudden disappointment. He was surprised at how badly it made him feel. Strangely, he wanted to do more for her, and so he dug deep into his recollections and pulled out what little information he had left.

"Look," he said, "I do know *one* thing. Whatever it is you're looking for, it's probably in the East."

Dylan's forehead creased with confusion, and her eyes squinted, as they travelled up from the pages of her mother's manuscript, and fixed themselves upon Kit. She didn't say anything, but her muteness spoke volumes. And so Kit went on with his story.

"Every power on Earth has its source," Kit elaborated. "The Aurora is no different. And the crest of Aurora in-and-of-itself tells us where that source is."

Kit held his index finger out towards the ancient book, and placed it upon its pages. He pointed to the two interlocked rings in the crest.

"These two circles," he explained, "the one on the right, that's *'Terra'* – the earth. And the one on the left is *'Sol'* – the sun. And this line here, piercing Terra, it points in the direction of the East. That's how we know that the source of Aurora lies there. But, unfortunately, that's all I know."

"It's not much to go on," Dylan noted, disheartened.

"Yeah," Kit replied, "I suppose that's why it's a secret. Otherwise, everyone would be scrambling to find the Aurora's source... It really is a priceless commodity."

"I don't care about that!" Dylan retorted. "I just care about keeping my sister alive."

Kit wasn't sure what more he could say. He watched, as Dylan continued to stare blankly at the pages of her family's journal – pages she would never be able to read. Until, a thought occurred to him. Dylan may never be able to read those ancient scribbles, he thought, and neither would he. But that didn't mean there wasn't someone else who couldn't...

"You know," he told her hopefully, "there may be another way."

Upon hearing his words, the glimmer in Dylan's eyes reignited. Her slumped shoulders straightened, and her ears were perked.

"I may know someone who could read it for you," Kit suggested. "It's a long shot," he warned. "She's a friend, but I lost touch with her a long time ago. If we could somehow track her down though, she'd be your best bet."

"What makes you think she'd be able to read it, when you can't?" Dylan asked.

Kit grinned at her question, and he answered: "Because she's old. Very, very old."

-- CHAPTER FOURTEEN --

HOLLY'S HOMECOMING

Dylan was sprawled out on top of her unmade bed, feverishly brainstorming and scribbling on a scrap piece of paper.

"Madison, Maria, Martha, Matilda…"

She spoke each name aloud, and then added them to her ever-growing list.

"Ma… Maa…Maaa…" she said, impatiently tapping the end of her pencil against the page, as she played with her syllables. "Magda! That's a new one! I haven't thought of 'Magda' yet."

Four days had passed since Kit had divulged the name of his supposed 'friend' to her. The friend who he presumed had the necessary skills to help decrypt her mother's journal.

To the best of Kit's recollections, the friend's name had been: 'Margaret Ma'. But Kit had warned this may no longer be the case. Apparently, Ms. Ma had a tendency of changing her name from time to time. The good news (according to Kit, of course) was that she'd always stuck to first names beginning with the letters 'M-a'. Names like: Mandy, Mackenzie, Marcy, etc.

Evidently, Ms. Ma chose to cyclically rotate through names similar to these every fifteen to twenty years. The bad news was that she was not as attached to her surname. 'Ma' would be long gone by now. And there was no guarantee that her *new* last name would be in any way related. It could literally be anything under the sun, Dylan thought. Smith? Johnson? Brown? According to Kit, they were *all* fair game, almost like looking for a needle in a haystack.

"What kind of freak changes their name so much, anyways?"

Although annoyed, Dylan whispered to herself quietly, so that Kit wouldn't overhear her from the next room. After four days cooped up with him in her tiny apartment, Dylan had learned to keep her voice down. In addition to his lightning-like reflexes, it seemed that Kit had also been gifted with *awfully* good hearing.

Dylan had caught him, on more than one occasion, inadvertently eavesdropping from afar. As a result, she'd started taking her phone calls outside of the apartment. It was a nifty trick, Dylan thought. Impressive. But it also made her feel a bit like she was being spied on, twenty-four hours a day.

Despite his annoying traits, it had been nice having Kit nearby. He'd spent the last three nights sleeping on Dylan's living room couch. And with him here, Dylan somehow felt safer. She could close her eyes at night without worry of sleepwalking herself into trouble again. Holly had not yet returned from her trip, and Dylan felt better… just having another body in the house.

Since Kit's arrival, Dylan had not been to the hospital to visit Dani. She'd been too busy chasing down leads on the strange, yet important, Ms. Ma. Kit and she had spent their days searching different online databases for variations on Ms. Ma's last-known name. So far, they'd had no luck.

There weren't many clues to go on, but Kit seemed confident that they would find Ms. Ma somewhere in the state of New York. Margaret had loved New York, it seemed, and had never strayed too far from there. She'd owned several different New York homes in her life. Kit recalled a beach house in the Hamptons, and a trendy apartment in upscale Manhattan. Yet he couldn't remember exact addresses.

"It's been a while," he'd moaned back at her, when Dylan had pressed him. "You can't expect me to remember *all* the details!"

Dylan couldn't understand how Kit's memory was so fuzzy. Even getting Ms. Ma's last-known full name out of him had been a challenge. Dylan had bombarded him with questions, in order to extract *every* last piece of knowledge he possessed about their subject. But it was no use. His memory was full of holes.

Kit could not recall what Margaret Ma's profession had been, nor what events had even led to his meeting her in the first place. It was as though a lifetime had passed since Kit had last seen her, or like he was remembering her from the patchy, incomplete viewpoint of a child.

There really was no end to the bizarreness that was her new acquaintance. Much about Kit remained unexplained. However, Dylan was confident she would solve the puzzle of his past too... given enough time.

Just then, a piercing cry came ripping into Dylan's bedroom, wrenching her away from her wandering thoughts. A woman was shrieking. The cry had come from the kitchen.

"Oh no, Holly!" Dylan exclaimed, as she jumped from her bed and ran out of the room.

The scene that awaited her in the kitchen might have been humorous under different circumstances.

Kit was standing straight as a board, a look of dumbfounded-ness frozen into his face. He held a single drumstick of leftover chicken in his right hand, and his left hand held the door of the refrigerator open. He faced Holly, who'd come home early and surprised him rummaging through their food stores.

Holly was shouting. She obviously thought she'd happened upon a burglar of some sort, and was brandishing an umbrella in Kit's face, attempting to fend off his non-existent attacks.

Dylan guessed from Holly's apparel that she'd only just returned home. She hadn't yet removed her yellow raincoat, and was holding an assortment of new mail and subscription magazines in her underarm. Her cheeks were pink from the cold of outside, and they were growing redder with stress now.

If left to her devices, Dylan was unsure of what Holly would do next. She may have looked dainty, but Holly was no pushover. Thankfully, Dylan had arrived in time. She intervened before Holly could escalate to any 'real' acts of violence.

"Holly, it's OK!" Dylan yelled. "He's a friend."

Holly's face relaxed when she heard her friend's voice. A part of her had worried for a moment that the man raiding their fridge had done her harm. She turned, caught sight of Dylan, and immediately, her anxiety left her. She lowered her umbrella and sighed a sigh of relief. Her facial features returned to their usual gentleness, and she cleared her throat sheepishly.

"Oh." She nodded apologetically to Kit. "Sorry about that."

The tension in the room had gone, and Kit finally relaxed his grip on the refrigerator door and allowed it to close. He did not reply to Holly, and only resumed eating his cold chicken, as though nothing had happened.

The three of them stood without speaking for a minute, awkwardly exchanging glances, unsure of what to do next.

Holly was the first to break the silence. She threw down her fresh pile of post onto the kitchen island, and then placed the point of her long, wrapped umbrella on the floor, leaning it against one of the kitchen cabinets.

"Dylan," she signalled her friend, "can I speak with you privately?" Her tone was hushed, but insistent.

She and Dylan made their way out of the kitchen and over to the living room, from whence Kit was still visible to them, but safely out of earshot – or so Holly thought.

"Pickle," she said, a mixed look of concern and confusion in her bright blue eyes, "what is this? I'm gone a few days, and you're bringing strange men back to the apartment?"

Dylan opened her mouth to answer, but couldn't find a space to interrupt.

Holly was obviously a bit shaken. She spoke fast, her hands energetically bobbing along with her speech, and catching in her blonde hair.

"Who is this guy?" she asked. "I mean – on the one hand – I want to say: 'Hello! Look out, Michael!' He's absolutely gorgeous, Dyl. But – on the other hand – are you *really* ready for this? You know, Dani's not doing so good, and I really think you should think hard before jumping into something you might not be ready for."

Dylan's cheeks turned red, for she knew that Kit had definitely heard every word of Holly's 'big sister' lecture. In fact, she was fairly certain she'd glimpsed him smirking to himself in the background.

Holly was, of course, oblivious to her embarrassment, not sharing in Dylan's knowledge of Kit's somewhat superhuman hearing. She stared at Dylan, expectantly awaiting her response.

"Well," Dylan began, keeping the level of her voice much lower than her friend's. "Firstly, you don't need to worry. Because it's not like that. You've got it all wrong. He's just a..." Dylan wracked her brain for the right words. "He's just... helping me."

"I'm sure he is!" Holly laughed, her eyebrows jumping up and down suggestively.

"No!" Dylan corrected her, still very mindful of Kit's repressed sniggerings coming from the other side of the apartment. "He's not helping me like *that*!"

Dylan took a deep breath and calmed herself. She thought for a second about how she should explain Kit's presence to Holly. She considered weaving some sort of lie, but decided against it. Holly would see through her instantly. So she went with the truth, knowing fully that her friend would not be pleased.

"He's helping me find someone to translate mom's journal. You know, the old leather book I showed you? The one I found in the safe deposit box a few weeks ago?"

"Yes, I know the one you mean," Holly replied, a bit defensively. "But how can *he* help?"

She turned and examined Kit again, searching him for any signs of intelligence she may have missed. She then turned back to face Dylan, looking wholly unimpressed. In her opinion, 'good-looking' men were of no *real* use – except for maybe the occasional male-themed marketing campaign, selling men's shaving creams and deodorants to other men, and the like…

"Holly, it's *him*!" Dylan answered with emphasis. "The one from the hospital."

Holly's eyes grew wide, and she threw her head around to look at Kit again. Her eyes found his crazy reddish do, and she finally made the connections in her mind. Just as soon as she did, however, she also remembered all the *other* stories her friend had told her about this particular individual. And a storm cloud began brewing within her.

"Do you mean to tell me that you brought your *stalker* home with you?! Are you nuts? Dylan, he could be dangerous! What were you thinking?!"

Over the next few minutes, Dylan remained quiet as Holly loudly chewed her out for her apparent lack of responsibility and regard for her own safety. The hushed discussion between friends was long over. Holly didn't seem to even care if she was being overheard anymore. In her mind, Dylan had gone too far. She'd given her a wide berth for far too long, and it had to stop.

"He could be a crazy person!" Holly insisted. "He could have murdered you in your sleep!"

Dylan's frustration had reached critical level at this point, and she exploded, lashing out at her friend.

"He saved my life!" she blurted out loudly. Then, realizing what she'd done, she repeated herself. This time, in a more civilized tone. "He saved my life, Holly."

Holly was taken aback. She had not expected this turn in the story.

"What do you mean?" she asked, her voice now much softer than it had been minutes before.

"A few nights ago," Dylan answered. She too, was speaking much more calmly now. "It's a long story, and I'm fine now… but he did. He saved me."

Holly was at a loss for words. This was a lot to take in.

The two friends stood in silence for a time. Both felt ashamed at having addressed the other with such aggression.

Kit took this opportunity to finally instil himself into their discussion. He'd been hovering on the sidelines for a while now, anxiously awaiting a moment to interject.

"If you ladies are done," he started positively, "I have some good news."

The two girls looked at him with the same look of exasperation in their faces.

Kit really needed to learn some tact, they both thought. His timing couldn't have been worse. And as though he'd read their minds, he went on to explain.

"Sorry to interrupt," he said. "But you'll want to see this. I think I've found her. Look."

Slowly, Kit unfolded a magazine he'd been holding in his hand, and held it up in the air. It was one of the subscription issues Holly had brought home with her in the post.

The cover of the issue featured the image of a rather jovial looking woman. She had straight, white hair, and was dressed in a white chef's apron. The woman was smiling and holding up a silver plate of hors d'oeuvres in one hand. The caption read:

MAMA MAGGIE'S RESTAURANT RANKED #1 FOR SECOND YEAR IN A ROW

Kit was smiling widely and pointing ecstatically at the cover of the magazine.

"It's her!" he repeated with more zeal in his voice. "I'd never forget that face."

The woman's face was, in truth, quite unique, and Dylan could understand how it may have imprinted itself on Kit's mind. Regardless, she was a bit sceptical. Did Kit *really* expect her to believe that the woman they'd been searching for just *happened* to land the cover of a mainstream magazine?

Holly was rolling her eyes.

"Really?" she asked mockingly. "Maggie Morales? You're saying that *Maggie Morales* is your mystery translator?"

She turned and now addressed Dylan alone.

"Are you really going to listen to this guy? Pickle, common... he's obviously taking you for a ride!"

Dylan pondered a moment and then snatched the magazine from Kit's hand. She flipped through a few pages until she found the cover article on Maggie Morales.

Her eyes hungrily searched the text for any evidence to back up Kit's identification of her. The article was primarily a fluff piece on Mama Maggie's hit New York restaurant.

"How did you know her last name, Holly?" Dylan asked her friend, her eyes still searching the magazine article.

Holly folded her arms and shrugged her shoulders. She felt Dylan's question was irrelevant to the matter at hand, and wasn't in any hurry to answer her.

"Holly!" Dylan exclaimed again. "How did you know Maggie Morales' full name? The article only refers to her as 'Mama Maggie'."

Dylan's face was as hard as stone. Holly could tell her friend was being serious, and so she paused her cynicism for a moment and answered.

"She's one of the greatest chefs in North America," Holly told her. "We study her recipes in my cooking class sometimes."

"When did you first hear about her, then?" Dylan followed.

"I'm not sure," Holly responded. "Not long ago, I guess."

"Here!" Dylan nearly shouted.

She'd located an interesting quote in the magazine article, one that had restored her faith in Kit. She read it aloud:

… Since its unexpected grand opening a year ago, Mama Maggie's hit restaurant ETERNALATE has received nothing but rave reviews from all of New York's most respected food critics. Like Mama Maggie herself, Eternalate exploded over night, and has taken New Yorkers by storm. Although the hit chef seems to have come out of nowhere, it seems Mama Maggie is here to stay – with Eternalate, once again, being ranked #1 by both Citizen's Choice and Foods For You alike…

Having finished, Dylan looked up from the magazine, imbued with an air of satisfaction.

"So?" Holly asked, not seeing the point in her friend's selected quote.

"So…" Dylan said with pleasure. "The article implies that no one knows where she came from – that she popped up over night. And Kit said himself that Margaret, or Maggie, or… whatever her name is, is always changing her name."

"Talk about weak! That doesn't mean anything," Holly protested.

"Don't you think it's strange that a hit chef like Mama Maggie just appeared out of *thin air*, Holly? There should be a record of some sort! She must have studied somewhere. Talent like that doesn't just spontaneously materialize. Her restaurant's been #1 for a year. And still, no one seems to know where she came from? Even *you* have to admit it's weird, Holly. And it lines up with Kit's story."

Holly listened to Dylan's speech without breathing a single word of retort. She didn't like it, but her friend made some undeniable arguments. She silently worried about what was to come. Her eyes bounced back and forth between the two standing in front of her, and she wondered what crazy goose chase Dylan would be suggesting next…

CHAPTER FIFTEEN

ANOMALOUS AUTOPSY

"Sam! There you are! What are you doing?"

Dr. Beth Chandler had been roaming the halls of Sunrise Hospital and Medical Center for some time now, in search of her favourite resident. Her young pupil had been missing in action. But she'd finally found him, huddled away in one of the archive rooms in the north wing of the hospital.

"I've been looking for you," Beth Chandler said, coughing, as dust floating around the old filing room infiltrated her lungs.

"What have I told you about keeping the volume on your pager turned up? The nurses have been trying to reach you."

Dr. Samuel Wilson had barely noticed his teacher entering the dark room. He seemed quite absorbed by his task, hunched over at a large desk, with only the light of a small desk lamp illuminating the pages of the old patients' charts laid out before him.

"Oh," he answered distractedly, never lifting his eyes from the old files. "I must have lost track of time. Sorry."

"Stop apologizing, Sam," Dr. Chandler told him. "Just do your job! I'm tired of always having to cover for you."

Her reprimands were ignored, however, as the young doctor shifted the subject of conversation abruptly.

"Have you seen the autopsy report for Freddy Jones?" he asked.

"Who?" Dr. Chandler replied, somewhat irritably. "Not now, Sam. We have a mastectomy to prep for, and I don't want to delay. I'd like to get home at a decent time tonight."

Beth Chandler tapped her foot on the ground as she spoke and looked down at her wristwatch impatiently.

"Just one minute," said Sam, "please? I promise I won't bug you with it again."

Upon meeting with her young student's pleading face, Dr. Chandler's annoyance seemed to melt away. She sighed, made her way around the large desk and peered over her resident's shoulder.

"Alright," she said. "But just one minute."

"Great! That's all I need."

Samuel Wilson's hands shuffled through the photographs sprawled out before him. He selected one from the pack and handed it to his teacher.

"This is a photo of the trauma site in our stab wound victim of last week," he said. "You remember? Jackpot Jones?"

Dr. Chandler accepted the photo from her resident, but did not examine it just yet. Instead, she frowned and addressed him firmly.

"Yes. I remember him, Dr. Wilson. I *remember* telling you to close him up for his family. What I *don't* recall... is ordering any post-mortem exams."

"Just hear me out," Sam beseeched her. "No family ever came forward to claim the body, and I noticed something weird when I was closing him up."

Before Dr. Chandler could scold him again, Sam readjusted the desk-light and pointed with his index finger to a specific spot in the photograph.

"Here," he said, "this strange discolouration in the wound's wall tissues."

Dr. Chandler inhaled deeply and buried her aggravation. While Sam may have been a pain in her sides at times, she *had* to admit, he was a brilliant doctor. If her resident thought there was something of note here, then there probably was… And so, she decided to hear him out.

"It seemed atypical for a knife wound," Sam continued, "so I had the coroner take a look. This is what I got back."

He now held out a thin paper file towards his teacher, but did not pause his speech. Dr. Chandler took the file from her student and began flipping and examining its pages, whilst he continued to present his findings.

"It turns out that the odd discolouration was actually the product of burns." Sam looked excited now. "But not just *any* regular burns. The coroner found a huge disparity in the degree of burns spread across the wound. Some of the tissues presented with only minor swelling, while others had literally been charred away."

Dr. Chandler's interest was finally piqued. Her back straightened a bit, and curiosity ignited in her eyes. She'd had a dull day, full of commonplace surgical cases. But here was something unique. It was oddities like these that had driven her to study medicine in the first place. She sometimes forgot this, when lost in the mundane, repetitive procedures she was forced to attend to at Sunrise.

"Really?" she asked, unable to hide the enthusiasm in her voice. "The burns weren't uniform across the wound?"

Dr. Chandler's brilliant mind was racing now, as she systematically worked through and eliminated the different possibilities and explanations for Sam's observations. It only took her a minute to come to the same result Sam had arrived at independently.

"The burns suggest that Mr. Jones' killer used a heated weapon in the attack," she posited. "But a burn pattern like *this* seems extremely unlikely. The heat would have had to have been unevenly distributed across the blade…"

"Exactly!" Sam exclaimed, his eyes shining. "Have you ever heard of such a thing?! I mean, how is that even possible?"

"Impressive, Sam." Dr. Chandler praised her protégé. "This is a good catch. I doubt the police's M.E. would have picked this up."

"Wait!" Sam interrupted. "There's more."

He was standing now and held both hands up in front of him, signalling a stop. Slowly, he reached his hand out to the far end of the desk and lifted a second patient file from its surface.

"For days now," he began, handing the chart to Dr. Chandler, "I haven't been able to get the autopsy report out of my mind. Somehow, the results felt familiar to me. But I couldn't quite figure out how… and then it hit me! Do you remember our weird runaway patient from last month? The one that disappeared from the hospital after he woke up?"

"Ah! The alleged Mr. Cook," said Beth Chandler.

She recognized the case Sam was referring to immediately, for it had embedded itself in *her* brain as well.

"I remember he never paid his bills," she remarked.

Dr. Chandler paused sombrely for a moment, as she remembered the many odd details of her mysterious patient: his unusually pleasant voice, as well as his beautiful mess of scarlet-blonde hair…

"You know," she commented aloud, "I saved that kid's life, and he repaid me by lying to me and skipping out on us."

It was clear Dr. Chandler had been a bit hurt by her patient's actions. She didn't normally take cases so personally. But this particular patient had stood out to her. Secretly, she'd hoped to spend more time studying the strange 'Chris Cook'… if that was even his name… There was something special about him, she was certain.

His response to treatment alone had been unnaturally swift.

As usual, Sam Wilson remained blind to his teacher's emotional state.

"Yeah, that's him!" he said, in an unknowingly insensitive way. "It was *his* case that was nagging at me all this time. He came in with a stab wound really similar to Jones' – same size, same location in his abdomen…"

Sam reached over and opened the patient chart in Dr. Chandler's hands. He helped her flip to a specific page and drew her attention to a paragraph of post-operative notes that appeared to have been made by his hand. Beth Chandler recognized her student's messy handwriting.

"You may not remember," Sam said, "but in the OR, when you were sewing him up, you mentioned you'd spotted some unusual blistering in the trauma site. I thought it was interesting, so I marked it up in his chart after surgery, see?"

Sam was correct. His notes were clear:

Upon closing, Dr. Chandler noted unusual blistering in walls of patient's wound.

"I think the two cases are linked," Sam concluded. "The blistering in this patient's wounds *also* suggests burns, and the use of a heated weapon. What are the chances that two patients could present with such similarities in such a short period of time? I think Jones' killer… *also* attacked our runaway patient!"

Dr. Chandler's eyes were wide. She dismissed her prior negative feelings towards the purported 'Chris Cook'. As though he were not special enough, it would appear that his value had now skyrocketed.

"If you're right, Sam," she interjected, "it would mean that our patient, this… Chris Cook, could be an invaluable witness in Jones' murder. He might just be able to ID the killer!"

Sam's cheeks were pink with pride. He'd solved the case! His days of tangled thoughts and muddled memories had finally paid off. And he was glad his mentor agreed with his findings.

Sam flashed Dr. Chandler a large, closed lipped smile then. But it did not last.

"Like you said, though," he told her gloomily, "he's gone. He made a miracle recovery and then high tailed it out of here. Our runaway patient could be anywhere by now."

Sam sighed, and Beth Chandler proceeded to wrap her arm around his shoulders.

"Turn that frown upside down," she told him. "You shouldn't downplay your achievements so quickly. This is a major breakthrough! You're like a true blue detective, Sam! If it weren't for you, I don't think *anyone* would have made this connection."

"You think?" Sam asked, eagerness flooding back into his face. "Thanks, doc!"

Having cheered Sam up, Dr. Chandler now released her resident.

She re-adjusted her dark rimmed glasses, swept her hands along the sides of her white lab coat, and addressed Sam once more. Her tone was more formal now.

"Well," she said sternly, "are we done here? Let's go! We've still got a surgery to prep for."

Sam aligned himself with his teacher and matched her businesslike manner.

"On it!" he replied, as he made his way towards the door.

Dr. Chandler was filled with satisfaction, as she proudly watched her student fall into place. He was a bit rough-around-the-edges, she thought, but Sam never failed to surprise her.

CHAPTER SIXTEEN

DYLAN'S DEFIANCE

"Dylan, stop! You can't go!"

Holly was pleading with her friend. She held the straps of Dylan's favourite knapsack tightly in her hands, and was hanging on for dear life.

The two girls stood on the sidewalk outside the front door of their apartment building. Dylan was attempting to load some luggage into the trunk of her father's SUV, but Holly was making the task extremely difficult for her.

"You can't stop me, Holly," Dylan told her friend through gritted teeth, as she tugged repeatedly at the bag in her hands. "I'm going. Whether you like it or not."

She pulled at the backpack one last time, and finally managed to dislodge it from her friend's grasp. Holly stumbled forward a few steps after losing hold of the precious parcel, but quickly regained her balance.

She looked up at Dylan then, her eyebrows creased with worry.

Dylan, however, appeared unfazed by her friend's gloomy expression. Having won the tug-of-war, she simply tossed her bag into the trunk of her vehicle, and slammed the door closed. She looked at her friend with an air of defiance, and then proceeded to make her way around to the front of the truck.

Holly followed her and continued on with her badgering.

"I just don't understand why you have to go to New York!" she wailed.

"I've told you a million times already," Dylan replied, clearly annoyed. "There was a last minute cancellation at Mama Maggie's restaurant, and we managed to squeeze in a reservation. If we don't go now, then it could be months before another spot opens up."

"I don't understand why you have to go at *all*!" Holly clarified.

There was desperation in her voice. A lump formed in her throat, and tears welled up in her eyes. Watching Dylan pack up her things was proving to be more difficult than she'd imagined.

Holly had started the day off strong, convinced that she could reason with her friend and keep her from committing a serious mistake. But as the hours had rolled by, Holly had not even made a dent in Dylan's armour. It seemed that she was determined to leave.

"Pickle, this is insane!" Holly tried again, her emotions rearing up inside of her. "If you'd just *look* at yourself, for one second, you'd see I was right! All of these stories he's told you, they're ridiculous! It's a lie – a ruse! Why can't you see it?"

Dylan tugged at the handle of her driver's side door and pulled it open. Holly now had a clear view of her opposition – the inexplicably handsome redhead that had somehow managed to bewitch her friend, with whimsical tales of fantasy.

Kit was sitting comfortably in the passenger seat of the SUV, his head conveniently turned and facing out the window. He was going to great lengths to remain neutral in the girls' dispute. But Holly knew he was paying attention. Ever since his arrival, that boy had spelled nothing but trouble, she thought to herself.

"Leave him out of this, Holly!" Dylan commanded her friend. "This isn't about him. This is about you! Why can't you trust me? I know you don't understand. That much is clear. But can you not just trust in *my* judgment? I know that I've been off since dad died. And I'm so thankful you've been there for me. But I'm not a child. You don't need to protect me anymore!"

Holly was stunned and hurt by her friend's words. She felt betrayed. How was it that Dylan could trust in this stranger over *her* – her best friend? How could she just abandon Dani now, to go gallivanting about New York City? And on this *fool's* errand? The whole situation felt completely wrong to her. And no matter how she tried, she couldn't wrap her mind around it. She felt as though she was standing in between two speeding trains, travelling towards each other on a collision course – powerless in the face of the inevitable crash. Her friend was on a dangerous path, she thought, one that would only lead her to trouble and heartbreak.

"And what about Dani?" Holly cried.

If reason would not sway Dylan, then perhaps guilt would.

"She needs you *here*. You heard the doctor!"

Tears were visibly running down Holly's cheeks now. Her big, blue eyes were swollen and overflowing with grief.

"Don't you see that Dani's the whole reason I'm doing this?" Dylan replied. "If I can find what my dreams have been trying to tell me, then I can *save* her. And everything can go back to normal."

The sadness in Holly's heart suddenly turned to anger. She couldn't take it any longer. These foolish falsehoods of 'magic' miracles that were *somehow* going to wake Dani from her coma? The whole thing was rubbish! And she wouldn't hear of it anymore.

"Dani's already dead, Dylan! Accept it!" Holly screamed, finally unleashing all of the pent-up tension and resentment she'd harboured all these months.

As soon as she'd finished, however, she regretted her insensitive words. Dylan stared at her in disbelief, and Holly didn't blame her. She took a step back, tears still streaming down her cheeks, and then bowed her head in shame.

"Well," Dylan told her scornfully, "I guess I have nothing to lose then."

Carefully, she stepped up into the truck and closed the vehicle door behind her.

Through watery eyes, Holly could see Kit readjusting himself and buckling up his seat belt. Dylan turned the key in the ignition, starting up the engine, and before Holly could utter another sentence, they were gone. The big, black truck sped off down the street and around the corner.

Holly wiped the tears from her cheeks, as she watched the truck disappear from sight. The emotional tempest within her subsided, and remorse took its place.

She wondered whether Dylan would forgive her momentary lapse of compassion. Despite their disagreement, she prayed then for her friend's swift and safe return home.

CHAPTER SEVENTEEN

BREACHING THE BORDER

The windshield wipers swept back and forth, clearing away the rain, as it fell hard against the large front glass of Dylan's truck. The rhythmic swooshing they made, together with the splattering of rain against the glass, was soothing. Dylan finally felt herself beginning to unwind.

Since leaving Montreal, her mind had been racing, ever replaying her last exchange of words with Holly. The quarrel with her friend had left her feeling distressed and repentant. Holly had spouted some vicious words in the end. But Dylan knew she hadn't meant them. She wanted to let Holly know that she forgave her… to clear the air.

"Kit?"

Dylan addressed her snoozing travel companion, who was still seated in the seat next to her. He'd fallen asleep within a half-hour of leaving the city, and had left her to navigate on her own.

"Wake up," she said.

He didn't flinch at her voice, however. And so Dylan leaned over to gently poke him in the arm.

Kit stirred at her touch. He peered over at her then, his bizarre, red-brown eyes looking weary and unfocussed. He mumbled something under his breath, but Dylan wasn't able to make it out.

"Hey," she said, "could you send Holly a message for me? I left my phone in the glove compartment in front of you."

Although he appeared to be shaking off his slumber, Kit did not do as Dylan asked. He only straightened himself in his seat, and stared out at the road in front of them.

"Can't it wait?" he asked her nonchalantly. "You're driving."

"Kit, c'mon," Dylan replied. "I just want to let her know we're OK. Please, can you just get my phone? It'll only take a minute."

But still, Kit did not heed her request.

Dylan frowned and looked over at him. It was then that she noticed the shift in his demeanour. He looked a bit uncomfortable.

"What is it?" Dylan asked him.

"Nothing," Kit answered defensively. "I just… don't want to send your message for you. You should send your own messages."

His uneven tone of voice gave him away, though. It was clear he wasn't being entirely candid. Dylan even thought he looked a bit embarrassed. She smiled, and looked over at him repeatedly, never lifting her hands from the steering wheel.

If Dylan hadn't known any better, she would have thought that Kit was… nervous. His facial expression reminded her a bit of those her sister had made the first time she'd ever taken her riding. Dylan recalled how awkward Dani had looked, sitting atop of that tall horse. It was an expression she'd never imagined Kit could be capable of. He always seemed so confident, so cool.

"You can tell me," she pushed him, still smiling.

Kit's body turned stiff then. He looked over at her and considered. Though he wasn't accustomed to sharing his weaknesses with others, he somehow found it within himself to answer.

"It's nothing," he said, averting his eyes from her. "I just… don't really know how." His voice trailed off as he finished his sentence.

"What do you mean – 'you don't know *how*?'" Dylan replied.

At first, she was unsure what Kit had meant. But as she spoke, it came to her, and she laughed.

"You mean… you don't know how to use a cell phone?"

Dylan's laughs echoed all through the vehicle now, interspersed only by Kit's whiny complaints here and there. The atmosphere in the large vehicle had turned from lethargic to remarkably cheerful.

"I'm sorry," Dylan apologized whilst trying to maintain a straight face, "but… how is that even possible?" She struggled to hold in her laughter.

Kit didn't seem to share in Dylan's enjoyment of his apparent lack of cell phone skills. He frowned at her, as if pouting. He answered her question as though it was only natural that he be this way.

"I just… never needed one before," he told her self-assuredly, turning his nose up at her in protest.

Dylan's laughter had now been reduced to a very slight chuckle.

"Well," she told him, "it's not hard. I can show you, if you want."

Her manner was genuine. She looked back over at him and smiled sympathetically. Kit held her gaze in his and responded in kind, flashing her his blazing white teeth.

"You should smile more often," Dylan told him warmly. "It suits you."

Kit opened his mouth, as if to respond, but then shut it again immediately upon realizing where they were. The fun-loving and playful side of him had vanished in an instant. And the original, solemn and shrewd Kit was back and on high alert. He stared out in front of them and sat forward in his seat. His body language turned cold and rigid.

They were approaching the United States border, and for some unknown reason, Kit had grown edgy.

"Is everything OK?" Dylan asked him, worried.

But Kit ignored her, his eyes darting from side to side and taking in every inch of the border crossing ahead of them. It was clear he was stressed. But Dylan couldn't fathom a reason for his sudden onset of jitters. He shifted in his seat, examining every window, as if searching for a way out – for an exit.

"Seriously, Kit, what's wrong? You're starting to freak me out a bit…"

Dylan stepped on the brakes, and the truck grinded to a halt. They were only one car-length away from the Border Control booth now. A man in an official-looking uniform was circling the vehicle ahead of theirs, shining a flashlight through its windows and talking with its driver.

Kit watched this spectacle with what could only be described as horror, shining in his eyes. His skin turned pale, and every one of his muscles tightened. His hand darted to the passenger door's handle, and for a minute, Dylan thought that he might pull the door open and flee.

The border patrol's inspection of the vehicle ahead of them finished then, and Dylan observed the small car pulling away. It was their turn. But Dylan did not move their vehicle forward just yet. She was afraid to. Kit's unexpected nervousness seemed to be rubbing off on her.

"Kit," she said, the tension within her rising. "What's happening? Do you want me to turn around?"

But Kit wasn't paying attention to her. In thirty seconds flat, he'd unbuckled his seat belt and hopped over the back seat of the truck, out of sight.

"Kit!" she cried, truly panicked now. "What are you doing? You're going to get me arrested! Come back here!"

There was honking coming from in-behind them now. Dylan was holding up the line. She paid no attention to their commotion, however. Frozen in fear, she sat staring into her rear-view mirror and at the back seat of her SUV, hoping to catch a glimpse of Kit's flashy red hair. What was he thinking? There was *no way* he could hide back there. It was far too exposed. Border patrol would see him for sure, and then they would *both* be in major trouble.

The man in the uniform was now approaching her truck. *It's too late*, Dylan thought. He walked over to the driver's side door and knocked on her window.

Dylan's heart was beating a million miles a minute. There was nowhere to run. *I never should have listened to that redheaded devil*, she thought to herself, as she wound her window down and met with the border officer's eyes. *Holly was right.*

"Everything alright there, ma'am?" the officer asked her. "You're holding up the line. Would you mind moving your vehicle forward a few feet to the inspection zone?"

Dylan's throat had gone dry, but she nodded and pressed lightly upon the gas pedal, driving her truck up to the Border Control booth, as ordered.

The border officer followed her on foot, and then leaned his head back in close to her window. He examined her facial features carefully, before continuing.

"Are you alone, ma'am?" he said finally, his eyes darting to the passenger seat next to hers.

Dylan didn't answer him and only stared. She must have looked like a deer caught in headlights. She certainly had the requisite amount of fear in her for the part. Thankfully, the officer didn't seem to notice.

"Can I get your passport, ma'am?" he asked, as he straightened his back and began his stroll towards the back of the truck.

Dylan saw him pull out his flashlight, and her heart nearly

stopped. She watched with dread, as the officer lifted the light and pointed it into her rear windows. He peered into her vehicle from different angles, and Dylan knew that, any second now, he would spot her stowaway. She couldn't watch. And so she held her breath and slammed her eyes closed, bracing herself for the worst.

Minutes passed, but there were no sudden exclamations heard from behind. No alarms went off, and no dogs were heard rushing to the scene, barking.

"You know, it's funny..."

The officer was speaking to her again. He was laughing to himself. Dylan opened her eyes, only to see him approaching her window again, this time from the front of her vehicle. He'd come full circle, it seemed, and now finished his sentence:

"I was *sure* I saw someone sitting next to you when you first pulled up. I guess the old mind is playing tricks on me!"

Dylan couldn't believe it. Somehow, the border officer hadn't spotted Kit huddling away in her back seat. Today was her lucky day!

Pulling herself together, she reached over to the glove compartment, opened it and grabbed her passport from within. She handed the little booklet over to the officer, who was now leaning by her driver's side window, and flashed him the hugest, friendliest smile she could muster.

How Kit had managed to avoid detection – Dylan did not know. But she wasn't about to question it now. Not when there was still a chance she could get through this.

"How long you plan on stayin', ma'am? And the purpose of your journey? Business or pleasure?"

The border officer had switched back into official business mode, asking his standard border crossing questions. His eyes were glued to Dylan's open passport. He was reading her information and examining her headshot.

"I'm headed to New York city, sir," Dylan answered him, having found her voice again. "I'll only be a few days. Doing the tourist thing."

She kept her answers short and sweet. Her hope was to whiz through the rest of this interview, and to then high tail it as fast as possible across the border.

If I stay calm, I might just make it, she thought to herself hopefully.

The border officer nodded his head and stood up once more. He didn't appear to be in any way agitated or perturbed. He turned his back on Dylan then and reached over to his booth.

There was a faint clasping sound heard, as he slammed down his official border stamp in her passport. He then turned back to face Dylan's truck, reached his hand through her window, and handed her back her passport.

"Well," he said, "everything seems in order here. You have a lovely day, ma'am. Welcome to the United States of America."

The officer waved her goodbye, a big smile spread across his face, and Dylan slowly drove off.

It's a miracle, she thought, adrenaline still running through her veins. And as the distance between her truck and the border grew, so did Dylan's conviction. After a few miles, she allowed herself to smile and relax.

"I did it," she whispered to herself with pride.

Just then, Kit popped his head back into view. He appeared from out of nowhere, startling her once more.

"You!" Dylan cried. "How did you...? Where did you...?"

Dylan was *beyond* confused. She didn't even know where to start. She was furious that Kit hadn't warned her of his little stunt ahead of time. But she was also equally inquisitive about how he'd accomplished the feat *at all*.

Curiosity won out in this instance, and she set her fury aside for the time being.

"Could you please explain to me how that border officer missed you?"

Kit did not answer her question, however. He climbed back over to the front of the vehicle, and sat himself down in the passenger seat next to her. He had a preoccupied sort-of look on his face – one that may even have been described as sadness. But he didn't say anything.

"Hello?" Dylan pressed him again. "I deserve an answer, Kit. Do you have any idea what you just put me through?"

But Kit refused to speak to her. He did not even face her. He only stared out of the window and at the scenery passing them by.

Dylan tried a few more times to stir him to speech. But her efforts were in vain. It was as though Kit didn't even hear her.

Soon, silence fell upon them. The Big Apple was still a few hours away, but neither of them spoke again for the remainder of their drive there.

CHAPTER EIGHTEEN

MANHATTAN MOONLIGHT

Dylan finally understood now, why all of New York's most revered critics had given Mama Maggie their thumbs up. She and Kit had only just claimed their reservation at the hit chef's restaurant. But from the moment she'd stepped foot inside, Dylan was blown away by its grandeur.

Eternalate was located in the heart of Manhattan, atop one of those monstrous skyscrapers Dylan had only ever seen on her television screen back home. The restaurant took up the entire top floor. The space was large, but the atmosphere intimate. The ambient music and décor together, made guests feel at ease and peaceful. All of the table settings were spaced out, circling the edge of the building, each with a perfect vantage point from which to gaze out at the city through large glass windows. The walls in the interior had been strategically lined with full-length mirrors, which reflected the breathtaking views, and which also served to provide an illusion of floating above the metropolitan skyline.

From her table, no matter which way she looked, Dylan was faced with reflections of dozens of New York's tallest, most beautiful buildings, each glittering in the night sky. The lights in the restaurant were dimmed, so as to enhance the spectacle. And a single candle had been placed upon Dylan and Kit's table, its flame designed to boost the 'mood'.

The scene was absolutely flawless, and enough to drive Dylan to reverie. She imagined this place would provide the perfect setting for romance, that two people in love could easily share a perfect moment in time here. The thought brought a fleeting and tender smile to her lips, which was followed by a long disheartened sigh. Naturally her first dinner date in one of the world's most picturesque venues had to have been with such a *dreary* partner…

Kit was sitting opposite Dylan at the charming, candlelit table overlooking the sparkling city. To the untrained eye, he appeared to be the perfect companion – handsome and attentive. But Dylan knew better than the other women about the restaurant, who'd stealthily been eyeing him since they'd first walked in. Kit may have been stunning, but his personality needed a major overhaul, Dylan thought. His striking superficial features couldn't possibly make up for all of the dark secrets he chose to conceal beneath the surface.

Before the incident at the border, Dylan had thought she'd glimpsed a piece of him she could have connected with – a Kit who was less guarded and free. But sitting with him now, she was more convinced than ever that she'd made a mistake. This Kit, before her, had nothing to offer. He was closed-off and miserable, having chosen to isolate himself from any *real* friendships. He'd refused to engage with Dylan *at all* since their episode at the border. She wondered whether he even remembered why they'd come to New York in the first place, or whether he was already contemplating ways of leaving her.

Dylan shook away her morose thoughts. No matter what her travel companion was going through, she needed to remain focused. She was on a mission, after all. There was purpose to this madness.

She sat up straighter in her chair and stuck her neck out as high as she could, in order to get a better look at the other guests surrounding them, and at the waiters flitting to and from the kitchens. *That* would be where Mama Maggie was, she supposed. That is, assuming the celebrated chef was personally overseeing the preparation of meals that evening…

"Don't worry. She's here."

Kit had finally broken his silence. He'd read the concerned expression on Dylan's face and decided to ease her mind.

"Oh, so you're speaking to me now?" Dylan replied, somewhat passive aggressively.

Her tone was sarcastic, but her message was not meant as humour. The anger she felt towards Kit was real and palpable. But she put it aside for the time being. She would need Kit's cooperation in order to recruit Maggie to her cause.

"Never mind," she told him, shaking her head and brushing off her bad temper. "How can you be sure she's here?"

"Because she has a meeting," Kit answered her.

Dylan looked at him and squinted her eyes inquiringly. She was about to speak, but Kit beat her to it.

"I can hear, remember?" he clarified, with one finger pointing up to his right ear.

Dylan remembered then – Kit's handy superpower. In her irritation with him, she'd forgotten *all* about his little hearing trick. She grimaced involuntarily at the memory. It was too bad he was such a pain sometimes, as Kit *really* was a useful accomplice.

"OK then," she said, waving her hand in exasperation. "What do you hear?"

Kit was still. He stared out at the other end of the restaurant. He'd targeted a specific table by the windows, on the other side of the room, and was watching it determinedly.

"There," he told her, "the man at that table just inquired with the waiter about his meeting with her. He's sitting alone, the one sipping on a glass of red wine."

Dylan swung around in her chair and peered over at the table that Kit had indicated. Her manner lacked all subtlety. It was a good thing the subject of their prying was seated so far away from them; for he would definitely have caught her snooping had he been closer.

Dylan was a horrible spy, and Kit knew it. He chuckled at her eagerness, but caught himself in time to pass it off as a discrete cough.

Normally, Dylan would have defended herself against his mocking, but she was far too wrapped up in her observation of Mama Maggie's anonymous visitor to care. She held the back of her chair tightly in both hands, her chin uncomfortably resting over top. She strained her eyes for a clearer view of the man's face, and… eureka!

"I know him!" Dylan cried, her body turning back towards the table in a flash. Her eyes were wide, and her mouth hung open in awe.

"You do?" Kit asked her, surprised.

"You don't?!" Dylan replied incredulously. She seemed more excited by the presence of this stranger, than by the prospects of meeting Mama Maggie herself. This confused Kit, and so he questioned her with his eyes.

"That's Donald Dusk!" Dylan exclaimed. "You know, the famous late night talk show host? He's our favourite! Dani, Holly and I *never* miss his show. I didn't recognize him at first, without his blue suit, but it's definitely him. I wonder why he's here… maybe he's trying to get Maggie to appear as a guest. This is so exciting!"

She was babbling like a star-struck groupie. Kit couldn't believe his eyes. Her behaviour seemed positively alien to him. He had never understood how people could fixate so intensely upon television stars. These so-called 'entertainers' were nothing special, in his opinion. They had no *real* talents – nothing to set them apart from all the other 'regulars' of this world.

It was ironic that Dylan should be so enthralled by this nobody, Kit thought. For she, on the other hand, was someone who was *truly* unique. He wondered whether she'd even been able to grasp just how blessed she was, having been born into such a legacy as the

Aurora. Her potential, he believed, was immeasurable. But it was perhaps her ignorance of this… that made her all the more appealing?

Dylan had halted her blabbering, and Kit stared over at her from the opposite side of their candlelit table. The light flickered in her emerald eyes, and she was smiling. Her enthusiasm over spotting the famed Mr. Dusk seemed to have overtaken her, making her forget her prior feelings of resentment towards him. She was back to her old self again, calm and compassionate.

Kit realized then, that it wasn't just her birthright that made her stand out above the rest. It was also the warmth that regularly radiated from her, day-by-day. It had been a long time since Kit had met anyone as… wholesome, as she.

Kit regretted his most recent treatment of her. Dylan had been so generous, so forgiving, and he'd repaid her with reticence. He wanted to tell her – everything. But fear kept him from doing so. He'd been down this road before, and learned his lesson the hard way. People from *her* world… never understood. She would look at him differently, once she knew, Kit thought. He wasn't certain he'd be able to bare it. Not again...

"Could you make out what time the meeting was at?"

Dylan addressed Kit once more, tearing him away from his melancholic thoughts.

"Kit? Hello?"

"Sorry," he responded, shifting in his seat. "No. I didn't hear a time."

"OK then," she told him, picking up her menu. "We might as well eat. I don't know about you, but I'm starved."

Again, Kit didn't answer her. Instead, he rose distractedly from his seat. His face flushed faintly and his deep maroon eyes grew wide with recognition.

"Where are you going?" Dylan asked.

But Kit wasn't moving. He wasn't standing tall, nor was he sitting. His legs were bent awkwardly and his left hand still clasped the back of his chair. It was as though he couldn't decide whether he should continue to stand or sit back down. His eyes had not moved either. They only remained locked and mesmerized with something in the distance.

"What is it?" Dylan asked again. She pivoted herself in her chair, in an effort to find what it was that had disturbed her companion so.

A woman had emerged from behind a mirror-concealed door in the center of the room. There were a few of these doors around the restaurant. Dylan had observed the waiters making use of them earlier. She presumed that they led to the kitchens.

The woman who came through the door was short and rather stout. She wore a white chef's uniform, which suggested she was one of the cooks. Dylan couldn't see her face, for she had her back turned to them. But her hair was a bright blondish-red. In fact, it looked much like Kit's. Dylan had always assumed that Kit's particular brand of flamboyant fiery locks were one of a kind, so she was surprised to see the shade replicated here with such accuracy. Could it be coincidence? Dylan thought better.

She continued to watch the plump, little redhead, as the woman slowly made her way between tables and further afield from them. Dylan couldn't be sure, but she appeared to be headed for Donald Dusk's table. Dylan considered whether this redhead could be Mama Maggie herself, en route to her appointment. But she dismissed the thought. She recalled quite clearly, from Holly's magazine cover, that Maggie Morales' hair was a perfect white. But just then, the woman stopped, turned in their direction, and Dylan immediately saw her mistake.

Indeed it *was* Mama Maggie, in all her splendour. Dylan recognized her distinctive face straightaway, those cheerfully chubby cheeks, the glee in her eyes, and her large, toothy grin. Despite her change in hair colour, Kit had known *all along* it was she. He seemed to have a sixth sense for these things...

Maggie Morales had not yet made it to her meeting with the renowned Mr. Dusk. On her way, she'd been accosted by a number of 'fans', seated at one of the more central tables of her restaurant. She didn't seem bothered by the delay, however, and instead began busily shaking hands and conversing with her grateful guests. She took her time, and slowly, one by one, addressed each individually, her eyes wandering in between.

When at last she'd finished with her appreciative patrons, Mama Maggie straightened herself once more. She was about to continue on her journey towards the far end of the restaurant, but stopped suddenly. Before stepping away from her table of admiring clientele, she'd given the Eternalate dining room the once over and caught sight of something, or rather, someone… unexpected.

Maggie remained paralyzed in place for a time, staring in Dylan and Kit's direction. And then, as luck would have it, she abandoned her table of devoted supporters and made a beeline towards them. Dylan couldn't believe it. Maggie had recognized Kit! 'Operation: Find Mama Maggie' was turning out to be much simpler than she'd anticipated.

Dylan turned to face her partner, but Kit failed to notice, as he was otherwise preoccupied. He'd taken a step out from their table and was now standing with his back straight, shoulders back, preparing to formally receive his long-lost friend.

He wasn't smiling. Dylan noticed his facial features looked more proper than usual. He appeared serious, even by *his* standards, Dylan thought. *Like a soldier, readying himself to meet the general he'd not seen since times of war.* Funnily enough, the expression on Maggie's face looked to be one of amazement and disbelief. She looked at Kit as though he was one of her squadron, whom she'd presumed dead and fallen in battle.

Slowly, the two came together. Dylan watched their reception with great interest, for it was unlike any greeting she'd ever seen before.

When Maggie had come within a meter of Kit, he immediately lowered his gaze and bowed to her, his arms tucked tightly at his sides. He muttered something foreign under his breath. Dylan couldn't quite make it out, but she was certain it wasn't English. Stunned, yet also impressed, she continued to observe him like this. Dylan may not have known the meaning or origin of Kit's adopted pose, but she knew one thing for certain: the respect that he held for Maggie was... absolute.

From Kit's conduct, it was obvious that Maggie was one exceptional, perhaps even powerful woman. But try as she did, Dylan couldn't see it. Mama Maggie stood before her now, less than two steps from where she sat. But to Dylan, she looked like an ordinary woman. She was not *nearly* as old as Kit had portrayed her to be. Dylan guessed late forties to early fifties. Her height and build were similarly unimpressive. She couldn't have been more than five feet tall. Yet, Kit still seemed to revere her all the same.

"Kitsune?"

The first words from Maggie's lips were just as foreign to Dylan as Kit's last mumblings had been. However, it sounded like she may have been... calling him by name?

Kitsné?

Dylan repeated it in her head. It *had* to be Kit's full name. It occurred to Dylan then, that Mama Maggie might prove to be a great resource in unlocking the many riddles surrounding her mysterious companion. Maggie had only just arrived, and already, Dylan had learned something new of Kit's surreptitious past.

Meanwhile, Kit was still frozen in his bowed position, as though awaiting orders of relief. His eyes remained fixed upon the ground in a show of total deference. He'd been like this for more than a minute now, and it proved ample for Maggie.

"I knew it was you, Kitty!" she exclaimed, overjoyed. "Now stop that nonsense! Get up and let me see you."

Kit finally relaxed at her words. He stood back up, towering above her, and smiled warmly in her direction. Mama Maggie did not waste an instant more. She threw her arms open, inviting Kit to embrace her. The scene was… too much! Dylan had to hold her hand over her mouth to keep from laughing.

In a split second, Mama Maggie, the decorated general, had transformed herself into Mama Maggie, Kit's adoring great aunt or grandmother. There was no way that Kit would give in to her show of affection, though. Dylan was certain that her brooding companion was *far* too serious for hugs. But she was wrong… again.

Right there, before Dylan's disbelieving eyes, Kit leaned in towards Maggie. He clasped his arms around the merry, little woman and squeezed her wholeheartedly.

The display was adorable, really. Kit had given himself over to Maggie completely. He looked like a happy, little kitten, nuzzling its mother. Dylan wondered if the analogy was the foundation for Maggie's hilarious nickname for him: *'Kitty'*. Dylan would definitely be teasing him about that later.

She smiled to herself, still happily watching Kit and Maggie's embrace. The fascinating reunion was the best thing she'd witnessed in months.

Maggie had now released Kit from her embrace, and was holding him tightly by the shoulders. Her expression was no longer one of serenity and fondness, but of grave concern. In the short time that she'd held Kit in her arms, she'd noticed something was different about him. Something was wrong.

"What's happened, Kitty?" she asked with apprehension in her voice. "You're not well?"

Kit did not answer her query. He cleared his throat and, instead, held his arm out in Dylan's direction.

"Mags, this is Dylan," he told her. "I'm actually here for *her*." His introduction was noticeably meant to divert Maggie from her question. Dylan couldn't fathom what it was that had Maggie so shaken. But one thing was clear: Kit didn't wish to discuss it in her presence.

Before Dylan could protest, Maggie had taken Kit's hints on board and extended her hand towards her.

"It's lovely to meet you, Dylan," she said. "I'm not sure what's brought you here tonight. But I thank you. What a gorgeous surprise this is! I've gone far too long without a visit from Kitty."

Dylan was about to respond but restrained herself when she realized they were being observed. Maggie, being Eternalate's biggest star, had naturally drawn the attention of dozens of curious eyes about the restaurant. Her unusual reunion with Kit had also not helped matters.

Dylan took a moment to examine their surroundings. In less than thirty seconds, she'd spotted more than ten different neighbouring tables at which the dinner guests had lost interest in their food. The customers were watching them intently, probably wondering like Dylan, what the reason was for Maggie's strange exchange with the young man sporting a matching hairstyle to hers.

Thankfully, one of the waiters appeared then and interjected, before Dylan could speak.

"Excuse me, Mama." He spoke to Maggie in a hushed voice. "I don't wish to disturb you, but Mr. Dusk is waiting."

Maggie didn't seem alarmed, nor rushed, by her employee's reminder. She merely waved her hand up at him dismissively.

"Give him my apologies, would you, George?" she told him. "I have some unexpected family matters I must attend to now. I'll have to reschedule our appointment for another time."

"Yes, Mama," George replied, politely excusing himself from them.

With George gone, and her appointment with Donald Dusk taken care of, Maggie turned her attention back to Dylan and Kit.

"Well," she began, "we've got lots of catching up to do. I can tell. But, may I suggest we do so elsewhere? You're welcome to come back to my house. I'll cook us up something special, and we can talk *all* you like! What do you say?"

Dylan liked the idea of removing herself from the inquisitive eyes all around them. On the other hand, she didn't wish to intrude.

"Thank you," she said. "But, I hope we're not disturbing you. If you'd like us to come back later..."

Maggie interrupted her. "Don't be silly, dear. Donald can wait! It's not every lifetime that Kitty drops in." She paused and took Dylan's hand in hers before finishing: "...and accompanied by such a lovely girl." She smiled, and Dylan got the distinct impression that Maggie may have drawn some very *incorrect* assumptions about her relationship with Kit. She didn't correct her just yet, however, and simply flashed her a nervous smile in return.

Kit laughed. Sensing Dylan's discomfort, he took the lead and accepted Maggie's gracious invitation.

"Ah, Mags," he sighed, "we'd love to see your place."

Maggie propped up like a daisy upon hearing this. She was properly brimming with joy at the prospect of having guests.

"Perfect!" she cried happily. "I'll just grab my coat. Oh! I can't wait for you to see my new house, Kitty. It's a *wee bit* out of the way... but much quieter! And more private – I promise you. Besides, I have a feeling you'll both like it there... "

-- CHAPTER NINETEEN --

MAGGIE'S MANOR

Calling Maggie Morales' residence a 'house', Dylan soon learned, was in fact a serious distortion of the truth. When Maggie had, so cordially, invited she and Kit to dine with her at her abode, Dylan had expected *some* degree of luxury. A successful chef, such as Maggie, could no doubt afford herself some fairly comfortable living quarters. However, the magnificent gated estate to which Maggie had led them, following their departure from her lavish restaurant, had *far* surpassed Dylan's wildest imaginings.

Maggie's mansion had been built along what could easily have been a one-mile stretch of beach property in Long Island. Dylan and Kit had not been given the grand tour on their arrival. But upon entering the monstrous manor, Dylan had taken a peek down one of its two elongated wings. The two-story extension, Dylan guessed, must have stretched at least one hundred meters along the coastline. It likely could have housed more than ten or fifteen separate and equally sizeable rooms.

The manor's massive size was not its only virtue. Its interior, Dylan had seen, was just as opulent as its gorgeous Victorian exterior. The ceilings had been built so high, Dylan was certain they would give off the perfect echo. Of course, she had restrained herself from testing her theory, not wanting to appear ill-mannered.

The dining hall, where the three had set themselves up for the evening, was illuminated only by the light of an impressively large crystal chandelier, which hung from the ceiling above the rectangular dining table. The walls were painted a rich cream colour and lined with beautiful glass-door cabinets that matched the walnut flooring. The table itself spanned nearly the entire room, and Dylan estimated it could have comfortably seated twenty or so guests.

She and Kit were presently sitting at that very table, on either side of Maggie, who was sitting comfortably in her seat at its head. A pair of reading glasses were perched upon Maggie's nose, and she was delicately flipping the pages of Dylan's treasured, leather-bound book.

"It's impressive," Maggie told them. "I must tell you, I've never seen anything quite like it."

Dylan had been sitting quietly for some time, waiting, whilst Maggie had taken the time to examine the journal. Her impatience, steadily rising within her, now reached an all-time high.

"But, you *can* read it? Right?" she asked Maggie from the literal edge of her seat.

Kit, unlike Dylan, had kept calm throughout Maggie's inspection of the ancient text, probably on account of his delectably full stomach. The table was filled with empty dinner plates, which earlier had held a large selection of Maggie's most delicious foods. Kit had been responsible for devouring more than half of these dishes. Having gorged himself to his heart's content, he was now positively beaming with delight, his eyes closed and his back leaning against the cushion of his chair.

"Calm yourself, child," Maggie answered, flashing Dylan a warm smile. She gently placed her hand over Dylan's arm, squeezed it lightly, and finished: "There's no reason for alarm. Yes, I can read it. In fact, it would be my pleasure to do so."

Dylan breathed a sigh of relief and finally let herself go. She fell back into her chair and smiled widely back at Maggie.

"You know," Maggie told her, "you're very fortunate to have met Kitty when you did. I may very well be one of the only people left alive who can still read this ancient form of Hanzi."

"Hanzi?" Dylan asked.

Maggie smiled back at her and then clarified.

"It's a form of writing that originated over 2000 years ago, during the Han Dynasty. But, it fell out of common usage a long time ago."

Maggie looked back down at the book laid open in front of her. She flipped a few more of its pages and added: "But the entries in your family's journal aren't *all* written in the same style. Every few pages, the characters shift slightly, become more evolved, more modern. It's amazing, really. The writings in this book may very well document the complete evolution of Hanzi scripture in time…"

Dylan rolled her eyes.

"That's exactly what the doctor from the Smithsonian said."

"What doctor?" Maggie replied. Her expression had turned grave. She hurriedly removed her glasses from her face and took a deep look at Dylan.

Kit too, upon hearing Dylan's words, had stirred from his restful state. He sat straight in his chair and leaned forward, somewhat alarmed.

"Before I met Kit," Dylan answered, her eyes worryingly darting to and from her two companions. "I wrote to a linguist in DC. He said that he wanted to work on my mom's journal. I never met with him in person, but…"

Both Maggie and Kit relaxed again upon receiving Dylan's clarification. Each looked at the other with reprieve. It was as though they were silently celebrating some narrow escape.

"What? Was that wrong?" Dylan asked them, her curiosity at their shared understanding nagging at her.

"No, dear," Maggie told her soothingly, "you've done nothing wrong. But, when I said that your family's book might have some historical value, I never meant to suggest that you should *actually* hand it over to any museum… On the contrary, I'd like to impress upon you how important it is that you *never* do anything of the sort."

Her tone felt severe and out of character. Dylan was surprised. She hadn't imagined that Maggie was capable of such stern words. Until that moment, Maggie had been so cheery and light-hearted.

"Why do you say that?" Dylan asked her hesitantly.

Maggie did not answer Dylan immediately. She seemed to be considering her words carefully before speaking. Finally, she opened her mouth – but Kit spoke first, stealing her cue.

"Do you remember when I explained to you that the Aurora was a gift?" he asked Dylan. His tone impressed upon her the importance with which he spoke.

Dylan nodded, her eyes wide.

"Well," Kit continued, "like any other gift, it has value. And there are those that would give *anything* to possess it. They wouldn't hesitate to take it from you, or to hurt you in the process. Trust me. I know. The less people know about you, the better. There's a reason this book's been passed down through your family *in secret*."

He spoke with such assuredness, as though he himself had dealt with villains of the sort he described. There was pain behind his words. And so Dylan trusted him.

"OK," she whispered, her eyes trapped in Kit's intense stare. She wondered who in this world could have hurt him so. It was difficult to picture Kit as anyone's victim. To Dylan, he'd always seemed so worldly, so resilient.

The tension in the room had risen unexpectedly following Kit's speech, and Maggie thought it best to bring it back to a more civilized level. She raised her hand to her mouth and cleared her throat loudly. The sound was enough to rattle Kit and Dylan from their powerful connection.

"It's getting late, my dears," Maggie noted, "and we *all* need some rest, I think. You'll both stay here tonight. I've already had Alaeder prepare rooms for you."

She rose from her seat and clapped her hands together, summoning her manservant. A moment later, a man entered the dining room and nearly scared Dylan half to death. She'd not expected such a swift response to Maggie's call, nor had she been prepared for Alaeder's rather… shocking appearance.

The most startling thing about Maggie's butler was his height. Upon entering the room, Alaeder cast a shadow that traversed the entire length of the large dining table. He had a hunch in his shoulders that was fairly pronounced, most likely the result of always having to stare downwards at the people around him. Had he been able to stand straight, Dylan would have put him at about eight feet tall.

As though his height were not horrific enough, however, the skin of his face and of his hands looked greyish and sickly. At first sight, Dylan had imagined Alaeder was ill, the grimy pigment of his skin an ailment of some unknown disease. The expression on his face was equally grim, and his mouth was turned upside down with matching dull eyes. Had it not been for his impeccable dress in black blazer and tie, Dylan would have also thought him terribly unhappy.

Alaeder's entrance had caused Dylan to literally jump from her seat. He, most certainly, had noticed her offensive reaction. However, the giant manservant did not appear bothered by her obvious show of agitation. Not in the least. He simply carried on in his usual fashion, completely unaffected.

"What may I do for you, Madam?" he inquired from Maggie indifferently. His voice was incredibly soft and surprisingly soothing. It rung in Dylan's ear and immediately travelled to her heart. Like magic, she forgot Alaeder's unappealing exterior and saw through to his tender soul.

"Please, would you boil some water for our guest, Alaeder?" Maggie requested. "And meet us by the fountain?"

Alaeder nodded his ascent and exited the room. Dylan watched him go with interest. She was intrigued. Despite his monstrous size, Alaeder had managed to leave the room without so much as a creek from the wooden floorboards beneath him. His footsteps were lighter than those of a creature one-tenth his size. Dylan's head tilted unconsciously in confusion. She wondered how such a thing could be possible. But before she could question Maggie about her strange butler, she was interrupted.

"Come, darling."

Maggie bade Dylan to follow her out of the dining hall, and into the spacious corridors of the manor. Kit joined them, and the three travelled back the way they had come, through a dimly lit passage, and back into the main entrance hall.

This particular space was the first Dylan had seen when she and Kit had been admitted to Maggie's home earlier in the evening. It was just as spectacular now, as it had been then.

The floor of the entrance hall was made of solid marble, and there were beautifully carved white stone staircases circling the edges of the room, leading up to the second floor. The beauty of these, however, was nothing compared to that of the crowning piece of the room – a water element, in the very center.

The fountain was timeless and elegant. It was large, measuring almost five meters in diameter, and featured eight statues, all huddled up together and intertwined in the center. Each figure was unique, as though they had been modelled after the living. But each had been sculpted holding identical round disks, which they held up into the air at different heights. Water flowed up through the topmost of these disks, and then fell over its sides, onto the next disk down. The water fell upon each and every disk, one after the other, before landing at the very bottom of the fountain. The way in which the water moved, from disk to disk, was seamless and beautiful.

A ledge, which was about two feet high from the ground, framed the circular base of the fountain. It offered perfect seating from which one could observe the motion of the flowing water. Upon entering the entrance hall, Maggie went straight to this ledge. Carefully, she sat down upon the hard stone seat and beckoned Dylan and Kit to join her.

"Now, my dear," she began, looking at Dylan, "I expect it will take me a day or two to read through your journal. I want you to take this time to regain your strength. You said you've not been sleeping well... but I know of something that should help suppress those pesky nightmares."

Slowly, Maggie reached her hand down into the basin of the fountain and gently slipped it beneath the surface of the water there. Her arm dove a few inches deeper and wove steadily through the water, as though she was feeling around for something. Finally, Dylan saw Maggie's arm steady. She pulled at something beneath the surface, and a moment later, her hand and arm had emerged, dripping wet, from the water.

With her fingers, Maggie held what appeared to be a fairly large, white flower. The blossom was about the size of her fist and was composed of dozens of pointed petals, all stemming from a bright purple center. Dylan had never seen anything quite like it. It was exotic and strange looking. She wondered where it had come from, for it certainly had not been visible to her from where she sat.

Dylan stared down at the water in the base of the fountain once more. Her eyes searched its depths, but all she saw was the bottom of the marble basin. The water swirling around in the fountain appeared crystal clear. And there was no evidence of vines or plants of any kind. Her chin shot up into the air, and she looked at Maggie with question marks in her eyes.

Maggie chuckled softly at Dylan's reaction.

"They're called: '*Shen Jing*'. It means '*mirage*'," she explained. "They're a species of lotus flower that are all but extinct now. I keep a patch of them growing here. They have some amazing therapeutic properties, and are *guaranteed* to give you a good night's sleep."

At that moment, Alaeder appeared next to them, holding a large, silver food tray. He knelt down onto one knee, so as to lower himself to Maggie's level, and held the tray out towards her. On it, he had placed two glass mugs and a glass teapot. The teapot had been filled with boiling water, and there was steam escaping from its spout. Maggie lifted the glass top from the pot, and gently placed the lotus flower within. The blossom sank to the bottom and slowly began to steep in the hot water. Dylan could clearly see the reaction through the glass of the teapot. Pale violet streaks of colour began seeping from the lotus, and into the surrounding liquid.

"Thank you, Alaeder," Maggie told her giant manservant.

At her words, Alaeder stood up again. His thin frame shot upwards, elevating the silver tray high up into the air along with him.

Maggie took Dylan's hand in hers, and then wished her goodnight.

"Alaeder will take you to your room," she told her, "and by the time you reach it, the tea should be ready. A few sips is all you'll need. I promise you'll feel yourself a *whole* new person in the morning."

Although Dylan was a bit hesitant at sipping this unknown, purplish tea, she had to admit, she was tempted. After all these months, the thought of having a good night's sleep (free of distressing dreams) was like music to her ears. And so she decided it would be safe to try. After all, what harm could a few sips do? She took a deep breath and smiled back at Maggie.

"Thank you," she said, rising from her seat to follow Alaeder up the marble staircase, "and goodnight."

When she was halfway up the stairs, Dylan glanced back down at the entrance hall below, and found Kit staring back at her. She nodded to him warmly and then turned her attention back to the giant manservant leading her away.

Unlike Dylan's, Kit's gaze did not waiver. He kept a watchful eye on her as long as he could, until she had turned the corner at the top of the staircase, and moved out of his view.

-- CHAPTER TWENTY --

CUTS AND COALS

"How long do you think she'll sleep for?"

Kit spoke to Maggie.

"You didn't tell her everything about that lotus flower," he continued, chuckling lightly. "I still remember the last time you gave me a dose of that tea, after that debacle with Li... I must have slept for a week!"

Maggie joined Kit in his reminiscing. She laughed also, and then calmed herself before taking a sip of her drink. The two had retired to Maggie's study after Alaeder had escorted their precious Aurora to bed.

"Oh, stop that," Maggie told Kit, lowering her glass from her lips and resting it in her lap. "*That* was different. You were an absolute mess. Dylan probably only has a day or two of sleep to catch up on. She'll thank me when she wakes up."

She paused before adding: "You're *sure* you don't want a drink? It's just us adults now." She held her own glass up into the air and rattled it enticingly as she spoke.

Kit shook his head. His nostrils were tingling. He could smell the delicious earthy aroma emanating from Maggie's scotch glass, even over the burning smell of the flaming coals in the fireplace. It was tempting for sure.

"You know I can't," he answered finally.

"Suit yourself," Maggie replied. "But one day, you'll see that this 'diet' of yours is just ridiculous. There's nothing wrong with you, Kitten. You're perfect. Just the way you are."

She lifted her glass to her lips and swallowed the rest of her drink in one refreshing gulp.

Kit didn't say anything more. He was feeling a bit uncomfortable in his regal velvet armchair, and so he readjusted himself. He sat forward, resting his forearms in his lap, and stared deeper into the flames flickering under the mantelpiece.

The smell of Maggie's antique scotch had all but disappeared into her stomach now, and thus freed up Kit's senses. The taunting aroma now dissipated, he retreated once more into his thoughts.

Dylan.

No matter how hard Kit tried to focus on other things, he always came back to her. And try as he did, he couldn't quite understand why.

"You care for her, don't you?"

Maggie seemed to have read his thoughts. She always *could* read him like an open book, he thought. Kit didn't answer her, and instead, chose to remain tight-lipped.

Sensing his hesitation, Maggie didn't push him. She merely readjusted herself in her armchair, and went on.

"It's hot in here, yes?" she asked. "Perhaps the fire was too much?"

Her skin did appear a bit flushed under the heat of the flames. Kit watched in silence, as she slowly held her hands up to her head, gently ran her fingers along the back of her neck, up the bottom of her scalp and in under her gorgeous reddish-blonde hair. She fiddled with something at the back of her scalp, and a moment later, all of her hair came sweeping off of her head in one fell swoosh.

"That's *much* better," Maggie sighed, examining the bright red wig of hair in her hand. "You know, it's ironic that I wore this one today, of *all* days… almost like I knew you were coming."

Setting down the hairpiece, she took a long hard look at Kit. Her bald head appeared smooth and shining under the glow of the fireplace. Her face serious.

Though Kit had very obviously seen Maggie in her natural hairless state before, she'd nevertheless managed to grab his attention. He knew that she disliked being seen this way. Almost as much as *he* detested his own altered-self, following a few sips of the wrong cocktail.

"No more hiding, Kitsune. I'm *far* too old for your stubbornness, and it's about time you grew up. You're not a cub anymore."

Kit knew she was right. He sat up in his chair, looked Maggie straight in the eye, and then bowed his head again in shame.

"What's happened to you, Kitty?" Maggie asked him. "Something's different, and not in a good way. I'm not talking about Dylan. She seems like a lovely girl. But you're not telling me the whole story. I find it hard to believe that you just *happened* upon the Aurora by chance."

"You're right," Kit answered her, his tone defeated. He grabbed the bottom of his shirt and lifted it, revealing a horrendous three-inch scar running across his abdomen. "This is how I found her," he confessed.

Maggie gasped, raising her hand to her mouth in shock. She rose from her armchair and leaned down in front of Kit. Slowly, she raised her hand up to his now healed wound, and gently placed her fingers upon its edges.

"How could this happen?" she asked, bewildered.

She examined Kit's scar closely, almost as though she was attempting to convince herself of its existence – like she couldn't believe it was real.

"A scar like *this*…" she continued, and then paused.

Her eyes wandered away from Kit's scar and then shot upwards in alarm.

"Is this is why you've been… so different?" she asked. "Whoever did this, they took your…" She stopped herself there, as though the mutilation and loss Kit had been forced to endure was simply too horrendous to be put into words. "I'm so sorry, Kitten," she whispered, sounding genuinely dismayed.

Kit's eyes turned glassy then, and he roughly slammed his shirt back down. The same anger and hatred he had felt for L upon first waking in the hospital weeks earlier returned and began swirling inside of him like a hurricane.

"Yeah, well," he answered, struggling to keep himself composed, "I'll find him. I know what he looks like, and if I stick with Dylan, he'll show himself eventually. I think he's her uncle. But, it's strange. I don't think she knows him…"

"That *is* strange," Maggie answered, perplexed. "But wait, you 'think'? You mean, you haven't discussed it with her?" Her tone had shifted from concerned to irritated.

"Kitty," she berated him, "you have to tell her! You can't keep this from her. She'll never forgive you if she finds out you've been lying to her. I can tell you now, keeping secrets is bad… for *any* relationship."

Kit's face turned a bright shade of crimson, which naturally complemented his dashing red hair.

"You're talking nonsense," he huffed, embarrassed. "She's just a friend. Besides, I'm *going* to tell her. I'm just… waiting for the right time."

"I wouldn't wait too long, Kitten," Maggie advised. "The longer you wait, the worse it'll be. I guarantee."

Having finished cautioning Kit on the rules in dealing with the fairer sex, Maggie's thoughts turned back to his story.

"How was it that you came to cross this man, anyways?" she asked. "This… uncle of Dylan's?"

Kit frowned and leaned back in his armchair without answering her question. His expression looked a bit like that of a guilty child.

"Kit?"

Maggie pushed a bit harder, but then figured it out on her own.

"You've been *hunting* again, haven't you?!" she cried, plainly upset. "I told you! Nothing good would come of you chasing after that elusive treasure of yours! And see? Look what's happened! I hope you know you got lucky this time, Kitsune. If that man had held on to you any longer… you might not even be here anymore. You'd do good to remember: you're *not* invincible!"

Kit didn't answer her, and allowed Maggie to continue on her rant.

"I just don't understand your fascination with that thing. You already have everything you could *possibly* need – why do you need more? What *more* could it give you? I've told you before. It's *too* risky. Anyone who's anyone, and trying to make a name for themselves, goes after the Crepusculum. I hope you know you could have died, Kitty. Or worse… you could have been exposed! Why'd you do it? Tell me. Why?"

Kit shrugged his shoulders. He didn't have an intelligent answer for her.

"I don't know, Mags," he told her ruefully. "I guess… I just got bored."

Maggie sighed.

"Well," she replied, "I know how you feel. I've led a life much longer than yours. Or have you forgotten? But, do you see *me* hopping off and getting myself into trouble every time a new lead on some foolish legend rears its head?"

Kit lifted his hand to his chin and considered her question. His manner was exaggerated, and Maggie soon realized he was teasing her. She gave him a playful tap, and he laughed.

"What I'm trying to say," she said, holding back her own laughter, "is that I find *other* ways to distract myself – smarter, better, safer ways. And you can't shut yourself away like you do! If you'd just give them a chance, you'd see there are some *good* people out there, ones that are worthy of you."

The time for jokes had passed. Maggie looked upon Kit now, like a mother would upon her own child. Hope shining in her eyes.

"… like Dylan," she added quietly. "I have a good feeling about her, Kitten. I think she just might be… exactly what you need."

Kit grew quiet at Maggie's words. He listened intently to all she had to say, but refrained from saying anything further.

Maggie smiled at him with sincere affection.

"And don't you worry about that scar," she said. "I'll whip something up for you. That way, when you finally find this man, you'll be able to put things right again."

-- CHAPTER TWENTY-ONE --

BORN OF BLOSSOMS

There were birds singing. Dylan heard them happily twittering somewhere off in the distance. The sound acted as a gentle alarm clock, waking her from sleep. Unlike recent times, Dylan awoke feeling refreshed and relaxed. The cheerful chirping, like beautiful music to her ears.

Smiling to herself, she gently opened her eyes and took in her bright surroundings. The guestroom in which she'd spent the night had a glass-domed ceiling. In the evening, Dylan recalled it had offered her beautiful views of the night sky. Curled up in dozens of luxurious pillows, she'd fallen asleep with the stars shining down on her. But the night had now passed, and morning had taken its place. Dylan felt the warmth of the sun's rays beaming down on her.

Feeling full of energy, she sat herself up and stretched her arms far up into the air. With one fell swoop, she threw off the duvet and sheets that covered her legs. She hopped out of bed, taking in a full breath of fresh air.

The lotus tea Maggie had prepared for her had worked like a charm. Dylan hadn't felt this good in months. Her mind was sharp again, her body, young and strong. It would seem that a good, nightmare-free sleep was *all* that she'd needed, after all.

Dylan stood now, tall and revitalized, looking about. It had been dark the night before, when Alaeder had escorted her to her room. And so, she hadn't had the opportunity to properly appreciate it then.

The guestroom in which she'd spent the night was, in fact, the manor's most unique. Maggie had nicknamed it *'The Tree House'*, for it had been built to overlook the manor's greenhouse below (hence, the shared glass-domed roof).

Upon closer inspection, Dylan saw that *The Tree House* had only three walls. The fourth, which was located at the head of the bed, was more of a 'half-wall'. Being cut-off at chest height, it functioned more as a lookout point, from which one could observe the many flowers and trees flourishing below. Dylan crossed her arms and rested them upon this ledge now.

No wonder the air feels so crisp, she thought.

Sleeping in *The Tree House* was akin to sleeping above a flowering forest – full with life and energy.

From her vantage place at *The Tree House* lookout, Dylan could glimpse the entire floor plan of the greenhouse below. Down there, the glass-domed roof extended downwards and also made up the walls of Maggie's greenhouse. The space was large and shaped like a half-moon. A wooden pergola-style trellis ran all along the edges of the greenhouse, creating a border around the gardens. There were a multitude of vines and brambles climbing the trellis' posts, and spreading themselves across its top. Their flowers acted as a sort of sparse canopy – a makeshift shelter to the footpath below.

Within the pergola border was a small pond, a vegetable patch, a cluster of fruit trees, and rows of (what looked like) dozens of different fresh herbs and floras. The space was utterly vibrant. Each of the plants growing within the greenhouse appeared healthy and ripe with vitality. However, none were as beautiful as the jewel blossoming at its very center.

The majestic tree had been placed upon a small mound of grass, very near to the greenhouse's pond. Its branches were long and covered in what must have been hundreds of tiny pale-pink blossoms. The soft colour of the blooms sprouting from its twigs paled in comparison to the other brighter, and more exotic flowers growing all around it. However, this could not lessen its splendour – not in the least. The cherry blossom tree was like a shy, yet still sparkling star surrounded by boisterous, arrogant weeds. Dylan had easily picked the resplendent tree from the bunch, and once found, could not tear her eyes away from it. She stared until she saw through its many branches, to the mound of grass beneath. And it was there that she saw him again.

It appeared that Kit also had recognized the beauty of the cherry blossom tree. For there he was, lying under the shade of its branches. Dylan recognized his clashing red hair straight away, and meant to call out to him, before someone interrupted her.

"You're awake."

Dylan turned and found that Maggie had entered the room, with Alaeder trailing in-behind her.

At first, she hadn't recognized the jovial little woman, for Maggie was now sporting a new hairstyle, different from the one she'd seen the night before. To Dylan, it appeared that, overnight, her gracious host had dyed her hair a pale blue, and arranged it into clusters of loopy little curls. Admittedly, the hairstyle itself looked fabulous. Nevertheless, Dylan couldn't help but stare – if only, out of confusion.

"You're admiring my new 'do'," remarked Maggie then. She smiled as she stepped up next to Dylan, and joined her at *The Tree House* lookout.

Dylan's cheeks flushed in embarrassment, as she realized her host had noticed her gawking.

"Don't worry, dear," said Maggie. "It's normal to be curious." She placed a reassuring hand over Dylan's arm and went on. "It's a wig," she explained. "They're *all* wigs. You see, when I was a little girl, something... very strange happened to me. I was struck by an unusual illness and lost all but one of the hairs on my head. The doctors couldn't explain it. *'Witchcraft'* – is what they said it was." Maggie paused then and laughed. "It never did grow back," she said, still chuckling to herself. "I spent the better part of my early years looking for an antidote. But nothing ever worked. In time, I grew to accept it… These days, I use my bald head, much like I would a blank canvas. Just another means of expressing myself through my art."

When she'd finished, Maggie pointed up to her elaborate, blue hairdo and smiled.

Dylan couldn't help but smile back at her. It dawned on her then, how truly unique Mama Maggie really was. Dylan had never met anyone quite like *her* before. Being around Mama Maggie was like being around your favourite and fun great aunt. Somehow, you just knew she had something special in store for you… like a batch of freshly baked cookies in the oven, or a brand new puppy hidden in the closet. The thought caused Dylan's smile to widen, before the sound of rustling sheets nearby gently jolted her back to reality.

Since Maggie had joined Dylan at the lookout, it seemed her manservant had begun busying himself with his daily chores. Dylan watched Alaeder now, as he expertly made his way around *The Tree House*, changing and folding the sheets of the grand bed.

A night of rest had not improved his colouring in the least, Dylan noted. Alaeder's skin still appeared to be a sickly shade of grey. And now, under the glow of the morning sun, Dylan was able to discern further, even more unusual details in the towering butler's physique. The tops of his ears, for example, were not rounded – but rather, ever so slightly pointed. His fingers appeared unusually long and skeletal in shape. Dylan also noticed that each of his elbows and shoulders were unusually sharp and jagged, as though they might come tearing through the fabric of his prim uniform at any moment.

In spite of these ghastly details, however, Dylan saw that Alaeder's general aura – the way in which he, somewhat gracefully, moved about the room – also had not changed. His manner, she noticed, remained just as gentle as it had been the evening before. When taken as whole, in fact, Alaeder's tender demeanour somehow managed to temper his grisly exterior. The longer Dylan watched him, the more at ease she felt in his presence.

When he'd finished making up the bed, Alaeder respectfully bowed his head to his master, and proceeded to exit the room.

His departure was so quick, in fact, that Dylan was barely able to utter a "thank you," before he had gone.

"I see you've taken a shine to Alaeder," Maggie commented then, when she saw the affectionate manner in which Dylan had saluted her manservant.

"He's sort of *special*, isn't he?" said Dylan, a bit dazed.

"As are you, my dear," Maggie answered, "and Kitsune. And, I suppose, myself too." She paused before adding: "We're all unique in our own way."

There was silence for a moment or two, while Dylan considered if she should continue or not.

"I hope you don't mind my asking," she finally managed to say, "but, what exactly… *is* he?"

From the moment she'd laid eyes on him, Dylan had known that Alaeder wasn't quite '*normal*'. Though, up until then, she'd been too frightened to ask. Part of her had worried that her questions might be met with disapproval or contempt.

Fortunately, Maggie's reaction to Dylan's query was quite the opposite. By all accounts, she appeared all too glad to share the story of Alaeder's origins.

"His people," Maggie told her, "were called: the 'Faye'. A long time ago, they lived in one of the forests up in the Himalayas. Though, years ago, they were driven out by men and deforestation. Most of them died at that time... The Faye were a peaceful, kind-hearted people. They were never meant for this industrious, unforgiving world. It's very sad, but… I think they might be all-but extinct now."

Her expression turned even sadder, as she continued with her story.

"When I found Alaeder, years ago, his spirit was nearly broken. The villains who'd found him treated him like a slave. Day and night, they forced him to haul lumber across the very lands they'd stolen from him and his kin. What awful people they were. Luckily, their leader had been open to bribes… and I was able to take Alaeder away from there. He's been with me ever since. I thank my lucky stars that I found him when I did. I honestly don't know where I'd be today without him… All those beautiful plants you were admiring down there – that's *all* Alaeder. He loves tending to the greenhouse. He's got a real gift for botany, you know?"

Maggie stared down at the gardens again, proudly surveying her butler's work.

Dylan looked as well. The wheels of her mind had begun churning again. Maggie's story had only sparked further questions for her. She wondered what the lady had meant when she'd used the words: "*years ago…*"

For some time now, Dylan had suspected there was something a bit *'unusual'* about Kit too. Her mysterious companion had always seemed to her, a bit too wise and worldly for his age. He also possessed more than one extraordinary talent… talents that went *far* beyond 'ordinary' human abilities.

Since meeting Maggie, Dylan's suspicions had only intensified. It was clear that she too, was 'different' – like Kit. The way in which Maggie spoke, for example, always seemed so confident and authoritative. It was as though she'd already seen everything, been everywhere… and learned *all* that this world had to teach her.

Dylan wondered how her strange, new friends could have acquired their vast knowledge, peculiar skills, and unusually vast experiences. She'd eliminated a few theories already, and only one remained, burning in the back of her mind…

"Exactly… *how old* are you?" Dylan blurted out, unable to repress herself any longer.

She regretted her question almost immediately, and clapped her hand over her mouth by way of reflex.

"I'm sorry," she mumbled through her fingers. "I shouldn't have asked that."

But Maggie seemed to take Dylan's insensitive question much better than expected. She laughed heartily, as though she found the question rather amusing.

"I couldn't tell you, darling," she answered in between laughs, "even if I wanted to. I think I might have stopped counting… right around year: one thousand and two. Yes, it must have been then. I mean, at that point, it was just getting silly!"

It took a moment before Dylan was able respond. She had expected more resistance from Maggie, but in the end, was pleased to have the truth confirmed so freely, and with such candour.

The weight of Maggie's words burrowed themselves into her mind, and it was a minute or two before their meaning really impressed themselves upon her. When their significance became clear, Dylan's eyes finally widened and her mouth fell open in awe.

I was right, she thought to herself, utterly and unequivocally amazed.

Dylan had hoped with all her heart that such things could be true. *Eternal life* – and by extension, the legend of the Aurora itself. But even with all the strange happenings of the last few weeks, a small part of her had remained skeptical. Maggie's revelation had finally put all of those reservations to rest. *She* was the undeniable proof that Dylan had been waiting for: a *real* immortal, living and breathing, and standing right before her very eyes. Dylan could barely contain her delight. She *had* to know more…

"…how?" she managed to sputter, feeling a bit flabbergasted.

"Honestly," Maggie told her, "I'm not exactly sure. But I think it might have had something to do with that illness I spoke of before, the one I contracted as a child. Either that, or one of those remedies I cooked up had some unexpected side effects. I must have swallowed hundreds of crazy concoctions whist trying to get my hair back. I don't remember half of them! In any case, I didn't realize that I was 'different', until I was much older… when the people around me began to change and… I didn't."

Dylan couldn't quite shake her shock. She stared at Maggie, wide-eyed.

"…wow," was all she managed to say, as she took a deep breath and turned back to face the gardens.

Her mind was busy processing all of the wondrous, new information she'd just received, when she spotted Kit again, still lying in the shadows of the cherry blossom tree. Her excitement left her then, and her face went blank.

"What about Kit?" she asked apprehensively. "Is he also… like you?"

Maggie hesitated before responding. Dylan could tell that she'd made her feel uncomfortable, as Maggie's manner instantly lost its jolly undertone.

"I'm afraid I can't say," Maggie replied. "That's for him to tell you, darling… when he's ready."

Dylan felt she already knew the answer. She knew that Kit and Maggie probably shared in certain traits, but also… that there was something *more* to Kit, something that always kept him at arm's-length, something he was ashamed of, or maybe even… afraid?

"He's not human… is he?" Dylan asked, genuinely dismayed.

"Human?" Maggie responded. She took a deep breath, before continuing carefully: "No. I suppose, in the strictest sense, he isn't.

But what *is* 'human', really? Kitsune has ten fingers, ten toes, eyes and ears, just as you do. He has free will. He thinks, grows, bleeds... loves."

Dylan blushed. She had a feeling the final item in Maggie's list had specifically been placed there for her benefit.

"What more does one need, really?" said Maggie. "What other qualities would Kit need to possess, to be considered... 'human'?"

Dylan could not answer, nor did she want to. In fact, she felt embarrassed at having asked the loaded question in the first place. Her head was bowed shamefully, and she anxiously fiddled with her fingers.

Maggie took a step in closer towards her and placed her arm around her shoulders. Gently, she reached for Dylan's tender face, tucked her fingers under her chin, and lifted her head. She redirected Dylan's gaze until it had, once more, connected with the cherry blossom tree in the greenhouse below.

"He's been lying there under that tree for nearly two days now," Maggie told her, "watching over you. Tell me: does that sound like someone who's... *not* human?"

At this, Dylan's eyebrows furrowed unexpectedly. "Two days?" she said. "How long have I been asleep for?"

Although clearly disappointed at the turn in their conversation, Maggie answered Dylan's question forthwith.

"I'd say about sixty hours," she said, "give or take."

"Sixty hours?!" Dylan repeated. "Wow.... I mean... that has to be some sort of record, right?"

Dylan wasn't bothered at having been unconscious for such an extended period. Her reaction was more one of surprise. After all, no harm had been done. She was awake now... and feeling in better form than she had been in weeks.

Though, in turning over Maggie's newest revelation, a thought did occur to her, and she remembered then, what her purpose had been in coming to New York in the first place. Excitement burgeoned within her, and she asked:

"Two days. That must mean... have you finished with my mother's book?"

"Almost," Maggie answered. "We'll talk later this afternoon. I should be ready by then. I just need a couple more hours with it."

"Perfect," said Dylan, now smiling widely. "I really can't thank you enough for doing this for me, Maggie. Really."

"Don't be silly, dear. Like I said before, it's my pleasure. But, perhaps you should go down and see Kitty while you wait? I'm sure he'd like it if you did..."

At this, Dylan's face lost some of its glee, and her expression grew slightly sombre. Her eyes creased with concern before asking:

"You say he's not human, but... he's not... *dangerous*, is he?"

Maggie's mouth curled up into a sly smile, before answering.

"Not if you're on his good side," she said, with a small wink of her eye. Her tone thereafter grew more serious, and she added: "Listen darling, I know sometimes Kitty can be a bit... intimidating, or even... downright unpleasant. But, he's one of the 'good ones'. I promise you."

Her manner was warm and sincere, and Dylan couldn't help but feel comforted by her words. With a slight nod of her head, she left *The Tree House* lookout then, and began making her way towards the door.

"Wait," said Maggie. She pointed to the far corner of the room, and added: "Behind the wardrobe. There are stairs there that will take you straight down."

Following Maggie's directions, Dylan stepped up to The *Tree House*'s only wardrobe in the far corner of the room. She peeked her head around the back of it, and sure enough, found a set of tiny, downwards spiralling steps, hidden in-behind. The stairs were metal and narrow. Dylan guessed a larger person might not have been able to fit inside the small space. Though, she also judged herself sufficiently slender to pass.

Tentatively, Dylan placed one foot upon the top step, then the other, and slowly allowed her full weight to shift onto the rickety, little staircase. It held, and so Dylan relaxed, gripping the handrail tightly, as she carefully made her way down, one shaky step at a time. The manor's greenhouse was only one story below, and so it wasn't long until Dylan had reached the bottom.

Slowly, she left the shadow of the stairwell, and stepped out into the sunlight again. The air down in the greenhouse was warmer, and more humid, than it had been up in *The Tree House*. Though Dylan had never visited a tropical jungle before, she imagined it might feel a bit like this. She took a dozen or so steps forward, and when she had completely cleared *The Tree House* lookout, turned back to peer over her shoulder.

Maggie, she saw, was still watching her from atop her high ledge. Dylan immediately found her familiar smiling face in the distance. Their eyes locked, and Maggie began enthusiastically gesturing at her with her arms, obviously encouraging her to keep going.

Dylan smiled to herself and took a few more steps forward. She was now ascending the grassy mound, upon which Kit and the cherry tree were perched. Before reaching the top, she turned back one last time to look for Maggie, but found that she had disappeared from view. *The Tree House* lookout was empty. She and Kit were alone. It seemed that even the birds had vanished, as Dylan could no longer hear their cheerful song, floating on the air.

"You're up."

The sound of Kit's voice pierced the silence of the greenhouse and caught in Dylan's ear. She'd now reached the foot of the cherry tree and found him laying there, his eyes closed. He looked relaxed, more so than Dylan had ever seen him before. He was breathing deeply, taking long breaths, in and out through his nose. Dylan watched his chest rise and fall, as his breath entered and left him in turn.

"Don't just stand there," he told her abruptly. "Join me." He still did not open his eyes, however.

Dylan hesitated before taking her place next to him. She still wore her pyjamas, after all, and felt a bit uneasy, standing before him then, bare-footed in the grass. She considered briefly whether she should go back to *The Tree House* to change...

"Just lie down," Kit told her.

Finally dismissing her doubts, Dylan lowered herself down onto the ground. Slowly, she ran her fingers through the fresh grass in front of her and spread herself out next to him. She rolled over onto her back and stared up in the direction of the sky. Her head was in perfect alignment with his, and she could see his face out of the corner of her eye now. Their bodies were close. Dylan had only to reach her hand out an inch or so, and she could have easily connected with his. The thought caused her cheeks to flush unexpectedly, and she immediately redirected her gaze upwards, so as to avoid any further awkwardness.

The two of them lay in silence for a time. Kit, in his relaxed state, and Dylan, feeling the exact opposite. Her heart pounded in her chest, though she couldn't quite gather why. She was glad that Kit's eyes were closed, and that he couldn't see just how nervous she was. Slowly, she took in a deep breath and stared up at the overhanging branches.

Fortunately, the view from under the tree served as a perfect distraction. The space in between the branches was just enough to glimpse the clear blue skies up above. Dylan's anxiety was soon lost in the countless tiny blossoms flowering overhead. She inhaled deeply through her nose, taking in their sweet fragrance.

"Sakura."

Kit had opened his eyes and turned his head to look at her.

"That's what my mother called them," he said, turning his eyes back towards the sky. "They usually only flower in spring. But, leave it to Maggie to cheat Mother Nature." He smirked, flashing her his abnormally sharp teeth again.

Dylan smiled back at him, but did not respond. Maggie's words still rung loudly in her head. Dylan wondered if what Maggie had said was right. Was Kit *really* so different from her? Sure. There were oddities about him that set them apart. But were these differences *so* significant, that she should keep her distance from him?

Dylan felt conflicted. Her heart wanted to trust in Kit completely. But her head screamed: 'caution'. Kit was still keeping something from her, after all. She wondered what his secret was, and why it was so imperative that he hide it from her. *What could be so bad*, she thought, *to be better left unsaid?*

Thankfully, Kit chose this moment to interrupt her wandering thoughts. Without warning, he took her hand in his. His sudden show of affection intercepted her many qualms, and Dylan was surprised at how easily she welcomed his advance.

"My very first memories are of a place just like this one," Kit told her. His voice sounded different – softer than usual. "Under the Sakura tree near her house," he continued, "that's where she found me. My mother. I call her my 'mother', but... she wasn't. Not really."

Kit was speaking of his past, Dylan gathered. It was the first time she'd ever heard him speak of any sort of family. And so, she did not dare interrupt him, not even for a moment. Dylan took a deep breath, so as to ensure she'd remain completely quiet, while he went on.

"I was alone when she found me," Kit said, "weak and... nearly starving. She took me in, cared for me... raised me. I owe her everything. Even to this day, it's still the clearest, happiest memory that I have: my mother, coming towards me, under that Sakura tree."

Kit stopped. Dylan waited, but soon realized he would not be gracing her with anything further. His fleeting moment of candidness had passed, and all too quickly.

Dylan did not ask him any questions about his story, nor did she impose any comment on anything he'd said. She felt Kit preferred it that way. While his story may have been short, Dylan still felt it had spoken volumes.

Kit had had a mother, and a human mother, at that. He was adopted.

It's not much, she thought, *but it's a start.*

Dylan felt a sudden surge of affection for her mysterious companion then. Gently, she squeezed Kit's hand, and quickly felt him reciprocate the gesture.

Neither of them moved nor spoke again after the tender exchange. They simply remained as they were for a time, quietly lying under the Sakura tree.

-- CHAPTER TWENTY-TWO --

PEEK INTO THE PAST

Holly Andersen was pacing back and forth in the middle of her Montreal apartment. She looked frustrated, and was holding her cell phone up to her ear.

"It just keeps going straight to voicemail!" she cried, slamming her thumb down onto the 'End Call' button of her phone's touch screen.

She spoke to an older gentleman, who was sitting nearby on one of the kitchen island's high stools. The man looked to be in his mid to late fifties. He was slightly overweight, and had a full head of curly black hair, which had obviously been dyed. The man had a sympathetic face and gentle eyes, and appeared to be listening patiently to Holly's hysteria.

"I'm sure everything is fine," he told her, attempting to soothe her panic.

"But it's been over three days," Holly harped, "and she hasn't responded to any of my messages. I just know something's wrong. It's not like her."

At that moment, the front door of the apartment opened, and Michael Evans, dressed head to toe in his police uniform, stepped inside. Holly immediately looked to him with hopeful, shining eyes.

"I just spoke to my Captain," Michael told her. He paused, before going on: "I'm sorry, Holly. There's nothing we can do. If Dylan left the way you said, then... she's not exactly a missing person. And if she's also left the country, then... she's way out of our jurisdiction."

"That's insane!" Holly protested. "Tell him, Larry!"

She turned back towards the older man, whom she'd been speaking to prior to Michael's entrance.

His name was Larry Gibbons. He was a lawyer who'd been a friend of the family for, well... forever. 'Uncle Larry' is what the girls had called him as children. He'd attended college with Dylan's father, and after Dylan's mother had died, had made a habit of regularly lending a hand around the Dubois family home.

"I'm afraid Michael's right, Holly," he regretfully informed her. "If Dylan left of her own volition... then, it's not a kidnapping either. And the police can't intervene unless there's been some sort of crime."

"But, you don't understand," Holly pleaded with them. Tears welled up in her eyes. "This guy she left with... he's like, brainwashed her or something! The stories he told her – they were crazy. We have to do something. I can't just stand here and do nothing!"

It appeared Holly wasn't alone in her concerns, as the thought of an unknown man lurking about his ex-girlfriend also seemed to be causing Michael some distress.

"I know you're upset," Michael told her. "We all are. But... Dylan's clearly trying to work through something. She's changed, Holly. Everything's changed. For God's sakes, Dani's in a coma!"

He stopped himself there, realizing he'd lost some of his composure. The momentary rise in his voice, it seemed, had also triggered something in Holly. The tears she'd been repressing now came tumbling down her cheeks.

Taking a deep breath, Michael moved in closer towards her, and took her into his arms. He held her tightly, in the way one might hold a small, trembling child – with his chin resting atop her head.

"I'm sorry, Holly" he said. "I guess I'm a bit frustrated too. But there's nothing we can do right now. We just need to trust she'll come back… when she's ready."

Following these encouraging words, Michael released Holly from his embrace. He held her by the shoulders at arm's length, hunched forward, so as to look straight into her misty blue eyes.

"Are you going to be alright?" he asked her sincerely.

Though still a bit saddened, Holly managed to rustle up a reassuring nod.

"Good," said Michael, attempting a more positive and upbeat tone. "Now I'm still on duty, but I'll check in on you later? After my shift, OK? Chin up. Everything's going to work out. You'll see."

He waved to Larry and then quickly headed out the door.

Holly watched Michael exit the apartment, and then breathed a large disenchanted sigh. She took a seat on the stool next to Larry's, and then collapsed onto the kitchen island's surface.

Dylan's family photo album still laid open there in front of her. It had been weeks, and neither Holly nor Dylan had bothered putting it away. The mess of black and white photographs Dylan had collected from her parents' safe deposit box also remained. Feeling a bit restless now, Holly picked one of the black and white prints from the pile, and held it up in the air.

The photo was one of a teenage Lenora Dubois (Dylan's mother). In the picture, Lenora was holding a bouquet of flowers and smiling. Holly thought the flowers looked a lot like the yellow flowers Michael had given to Dylan weeks ago. But she couldn't be sure, for the photo had been printed in sepia tones. As she stared into Lenora's smiling face, Holly couldn't help but notice all of the family resemblances there.

Larry had been quiet for some time, but now chose to speak up once more.

"She really was beautiful," he said in a reminiscent tone.

Holly didn't answer, but diverted her eyes from the photograph – signalling to Larry that he'd captured her attention.

"'Nora'," he explained, "that's what JP and I used to call her. You kids were young when she passed. You never knew her like we did. Dylan's a lot like her, actually. Stubborn as an ox." He smiled and continued: "You never *could* tell Nora what to do either. She followed her own path, that one."

At this, Holly sat up straight and let out a small laugh.

"It must have driven Mr. Dubois crazy," she said.

"Well, it wasn't *always* easy," Larry answered, chuckling to himself, "and JP had his doubts now and then. I remember this one time… Nora had gotten it into her head that she was going to fly to Cambodia, of all places! She was about Dylan's age. It was before you kids were born. Anyways, the country was in total shambles at the time. Thousands of people were being killed and tortured under a new dictator. Not to mention, there was a conflict brewing with the Vietnamese too… and *our* Nora was utterly convinced that she needed to help, that she could make a difference if she tried."

Holly looked at Larry, bewilderment shining in her eyes.

"I had *no idea* that Dylan's mom was such a daredevil," she said.

"Not quite a 'daredevil'," Larry corrected her, "more like a… righteous soul. For as long as I knew her, Nora would always go out of her way to help the people around her – sometimes even to her own detriment. It was almost as if she'd been trying to make up for something… like she was searching for redemption from *some* mistake she might have made in the past. This is all conjecture, of course. I suppose neither JP or I ever *really* understood her in that way…"

Larry's voice had trailed off, but Holly continued to stare at him expectantly.

"And?" she pressed. "What happened with Cambodia? Did she go?"

"Ah yes," Larry replied. "JP pleaded with her endlessly not to. But Nora, being who she was, didn't listen. She hopped on a plane and disappeared from our lives to go volunteer in a hospital somewhere along the border. I remember JP was beside himself with worry. Lots of sleepless nights... Of course, Nora came back a few months later. Not a scratch on her. And life went on, as if nothing had changed."

"Amazing," said Holly. "I never heard that story before."

"JP put the entire incident out of his mind after Nora returned," Larry explained. "I guess he was just happy to have her back, safe and sound. Although, every so often, Nora would come up with some *new* humanitarian errand... and JP would have to suffer through it also." He laughed. "The Cambodian mission was the worst of the lot though, and by the time Dylan was born, Lenora's so-called escapades were all but over with."

Holly leaned her head into her hand, as she listened intently to Larry's tale – her elbow perched upon the kitchen counter.

Incredible, she thought. How strange it was, hearing of the fabulous deeds parents and mentors had undertaken in their youths, the goals they had pursued, aspirations they'd had. Holly now had a whole new appreciation for the woman that had been Lenora Dubois.

I guess now I know where Dylan gets it from, she thought to herself quickly.

"I should probably get going," said Larry then, rising from his seat and looking down at his watch.

"Yeah, of course," Holly replied, jumping from her chair. "Thanks so much for stopping by on such short notice," she told Larry, as she made a move to retrieve his coat from the closet. "And sorry to drag you out in such a panic."

"Don't be ridiculous," Larry responded, dismissing Holly's apologies. "No thanks required. You know you girls are like family to me. I'm always happy to help."

"Before I forget," he added, now slipping his arms through the sleeves of his trench coat. "I wanted to let you know that I heard back on those insurance claims I filed. There weren't any issues, and the paperwork's all gone through now. We should receive the funds in the next week or two. When you hear from Dylan, let her know that I'll spread the money evenly over the family accounts. There'll be more than enough to deal with Dani's medical bills. So she shouldn't worry."

Larry placed his hand over Holly's shoulder then, before adding: "and neither should you, darling. Dylan's tough, like her mom. I'm confident you'll be hearing from her soon."

Holly gave her uncle a forced smile, and nodded her head.

As Larry leaned over to put on his shoes, she shoved her hands into her jeans and felt something there with the tips of her fingers. Gently, she pulled the item out from her pocket, and immediately recognized it.

All these weeks, Holly had kept the photograph of Lenora's unknown relative folded up in her pocket. She'd deduced the boy in the photo was a relative of Mrs. Dubois' (it seemed the most plausible explanation, given his familiar look and frequent appearance in the old black and white prints). Still, despite her best efforts, Holly had been unable to place the boy. The mystery had continued to nag at her from time to time.

Staring down at the face of the mysterious boy now, with Larry close by doing up his shoelaces, Holly realized she'd overlooked a significant avenue of inquiry. After all, Larry had *known* Mrs. Dubois personally. Perhaps *he* could shed some light on the identity of the unidentified boy from the picture?

Silently cursing herself for her foolishness, Holly asked him now: "Uncle Larry, one more thing before you go? About aunt Lenora? By chance, did you ever meet any of her family? Like, did she ever have any cousins come around, or anything like that?"

Larry had finished tying his shoes at this point. He stood with his hand hovering over the front door knob, but stopped when he heard Holly's question.

"No," he said, crinkling his eyebrows curiously. "Why do you ask?"

"I just wondered if… maybe you knew who *this* was?" Holly held the photo of the smiling boy up in the air, so Larry could see.

"We found it in some of aunt Lenora's old things," she added. "There were other photos of him too. The two of them looked… pretty close."

Larry's brow creased as he stared hard at the photograph Holly held up for him.

"He doesn't *look* familiar," he said. "I'm sorry, Hol. I don't think Nora ever mentioned any family. She was adopted, you know?"

"Oh yeah," Holly recalled. "I keep forgetting…"

Larry turned the knob of the door, and Holly heard it gently creak open. The sound only lasted a second, however, for Larry stopped himself once more. His eyes travelled upwards, and Holly could tell he'd lost himself in a thought.

"What is it?" she asked.

Larry loosened his grip on the knob, and then lifted his index finger up into the air.

"Now that you remind me, though," he said, as he let go of the door completely and allowed it to close behind him, "there *was* that strange guy after Nora's accident."

Holly drew in a sharp breath, in anticipation.

"I never met him myself," Larry said. "But JP told me about it, after the fact. It happened before the funeral. There was a man that accosted JP out in the street. He was crazed, and caused quite a commotion. Kept claiming to be Lenora's brother! It was the strangest thing, because... JP said Nora had never mentioned a brother before."

"I never knew Dylan had an uncle," Holly said, without thinking.

"Well, I don't know if it was true," Larry clarified. "The man could have been lying. We never saw him again. JP filed a police report, and that was the end of it."

"Oh," Holly answered.

A moment of silence passed, and Holly spoke again: "Did you say this man came to aunt Lenora's funeral?"

Larry's account, muddled as it was, had somehow managed to knock loose some of Holly's own memories... of another, more recent funeral...

"Actually," Larry said, "I think he showed up sometime during the wake..."

But Holly wasn't listening anymore. She'd finally figured it out. How could she have forgotten? After all, it had been such a peculiar incident...

Larry was still droning on. Holly guiltily wished that he would finish, so she could focus on her new lead. When an opportunity finally presented itself, she did her best to wrap things up with him as fast as she could.

Minutes later, Holly had ushered Larry out the door and was sprinting towards her bedroom. Excited, she entered the room and darted straight towards her bedside dresser. With haste, she threw open the topmost drawer and began rummaging inside.

The memory which had her so worked up had now taken full shape in her mind.

The boy from the photograph, I've met him, she thought, *after Mr. Dubois' funeral.*

Although he wasn't so much a *boy* anymore… but a man. A man with dark eyes, and a big scar running down his face. Holly saw him all too clearly now. She remembered her encounter with him like it was yesterday.

Dylan had been completely distraught after the funeral. Holly had spent the better part of an hour attempting to comfort her. She'd then decided to grab some fresh air, and it was then that he'd shown himself.

The man with the scar had claimed to be a friend of the family. He'd explained that he'd been away for much of Dylan's life, and that she wouldn't remember him. He'd kept away from the funeral, he said, because he hadn't wished to intrude at such a sensitive time. He told Holly that he was only passing through, that he spent most of his time abroad. However, he'd also said, that if Dylan should ever need him, she should contact him.

Holly was certain the man had given her a card with his contact information. With everything going on, she'd forgotten all about it. But she also knew she hadn't thrown it away.

Holly fumbled around in her bedside drawer, searching for the elusive card. She waded through layers upon layers of junk, and finally emerged victorious.

"Found it," she said aloud, with a sigh of satisfaction.

The little card, which she now held in her fingers, was simple. At one time, it must have been blank, for there was no formal printing on it. Rather, it had functioned as a note of sorts, for the man with the scar had merely inscribed his name and telephone number on it by hand. The handwriting was slanted, and the letters cursive. Holly had to read it a few times over, but eventually was able to make it out.

The name on the card was: 'Luca Lynch'. And the phone number was an international number – area code: '852'.

Holly wondered whether this 'Luca' was the same man from Larry's story, and whether he might *actually* be Dylan and Dani's long-lost uncle.

Maybe you can help me? She thought to herself, as she stared at the slanted writing on the little card.

-- CHAPTER TWENTY-THREE --

JADEITE

Dylan and Kit found themselves, once again, sitting on either sides of the manor's large dining room table. Only this time, instead of dozens of empty dishes and used utensils, the table's surface was covered with dusty old books and maps. Over the past two days, Maggie had transformed the dining room into a makeshift research center.

She was currently seated at the head of the table, peering at the screen of a large laptop computer. The focus of her studies, Dylan's mother's text, was lying open in front of her. The ancient text had obviously been scrutinized quite closely, as evidence of Maggie's translations was quite literally protruding from its pages. The journal had been marked in various places with coloured tabs, and there were small pieces of notepaper stuck everywhere to its pages. One look at the old book told Dylan that Maggie had been *extremely* diligent in her task. She could hardly wait to hear her conclusions.

"So?" Dylan asked hopefully. "Have you found anything?"

Maggie tore her gaze away from her computer's screen to look up at Dylan. Her expression was not one of triumph, however, and so Dylan's heart immediately sank.

"There's good news, and there's some bad news," Maggie told her. "Which would you like to hear first?"

Dylan was caught off guard. She hadn't expected there to be any *bad* news to be had from her mother's manuscript. Somehow, she'd thought the hard part was behind her. She looked to Kit for guidance, but he merely stared back at her blankly.

"Give me the good news," she answered finally.

Maggie nodded her head and then picked up the ancient text from the table. She leaned forward, so as to be closer to Dylan, and then placed the text back down on the table's surface, tilting it slightly so Dylan could have a better view of it.

"This book," Maggie explained, flipping through the journal's pages, "may very well be one of the *richest* and most precious texts I've ever had the privilege of reading. Its pages are filled with the knowledge and experiences of past Aurora – recipes and step-by-step instructions for performing specialized rituals, and for brewing some very *rare* and complex remedies. I'd always known that the Aurora was out there, and that her powers of rejuvenation were unmatched... but, even *I* was amazed at the contents of this manual."

Dylan stared down at her mother's book, completely enraptured. She held her hand out and touched it, gently running her fingers over its worn pages.

"You think there's something in here that will help me save my sister?" she whispered.

Maggie smiled at her.

"After reading this," she answered, "I'm more convinced than ever that the Aurora can save *anyone*. There are no hopeless cases, as far as I can tell. Where there is life, even the most faint, the Aurora can preserve and protect it. And it will flourish under her care."

Upon hearing Maggie's words, Dylan's heart swelled with joy. Finally, she was getting somewhere, she thought. Here was some hope for Dani, after all.

But her thoughts in this were premature, as Maggie had not yet finished relaying her findings:

"I found no specific reference to treating people in comas," she cautioned. "The medicines described in your mother's text were developed to treat injuries and ailments more *vile* than that – infections that I doubt even Kitty would recognize. The cures described in these pages aren't meant for treating your run-of-the-mill sicknesses. You wouldn't find any of these afflictions in any common hospital..."

Confused, Dylan looked up at Maggie enquiringly.

"Don't worry, darling," Maggie reassured her. "The book doesn't lay out methods for treating everyday injuries. But I think I know why. The most plausible explanation is that the Aurora doesn't *need* any help in healing these. And so, the medicines described in the text were only meant for those wounds or diseases that proved more resistant than average. Whenever an Aurora encountered something novel, she made an entry in this journal, so that the next Aurora could learn from her encounter with it. It's truly remarkable. There are entries in this book that, I'm sure, pre-date even me. Countless generations of Aurora have contributed – some more than others, of course."

Maggie took a deep breath and then continued relaying her findings.

"That being said," she clarified, "it looks that even those Aurora that had no new expertise to impart wrote in the journal anyways. Some of the entries, I found, read more like snippets of a diary, recounting mundane and sometimes even personal occurrences. Soon after I began reading, I realized that this text isn't just an instruction manual. It chronicles the lives of your ancestors, all of the Aurora that lived before you – like a sort of... family autobiography. We should all be so lucky to have such a well-preserved record of where we came from."

Maggie sat back in her chair when she'd finished. She seemed pleased with her work, and was watching Dylan's reaction.

Dylan's throat felt a bit tight. There was a lot to process here.

She flipped through some of the pages in front of her, and hurriedly read some of the notes Maggie had left within her mother's book.

One of the translations referred to something called: "the Purple Plague", and another appeared to describe a treatment for: "poisonous harpy bites". Dylan wasn't sure what a 'harpy' was. She assumed it was some kind of animal. Quickly, she flipped through another few pages, but the translations she found there were no more enlightening than those that had come before.

"And my mother?" Dylan asked. "Did *she* write?"

Maggie frowned and shook her head. "I'm sorry, dear. The last entry is *far* too old to have been your mother. For some reason, she never wrote in it."

"Alright," Dylan replied, clearly disappointed, "and the bad news?" She bit her lip, as she awaited Maggie's answer.

"The bad news," Maggie replied in a more delicate tone, "is that I didn't find any clues as to the location of the Aurora's source. None of the entries explain what steps you should be taking *now*, in order to answer the calls in your dreams. I get the feeling that Aurora always made a point of passing *that* particular lesson along *orally* to her successor… and so there was never any need to write about it."

Dylan drew in a sharp breath. It was just as she had feared. How was she to help Dani now? An ancient book of cures was, no doubt, an invaluable asset to have. But of what use was it to her… *without* the power required to perform them?

Kit had been listening quietly from across the table. But now, seeing the panic bubbling up inside of Dylan, he cut in.

"Let's slow down for a second," he interjected then, holding his hands up in the air. He closed his eyes and considered for a moment. "You may have missed something, Mags," he suggested. "There might *still* be something useful in these pages, no? Maybe something you dismissed, something you thought wasn't relevant… like one of those diary-type entries maybe?"

It was clear Kit was grasping at straws. But Maggie nevertheless took his crude suggestion to heart.

"Kitty may be onto something," Maggie chimed.

She cleared some space in front of her and spread one of the maps she'd been looking at earlier out on the surface of the table.

"It's true that none of your ancestors gave away any information regarding the location of the Aurora's source," she said. "But there *was* one clue to be had. In the very *language* they used to recount their experiences. The early entries, especially, used very unique expressions from some very distinct and ancient dialects. If I had to guess, I'd say their authors most likely hailed from the North. By today's map, maybe Hebei or Shanxi Province…?"

Maggie used a pen to circle the relevant areas on the map. And Dylan leaned in closer for a better view.

"China?" she remarked aloud. "I guess I shouldn't be surprised. Kit had said it would be in the East. I guess I just never thought it would be *that* far east…"

"Well," Maggie continued, "I could be slightly off. Really, it could be anywhere in that general region… perhaps even Inner Mongolia. The hard part is pinpointing the *exact* location. I'm not about to send you backpacking in northern China without a *single* lead as to where you're headed."

"OK," Dylan answered determinedly. "How can I help?"

"Fortunately," Maggie explained, "I know the region quite well. And so does Kitty… I think?" She looked over at Kit, and he nodded, confirming her assumption. Maggie then went on: "Maybe if you tell us more about the dreams you've been having? It might spark something… help us narrow things down?"

It seemed a good plan. Though Dylan worried whether the dreams would be able to fill the gaps. Ever since they'd began, her nightmares had done nothing but cause her grief. She doubted now whether they could be of any help.

"OK," she said, somewhat sceptically. "I'll try."

Dylan closed her eyes and tried her best to recall every detail of her recurring nightmare.

"The dreams have changed over time," she said. "But there are some things that are always the same. I'm always in a field, a really *big* field. The grass is tall. And there's a sort of cave in front of me – this… dark space. At first, it's closed off to me and I can't get in. But later, it opens, and there's a light inside of it. I feel like I have to reach it… like there's something there, calling to me – an object of some kind. It's a really *strong* feeling. It's hard to describe, but in the dreams, I just know… I need to get to it."

Dylan opened her eyes then, only to find both Maggie and Kit still staring at her intently. Her retelling of the nightmare had obviously been lacking. And so, she closed her eyes again, wracking her brain for further details.

"There's water nearby," she added, "because I can always hear it. A river, maybe? And there's an animal in the cave. It growls at me, but I never actually see it, so I can't be sure what it is. The growl is really throaty and deep… like a lion's."

Dylan could still feel her companions' eyes boring into her like daggers. Though she wasn't sure what more she could say. The dreams, she realized, had actually been quite mediocre and vague. What other details could she provide?

There isn't anything else, she thought to herself, growing more nervous then. *What'll happen to Dani if Maggie and Kit can't pinpoint the source? What will I do?*

"There must be something else," Kit pushed her. "Anything?"

His forcefulness was not helping matters. Dylan already felt pressured enough. She began fidgeting with her fingers, and nervously running her hand over her forearm.

"The grass!" she cried suddenly. "The grass in the dream. At first, it seemed regular. But later, it turned a different colour – a sort of palish red… That's different, right? Does that help?"

But the look in Maggie and Kit's eyes remained vacant.

"No," Maggie told Dylan. "I'm afraid none of what you say rings any bells… Perhaps, if you take some time, something else will come to you?" Her tone was gentle and encouraging. But Dylan wasn't comforted in the least.

"No!" she cried, jumping from her seat. Her voice was panicked. "You don't understand," she said shakily. "There *isn't* anything else. That's *all* there is…" She grabbed anxiously at her wrist and fiddled with her jewellery, as she spoke. "What am I going to do?" she added, her eyes wide with worry. "If I can't help Dani, what'll happen to her?"

Kit was at a loss for words. He seemed genuinely saddened at seeing her so distraught.

Maggie, on the other hand, appeared unfazed by Dylan's sudden show of sorrow. She seemed distracted, her gaze drawn to Dylan's wrist.

"What's that you're wearing?" she asked abruptly. She pointed to one of the bracelets Dylan had been anxiously twirling in her frenzy.

The lady's question caused Dylan to stop suddenly. She looked down at the white bangle on her wrist.

"Oh," she answered. "It's nothing – just my mother's jade bracelet."

Without a second's hesitation, Maggie took the girl's arm roughly into her hands, and leaned in for a closer look.

"This is *real* jadeite," she observed, as she twisted the stone bangle around with her fingers and examined it carefully.

"Yeah…" Dylan replied, a bit confused by Maggie's sudden interest in her family heirloom.

"Well," Maggie exclaimed, "don't you know that white jadeite like this is *extremely* hard to come by?"

But both Dylan and Kit looked upon Maggie with blank faces. It seemed neither of them had any knowledge of this particular fact.

"Jadeite is China's most precious stone," Maggie explained, "but normally, it's green. Of course, it can be found naturally occurring in other colours too – yellow, orange, violet, etc. But *white* jadeite is particularly rare... and *pure white* jadeite – like the kind your bracelet is carved of – even more so! In fact, I've only ever heard of *one* mine in China that ever turned out such perfect specimens. And it was exhausted hundreds of years ago!"

Maggie let go of Dylan's wrist then, and hopped over to her computer. She began furiously typing something, and then slammed her finger down on the 'Enter' key.

"Ah ha!" she yelled, as the results of her Internet search appeared on her screen. Her exclamation caused Dylan and Kit to jump involuntarily. They both waited for her to share her breakthrough.

"I've got it!" Maggie exclaimed, smiling widely. "I've got the coordinates, right here! It's in Hebei Province, just as I predicted."

"How?" Dylan asked, slightly shocked. But she too, was smiling.

"The mine," Maggie clarified. "I remember it well, as I was in Beijing at the time when the sudden influx of white jade jewellery hit the streets. It was a *real* scandal. When the government got wind of it, they took possession of the mine so they alone, could reap the profits. They sold the jade at inflated prices for years, and made a killing. In any case, before the mine was depleted, whilst it was still an active site, they built up a tiny town around it to house the miners. 'Bai Yu' is what it was called, after the precious stone that essentially founded it."

"So," Dylan began, "you think that this abandoned town, Bai Yu... is somehow connected to my family? ... I'm not sure I follow."

Before answering Dylan's question, Maggie reached for her

family's journal. Carefully, she flipped through the coloured tabs she'd placed in the book, looking for a specific entry. Once found, she flipped the book open to the relevant page, and then handed it back to Dylan, pointing her to the right passage.

"*This* Aurora," she said, "her name was: 'Kai'. She didn't write much, because she didn't really have anything new to contribute (in terms of healing practices). But she *did* fill a few pages with some pertinent details about her life. From her writings, I gather she was quite timid and never left her home village. She was, however, deeply in love with a man who lived in a neighbouring town. She describes her time with him quite vividly. It was really lovely, actually. But that's beside the point. In one entry, she describes a beautiful white stone bracelet that he gave to her as a gift. Don't you see?! She must have passed that bracelet down to her daughter. And since then, it's come all the way down to you. The man she spoke of, her lover, he must have been one of the miners of Bai Yu!"

Dylan considered Maggie's deductions carefully. Her logic seemed sound, but there was one shortfall to her thinking.

"Even if you're right," Dylan posited, "and this bracelet really *is* made from stone that was mined in that little town. How can you be sure it was a miner that gave it to her? Couldn't her lover have just bought it for her, from one of those merchants you mentioned?"

"No!" Maggie answered. "You're not understanding just how *rare* that bangle is. It's priceless! I expect only a few of Beijing's elite would have been able to afford it back then. It would have been worth a small fortune. It's highly unlikely that Kai's lover was the type to have had *that much* disposable income. No. He must have stolen some rock straight from the source – at the Bai Yu mine. Find Bai Yu. And I bet you, you'll find your source!"

Exhilarated, Maggie proudly slapped the palm of her hand down onto one of the dozens of books littering her dining room table. After days of work, she'd finally arrived at the answer.

Both Dylan and Kit looked at her with big smiles spread across their faces.

"I guess I'm going to China," Dylan said, her eyebrows raised in disbelief. "I think I might need a visa." Her forehead creased with concentration, as she began listing off the preparations she would have to make before embarking on the trip.

"Forget all that, darling!" Maggie cried, waving her hand up dismissively. "No need to worry. I'll arrange everything. I'll charter a flight for you and Kitty ASAP. No need to bother with all that red tape. I have friends over there that will take care of everything! This is so exciting, isn't it Kitty?!"

But Kit did not answer. In fact, he'd turned white as a ghost at the mention of Maggie's proposal.

Dylan didn't seem to notice, she, like Maggie, having lost herself in the excitement. Things were finally moving in the right direction, she thought.

Hold on, Dani. Just a little longer.

-- CHAPTER TWENTY-FOUR --

TWO TALKS ON A TARMAC

It was a cold, grey day. Winter's first snowflakes could be seen falling from the dark clouds littering the sky.

Maggie was bundled up, standing with her arms crossed upon one of the private runways at Long Island Airport. She wore black leather gloves and tall winter boots. It was clear she was *not* a fan of the cold. Her eyes watered as freezing wind brushed by her, and she shivered, ducking her head further into her warm winter coat.

"Aren't you cold?" she asked aloud, her teeth chattering.

She spoke to Kit, who was standing by her side in nothing but a light windbreaker.

Kit's flamboyant reddish hair was blowing around in the wind. Unlike Maggie, he didn't seem to mind the freezing gusts brushing against his skin. And so he ignored her question.

The cold seemed to be the furthest thing from his mind. A look of utter dread plastered on his face, he stood erect and tense, staring directly ahead at the object of his fears.

The private jet airplane Maggie had so kindly chartered for Kit and Dylan's journey was parked a mere ten or so feet away from them. It had a height of about twenty-two feet, and a wingspan more than double that. A beautiful plane it was – top of the line in comfort, speed, and fuel efficiency. Not that any of these specs had swayed Kit from his apprehensions. To him, the large, metal bird was *still* just a flying 'death-box'. Maggie may as well have chartered him a steel coffin with wings...

"Oh! Stop being so melodramatic, Kitty!" Maggie cried in an irritated tone through the woolly scarf covering her face. "There's nothing to be afraid of. It's *just* a plane. People fly in them every day. It's not how it used to be. It's safe, and it's about time you took a ride in one anyways. Now, would you please loosen up? I don't want you to scare Dylan. She's got enough on her mind as it is."

Coincidentally, Dylan appeared then in the distance, out from the jet plane's side door.   Smiling and unaware of her mention in their conversation, she waved to Kit and Maggie, before beginning her descent of the steps leading down to the tarmac. She and Alaeder were busying themselves loading luggage onto the plane.

Upon seeing Dylan's innocent smile, Kit straightened himself momentarily. For a second, it seemed he had forgotten his horror. But this fleeting cheer was short lived. A second later, Maggie saw his body tense up with dread, once more.

She chose this moment to interrupt his morose thoughts.

"Speaking of Dylan," she said. "Can I ask... have you told her yet?"

Kit did not answer.

"She *needs* to know, Kitty," Maggie urged him. Her tone turned serious. "You have a *long* flight ahead of you. I really think you should take this opportunity and speak frankly with her. I've thought about what you told me, and I think there's a real possibility she might be in danger. That uncle you mentioned – the one you call 'L'? There's something... *not* right about him. If he's truly from the Aurora's bloodline, it seems wrong that he should also be searching for the Crepusculum. And the fact that he's somehow estranged...? That Dylan doesn't seem to know him? It doesn't make sense. He may be more of a threat than you know. I fear he has ill intentions for her."

Kit nodded his head, but still did not answer.

Overwhelmed as he seemed, Maggie couldn't be certain Kit would take her suggestions to heart.

"Kit?" she tried again.

But it was no use. Her redheaded companion seemed a million miles away.

"Kitsune, please? Just watch out for her over there, OK? I fear there's more at stake here than we realize. The faster you get Dylan to the source, the better."

Again, no answer from Kit. Maggie finally gave up her attempts to counsel him.

Kit stepped away from her then, without so much as a "see you later". Having sufficiently psyched himself up for the trip, he now headed towards the foot of the airplane's staircase.

"What's wrong with *him*?"

Dylan had finished loading her belongings onto the plane. She'd come to say her final farewells to Maggie before leaving, but on her way, had crossed paths with Kit. Confused by his ghostly demeanour, she turned her head now, only to see him stumble as he took his first steps onto the plane's boarding staircase. Alaeder, she saw, had to help him up the rest of the stairs and into the plane.

"Ignore him, darling," Maggie answered her. "Just a touch of aviophobia, that's all."

"No way," Dylan exclaimed, nearly laughing. "I wouldn't have thought Kit was afraid of anything."

"Yes. Well..." Maggie replied. "I suppose there's much you don't know about Kitty..."

She frowned disapprovingly.

If only there was some way of compelling him to tell her, Maggie thought to herself. And just then, it hit her, like lightning: the plane (and Kit's fear of flying, of course) presented the *perfect* opportunity for forcing his stubborn hand.

A plan materialized in Maggie's mind, and she smiled to herself slyly.

Of course, Kit won't be happy with me, she thought. *But he'll forgive me in time. What's a little meddling in the long run, anyway?*

Maggie drew in a breath of cold air, and turned her gaze determinedly on Dylan.

"Kitty's always been a bit nervous of airplanes," she told her. "He'll deny it, of course. Too proud for his own good. But fair warning, he'll probably be a *real* pain on the flight." She paused then, before continuing: "Luckily, I know the perfect cure! It'll put Kit right to sleep and make the journey far more comfortable for him. And for you, of course."

"Your lotus tea?" Dylan asked, cleverly holding up a thermos filled to the brim with the familiar purple liquid.

"No, no," Maggie chuckled. "That's for you, dear. It's much too precious to waste on something as silly as this. Be sure to conserve it! No. I had a much simpler solution in mind for Kitty." She lowered her voice then, making extra certain she wouldn't be overheard by Kit's long-range ears.

"Just between you and I," Maggie whispered, "Kit's a *real* lightweight. So when you get up in the air, *all* you have to do is spike his drink with a little gin. He'll fall straight asleep! Guaranteed to work like a charm." At this, she gave Dylan a subtle wink.

"I don't know, Maggie," Dylan replied, evidently a bit concerned. "I'm not sure I'd feel comfortable…"

"Don't be ridiculous, child!" Maggie exclaimed. "It's for his own good. All that stress isn't healthy. The gin will relax him and allow him to get his rest. Besides, you'll need him to be in full form when you land. Trust me! It'll be fine."

Although still a bit uncertain, Dylan agreed to Maggie's suggestion… if only to appease her.

"That's a good girl," Maggie told her. "It's for the best. You'll see. There's a bottle at the back of the plane. They usually keep it in the bottom cabinet. Be sure to use the gin though, and not the other alcohols on board. Mix it with some juice, and he won't notice a thing!"

Having successfully put her brilliant plan in motion, Maggie opened her arms wide and invited Dylan to hug her.

"Be sure to let me know how you get on," she told her, taking the girl into her arms and squeezing tightly.

"I will," Dylan answered.

The two women were still in mid-embrace, when a shrill ring was heard emanating from Dylan's coat pocket. Startled, she withdrew from Maggie's hold and roughly jammed her hand into the pocket, pulling from it her ringing cell phone. Glancing down at the display, Dylan's face seemed to contort with concern.

"Everything OK?" Maggie asked her.

"It's just my friend," Dylan answered, a bit distracted. "She's not exactly been the most supportive lately – with everything that's happened, and with Kit especially. I guess I've been sort of avoiding her because of it. But I should probably tell her what's happening before we leave… I think I'll try calling her back." At this, she waved goodbye, turned and headed for the plane.

Maggie too waved goodbye and shoved her hands deep into her coat's pockets. She watched in silence, as Dylan climbed the steps leading up to the jet.

You be safe now, she thought to herself, as she watched the jet's passenger door close behind Dylan. *I've done all I can for you. It's up to you now. Just please… be careful.*

Alaeder had finished with his duties on the plane and now re-joined his employer on the tarmac. He stood next to Maggie (almost twice her size) and looked down at her.

"Would you like me to pull the car around, Madam?" he asked, in his usual gracious manner.

"Yes, Alaeder," Maggie replied thoughtfully. "But we've not far to go. I've got a second plane waiting for us on the other side of the airport. We're taking our *own* little trip."

Alaeder bowed and obediently removed himself to fetch their vehicle. As he walked away from her, Maggie watched airport workers wheel away the staircase from Dylan and Kit's plane. It wouldn't be long now before lift off.

Almost there, she thought to herself. *Just one last loose end to tie up, whilst the kids are away.*

-- CHAPTER TWENTY-FIVE --

SECRETS IN THE SKY

Dylan loved flying. Not that she'd had much opportunity to do so in her life – a few family vacations, mostly. But each time, she'd come away from the whole airplane 'experience' even more exhilarated than the last. There was something *magical* about being up at 40,000 feet – and staring back down at the Earth through those little fishbowl windows every plane has. Everything always seemed so small and insignificant from up high in the sky.

Dylan had always imagined that, if Heaven were a real place, then *flying* was the closest she would ever get to it (that is, without the messy consequence of her untimely demise). She enjoyed staring out at that heavenly sea of white clouds floating below the metal wings of her plane. It was hard to believe those same clouds were mere masses of condensed water vapour. They looked so real, like clusters of delicious cotton candy suspended in the air. Dylan couldn't help but envision herself stepping out and falling into them, like fluffy, white cushions. She imagined she could spend countless hours hopping around the sky from cloud to cloud, never tiring – free as a bird.

Her sullen companion, however, seemed to have a very different opinion of flying. Whilst Dylan drifted effortlessly through blissful fantasies, Kit it seemed was suffering silently through his *own* private tribulations.

Unlike Dylan, Kit felt that flight was something best left to those who'd been blessed with wings at birth. As far as *he* was concerned, he'd been given legs for a reason. Nature had intended him to be a land dweller – *not a swimmer, nor a flyer*! His feet were meant to be on the ground at all times. To presume he could fly, Kit thought, was both egotistic and greedy. He couldn't understand what had possessed the human race to develop these 'flying machines' in the first place.

Only an hour or so had elapsed since Dylan and Kit's plane had taken off from the runway. And in that time, Kit's emotional state hadn't shown any signs of improvement. He'd been jumpy from the start, and his anxiousness had only grown since.

When the jet engines had first started, Dylan had worried her companion was going to be sick. All the blood had drained from his face, and his skin had taken on a greenish hue. The plane had roared down the airstrip, and Kit had gripped the armrests of his chair so tightly, Dylan had thought he might leave claw marks in their gorgeous leather coverings. He'd calmed himself a bit after lift off, but hadn't spoken a single word to her since.

Dylan turned herself away from her window now, to check on her terror-stricken travel companion. Kit still had not moved. He sat in his large, luxurious sofa chair, his back straight, and his eyes locked in a forward stare. All of his muscles seemed to be engaged. He was so tense, he could have been a stone statue, Dylan thought

She couldn't understand it. The private jet on which they travelled boasted some of the most lavish accommodations Dylan had ever seen. The cabin was the epitome of comfort. And yet none of this seemed to alleviate Kit's stress.

The jet's passenger compartment could easily have held a dozen or more passengers. But Dylan and Kit had the space all to themselves. The floor of the cabin was lined with beautiful off-white carpets. And the furnishings were all constructed of elegant, dark woods and soft cream coloured leathers. There were a few rows of spacious, forward facing seats up near the front of the plane, right in behind the cockpit. But these were all empty at the moment.

Dylan and Kit had settled themselves in the tail portion of the plane, which had more of a 'living room' feel to it. It was furnished with two swivel sofa chairs to one side, and a larger, elongated couch on the other. The two seating spaces faced each other, and were separated only by a slim coffee table, which was bolted down to the floor between them. Dylan had curled herself up in a blanket on the longer sofa. She stared over the aisle at Kit, who still sat uneasy in his armchair across the way.

"You doing OK over there?" Dylan asked with concern.

Kit seemed to grumble something in reply, but did not move. The same look of dread remained frozen in his face.

It was looking more and more that Maggie had been right about him. Dylan had never seen anyone so completely mortified before. This wasn't your average 'garden-variety' fear either, Dylan thought. Kit's tormented state appeared far more severe. *A real-life phobia.* Maggie had told her that Kit was afraid of flying, but Dylan had not expected *this level* of anguish from him. It all seemed so out of character...

Dylan checked the time on her phone.

3:30pm Eastern Time, she thought. The jet would not be landing for another twelve hours. She wondered if Kit could even make it that long... and whether she would be able to stare at his petrified figure for the remainder of their journey. *Twelve hours is a long time,* she thought.

Dylan wracked her brain for topics of conversation. *There must be something I can say to distract him*, she thought. But Maggie's suggestion from the airport seemed to be drowning out all other thoughts in her head. Dylan pushed that plan aside, determined to use it only as a last resort.

"So... you've been to Beijing before?" she asked her companion, casually. "Back at the manor, I thought Maggie said you had…"

Upon hearing her question, Kit seemed to break free from his panic spell momentarily. Long enough to look her in the eyes.

"Yeah," he said, his manner a bit uncertain.

Dylan smiled back at him and sighed, relieved to have caught a glimpse of the fearless and sturdy Kit she'd come to know so well.

"Would you tell me about it?" she asked him gently.

She must have spoken too fast, however, for Kit's face turned sour at her request.

"It was a long time ago," he answered after a short pause. "It's not important."

His voice was pained, as though he were recalling memories he preferred to keep buried. He turned away from her then, rudely signalling his withdrawal from their dialogue. His eyes found the window next to his seat, and Dylan saw the apprehensions return to his body as he caught sight of the clouds floating by outside of the jet.

It was then that Dylan resolved herself to put Maggie's controversial plan into action. She'd tried conversation. But it was clear from Kit's reaction; he had no interest in helping his situation.

Dylan rose from her seat, tossing the blanket she'd been wearing onto the sofa behind her. From the corner of her eye, she watched to see whether Kit would notice her departure. He, however, seemed uninterested in her movements, and did not stir at her leaving.

The plane's kitchen wasn't far. Slowly, Dylan made her way through the narrow passage at the rear of the plane, past the jet's only lavatories. On the other side of the passage, she entered the kitchen and pulled a curtain which hung from the small doorway behind her.

Once safe from Kit's prying eyes, she immediately went to work, opening and closing all of the cupboards she found. In less than a minute, Dylan had found two stunted drinking glasses in one of the top cabinets, filled these with ice from the freezer, and pulled the only bottle of gin she found out from the lowest cupboard. Carefully, she poured the clear liquid out from the flask and into the two glasses, filling them just below the halfway mark.

All she needed now was some sort of 'mixer' – something to conceal the taste of the liquor. She found a few options: club soda, ginger ale, cranberry or apple juice. Convinced that none of these would suffice on its own, Dylan got creative, adding a little apple juice for sweetness, some ginger ale for bubbles, and finally, the cranberry juice, thinking its bitterness was her best bet at masking the gin. Having mixed two glasses of her wild concoction, Dylan tested one and was pleasantly surprised to find it had an enjoyable taste. Refreshing – yet not too sweet.

"This might actually work," she whispered to herself, after swallowing a mouthful of her delicious brew.

Swiftly, Dylan disposed of her used cans and stored away the bottles of gin and juice. She pulled open the curtain, which led back to the cabin, collected her freshly mixed drinks, and exited the kitchen.

She found Kit exactly as she had left him, still brooding away in his sofa chair at the rear of the plane. Slowly, Dylan lowered herself back into her spot on the couch across from him. She placed the two glasses she'd carried back with her on the coffee table, and waited.

At first, nothing happened. Kit did not even turn his head at her arrival. She tried sliding the drink she'd prepared for him in his direction.

"I made you a drink," she told him hopefully. "Thought you might be thirsty."

Still nothing.

Dylan lifted her own glass from the table and took it to her lips. She sipped at the cocktail and continued to watch Kit in silence, hoping he might eventually turn to acknowledge her. She sat patiently for ten or fifteen minutes, and had almost given up hope, when finally, he moved.

By this time, Dylan had finished her own drink, and the ice in her companion's glass had all but melted away.

Slowly, Kit took the drink into his hand and raised it to his mouth. Dylan's eyes widened as she watched him take his first sip. She wondered whether he would notice the 'secret' ingredient, and how mad he would be if he did. Bracing herself for his reaction, her muscles tensed and she held her breath.

For a second, Dylan thought that she was caught, that Kit's tongue would undoubtedly notice something *'unusual'* in the refreshing beverage. It seemed plausible to her that her strange companion would have 'killer taste buds' to go along with all those *other* heightened senses she knew he possessed. Thankfully, she was wrong.

Minutes passed, and the outrage Dylan had expected from Kit never came. He carried on as usual, quietly sipping at the 'trick' cocktail in his hand. Dylan was relieved, but wondered whether her sneaky scheme had even been worth the trouble. After all, she herself had never been much of a drinker. Yet she'd downed her entire glass, and could barely feel the alcohol's influence on her body. She doubted the same amount of gin would have *any* calming effects on Kit, who was much larger than she – weight-wise.

No matter, she thought to herself, as she shrugged away her concerns. *I can always make him another, if he needs it…*

Feeling satisfied at having succeeded in her secret scheme, Dylan kicked back in her large sofa. She leaned her head against its soft pillows, closed her eyes, and breathed in deeply. Perhaps once Kit had fallen asleep, she too, would be able to get some shuteye? The vibrations and low pitch humming of the plane's engines seemed a perfect lullaby.

◆

Dylan was well on her way to dreamland, when there finally

came a sound from Kit's direction – a weak thud. Roused by the noise, Dylan re-opened her eyes and sat up straight. She quickly found the source of the thump. Kit had fallen asleep and dropped his glass onto the floor next to him.

For a moment, Dylan watched him without moving. She couldn't believe it. The gin had worked! Kit looked so peaceful now, slumbering away in his plush sofa-chair.

Dylan stood to get a better look at him. His behaviour since boarding the jet had been so irritating, she'd almost forgotten how handsome he was – with his striking features and bright reddish-blonde locks. He was quiet now. Calm. And like a crying baby that had finally went down for its nap, Dylan was again able to appreciate just how truly special Kit was.

Careful not to make any sudden movements or sounds, she covered him up with her own blanket, deciding it was the least she could do.

I did essentially drug him, after all, she thought to herself, slightly ashamed at her actions. *But it'll be alright. I'll apologize later.*

Having had her fill of gazing upon the serenity of her sleeping companion, Dylan turned her attention to the fallen glass by his seat. As she knelt down to pick it up, a look of distress washed over her face. Kit, it seemed, had not finished consuming the contents of his glass before dropping it. The cocktail had spilled onto the floor and formed a large, slopping puddle on the ground. The pale red liquid was now seeping into the jet's gorgeous white carpet.

"Shoots!" Dylan cried, as she ran swiftly towards the kitchen, grabbing a roll of paper towels and the bottle of club soda from the fridge.

She made it back to the foot of Kit's chair and hastily began cleaning up the mess – scrubbing and flushing out the spot with the clear, fizzy solution. She rubbed at the blemish in the carpet until her arms hurt and tiny beads of sweat began forming on her forehead.

Furiously, she laboured, losing all track of time, never distracting from her task. Her eyes remained locked on the spot until, finally, it was done.

Dylan sighed with satisfaction and sat back on her knees, quietly admiring her work. The carpet was wet – but spotless. She'd been lucky. Had the drink been pure cranberry juice, she surely would not have succeeded in her task.

Wiping the sweat from her brow, Dylan now rose from the floor and looked back over at Kit's chair. She hadn't heard a peep from him this whole time, which she thought a bit strange. She presumed the alcohol had simply had a greater impact on him than she'd anticipated – that he was out cold. But when Dylan finally looked back up at her friend's seat, she was confused by what she found.

The chair. It was empty.

Well, not empty *per se*.

The blanket Dylan had lain over Kit's slumbering body was still there. But Kit wasn't. He'd vanished from right under her nose in yet *another* unexplained disappearing act. Dylan couldn't understand it. First, the dead-end alley back home. Then, the truck at the border. And now *this*. How was he doing it?

Stunned, Dylan whipped her head around and searched the rest of the cabin with hungry eyes. Kit was nowhere to be found. Her mind began working furiously, desperately trying to make sense of her situation. She'd been hunched over at the foot of Kit's seat this entire time. It wouldn't have been possible for him to slip by without her noticing. She would have *seen* him, *heard* him… or even *felt* him move.

All at once, feelings of bewilderment and frustration flooded her. Dylan held her hands up to her head and ran her fingers through the roots of her hair. What was happening? How could he be gone? It just didn't make any sense.

And then, it happened. The clue Dylan had been awaiting for so long finally reared its quirky, little head. Quite literally.

Out of the corner of her eye, Dylan caught sight of movement coming from under the blanket she'd placed in Kit's chair. Caught off guard, she jumped backwards – startled by what she'd seen. Had she not known any better, Dylan might have thought that a rat had smuggled itself onto their plane and into Kit's seat. As unlikely as that seemed.

Curious to know what had caused the rustling from under the sheet, she leaned in for a closer look.

The movement came again, and this time, Dylan saw it clearly. There was *most definitely* something alive there, wiggling around under the warm, woollen blanket. It was much larger than a rat, however. Dylan guessed it was more the size of a cat. Whatever it was, she was determined to find out. And so, slowly, she reached out a hesitant hand and pulled at the fabric. The sheet slipped closer towards her gradually, until finally, it fell away, revealing what had been hidden beneath it.

Kit's clothes (the same ones he'd worn when boarding the plane) were lying there, crumpled up on the leather surface of the chair. The creature, which had caused the rustling from under the blanket, was curled up, right smack in the middle of these – like a kitten, cosily tucked away in a linen basket. Dylan couldn't make out what *type* of animal it was just yet, for its back was turned to her. However, she quickly ruled out both rats *and* cats. This creature, she realized, was unique. The bright reddish coat of fur on its back was unlike any she'd ever seen – and yet, it also felt oddly… familiar.

Dylan wasn't afraid. The animal hadn't noticed her. It seemed to be sleeping, and was breathing heavily. Its front was hidden from view, obstructed by Kit's shirt. Dylan had only to lift the bottom of the garment in order to unveil the animal hidden beneath. And so she did, meticulously, so as not to make any direct contact with the creature.

With the shirt out of the way, the animal was exposed, and Dylan finally learned its identity.

It was a fox! The healthiest, largest, and most fine looking one Dylan had ever seen – but a fox, nonetheless. The creature had a long, narrow snout, big, pointed ears, and thick, black whiskers – all of which were most definitely canine. It looked harmless really, and was far too elegant to be a dog. The features of its face were delicate and attractive-looking. Its eyelids were shut lightly, and Dylan could see that it was dreaming, as its eyes were rapidly rolling back and forth underneath. Its long, bushy tail was wrapped tightly around its small body, like a beautiful fur scarf. And its ears were turned down and backwards behind its head.

Fascinated by the animal before her, Dylan knelt down so as to be nearer to it. She yearned to be closer to the magnificent creature, and felt herself being drawn to it, pulled – much like a magnet to metal. She longed to connect with it, to touch it. And although her instincts cried caution, she reached out a shaky hand then, and placed it upon the creature's fur coat.

The hairs on the fox's back were softer than Dylan had expected, like silk – smooth and supple. The creature was warm. It radiated heat and comfort, which only encouraged Dylan's advances. Gently, she ran her hand down the creature's body, and found a spot on its side where she felt the beating of its heart. Her hand lingered there a moment, and slowly, she took in and processed all that she was seeing and feeling.

This wasn't just *any* fox, Dylan realized, her hand still resting upon the creature's reddish fur. Somehow, she *knew* this animal. She felt… acquainted with it – like she'd met it once already. Not only did its presence feel familiar to her, but she also felt… close to it in some way. Her eyes fixed themselves upon the gorgeous red fur in between her fingers, and suddenly, *she knew the truth.*

It was Kit. He'd been here all along, Dylan realized. Kit and the fox – the two were one and the same! He hadn't disappeared at all. He'd only *changed*, transformed! Kit *was* the creature before her. *He* was the fox. Dylan recognized the unique crimson hue of her friend's hair in the bright red flush of the fox's fur. And then, everything made sense to her – his unusually powerful hearing, his quick reflexes, the way he always moved about… so nimble and swift. Dylan had always known that Kit was… *different*. But now, she knew why. All of Kit's strange and unusual 'gifts' – they weren't just inhuman, she realized, they were *animal*. The traits of a fox!

Having finally solved the mystery that was her enigmatic friend, Dylan's mouth fell open in wonder. Her hand fell back to her side, and she pondered the many implications that this discovery brought.

Maggie had warned her of this, she recalled. Kit *wasn't* human. But just how *'animal'* was he, Dylan wondered. Obviously, Kit was able to take on a human form. Or… was it the opposite? Was he, rather, a human… able to take on animal form? What came *first*, Dylan asked herself: *the fox or the man?*

Dylan sighed, as she realized her discovery had only propped up further questions for her. She would have to ask him, she supposed. Hopefully Kit would be more forthcoming, now that she'd uncovered his secret. She also decided then, that no matter what his answers were, she would keep an open mind. It didn't matter *what* Kit was, Dylan decided. To her, he was still the same Kit she'd known all along – the same boy who'd rescued her on that rainy night back home, and who'd helped her on her journey. He was *good* – through and through. Her heart knew this.

Heavy with her recent discoveries, Dylan now made a move to lift herself from the floor. Before rising, however, she spotted something tucked under some of the clothes on Kit's chair. It looked like a chain of sorts, hanging from one of Kit's pockets. Without thinking, Dylan reached for the dangling metal and took it into her hand. She meant to tuck it back into Kit's pocket, but as she made contact with the chain, it loosened and fell loosely into her palm.

Dylan saw immediately that it was a necklace with a locket strung onto it. It was gorgeous. Vintage, and decorated with a beautiful floral-like pattern. Dylan wasn't normally in the habit of snooping, but in this instance, couldn't quite help herself. The locket had already been opened a crack. Surely there would be no harm in taking a peek?

With the tips of her fingers, Dylan gently opened the oval shaped locket fully. Slowly, she re-adjusted her eyes and looked upon the photos it contained.

Within moments of gazing upon the pictures, Dylan's features fell. Anger began to swell within her, and her mood turned black. She'd recognized the faces staring up at her from the locket almost immediately.

How Kit had come to possess this particular necklace, she did not know. For this was *not* his family, she thought, but *hers*. The photo in the rightmost half of the locket, in particular, was of her mother – Lenora Dubois.

Dylan shut the locket forcefully in her palm and made a fist around it. Her mouth turned hard, and she rose to her feet. She stared back down at Kit, who was still asleep in his chair, peacefully unaware of her recent discoveries.

He would have some *major* explaining to do when he woke up, Dylan thought. For as far as she was concerned, there was *no good reason* Kit should have kept this secret from her.

It seemed her travelling companion was more than just a fox. He was a sly one, at that... and he'd had her completely fooled.

CHAPTER TWENTY-SIX

UNMASKED

After a near twenty-four hours of unconsciousness, Kit finally woke from his alcohol-induced slumber. His head was pounding, and his stomach felt like it'd been wrenched around in his abdomen a few times over. He felt like he'd been run over by a tractor.

Slowly, he opened his eyes. The room around him was pitch dark, and he was lying face down in what appeared to be a large bed, dressed in what felt like some sort of bathrobe. He couldn't remember the chain of events that had brought him there, nor where his clothes had gone. His last memories were of the plane... and of Dylan.

Instinctually, Kit called out to her now.

"Dyl..." he tried, but his voice was hoarse and dry. The call came out as a mere whisper.

His heart thumped hard in his chest, as his worst fears for her sprang into his mind. Whoever had brought him here must have overpowered him somehow. Although, Kit couldn't imagine how that could be. Nevertheless, with him out of the way, Dylan had been left completely defenceless. She was so fragile, Kit thought. He would never forgive himself if she'd been harmed.

Despite the aching in his body, Kit managed to push himself up into a seated position. He cleared his throat and then tried calling for

Dylan once more. The call came out much clearer this time.

"Dylan!" he cried with worry.

The words had only just left his lips when, all at once, the lights turned on.

Kit was blindsided by the sudden illumination in the room. He ducked his head and raised his forearm up into the air, shielding his eyes from the glare, whilst desperately trying to adjust. Tears welled up in his eyes and blurred his vision. He couldn't quite see yet, and so he relied on his hearing instead.

Someone had turned on a faucet. There was water running. But then, it stopped, and he heard footsteps coming towards him. They grew louder, drawing nearer, and a minute later, they'd reached the foot of his bed.

"Here, drink this."

The voice was familiar, but it lacked the softness and care that Kit had grown so accustomed to in past weeks.

Confused, Kit lowered his arm from his face. His eyes had adjusted themselves to the ambient light, and he could now clearly see Dylan before him. She stood next to his bed and was holding out a glass of water for him.

"You'll feel better after you drink," she insisted. "You're dehydrated."

Her voice sounded detached, distant, and her features were cold and hard. Kit noted the differences immediately. Something was wrong. Her manner was strange.

Kit was unsure and wary. But even he knew she was right. He felt groggy, and his head was sore. Someone had done a real number on him. His body was crying out to him with twinges of pain from just about everywhere. And so, he cautiously took the glass from her and sipped at the water. It was refreshing.

Meanwhile, Dylan pulled a solid wooden chair out from a nearby desk and placed it next to Kit's bed. She sat herself down, crossed her legs, and watched him drink, patiently waiting for him to finish. Her body language remained the same, impassive and icy. Kit could feel her piercing stare boring into him like knives. He wondered what he'd done to merit this hostility from her. What had happened on that plane? What was he missing?

Kit wracked his brains. He struggled to recall his memories, to find the missing pieces to the puzzle. His eyes wandered about the room, searching for clues.

The suite in which he found himself appeared large. Kit noted the adjoining bathroom and what looked to be a sitting area, right outside the bedroom door. Could it be that their plane had reached its destination without his being aware? It was the only explanation. This *had* to be their hotel room – the one Maggie had booked for them in Beijing.

Kit continued to question himself. How had he gotten here? Surely, Dylan hadn't carried him all the way from the airport? How could he not remember checking into the hotel? And what could have caused Dylan's sudden emotional shift towards him? Why, he wondered, was she so cross?

Kit was silent for some time as he ran over all of these questions in his mind. Dylan soon grew impatient with him. She spoke then, and interrupted his contemplations.

"I finally figured it out," she said blankly. Her tone was almost scornful. "'Kitsné'. It's tricky, but... your mother must have had a *real* sense of humour, naming you that."

Dylan laughed before she went on, a forced, unsettling sort-of laugh.

"It took me a while to get the spelling right. But I got it eventually. 'K-i-t-s-u-n-e'. I looked it up while you were sleeping." She paused and lowered her gaze, smiling to herself. "It's kind of funny, actually. Japanese for 'fox' – right? Clever. It's a good name."

Kit's eyes widened in disbelief, and he felt his skin begin to warm. He finally understood what was happening, and he was humiliated.

Dylan *knew*. She'd seen him. He'd exposed himself somehow. But how? Kit couldn't imagine that he'd revealed his *alter ego* to her voluntarily. He would remember *that*. There could be only one other explanation… Suddenly, the thumping in his temples and the queasiness in his stomach all made sense.

"You poisoned me?" Kit mumbled miserably. His face was flushed with shame. He could feel the sting of treachery in the back of his throat, and materializing in behind his eyes. He felt a fool. He'd trusted this girl, even cared for her, and she'd fed him *poison*? Unknowingly or not, Dylan had stripped him of his sovereignty. She'd taken from him the one thing he'd worked so hard to build – his most treasured possession – the control he held over his mind and body.

Kit recalled the drink Dylan had prepared for him on the plane. One drink – just one. He remembered how small the glass had been, how little it had held. In order to subdue him, Dylan would have had to have used the right spirit, one to which he had no tolerance – gin, perhaps? Or maybe… vodka? But how could she have known? This was no coincidence. And it dawned on him then – Maggie. She'd had her hand in this, Kit was sure. The disgrace and betrayal he felt now turned to frustration, to anger. Always the meddler, Maggie was…

Dylan, it seemed, was unaware of Kit's inner turmoil – and of the apparent violation she'd inflicted upon him when she'd administered him alcohol without his consent. As far as Dylan was concerned, *she* was the victim here. Kit had encroached upon *her*. He'd lied to her. And her only concern now was of extracting the truth from him – once and for all.

"It's a neat trick," she told him, nodding her head, "that 'morphing' thing you do. I missed it on the plane, but caught the second show a few hours ago, after we got to the hotel. You were totally out cold, so I had to carry you in my arms. You make a really cute fox, I have to say… with the little whiskers and feet. Very sweet."

Her words were kind, but her voice betrayed her true feelings. She was angry with him, and Kit couldn't quite comprehend why. Certainly, it was understandable that he should want to keep this particular part of him secret? At least, until he could be sure that she was trustworthy?

"I found you on the plane," Dylan continued, "but I wasn't absolutely convinced it was you. Not until we got here and I put you down. It happened right there in front me. Just like that, you changed back into yourself. It was… really amazing to watch and… yeah! It explained so much! I've had tons of time to think since then, and I've been going over it *all* in my head – all those special talents of yours… how fast you are, and how you can hear a pin drop in the next room. Not to mention, that disappearance stunt you pulled on me in the truck at the border. Hiding under the back seat, right? Out of sight? Good one. Really… very cool. I get it now." She stopped and gazed at him, wide eyed. But Kit could tell – there was more.

"The one thing I haven't quite figured out yet is the alley," she said. "You know, the one I chased you into? You're going to have to help me out there. I thought *for sure* I had you cornered. And I must have searched that cul-de-sac top to bottom. There was nowhere to hide, even for the smallest of critters. So… how'd you do it?"

Dylan leaned forward and stared intensely into Kit's eyes. She squinted inquisitively at him and waited for his answer.

Kit's jaw was hard, and his body felt stiff with resentment. But there was no use hiding from her anymore.

"I jumped," he answered, his voice trembling. "The barricade, it wasn't that high… easy enough to scale."

Dylan sat back in her chair. She tilted her head back and sighed:

"Of course. Why didn't I think of that?" Her tone was sarcastic, and she ran her hands over her head as she spoke. It was clear she was feeling exasperated.

"You're just full of surprises, aren't you?" she asked in a cynical tone. "Well, at least I know it *was* you following me that day… but what about before that? You never *did* tell me where you came from, or what brought you to me. That day I bumped into you at the hospital – that wasn't an accident, was it? You'd been watching me? For how long? And… why?! Why are you helping me now, Kit? Does it have something to do with this?"

And then, as though it had been her plan all along, Dylan lifted her hand into the air and let drop the locket she'd found amongst Kit's clothes on the plane. The metal pendant fell swiftly from her grasp and then bounced a bit, when it had reached the end of the chain to which it was tethered.

Kit watched the necklace suspended from Dylan's fingers sway back and forth in front of him, as if hypnotized. And his face turned pale. The offending piece served as a vicious wake up call for him. One look at it, and he was reminded of his *own* offences against the lovely girl before him – how he'd planned to use Dylan as a conduit for his own benefit, and how he'd then kept the truth from her, regardless of the numerous opportunities to come clean. If only he'd been honest with her from the beginning… things could have been different, he thought. He could have avoided this mess. Perhaps *he* was the one to blame for her subsequent move against him? Could he really fault her, knowing what he'd done? The anger and bitterness he'd felt evaporated from his mind then. All that remained now was guilt, and regret.

"No more lies, Kit. Please. Just tell me what's going on. Tell me where you got this locket."

Dylan's patience was up. She was anxious for answers. Kit, however, did not seem ready to provide these. He was sitting on the edge of the bed, his shoulders slumped and his head hung in disgrace. He had the air of one who'd been defeated, an aura of hopelessness about him. He avoided Dylan's gaze and refused to look at her.

"You *have* to tell me," she pushed him. "I deserve to know. This is *my* family, Kit! There's a picture of my mom in here. Is this how you found me? Why do you even have this? Tell me!"

But Kit remained tight-lipped. His confessions burned in the back of his throat, and as much as he wanted to, he could not bring himself to speak. Fear and shame kept him locked up tight. It was the only coping mechanism he knew.

"You're not going to tell me, are you?" Dylan asked him finally. Tears welled up in her eyes when she realized she was getting nowhere with him. She rose from her seat and headed for the door.

Before leaving the bedroom, she turned back and added sadly: "Just so you know, it wouldn't have mattered to me where you came from or… 'what' you were, Kit – whether you were human or animal or… even something in-between. *I* always knew who you were. I just wish you'd trusted me too."

Her words dug into Kit's conscience like a drill. He lifted his head in time to see her wipe away a few salty tears from her cheeks and leave his sight. He didn't try to stop her. He didn't know that there was anything he *could* say to make things right again.

Minutes later, he heard rustling coming from the far end of the next room, and then a door gently being opened and closed. He knew Dylan had gone. He was alone again. She'd left him… to wallow in his misery, and shame.

-- CHAPTER TWENTY-SEVEN --

HOLLY'S HEART

"What do you think?"

Holly was hunched over the little table at the foot of Danielle Dubois' hospital bed, staring intently into the face of Michael Evans. It was visiting hours at the Montreal General, and Holly was paying Dylan's sister her daily visit. She'd summoned Michael because she'd received a rather worrying voicemail from Dylan, which she wanted him to hear.

"I'm not sure *what* to think," Michael answered her. "She sounds normal in the message. There's no hesitation in her voice – which seems strange, given what she's saying."

"She's gone to China for crying out loud!" Holly yelled unexpectedly.

Her sudden outburst, being quite loud, drew some attention from outside. A couple of nurses shot some dirty looks at her through the glass window of the hospital room. Holly grimaced in response, but still lowered her voice before continuing.

"This is getting completely out of hand," she cried. "How can she think that this is OK? She's gone mental! Running off like this without consulting me..." Holly lowered her voice even further before finishing. "Dani's doctors have been asking to speak with her," she whispered crossly. "They're pushing for us to decide on a course of action for Dani. What am I supposed to tell them? 'Sorry Doc, Dylan's decided to take an impromptu vacation with her psycho boyfriend'!?"

Her tone was sarcastic, but Michael still reacted adversely. His face flushed at Holly's uttering of the 'BF' word, and he lowered his gaze, hiding his momentary slip of emotion from her. Recent events had forced Michael to accept his relationship with Dylan was over and done with. Nevertheless, it seemed the thought of her having potentially moved on still stung.

Feeling a bit guilty at her carelessness, Holly refrained from speaking again. She waited a minute or two, whilst Michael collected himself and finally addressed her.

"I agree. This *is* out of character for her. But we've been through this already. There's nothing we can do."

"But what if there *was* something?" Holly countered. She handed him the card she'd received from the mysterious man at the funeral.

Michael accepted the card from her and examined it.

"Luca Lynch" he read aloud. "Who's that?" He sounded intrigued.

"I met him after the funeral," Holly told him. "He said he was a friend of the family and that I should call, if Dylan was ever in trouble..."

Michael squinted his eyes. He didn't quite understand how anyone (even a 'friend of the family') could help them in their present predicament.

"I talked to Larry," Holly clarified, her eyes growing wide. "And I think this guy might be related to Dylan's mom. He might have been her brother... As in, he may be Dylan and Dani's uncle – a blood relative."

Holly paused her speech for effect, wishing to impress upon

Michael the importance of her discovery.

"Dylan won't listen to *us*," she said, "but maybe… she'll listen *to family*."

Michael sat back in his chair and took a long, deep breath. He considered Holly's idea a moment. True. Her proposal had merit. But it also came at a price. Contacting this man without Dylan's blessing would mean stepping over some lines that Michael felt were better left uncrossed. After turning it over a couple times in his head, he finally came down hard against the idea.

"No," he told Holly, his tone commanding and righteous. "That's going too far. I know you grew up with her. But Dylan wouldn't want you calling this guy behind her back. I may not know what's going on with her right now. But I *do* know that. You're like a sister to her, Hol. But *this*… this isn't your call to make."

"She's not leaving us any choice!" Holly protested. "This is the only way. The number on the card – I looked it up. It's a Hong Kong area code! Dylan may be half way around the world by now. But this guy's right around the corner from her! It's our best bet at bringing her home."

Michael was angry now. Holly was trying his patience. His forehead became creased with frustration, and he rose from his seat. Standing tall, he repeated his objections once more.

"Stop it, Holly," he ordered her. His manner was powerful and authoritative. "I don't want to hear another word. You asked me for my opinion. And I'm giving it to you. You should leave it alone."

At that, he turned his back and made a move to leave the room. Before exiting, he threw the little card Holly had given him onto Dani's hospital bed and gently took the slumbering girl's hand in his.

"Sorry, Dani," he said in a soft voice. He lowered his head in a show of respect, and a moment later, was out the door.

After Michael had left, Holly rose from her seat. Carefully, she made her way over to Dani's bedside, taking up the little card from the hospital bed and lifting it from its resting place. Her face was stone cold. Silently, she read the phone number on the card again, and looked over at Dani.

Holly barely recognized the face of the patient lying in the bed before her. Since falling into her coma, Dani's condition had deteriorated rapidly. The changes in her appearance over the last month, alone, had been drastic. Her body was fading, withering right before Holly's eyes. Her face, which had once been so full and lovely, was now sunken and empty. Her hair, once a beautiful shade of honey, now looked dull and dead. This person was no longer the Danielle Dubois that Holly knew and loved. She was a stranger.

Before the fire, Dani had been so young and joyful – always so full of life and laughter. But that was the past, Holly thought. That beautiful girl was gone now – brain dead. The body lying here was just an empty shell. A shell that had once housed a magnificent spirit – but a shell, nonetheless. Dani wasn't there anymore. She'd left them long ago.

Holly wasn't even moved anymore, staring down at Dani's cadaverous body. She'd finished mourning and cried her last tear. She'd said her goodbyes and let Dani go. It was time that Dylan did the same.

Her mind decided, Holly reached into her pocket and pulled out her cell phone. Referring to the little card in her other hand, she dialled the number for Dylan's suspected uncle. The Hong Kong digits for Mr. Luca Lynch.

"I'm not losing you too, Pickle," she said aloud. "This family's already lost too many members by my count. I don't care what Michael says. I'm doing this."

She held the phone up to her ear and heard the ringing from the other end of the line. Her jaw was tense, and she swallowed nervously, as she waited for someone to answer.

-- CHAPTER TWENTY-EIGHT --

SUNRISE SERRADA

It was the wee hours of the morning. The sky above was still dark, but there was a hint of an orange glow on the horizon in the East, marking the dawn. A new day was beginning.

Dylan, however, being jet lagged with the time change on her side, was already miles ahead. She'd gotten her head start hours earlier, after leaving the hotel room back in Beijing.

Upon first leaving Kit in the middle of the night, Dylan had hesitated. Could she go on without him? She'd asked herself that question whilst uneasily pacing back and forth in the hotel lobby. Part of her had hoped that he would come to his senses, that the next dinging of the hotel's elevators would signal his arrival, and that Kit would come barrelling out of those opening doors, full of apologies and confessions. Her heart had longed for reconciliation. If only he had come to her, she would have forgiven him. She could have forgotten, she thought, if only he'd explained.

Alas, her hopes had gone unanswered. After waiting a respectable amount of time, Dylan had taken up her gear and started out without him. Perhaps *this* was how things were supposed to turn out, she told herself, in attempts to soothe her disappointment. Kit had taken her this far (for which she was grateful), and she was now meant to go on alone.

A hired car had taken Dylan three hours north, out of the city and into the wilderness. She had then continued her journey on foot, as the road had come to an abrupt end, not far outside a little village her driver had called: *'Bian Yuan'* – "the edge". There, Dylan had strapped on her winter boots and parka, before setting out across the barren, snow-covered landscape of northern Hebei province.

Nearly an hour had passed since she'd left the comfort and warmth of her hired vehicle. But Dylan felt that she was no closer to finding her target. The terrain around her looked the same to her as it had when she'd first stepped out – flat, with the occasional snow-sprinkled boulder here and there. She was alone out here. The country around her was cold and desolate. No one had walked these lands in a long time. Still, she pressed on, never looking back. It couldn't be much further, she told herself hopefully. She had to be on the right track.

The atmosphere was growing brighter now, and with every step, Dylan could see the sun rising higher in the sky. She squinted her eyes against the light, and felt an icy breeze blow past her. The wind froze her cheeks and made her eyes water. She could no longer feel the tip of her nose, as it had gone numb in the cold. Her fingers too, felt stiff – the freeze having worked its way through her leather gloves. She was breathing heavily. Her body was weary of the incessant trudge across this difficult terrain. But she did not stop, for her resolve could not have been stronger. Onwards she went, pulling her fur-lined hood tighter around her head and rubbing her hands together for warmth.

All was quiet around her, and for too long, it seemed that the only sound was that of the snow crunching under her feet. The constant drone had turned Dylan's mind to mush, and so she welcomed the ear-splitting tone that suddenly sounded from within the knapsack she carried on her back.

Startled, Dylan very nearly missed her step when she heard the alarm go off. But she quickly shook her surprise, and withdrew her arms from the straps of her bag. The high-pitched sound could only mean one thing, she thought, smiling to herself.

Hurriedly, Dylan unzipped the backpack and pulled out the handheld machine that was emitting the piercing sound. Her eyes found the device's display screen, and her heart leapt in excitement. A series of numbers flashed across the monitor, and Dylan knew then that she'd finally reached her goal. The instrument ringing in her hands was a Global Positioning System designed to track her movements across this snowy wasteland. Before leaving, Dylan had programmed it with the coordinates to the abandoned town of Bai Yu. The machine was simply alerting her of her arrival there.

With the shrill ring of the GPS sounding in her ear, and her heart racing in her chest, Dylan threw her head around in every direction. She strained her eyes against the blinding light of the rising sun, and looked far into the distance, searching for her prize. She ran ahead a few paces, pushing against the snow blocking her path, and that was when she came upon it.

The even and mind-numbing terrain that Dylan had travelled across now came to an unexpected end. The land before her fell away in the form of a steep, rocky-looking slope. After hours of journeying, Dylan found herself perched upon a tall, snow-covered hill. The scenery she beheld from the top of the peak was breathtaking, and Dylan couldn't help but stop herself. After storing away her GPS device, she stood for some time, taking in her bird's-eye view of the frozen country stretched out at her feet.

From way up here, she could clearly see the remnants of what she assumed was the ancient mining town of Bai Yu – located less than a kilometer off from the foot of the stony hill. There looked to be a dozen or so structures strewn over the snow-covered landscape. But Dylan couldn't quite make out any details. She would have to get closer, she thought.

Further afield, past the ruins of the little town, were the

beginnings of an enormous forest. The trees, Dylan saw, stretched far out towards the horizon and met with the sky, which was now ablaze with a morning tapestry of pink and orange light.

Anxious to reach her destination, Dylan took a deep breath and began her descent of the rocky slope. Carefully, she weaved her way through the maze of icy boulders that garnished the hill. The snow upon the ground made the hike even more treacherous. But Dylan remained surefooted, never slipping. Even Kit, with his unnatural powers of agility and nimbleness, would not have fared better against the icy obstacles blocking her path. And so, the further Dylan made it down the slope, the more assured she became. By the time she'd reached the bottom, she was beaming with confidence and optimism over her achievement.

"I made it," she said aloud to herself, a large grin spread across her face.

Her spirits were up, as she embarked upon the last leg of her journey – the short and final stretch to Bai Yu.

It wasn't long after she'd reached the little town of ruins that Dylan recognized it for what it truly was – a dead end. Bai Yu, it seemed, was nothing more than a set of ancient, dilapidated and roofless structures – set upon cold and deserted grounds. It was hard to believe that the few crumbling walls of rammed-earth still standing in this forsaken place had once been a village of bustling miners. Time had laid waste to all. Not a shred of life remained, no fragments of the once thriving and prosperous town. Bai Yu had become but a long-lost memory, buried in the shadow of a towering hill.

Unable to accept the evidence before her, Dylan swept through the town remnants, desperately hunting for clues. In and out of the skeletal structures she went, testing the battered walls and digging at the snow, hoping to find some sign as to her next move. Denial fuelled her. Perhaps an ancient relic had survived all these years, and now laid in wait under a layer of snow? Or maybe an antiquated carving had been left for her to find in one of the town's vestigial walls? She was wrong, however. There was nothing. After an hour of searching, even Dylan was forced to admit her defeat. Feeling squashed at her failure, she made her way to the far edge of the ruined town and collapsed onto the ground. She sat herself down on her knees, and quietly stared at the rays of the rising sun, which now blanketed the forest to the East.

Who am I kidding? Dylan thought to herself. *I'm no treasure hunter or explorer. What do I know of tracking supernatural sources of power? Kit and Maggie are wrong about me. They've got the wrong girl. I couldn't possibly be this Aurora they speak of... How could I be? One day on my own, and I'm already stuck... I'll never make it to the source on time.*

Images of Dani lying comatose in her hospital bed back home now flooded into Dylan's mind – her little sister, in need of help... beyond the reach of modern medicine. The Aurora had been Dani's only hope. She would never wake now, Dylan thought. And Dylan would never again hear the chime of her laughter, or the softness of her voice. Her heart ached at the thought, and her throat tightened in sorrow. Tears filled her eyes, and just as she was about to give in to the grief, she saw something...

In the distance, on the very edge of the vast wood, there came a sparkle – a golden glimmer by the trees. It called to Dylan, like her dreams had months before, and she knew then... It was a message, come to show her the way. Her resolve returned to her, and in an instant, Dylan was on her feet, sprinting towards the forest and the twinkle shining on its brink. She ran as fast as her legs would take her, against the icy wind that burned her face, her eyes locked upon that flicker of gold.

What is it? Dylan thought, her mind racing as fast as she. *Some kind of metal signpost? Or maybe a mirror?* She couldn't quite make it out yet, but the shining object on the forest's edge appeared small – no more than a foot tall.

As fate would have it, none of Dylan's predictions had hit home. The sparkling body at the edge of the wood was neither artificial, nor manufactured. In fact, it was the exact opposite – the most delicate and natural of things. A flower. But not just any flower… a *Serrada*.

Dylan recognized the blossom from her mother's favourite fairy tale as soon as she saw it, bursting from the snow on the ground as though it had a mind of its own – stubborn, and persisting through even the harshest of winters. The flower was different from those her mother had brought home to her as a child, however. It was far more beautiful and bright. It had the same cone-shaped petal Dylan had seen on other species of Calla Lily, but differed from these in one main respect. The single stem of pollen rising up through the center of the bloom seemed to sparkle in the sunlight. It was formed from (what appeared to be) tightly knit clusters of gold dust. Evidence of this golden residue could be seen lightly powdered upon the bright yellow petal, which was wrapped tightly around the flower's stigma.

This is it, Dylan thought, *the sign I've been waiting for*. With a sigh of relief, she knelt down next to the shining Serrada.

Upon closer examination of the plant growing out from the frozen ground, Dylan noticed something else. The open blossom, it seemed, did *more* than just reflect light. It also looked to be bioluminescent. The warm glow that the flower emitted was faint, but Dylan saw it clearly now, radiating from deep within its tissues. Dylan had heard of such phenomenon in fish before… but never in plants. She knew then how special the flower truly was – a veritable treasure… sent to her by the Aurora's source.

Slowly, Dylan removed her gloves. She reached her hand out and lightly brushed her fingers across the surface of the Serrada's one large, curved petal. Some of the blossom's golden pollen was lifted and smeared across her fingertips. The gold dust felt light and fluffy upon her skin. Dylan rubbed her thumb together with her fingertips, and felt the plant's golden residue easily spread across her skin's surface – much like a fine powdered sugar. She wondered whether the blossom smelled as sweet as it looked. Compelled by curiosity, she raised her pollen-covered fingers to her nose and breathed in deeply. Gently, she closed her eyes as the sparkling pollen's aroma travelled up through her nasal passages and triggered something within her.

A series of images, all strung together like a poorly edited film, began streaming in from behind Dylan's eyelids. The vision was quick and blurry. It lacked specifics, and yet… felt so real, familiar – like an old memory recalled from the depths of her mind.

Dylan saw her mother's face, heard the sound of her voice. She couldn't quite make out her words yet. There was laughter also. The laughter of a child, a girl. It took Dylan a moment to place the memory, but soon enough, she remembered.

Dani couldn't have been more than four or five years old. Her little sister had been violently ill for days. That was it – the day her mother had brought home their very *first* Serrada. Dylan remembered then… lying next to her sister, the shining yellow flower tucked in between them. Their mother had told them the Tale of the Lovely Young Maiden in the East for the very first time. Dylan recalled the change in her sister's features, as her mother had laid her hand on her forehead and softly recounted the tale. She saw it now – the serene look in her mother's eyes, the soft glow reflected in her cheeks, the warmth of her smile as she watched both her daughters, laughing and gazing back up at her.

The images lasted only a moment, but it was enough. Something changed in Dylan then. It was as if a key had been turned and a whole series of memories unlocked from somewhere deep within her. The visions began anew, and Dylan saw a slew of new faces flashing before her eyes, one by one. Though she knew she'd never seen them before, the faces *also* felt familiar to her, and Dylan realized, she knew each of their names too. Lenora, Dylan's mother, came first. Then, there was Lei, and Meilou, Kai, Lilu, Billi… Dylan saw the Aurora's history in reverse – each of the Aurora that had come before her. It was as though she was travelling back through time, one Aurora at a time. The images flew by faster and faster, hundreds of them. And soon, each face passed so quickly that Dylan could barely perceive them anymore. Suddenly, just as quickly as it had begun, the slideshow came to an abrupt halt. The visions settled upon a *single* face, the last face – *and the first*. The first Aurora. Unlike the others, Dylan couldn't quite remember her name, though she recognized her all the same. It was *her* – she was sure of it. The Maiden from her mother's story.

The scene panned out, and Dylan saw the Maiden travelling west through the forest, accompanied by the Emperor's messenger, just as she had in the story. She saw the Maiden leave her home – nestled deep within the Eastern Wood, saw her journey through the boundless forest and towards the Emperor's kingdom. Endless trees, rivers and waterfalls paved her path, followed by more trees, more rivers, more water... At first, Dylan couldn't quite understand the significance of what was being shown to her. But soon, the message became clear. The Maiden's voyage across the Eastern Wood – *It's the way to the Aurora's source!* Dylan realized. She'd known it all along. It had always been there, buried deep within her own mind.

The visions stopped then, and Dylan gently willed her eyes to open once more. She rose up from the ground and stared directly ahead, past the border of the wood and through to the many trees growing in the vast forest. In an instant, she recognized the way. Her path now laid bare before her.

There was no time to waste. She collected her things and started for the wood. Dylan left the glowing Serrada behind her, and moments later, crossed the threshold and passed into the fated forest.

-- CHAPTER TWENTY-NINE --

MAGGIE'S MISSION

What a circus, Maggie thought to herself, sitting and staring from the backseat window of her luxurious, rental sedan.

Las Vegas.

Maggie had never understood the appeal that this city held for so many. A modern day *Never Never Land* it was. A place to which men (especially) seemed to flock, in order to relive the glories of their youths. Every year, millions would come to play, to gamble, to revel in the perpetual bravado – the pizazz. But it was merely a show, Maggie thought, a charade, a temporary escape from which *all* must eventually return.

"I *do* wish that Kitty would stop coming here," she said. "He always leaves it such a mess."

She spoke to Alaeder, but her trusty butler did not answer. He was otherwise engaged at the wheel, manoeuvring their vehicle through the hustle and bustle of the Las Vegas Strip.

There were crowds of tourists everywhere, shuffling in between the palm trees and bouncing in and out of the grand hotels and lavish casinos. Honking cars, flashing lights, and giant billboards. The streets were chaos. It was midday in Sin City, and Las Vegas Boulevard was literally overflowing with guests, all come to visit its sparkling sights and entertainment... Or, as Maggie saw it, to peruse through its cesspool of commercial cons and consumerism.

Bored with the view from her tinted car window, Maggie turned her head away from the sleazy crowds and the monstrous buildings lining the street. She readjusted the taupe coloured scarf, which was draped over her head, and carefully placed a pair of dark sunglasses over her eyes. Overall, her ensemble appeared tame. A real change from the flashy looks she normally sported, but a necessary precaution, she thought. The probability of her being recognized here may have been low. But the famous *'Mama Maggie'* was better safe than sorry.

It had been many decades since Maggie had last visited this city. Part of her had hoped that she would never again be forced to return. Wishful thinking that had been on her part, for here she was again, just like old times: *Still cleaning up after Kitty's ridiculous escapades…*

Maggie remembered a time when she had journeyed to Las Vegas on a somewhat regular basis (once, sometimes twice a year) in order to rescue her foxy friend from his slip-ups. Obsessed with finding his elusive treasure, the Crepusculum, the crown jewel of the Wild West, Kit had come again and again to this miserable town, following lead after lead, and *always* ending in disaster.

Usually, Maggie's visits had consisted of but a few stops – a couple of dead-end bars, maybe a games room or a lounge. But this was the first time a hospital had ever been involved. It was his biggest blunder yet, she thought – *an entire week in a hospital bed… with doctors and nurses combing over his body and through his things.* Who knew what they might have discovered, what they might have noticed was… 'different' about him. Maggie only hoped that she'd arrived in time to reverse any damage Kit may have caused for himself.

Alaeder was now turning a corner, veering their car off of the busy Las Vegas Strip and onto a much quieter road. Maggie saw in the distance a grouping of boxy-looking buildings. *Sunrise Hospital and Medical Center,* she presumed.

Let's make this quick, shall we? she thought to herself optimistically.

At this, Maggie dug her hand into her purse and pulled from it a small glass vial filled with what appeared to be a finely ground, black powder. Holding it up to her nose, she shook the tiny container whilst examining its grainy contents. *I hope it's enough*, she thought.

Over the years, Maggie had perfected the recipe to this particular powder. When grave mistakes were committed, she would turn to her black concoction for help. Administered in the right amount, the exceptional powder could erase days, weeks, even months of its recipient's memories. Peculiar or unexplained encounters with mysterious red-haired strangers were completely forgotten – lost forever, along with the rest of its recipient's most recent recollections.

Maggie's one-of-a-kind powder had worked miracles in the past. In fact, it had saved her young friend from more than a few tight spots. The two of them had come to rely on it with such frequency, that Maggie had even composed a little poem in its honour. The rhyme had also served as a helpful reminder when mixing the blackened powder, as it also contained a list of its obscure ingredients:

> *To the city, Kitty always comes,*
> *to indulge in play and pleasantry;*
> *But not to worry, for I've a remedy,*
> *a sure way to hold their tongues;*
>
> *Some peel of pearl and daisy powder,*
> *a dash of elderberries;*
> *Grind with sesame and silver celery;*
> *make for emptied memories.*

Maggie stepped out from the shade of her lavish sedan, all the while, quietly humming to herself and softly reciting the words to her catchy, little jingle. Having removed herself from the vehicle, she called out to Alaeder before closing the door behind her:

"I shouldn't be more than an hour or so. Please return for me then, darling!"

"Yes, ma'am," he replied, as he pulled their vehicle back onto the street.

With the car gone, Maggie began her journey up some steps and into the busy hospital. The air inside was even drier than it had been out under the blazing desert sun. Maggie found the halls stuffier than expected, with all those warm bodies loitering together, awaiting their turns in triage. The signage in the medical center was also confusing and difficult to follow. Maggie was forced to stop for directions along the way. After roaming the disturbingly bland corridors for a time, she finally arrived at her destination – Sunrise Medical's surgical wing.

Not wishing to waste any time, Maggie stepped up to what appeared to be a sort-of reception desk, located along the far wall of a rather small waiting area. She addressed the young nurse manning the station in her most warm and wholehearted tone.

"Hello," she said. "My nephew was treated here a month ago. And I was hoping I could speak with his doctor? A Dr. Beth Chandler?"

"Sorry. Dr. Chandler isn't in today."

The young nurse seemed engrossed in her work. She didn't even look up from her files in answering. Maggie examined her further, before addressing her once more. Her name, which coincidentally appeared to be 'Margaret', was clearly displayed on her uniform.

"Margaret?" Maggie tried again, smiling. "What a lovely name. I wonder. Could I possibly trouble you for the names of the nurses who handled my nephew's case? Or perhaps, you could refer me to another doctor who tended to him?"

Upon hearing her name spoken with such warmth, Margaret finally looked up from her charts. It was clear she was not accustomed to being treated so pleasantly, as she offered Maggie a smile then.

"I might be able to do that," she answered, her manner having shifted quite abruptly. She turned in her chair in order to face her computer's screen. "I'll have to pull up his file, though. What was your nephew's name again?"

Maggie had been waiting at the ready with Kit's usual alias – 'Chris Cook'. She was about to provide it to the nurse, when something stopped her.

Maggie saw something then, hanging on the back wall of the little waiting room. A drawing. The police sketch had been pinned to a cork bulletin board behind the nurses' desk. It took Maggie only a moment to recognize the beautiful pencil-drawn face on the page – those prominent, dark eyes, that luscious head of hair. It was Kit. Clear as day. His face had been mounted on the wall. Put up on display for everyone to see, and there were big, black letters printed beneath it, which read:

WITNESS WANTED FOR QUESTIONING

IN MURDER INVESTIGATION

Maggie's eyes grew wide in spotting the drawing hanging upon the wall.

This won't do at all, she thought to herself crossly, tightly clasping in her hand her precious vial of memory-stripping powder. *No amount of my special powder will be able to fix this, Kitty… not this time, I'm afraid.*

"Are you alright?"

Margaret was staring at Maggie with a confused expression on her face.

"Yes," Maggie finally mustered, after having taken a moment to collect herself. "I just realized something. I'm sorry, but… I have to leave. My apologies. And, thank you for your help."

At this, she rushed away from the young nurse, and hurriedly made her way out of the hospital's surgical wing. With haste, Maggie scurried back through the corridors by which she'd come, and finally found her way out of Sunrise.

Sighing, she stood upon the pavement by the hospital's front entrance, and patiently awaited Alaeder's return.

I told him these treasure hunts of his would bring him nothing but trouble! Maggie thought to herself angrily. *Even I can't clean up this mess. My dear Kitty, how are we going to get you out of this one?*

-- CHAPTER THIRTY --

WALK IN THE WILD

Hours had passed, and Dylan continued to be amazed as she hiked further and further into the wood. Even now, she failed to grasp exactly *how* she managed to stay on course, but trusted her instincts all the same. She made her way forward, basing her steps on the vision that had been shown to her, adjusting her course when coming upon familiar-looking boulders or trees. While Dylan knew she'd never visited these woods before, she still felt acquainted with them somehow – as though *she* herself had been that young Maiden, so many years ago, taking the opposite path towards the Emperor's Kingdom. It all felt *so right*. Like she was finally coming home, after a long sojourn away.

Deeper and deeper into the forest Dylan delved, faithfully following the road map which had so seamlessly been laid out for her in her mind. The rolling images would recur from time to time. But Dylan was still uncertain as to how much further her journey would take her.

Upon first entering the forest, the way had been difficult. Dylan had tired quickly, dragging her feet through the thick snow, whilst also dodging in between the tightly packed tree trunks of the wood. The bare branches of the dormant trees had scraped at her face and blocked her path. But after a few miles, the trail had improved. Gradually, the layer of snow on the ground had thinned, as had the density of the trees. At first, Dylan had thought this transition in the forest was but a lucky break. It wasn't long, however, before she'd realized… it was much more than that.

The snow at Dylan's feet and the frost in the air continued to lessen as she moved further into the forest. Soon they had disappeared completely. The ground turned soggy, and the atmosphere warmed. Dylan spotted a few budding branches up above her head, and heard the chirping of wayward birds.

In just a few miles, the character of the forest had changed dramatically. *This isn't a winter wasteland anymore*, Dylan realized. The forest had transformed itself into a burgeoning wood – in the midst of a glorious spring. Somehow, the seasons had shifted and the forest found new life.

Dylan knew the manifestations she witnessed couldn't be natural. Rather, it appeared that something *mystical* was fuelling the forest. The wood was being re-energized, it's growth stimulated and encouraged.

She is life itself, eternal and undying.

Kit's words rung loudly in Dylan's mind then. She remembered the way in which he had described the Aurora to her – as if it was only yesterday. That was the night everything had changed for her. Kit's explanations had lifted her out from under the dreams that, for *so long*, had bombarded her sleep. In darkness, his words had brought her clarity and light, helping her onto her rightful path. Yet Dylan hadn't wholly appreciated their meaning until now.

It's the Aurora, she realized, or rather, the Aurora's source.

It was responsible for the transformations Dylan now saw in the forest. The source of the Aurora's power was greater than Dylan could ever have imagined. It seeped into the ground and flooded up into the trees, waking them from their winter's sleep. The Aurora's magic hung in the very air that Dylan was breathing. It warmed the woods, bringing life back to its wild undergrowth. At this rate, Dylan thought that spring would soon pass, and a forever summer would come over this forest. *The most beautiful and flawless summer anyone has ever known...*

Dylan smiled to herself. She knew now she was getting close. The changes she observed to the forest would likely become more and more pronounced as she neared the Aurora's source. Dylan had only to continue on her way and watch, as the trees around her blossomed into their fuller, more vibrant versions. *They* would lead her to her destination, she thought. The remainder of her journey would be a pleasant one.

♦

Dylan's path through the remarkable wood did indeed become easier as she continued to advance. The sun rose higher into the sky, feeding the forest with its rays. Slowly, the buds in the trees opened to reveal a crowd of healthy green leaves overhead. With the snow all gone, the harsh cold of winter now seemed but a distant memory. The ground upon which Dylan travelled grew firmer, as moss and grass began to grow, their roots tugging and pulling at the loose earth beneath her feet. And just when the forest's newfound heat and humidity had caught up with her, when Dylan's thirst had reached new levels of unbearable, there suddenly came the sound of running water on the air.

Dylan did not question her good fortune in this. It seemed only natural to her that the powers imbued in this forest should help her on her way. She followed the echoes she heard floating upon the breeze, and found her way down to a shallow river.

Standing on the riverbank, Dylan took a moment and examined her surroundings. The river, she saw, was about five or six meters across, and only a foot or so deep. Its waters ran clear over a bed of smooth, sand coloured stones. Dylan reassured herself it would be safe to drink. Out here, she was far enough from civilization. The river would be free of any man-made contaminants or chemicals...

not to mention, her fancy filter would remove any other common impurities and bacteria.

Pulling her bottle from her bag, Dylan made her way down to the river, stepping lightly over a dozen or so large stones strewn out along the bank. She knelt down to the water's edge and collected some of it in her container. Hopping her way back up to the grass, she held the bottle up in the air. Most of the water she'd gathered was still trapped above the filter. It would be a few minutes before every drop had passed through.

While she waited, Dylan wrestled with her remaining layers of winter wear. She'd already shed her gloves and parka earlier on. But the forest had grown much hotter now, and Dylan felt it time she also lost her sweater and changed her boots. Here by the river, the summer's rays beat down on her, causing her to overheat and perspire. There was no shade on the riverbank, no trees offering protection from the scorching sun.

Dylan removed her sweat soaked garments, swapping them out for more suitable apparel she pulled from her backpack. She put on a fresh sleeveless shirt, switched her socks, and strung up a pair of old running shoes on her feet. When Dylan had finished changing, she glanced back over at her bottle and found that her filter had finished its job.

Anxious to satiate her thirst, Dylan lifted the bottle's spout to her lips and squeezed the cold water into her mouth. She drank voraciously until her belly was satisfied, and then poured water into her hand, dousing her face and neck with the cold liquid. The water felt nice and cool against her burning skin. Feeling refreshed, she sighed and refocused herself upon her objective.

In the visions the Serrada had given her, there *also* had been water. Dylan remembered large volumes of flowing freshwater leading up to her destination. She closed her eyes and saw the images once more. Hazy at first, the visions grew clearer and more refined as she concentrated her mind on them. Dylan knew she was on the right track. She'd seen this setting before. The Serrada had shown it to her. *This stream will take me the rest of the way*, she thought. The source, she knew, laid in wait for her at the river's end.

With her water bottle still in hand, Dylan started out once more. She kept to the grassy parts of the riverbank, as the terrain nearer the river was slanted and slippery. She continued to drink as she marched, occasionally stopping to refill her bottle at the water's edge. The river, after all, provided an inexhaustible source of hydration. Dylan only wished that it had also delivered food. She'd already eaten much of her provisions, and had to preserve what little rations she had left for her return journey.

Strangely, even with her stomach growling as it was, Dylan's energy levels seemed to be on the rise. More than a day had passed since she'd slept. Dylan imagined she should have tired by now, and yet, the opposite was true. The farther she moved downstream, the more alert and lively she felt.

Presumably, the Aurora's source was beginning to affect *her* too. Its power wasn't limited to the vegetation of the forest. Even now, Dylan could feel it breathing new life into her body, reinforcing her muscles and boosting her movements. The feeling was intoxicating, and Dylan relished in it.

Faster and faster she went downriver, gaining speed with every bound. Invigorated, she revelled in the rush she received from the wind brushing past her cheeks and flowing through her hair. The ground passed quickly beneath her feet, and soon, the grassy riverbank turned to pastures of jagged rocks and stones. The nature of the river at her side *also* turned rampant. Its waters grew more turbulent and choppy the further she travelled. But Dylan did not slow. She continued to hop effortlessly across the rocky terrain… until her run was brusquely interrupted.

Dylan came upon a cliff and was forced to a halt. She stood tall and gazed out at the landscape before her. All of the river's waters rushed to this very spot, where they now spilled over and downwards in the shape of a whooshing waterfall.

This is it, she thought.

Cautiously, Dylan crept to the cliff's edge and lowered herself down on all fours. She drew in a breath of crisp air, and looked down at the waterfall's base. Her eyes squinting, she peered through the mist rising up from the booming waters below, and searched for further signs or clues in the chasm.

The drop down to the bottom of the falls was a good eighty to ninety feet. For a second, Dylan was overcome with vertigo, as she stared down at the crashing waters of the cascade. She imagined what it would feel like to plunge into the pool below. Chances were, even if she managed to survive the fall, she would still drown. Dylan doubted that even the strongest of swimmers would be able to withstand currents caused by a waterfall of this height. The thought turned her stomach a bit, and after dwelling on the foreboding imagery a minute or two, she pushed it from her mind.

Instead, Dylan turned her attention to the cliff's walls. Her eyes searched the wet, mossy surfaces of the ridge below. It wasn't long before her efforts were rewarded. Below her, less than twenty feet down, Dylan spotted something glittering in the sunlight. It was the same sparkle that had first drawn her to the forest's edge, hours earlier. Only this time, the light Dylan saw was more concentrated and intense.

"Another Serrada," she whispered to herself eagerly.

The glimmer came from somewhere inside of the cliff's walls, from within some hollowed space in the bluff. Dylan guessed there was a kind of ledge there, but couldn't be certain as her view was obstructed. She strained her neck out as far as she could, but it was no use. The cliff's edge kept her from properly seeing into the crag below. She would have to get closer.

Sighing, Dylan pushed herself back up and away from the stone precipice. She sat and pondered her predicament. She hadn't expected to encounter such a daunting obstacle. As a child, Dylan had taken *some* rock climbing lessons. But never in her life had she attempted *anything* like this. In the past, Dylan had always had experienced climbers with her. The cliffs she'd practiced on also had never been quite so precarious. One false step, she thought, and it would be the end of her.

For a moment, Dylan wished that she'd waited longer for Kit at the hotel. She would have felt safer taking on a task like this with him by her side. At least then, she wouldn't have been alone. In past weeks, it seemed that Dylan had grown accustomed to the fox's presence. He wasn't always a pleasure to be around – what with his brooding and occasional fits of indifference. But Dylan couldn't deny that she missed him now. Despite his faults, Kit had been there for her when she'd needed him. She doubted she could have made it this far without his help.

But he's not here, Dylan thought to herself sternly. *I have to do this on my own.*

Rustling up her courage, Dylan rose to her feet and got to work. She pulled some rope and a climbing halter from her backpack, and began clipping pieces together. When done, she found a cluster of very large, tightly packed boulders a few meters off from the edge of the cliff – and strung her rope around them. With her rappelling line safely anchored, she slipped into her climbing harness and secured herself to the rope via a metal belay device. By this time, her heart was racing, and her breaths had grown short and shallow. Fear was catching up with her. She struggled to keep it at bay, quietly muttering positive affirmations to herself.

"I can do this," she repeated softly over and over, as she fought to maintain her calm. "This is nothing. I can do this."

The setup nearly complete, Dylan had only to put a few final touches to her rappelling system. She tied a couple of large stopper knots in the ends of her two ropes, slipped her bag back over her shoulders, and threw the lengths of her lines down into the gorge.

She leaned back into her harness and tested the rope, allowing her entire weight to rest in her climbing halter. It held. Her system was set. She was ready.

Slowly, Dylan backed herself up, stepping away from her anchor and closer to the cliff's edge. She let the rope slide through her hands and through the belay device, which she held firmly by her left hip. She kept her line taut by her side, and allowed herself to move backwards in a gradual and controlled manner. Everything seemed to be going smoothly…

But what if something goes wrong? A little voice spoke from the furthest recesses of her mind.

Dylan had now reached her launch point on the edge of the cliff. She slammed her rope down hard in her belay device, applying the brakes. Wracking her head around, she peered down into the abyss over which she was now suspended. Panic took hold of her, and she felt the wind knocked out of her. Her whole body shook like a leaf on a breeze, as she struggled to catch her breath. Her heart beat so loudly in her chest and in her ears that Dylan could barely hear the sound of the raging waterfall anymore.

"Courage," she told herself firmly. "You've got this."

Refusing to allow herself even a single, further moment of self-doubt, Dylan took her fated plunge. Quickly, she drew in three breaths, leaned into her halter and stepped off of the cliff. Her feet found their way onto the surfaces of the cliff's walls, and gently, she began her descent, one shaky step at a time.

It took Dylan only a minute or two to rappel herself down to the crag in the cliff. It wasn't far (only about eighteen feet). When she'd finally reached it, Dylan knew immediately she was in the right place. Braced, standing over the ceiling of the hollowed ledge, she now had a perfect view of the little cave below her.

The hollowed space in the cliff's wall was much larger than Dylan had expected. In fact, it seemed to extend along the entire length of the cliff, past the falling waters and beyond. A large portion of the crag was still hidden from Dylan's sight, however – conveniently concealed in behind the waterfall. It was the perfect disguise – a veil of water masking the ledge from prying eyes. None except those who (like her) elected to actually scale the cliff on foot would be able to find this place. The ledge could not be seen from above. Nor would it be spotted by any chance passers-by below. To find it, one needed to know exactly what to look for: *the golden glow of a shining Serrada.*

Staring now at the hollowed cave before her, Dylan understood why the glimmer she'd glimpsed before from the top of the cliff had been so intense. There must have been over fifty or sixty Serradas here. The crag's interior was covered with them. The flowers themselves appeared to be prospering. Their growth spread far into the shallow cave, and also extended into the space hidden under the waterfall. Even from her spot standing braced over the cave's ceiling, Dylan saw the faint glow piercing through the curtain of tumbling water – not five feet away from her. The flowers were all over, bursting from the stone floors and popping out from fissures in the cave's walls. Their combined radiance illuminated everything. This space, which should have been dank and dark, instead was warm and bright.

Now, how do I get there? Dylan thought to herself, staring at the impossible ledge beneath her feet.

The task would require some finesse on her part. The ledge below was much further into the receding cliff than Dylan would have liked. She guessed about four to five feet further than the ceiling on which she now stood. The only way to reach it would be to swing herself directly into the crag below.

Before attempting the jump, Dylan resolved to first test the movement with something smaller. Carefully, and always with one hand holding her rappelling line tightly in a braked position, she removed her bag from her back. With her free hand, she swung the knapsack out and away from the cliff, and then quickly guided it back in towards the ledge below her. Releasing the backpack from her grasp, she allowed its momentum to carry it to its destination and heard it land safely amongst the flowers in the crag.

Relieved that her bag hadn't gone tumbling down into the abyss, Dylan sighed. Now, she had only to repeat the movement herself. Her heart thumping in her chest, Dylan somehow managed to formulate a plan. Methodically, she ran through each and every possible scenario in her mind for achieving the right speed and perfect landing, and finally settled upon a strategy.

Leaning back in her harness, with her feet planted solidly upon the cliff, Dylan prepared herself. She concentrated on her breaths. In and out, in and out they went – until her breathing became regulated and steady. It was a while still before Dylan had sufficiently revved herself up for the jump. But soon, she was ready.

 Bending her knees, she summoned all of her strength and pushed herself off from the cliff face. Having propelled herself into the air, Dylan simultaneously let loose the rope at her side, allowing it to unravel through the belay device at her hip. As she flew through the air, the weight of her body lengthened the line. When she felt she had reached the optimum point, Dylan tightened her grasp over the rope once more, pulling hard so as to apply the brakes again. Her body jerked in mid-flight and suddenly, she found herself falling fast. Her body jerked again when the line had stretched to its maximum and turned stiff. But Dylan held fast, despite the rope chafing and burning in the palm of her hand. She was now swinging through the air, gaining speed and coming in for her landing in the cliff's crag.

It wasn't long after she'd cleared the ceiling over her destination that Dylan recognized her mistake. Something had gone terribly wrong. She'd made a miscalculation. The rope caught on the rocky ceiling above her, and almost immediately, Dylan lost momentum.

I'm not going to make, she thought to herself, terror taking hold.

Panicking, Dylan lost her grip of the rope, and the line quickly unravelled further through her fingers. She caught it again, but not fast enough. She'd overshot the ledge. The rope had gone too far.

Dylan screamed as she went barrelling straight into a wall of rock. She felt her shoulder collide with the stone, and cried out again in pain. Things went from bad to worse then, as her body began bouncing uncontrollably on the outstretched line. Again and again, she collided with the cliff, knocking and scraping against its sharp surfaces. Her rope gone completely awry sent her within reach of the water's edge. Dylan held her breath and closed her eyes, as she braced herself for impact with the cold deluge.

CHAPTER THIRTY-ONE

BLESSINGS ON THE BRINK

Dylan was drenched head to toe in freezing water as she collided with the waterfall. Fortunately, the dousing managed to slow her movements, and her body finally came to rest against the cliff.

Cold and shaking, she found herself dangling helplessly from her rope. Frantic, she clung tightly to her lifeline. Her body was battered, and yet, she'd survived the fall. Summoning what strength she had left, she dug her fingers into a stone crevice, thus stabilizing herself against the cliff's face.

As she scrambled to find her footing, Dylan began to recognize the full extent of her misfortune. The rope that held her wasn't long enough. It didn't extend to the bottom of the gorge. This meant that rappelling herself down to safety would be impossible. In essence, she was stuck.

With her options limited, Dylan gazed upwards in an attempt to locate her target ledge. She found it almost immediately, nearly ten feet above her head.

My only only chance is to make it back up there, she thought.

The climb would be difficult. The cliff's surface was sheer and slippery – due to the mists rising up from the falls. In her injured state, Dylan felt it was unlikely she would make it. Fearing for her life, she now tried screaming for help. Her voice echoed in the chasm, but there was no one around to hear it. After a few failed attempts at wild cries, she felt it best to conserve her energy.

A few calming breaths, and Dylan resolved herself to attempt the climb. She began her ascent of the cliff, placing one sure foot onto the cliff's uneven walls. Her clothes were wet, fingers bleeding, cuts and scrapes covered her arms. Yet Dylan clung to the cliff's walls with every last ounce of power remaining inside of her.

I can do this, she told herself with difficulty. *I can make it.*

Over the next half-hour, she managed to push herself a considerable distance up the cliff. Through sheer determination alone, Dylan scaled four feet of rock. She calculated that no more than five or six feet now separated her from the bright ledge above.

Almost there, she thought, ignoring the searing pain in her ankle and the burning in her thighs. Her hands were a bloody mess of rope burns and slices, but she ignored these too.

With her left hand still holding her rope taut in a braked position, Dylan mostly relied on her legs to propel herself up the cliff. She did so again now, consciously choosing to disregard her many aches and pains. With her eyes turned downwards, she searched the rocky surface for suitable footholds. Having spotted one, she raised her leg upwards and bent her knee. Slowly, she pressed her foot down onto the little ridge – only to feel it crumble and give way under her weight.

Dylan clung harder to her rope, as she dug her fingertips into the stone and found her footing again. Scared and shaking after her close call, she pressed her cheek against the rock in an effort to catch her breath. Her heart was racing. She closed her eyes, and again, attempted to calm herself.

It was in *this* moment that it finally occurred to her – *perhaps her luck had simply run out?* All at once, the misgivings Dylan had been suppressing bubbled up inside of her. Tears welled in her eyes, as she realized the hopelessness of her situation. She wasn't going to make it. The climb was just... *too difficult*. The courage that had once lived in her heart turned to despair, and her throat began to burn with regret.

Why did I even come here? Dylan thought to herself wearily. *Was it all for nothing? Simply to die like this... all alone, in this godforsaken place?*

Lost amongst her newfound feelings of sorrow, Dylan failed to notice the onset of a light tugging at her rope. The pain in her palms having somewhat numbed her skin, prevented her from feeling the pull on her line. That is, until it had stretched so far as to begin yanking at her body harness. Startled by the sudden jerk at her hips, Dylan shot her chin up into the air. *Someone's up there*, she thought, *up on the ledge*. They'd grabbed hold of and begun pulling at her ropes.

Dismissing all the useless thoughts bouncing about her head, Dylan clenched her leg muscles one last time and wrapped her hands tightly around her line. With the extra hauling power now being supplied by her saviour above, she was able to scramble her way up the cliff with ease. One step at a time, she walked herself slowly up the ridge, until she had reached her target. Carefully, she released one hand from her rope and threw her arm up onto the sparkling ledge. As soon as she'd made contact with the floor, Dylan felt the stress on her rope disappear, as someone released the line and came rushing forward to help her. She felt a warm hand take grip of her bicep and force her upwards. Soon, her head had cleared the ledge, and she came face-to-face with her rescuer.

It was Kit.

Dylan could hardly believe her eyes. A wave of relief washed over her, as she saw him standing there, up above her, clad in matching climbing gear to hers. He'd come for her, even after everything that had transpired between them...

It felt like a dream. For a moment, Dylan had thought that all was lost. But now - Kit was *here*. He'd swooped in in the knick of time, just as he had before – all those weeks ago on that rainy night... Even with legs dangling helplessly off the ledge, Dylan had to stop herself in order for reality to sink in.

Kit's really here, she thought to herself reassuringly. *He's here, and now everything's going to be OK.*

Dylan still clutched at the stone floor – her feet swaying freely in the wind. Kit wasted no time. He planted his feet and stretched out towards her. With his free hand, he grabbed her arm tightly and began hauling her over the edge. When Dylan's torso had cleared, Kit helped drag both her legs over, one at a time. He did not release her again until Dylan was sprawled safely over the cold floor of the crag.

The terrible ordeal finally behind them, the pair sat upon the ledge in silence, as they caught their breaths. The air was cool, and yet, a warmth seemed to be radiating from the pack of golden flowers surrounding them. Dylan lifted her gaze, only to find Kit already staring at her, wide-eyed and worried. His brow creased and his lips quivered with unspoken words.

For a time, the two simply sat there, unmoving – their eyes locked, silently exchanging all of the thousands of thoughts and feelings neither had had the strength to speak aloud. But as Dylan stared deeper into those familiar, yet still mysterious eyes, her heart swelled, until she could contain herself no longer. She threw herself towards him then, wrapping her arms tightly around his neck and shoulders.

Kit, though surprised by her sudden show of affection, seemed to welcome Dylan's advance. He took her into his arms and held her firmly, before gently running his fingers up the back of her neck, and taking her head into his hands. After brushing a few loose strands of hair away from her face, he gazed into her eyes and asked with concern:

"Are you *hurt*?"

"I'm fine," Dylan answered, smiling up at him.

The gladness she felt at being reunited with him had no doubt caused her to forget all those pesky cuts and bruises she'd suffered in her fall. Luckily, Kit was not so easily thrown off.

"No you're not!" he cried, as he caught sight of the dried blood on her hands and took them into his own.

"Kit, I'm alright. Really. Superficial wounds. That's all. I promise."

He was sceptical at first, but finally seemed to accept her assurances with a nod.

"I don't know what to say, Kit," Dylan told him, finally. "I can't believe you're actually here. I didn't think I'd ever see you again really... not after I left like that..." She lowered her gaze, turning her eyes away from him.

At this, Kit carefully tried to interrupt. "About that..." he said. But his voice, being but a whisper, was so low that Dylan failed to hear him.

Completely unawares of his attempts to stop her, she went on: "How did you even find me?" she asked. When Kit didn't answer immediately, she added in a mumbled tone: "...not that I'm complaining or anything..."

There was a short pause, while the fox considered her words. Dylan watched with trepidation, as his expression slowly turned to that of a sly smile.

"I would have thought you knew by now," he told her, "... I'm an *expert* tracker."

"What do you mean?"

"Well," he said, "it was easy enough to follow your footsteps in the snow. After that, you could say I... relied on some of my more *special* skills to get me the rest of the way."

Dylan squinted her eyes inquisitively, as the grin on Kit's lips softened. He raised his index finger up into the air and pointed to his nose.

"You could smell me?!" Dylan exclaimed, now smiling widely. "No way!" Her mouth fell open, and she stared at him. Her emerald eyes sparkled in the light of the shining Serradas.

Kit shrugged his shoulders and beamed back at her.

"What?" he said, his cheeks now flushed in embarrassment. He averted his eyes from her and added in a hushed tone: "You smell kind of... nice, actually."

At this, the two burst into laughter. Each was overflowing with joy at being reunited. They held each other tightly – at long last allowing their affections to flow freely between them. When their laughter had subsided, Dylan shuffled in closer towards Kit and gently rested her head against his shoulder.

The atmosphere grew quiet again. Kit wished for nothing more than to simply remain as he was, holding her in his arms. He tried his best to push aside the tumultuous thoughts that now resurfaced in his mind – to savour this tender moment. And yet, he could not go on. There was *too much* he needed to say, too many confessions and confidences which needed to be made, before moving forward.

"Dylan," he said, slowly pulling himself away from her. "I need to tell you something."

He took her delicate hands in his and opened his mouth, as if to speak, but hesitated – swallowing nervously.

"I'm... so sorry," he said. His voice was shaking. "I should have told you before. I just didn't know *how*..."

Dylan laid a hand over his shoulder and gripped it reassuringly.

"I knew that if I told you about that locket, " Kit confessed, "if I told you about how I came to find you... Then I would have had to tell you *everything*. There would have been questions – questions I wasn't ready for." He took a deep breath, before going on.

"I didn't want to tell you..." Kit told her softly, "about *me* – about what I am. About my... *condition*."

"Condition?" Dylan answered. "You make it sound like some sort of disease. But I know it's not like that. Maggie told me…"

"No, Dylan," Kit interjected. "That *is* what it is. You don't understand. You haven't lived as I have… as *long* as I have. You don't know how I've struggled with it, or anything about it. It took me years. No. Decades… Lifetimes! And even now, I can't always control it. Every day, I feel it inside of me – that vile animal, scratching at my insides, trying to get out. I'm older now. I've learned to control it somewhat. But, there are *some* things that still bring it out of me… I'll never be free of it. It'll always be there, lingering inside of me."

He laughed a hollow, defeated sort-of laugh – and buried his face in his hands, as if ashamed.

Dylan waited a time, before asking him tentatively: "Tell me, then. How long?"

She'd expected some kickback to her question. But Kit didn't seem offset in the least.

"I'm not sure exactly *when* I was born," he told her. "But for all intents and purposes, my life started in 1275. That was when my mother found me and took me in. You know she was human? Like you."

Kit struggled to speak as memories of his mother came rushing back to him.

"It all started under that Sakura tree," Kit told her finally. "Back then, I wasn't like I am now. I was new and… hadn't learned to take shape yet."

"You mean, you were…?"

"The fox, yeah," Kit clarified. "At the beginning, there was *just* the fox. I… I came later."

He paused, and then laughed as one of his more pleasant recollections came to mind.

"You should have seen the look on my mother's face when I turned for the first time! She got more than she bargained for that day – that's for sure. Thought she was nursing a wounded animal back to health, but ended up with *me* instead. There I was – in all my glory – standing before her on two legs instead of four. Took her breath away… but, you know… she was never afraid. I was so young then – just a harmless little boy. She didn't hesitate for even a second. Adopted me, right then and there. Said I was… some sort of *miracle* child."

At this, Kit's features turned dark.

"She wasn't like the rest, my mother. Others… well, they weren't so welcoming. When the men in our village found out about me, they ran us out of town. *'Demon'* – that's what they called me. I was just a kid. I'd never harmed anyone. But they hated me anyways. I was different, and that was enough. After that, we bounced around from place to place. Times were tough, and my mother… she tried *so hard* to make a life for us. It didn't matter, though. Somehow, I always managed to make a mess of things. She *loved* me… but all I ever brought her was trouble. I just… *couldn't* get it together. I kept turning over and over, and at the *worst* times! Again and again, I was found out, and we'd have to start over. It went on like that for years. Until… one night… she finally got caught in the crossfire. They came looking for me, but found her instead. I was fourteen."

"I'm sorry, Kit. I didn't know," was all Dylan was able to muster.

"Well now you do," Kit said. "So maybe now you'll understand why I didn't tell you. Don't you see, Dylan? Those men. They were *right* about me. There's a monster inside of me, Dylan, and it got her killed. I didn't want you to find out. I didn't want you to see me… like that."

Dylan held her hands out towards him.

"You can't blame yourself for what happened," she said, taking his hands in hers. "Those men were wrong about you, Kit. They didn't know you like your mother did. She *saw* something in you –

like I do. Do you really think she would have given her life, if she didn't think you were someone worth saving? Your mother *died* so *you* could live. So you'd survive. ... and what a life you must have had. 1275? What is that? Like, six or seven hundred years? I'm certain your mother would have been proud to see how far you've come."

Kit smiled at her – but it was a sad sort of smile.

"I'll never understand it," he told her, "how you humans prize longevity so. You think eternal life is this *blessed* gift. But you're all blinded to the truth. I told you before, Dylan. It's a *curse*. It's not the wondrous thing you think it is. It's just the opposite, actually – just another symptom of my *disease*..."

"You don't mean that," Dylan replied.

"Yes, *I do*," Kit told her, more forcefully this time. "Think about it. I *watched* my mother die because of what I am. Do you think that was the last death I ever had to suffer through? There were plenty of others too – friends, people I loved! Do you have any idea what it feels like, to be the last one standing all the time? To see all the people you ever knew... die, over and over? Even when I do *everything* right, when my secret is kept 100% safe, people *still* die! They grow old and I just... don't."

Dylan was speechless. She hadn't considered that side of it. To her, immortality had always been a thing of fairy tales – a chance for endless adventures. She realized now, how misguided she'd been – buying into those countless Hollywood films that told glamorous tales of fountains of youth and never-ending life.

"Tell me," Kit asked her. "How would *you* feel, if everyone that ever mattered to you was gone? Would you even be here now, if you didn't have a sister who needed you? If you didn't have Holly? Our friends and families are what drive us. Without them, there's nothing left to strive for – nothing pushing us to better ourselves. I'm sure you have a list too, right? A list of things you want to do before you die? Everyone does. Now think... what would you do if you'd already checked *everything* off of that list? What if *all* those things you'd ever aspired to… what if they were gone too? What if you'd accomplished every dream you ever had? Been everywhere you ever wanted to go? What would you live for then?"

Dylan didn't have an answer for him.

"*I* know," Kit told her, "because I've lived through it. And it's *no life* at all. When all those things are gone, the future stops being this mythical promise land full of hopes and dreams. It's empty, and never-ending. Sure, there's the occasional thrill that comes along, now and again. But they're always short lived. Nothing *really* matters to you anymore. And so, you drift from place to place with no purpose, and nowhere left to go…"

Dylan had held her tongue throughout the entirety of Kit's disheartening speech, but by the end of it, was positively livid.

"Stop it, Kit!" she snapped, having finally found her voice again. "Do you *really* think you're the first person to feel this way? What you're describing. It's not unique to *your* situation! You don't need to be immortal, to feel alone or purposeless. There are plenty of 'normal' people out there who've been exactly where you are! And look at Maggie! If I'm not mistaken, she's a good deal older than you. Yet, she seems to be doing just fine. You need to stop wallowing, and pick yourself up! So what if you've accomplished all of your dreams. Make new ones! I know deep down you want to live as much as I do. Otherwise, you would have ended it by now. You would have thrown yourself out from one of those airplanes you're so afraid of, or… impaled yourself with a samurai sword – or something! But you *haven't*! Because you're kidding yourself, Kit. You may *think* you have everything figured out. But really, you're just as flawed as the rest of us. And I'll be damned if I let you speak another word of this… nonsense!"

When she'd finished, Dylan stood up suddenly and planted both her feet firmly on the ground. She looked down into Kit's startled face, and held her hand out towards him.

"Now get up," she told him. "You're going to start by helping me search this ledge."

Kit didn't move at first. After shaking his shock, he took Dylan's hand and rose to his feet. Once standing, he paused a moment and pondered.

There was a noticeable shift in his demeanour then, as he looked down at Dylan and finally flashed her his usual, sly smile – sharp, shining teeth and all.

"Alright then," he told her, "I guess we've got work to do."

CHAPTER THIRTY-TWO

KIT'S KEEPER

"Wait. Are you sure about this, Kit?"

The look on Dylan's face was one of absolute confusion and dumbfoundedness. She and Kit had been searching the ledge beneath the waterfall for some time now. And whilst they rummaged through the thick layer of glowing gold Serradas covering the ground, her friend had told her the convoluted story of the notorious locket – of his attack in Las Vegas, and of the way in which the locket had then led him to her.

"I don't have an uncle," Dylan said. "My mother was an only child. She was adopted."

"I know," Kit replied. "I found the adoption records. But your mother's wasn't the only name on it, Dylan. She had a brother. They were adopted together."

"Wow," Dylan muttered under her breath. "Come to think of it, there *was* that strange boy in all of my mother's photographs. I think his name was Luca, too. For the life of me, I couldn't figure out who he was. But... I guess this explains it." She collapsed onto the ground, having finally grown tired of hunting through the thick mass of radiant flowers. "... and I never knew," she said. "This is *huge*. I wonder why she never told us?"

"I don't know," Kit answered, still delving and peering through the endless supply of shining blossoms at their feet.

Dylan had halted her search efforts for the moment. The expression on her face turned to one of deep concentration.

"Maybe she was protecting us?" Dylan said. "But that doesn't seem right… If he was dangerous, you'd think my mother would have warned us."

Kit did not reply, and only kept wading through the shimmering flowers around them. They were losing light. The sun was now setting on the horizon. Soon it would be dark, and Kit knew their investigations of the ledge would become more difficult then – even despite the bioluminescent plants lighting their way.

Dylan, on her side, remained absorbed in thought. She sat motionless amongst the lustrous flowers, staring blankly at the curtain of water falling before her eyes. The sound of the waterfall's smooth and continuous flow was calming, and allowed her to think more clearly.

"I can't believe he attacked you," she said suddenly, turning away from the cascade and facing her friend. "That's horrible. But… why follow him all the way to me? Why search for him at all? You know there are police for that? Besides, what makes you think he'll come looking for me anyways? After all this time?"

Her questions finally caused Kit to stop. By now, he had finished his search of the crag's floors and had graduated to its walls. He paused in order to consider Dylan's queries, but did not turn to face her. His hands, instead, remained still and lost amongst the many stems of golden Serradas protruding there.

"He *stole* something from me," Kit answered, his eyes still locked in a forward stare. "And… I want it back." There was an aggressive shift in his voice as he spoke. Dylan heard it clearly. She waited a moment, before asking him, carefully:

"What did he take?"

Kit hesitated, but finally removed himself from the crag's walls, and turned to face her.

"Before I tell you," he said, "I want you to know… it stopped being about that weeks ago. I may have started out seeking revenge against him. But I'm here now, because I *want* to help you… to protect you from him."

"I know," Dylan answered, standing up and looking at him. "It's OK, Kit. You can tell me."

He took a step towards her, and took her hands delicately in his. "OK," he said. "Well… you know how you're always going on about how I have all these *'special'* talents? Like my hearing, and… how I can jump and run really fast…?"

"Yeah…?" Dylan replied, her eyes growing wider with interest.

"What if I told you that those weren't my *only* 'special' skills? That I used to have another one? One that was even better… and that your uncle took it from me?"

Dylan smiled before answering: "I would say… 'is that even possible?'"

"It is, if you have the right tool." Kit released her hands. He lifted his shirt up, and Dylan gasped as she caught sight of the horrible scar running across his abdomen.

"*He* did this to you?" she sputtered, unable to turn away from the gargantuan mark on Kit's belly.

"Yeah," Kit answered, as he roughly pulled his shirt back down. "That's how I know he'll come for you."

Kit turned away from her then, in order to continue his task of combing through the Serradas popping from the cave's walls.

"Your uncle's a power seeker, Dylan. He wields a very rare and dangerous weapon called an *'Extraction Blade'*. How he came to possess it, I don't know. Maggie told me stories of cursed daggers that could extricate gifts and talents from their victims – leaving them crippled and disabled. But I'd always assumed they were pure legend – made-up stories to scare people like me. I never thought they could *actually* exist. According to the stories, Extraction Blades store their victims' talents inside their hilts, allowing their bearers to then summon the skills they've stolen whenever they wish. They become theirs to use as they please. It's *sick*, really – like cutting someone's arm off, and then using it as your own."

As he spoke, the expression on Kit's face grew more and more perturbed. His brow creased, and his mouth scowled as he contemplated the wretched violation that he himself had been subjected to.

"The blades are said to drive their owners mad with power lust," he said. "With every skill they collect, they grow more and more greedy and envious of those around them. What may have started as a casual jealousy, soon turns to obsession and grows darker. Until their desire for power is all-consuming."

Kit paused and took a deep breath before finishing:

"Your uncle fits the profile, Dylan. He probably grew up alongside your mother – standing by and watching as she inherited and developed the Aurora's incredible gift. All the while, *he* remaining as he was – powerless and weak. I can only imagine the resentment he must have felt to resort to seeking such a cursed weapon. I didn't get it at first. But now I see… He means to correct the situation. You're his endgame, Dylan. He's going to try and take from you what he feels was rightfully his, all along. He's been biding his time since your mother died, waiting patiently for you to answer the Aurora's call – preparing to strike. He's coming for you, which is why we need to be quick."

At this, Kit began furiously uprooting Serradas from the rock wall in front of him. He'd found something hidden in behind one of the patches of golden blossoms there. When he had pulled five or six flowers from the wall, Dylan was able to see it too.

It was a crawl space – a sort of tunnel in the stone. Dylan had to rise up onto her tiptoes to see into the passage. But when she did, she saw a faint light shining through from the other side. The same instincts that had guided her through the forest, and down the cliff, now kicked her once more.

"You found it," she said, her heart skipping with anticipation. "This is it."

Kit didn't waste any time. He interlocked his fingers, leaned over and helped boost Dylan up to the opening. With her foot lodged between his hands, he hauled her upwards, until she was able to safely insert herself through the hole. Her hands found the rocky surface of the tunnel, and then her knees. The space was small. Dylan had to duck her head down in order to safely crawl through. For a moment, she was afraid Kit would be too big to follow her. But her worry was soon put to rest, when she heard him squeezing his way into the passage behind her.

The two of them inched their way through the stone tunnel in silence, their hands and knees scraping against the rock.

As they moved forward in the crawlspace, Dylan kept her eyes focused upon the light shining through from the other end. There was something *familiar* about it, she thought. She'd seen this light before – in her dreams. Only, it was different. Unlike the light from her dreams, *this* particular light was not out of reach to her. Slowly, Dylan saw it grow nearer, as she crawled her way forward and finally emerged on the other side.

She could hardly believe her eyes, when she pushed herself out from the rock and took in the scenery on the other side of the tunnel. It felt as though she'd stepped out of the dark and into some fantasy. The meadow was just as Dylan remembered it. The grasses surrounding her were thick and tall. Not a single blade was out of place. All those nights tossing and turning, lost in those nonsensical visions... suddenly, they all made sense. Here it was, after everything. The field from her dreams – it was *real*.

Dylan's heart skipped in her chest, as she stood staring at the pasture of towering grasses. It wasn't until Kit had also emerged from the tunnel and stepped up next to her, that Dylan was shaken from her trance.

"Where to now?" he asked her, somewhat urgently.

"What's the rush?" Dylan answered. "I hear what you're saying about Luca, and I agree. We'll be careful. But… there's no way he can get to us here, right? We're safe. We have time?"

Kit only stared, as he moved uneasily before her. He shifted his weight nervously from one leg to the other, lifted his arm and anxiously ran his fingers through his red-blonde hair.

"What is it?" Dylan said, but he didn't answer her. His jaw tensed, and he began grabbing and wrenching at the back of his neck.

"Kit?" Dylan tried again. "Just tell me, already!""

Her abruptness caught him off guard, and he was spurred into answering: "Alright!" he responded. "I'll tell you… just, don't hate me, OK?" After taking a deep breath, he went on: "You remember that skill I told you your uncle stole from me…?"

"Yeah…?" Dylan replied.

"Well, it took me a while to master it… so I might be wrong about this. But, if I'm right and somehow, he's gotten the hang of it…" He paused again, and frowned.

"Kit, just say it!" Dylan told him.

Her patience was clearly wearing thin, and so Kit dove headfirst into his confession.

"He could be here any second!" he blurted out, without another thought. After taking a moment to collect himself, he went on again, in a firmer, more assured tone: "What I mean to say is: if Luca's figured out how to *use* my ability – the one he stole from me. And if, somehow, he's gotten wind that you were coming *here*. Well… let's just say, it wouldn't matter how much of a head start we had on him. He'd catch us. And fast."

Dylan didn't argue with her friend. It was clear from the apprehension in his tone that their situation was dire. If Kit felt they were at risk, then… time was of the essence.

"I guess we'd better go then," Dylan told him. She pointed towards the horizon, and said: "It's that way."

Kit breathed a sigh of relief in response and smiled at her. He wrapped his arm around Dylan's shoulders and pulled her in closer towards him. After a quick exchange of nods, the pair set out together across the field of towering grasses and towards the sun, which was now setting in the distance.

-- CHAPTER THIRTY-THREE --

MONSTER IN THE MEADOW

"This might sound a bit strange. But, I feel… kind of… great!"

Dylan had her head tilted up towards the sky. She was admiring the full moon and the twinkling stars overhead. The sun had now set over the vast field in which she and Kit found themselves. It was a beautiful night. The air was fresh, and Dylan couldn't help but relish in the splendour of it all. It seemed only yesterday this place had been but a mere figment of her imagination, a simple night-time reverie. Yet, here she was now, walking amongst the towering grasses of her mind's eye.

"It's this place," Kit answered. "The earth, the air… I feel it too. The Aurora's energy. It's everywhere. The fields are coursing with it."

Dylan knew he was right. The Aurora's source appeared to be having an even more profound effect *here*, than it had in the woods from whence they'd came. Not only was it granting them added strength and endurance, she realized. It also seemed to be accelerating their restorative systems – imbuing their bodies with superior powers of recuperation.

Since entering the hidden meadow, the pain in Dylan's legs and arms had all but disappeared. The burning in her muscles had faded. Dylan was fairly certain she'd sprained her ankle earlier, in her tumble down the cliff. But that injury seemed to have miraculously evaporated as well. The skin of her hands felt smoother, as though the cuts and scrapes she'd sustained there had also healed themselves.

"Whatever it is," Dylan commented aloud, "it's amazing! I mean… It's almost like it never even happened – like I never fell…" She ran her fingers over the palms of her hands as she spoke, and felt for herself the spectacular difference.

Kit didn't respond. He wasn't paying Dylan much attention at all, actually. Whilst she was busy admiring her hands and evaluating the extent of her astonishing recovery, Kit was on full alert. He kept watch over the suspiciously tranquil grasses around them. Dylan continued on with her ceaseless chatter. Meanwhile, Kit's ears were perked and listening intently for signs of intruders. His eyes darted back and forth across the field, constantly searching. For some strange reason, he couldn't shake the nagging feeling that someone, or something, was following them – stalking them silently from the shadows.

"Shhh!" he hissed, sharply interrupting Dylan's prattle. Simultaneously, he threw his arm out in front of her, thereby stopping her from moving any further. "Do you hear that?" he whispered, now lowering himself closer to the ground and assuming a defensive position.

Dylan had been so preoccupied. She hadn't noticed how restless her friend had become. His sudden shushing of her had come as a bit of a surprise. Kneeling in behind him, Dylan leant her ears to their surroundings, as she too, began searching the grasses with wide eyes.

"What is it?" she asked, creeping in closer towards him and taking hold of his shoulder. "I don't hear anything."

"Quiet," Kit told her. His eyes were fixed on the tall grasses directly ahead of them. He was honing in on something in the distance. "It's coming closer," he whispered.

Dylan could feel Kit's muscles tense up in his shoulders, as he took hold of her and pushed her even closer in behind him, cradling her thigh with his hand. From this angle, it seemed he intended to use his own body as a human shield against whatever was coming for them.

"Shouldn't we run?" Dylan asked him anxiously.

"We can't," Kit replied, somehow managing to maintain his composure. "It's too late. It's here."

It was then that Dylan finally heard what she assumed Kit had heard minutes before – a nearly inaudible rasping, coming from the tall grasses ahead… and it was growing louder. Something was closing in on them, something large. And this creature, Dylan thought, was *anything* but human. Paralyzed, she heard it draw in closer towards them, her ears now filled with the sounds of the creature's rough breathing and intermittent snarls.

With her heart beating quicker in her chest, Dylan strained her eyes against the dark in a desperate attempt to glimpse the animal threatening them. The creature was circling. Dylan saw the tall grasses being parted, as it moved smoothly and stealthily through the field around them. Still, she couldn't quite pick out the creature *itself*. It couldn't have been more than two meters away, she thought. And yet, it remained completely invisible to her.

Kit continued to hold Dylan in close behind him, gently rotating her along, keeping her shielded, whilst simultaneously following the creature's ensnaring movements around them. They were trapped. The creature had them cornered and completely at its mercy. It was moving even faster around them now, tightening its hold, as if herding them like prey – until…

It stopped. The creature came to rest in a patch of grass not three feet in front of them, and for a time, remained completely still. Filled with dread, Dylan held her breath and waited for the inevitable ambush. She heard shuffling in the grass and, fearing the worst, slammed her eyes shut, all the while digging her nails deep into Kit's shoulder.

The onslaught she had expected never came, however. Instead, the clandestine animal stalking them from the field merely repositioned itself in the grass. Silently, it slunk its way through the meadow until it was facing them, and Dylan was finally able to catch a glimpse of it. Two big, round and glowing yellow eyes, peering at them from its hiding place in the towering grasses.

Dylan felt her breath escape her. The creature was even larger than she'd anticipated – at least five feet tall and ten feet long. Slowly, it stepped its way in closer towards them, and Dylan heard its giant paws weighing heavily into the ground at its feet. When it had moved within arm's length of them, Dylan was able to appreciate the creature even further.

Upon closer inspection, she noticed a unique lustre in the animal's pelt. The glint was faint, yet Dylan quickly came to understand its significance.

The creature was cloaked, she realized – covered in, what Dylan could only describe as, 'chameleon-like' fur. *That* was the reason it had been so difficult to discern in the first place. The hairs on the creature's body changed in colour, depending upon the different plants and surfaces they came in contact with. Even now, as it continued to step closer towards them, Dylan saw the hairs of its back and face continuously shifting in tint and shade with every passing blade of grass. The effect was mesmerizing, like staring directly into a transient illusion or mirage.

It's beautiful, Dylan couldn't help but think to herself.

Aside from the camouflage fur, the creature itself looked to be 'feline' in appearance. Its shape was akin to that of an oversized lion or panther. Dylan also thought she saw tiger-like stripes interspersed along the length of its body. Like other big cats, it had a large, rounded sort of head, short ears, four powerful looking limbs, and a long, slim tail.

"What *is* it?" Dylan mumbled under her breath. Her eyes were spread wide, and her tone sounded more intrigued, than fearful. Since laying eyes on the magnificent animal, something had changed within her. Her panic had all but dissipated. All that remained now was curiosity…

Kit, meanwhile, appeared to be having a very *different* reaction to the creature's advances. The closer it came, the more unsettled he grew. He kept his back pressed up to Dylan's body, and was pushing against her, gently trying to grow the space separating them from the monstrous creature approaching.

"If I had to guess," he told her with alarm, "it's some sort of apparition? A kind of… manifestation of the Aurora's energy."

"But why?" Dylan asked, still fascinated by the animal coming towards them.

"You didn't *really* expect the source to be unguarded, did you?!" Kit answered, clearly surprised by the lightness in her tone. The creature was now close enough that he could feel the warmth of its breath on his skin. Its growls reverberated within his chest, and he felt its gaze burning into him like fire.

Soon, the animal had moved so close, that Kit could no longer hold his ground. He stumbled backwards, pushing Dylan in the process, and moving her further afield from the source's guardian. The creature reacted adversely to Kit's sudden movements. It roared and bared its teeth for the first time. Ducking its head beneath its powerful shoulders, it proceeded to pounce, landing amongst the grasses behind them. With a single leap, the guardian had bypassed all of Kit's defences and come within reach of its primary target – the Aurora herself.

Dylan was not afraid, however. And when Kit, with his lightning-like reflexes, attempted to counter the beast's move by throwing himself between them once more, she stopped him.

"Wait," she said, holding her hand out and blocking Kit from interfering. "Don't move. Just wait."

Kit again, seemed surprised at Dylan's relaxed reaction to the guardian's obvious aggression and hostility towards them.

"Trust me," Dylan reassured him. She knelt down and placed herself squarely in front of the agitated beast. She was firm in her actions, and continued to hold her hand upwards in Kit's direction, thus warding off his attempts at intervention. Kit had no choice but to respect her wishes. He held his breath and watched helplessly, hoping without hope that she knew what she was doing.

Meanwhile, the creature continued snarling. Its eyes were now interlocked with Dylan's, and it was watching her intently. Its jaw hung open, and its thick lip kept curling up and down, by way of warning – showing off its collection of sharp teeth. It was clear the animal was restless, for it was breathing heavily, blowing puffs of hot, humid air out from its mouth on every exhale. Every muscle of its body too, was clenched and at the ready.

Dylan did not waiver in the face of this demonstration. She held – steadfast and unyielding – against the guardian's further rumblings and growls. It tested her, but she did not flinch, for she was determined to prove her worth to it. The Aurora was *her* legacy, after all. Left to her by her mother… and by *her* mother before her. Dylan was not *some* burglar, come to pillage the treasures of another. The guardian's powers were void against her. She was *entitled* to be here. This was *her* realm. This creature would have to submit itself to *her* claim.

Minutes passed, and Kit continued to watch from the sidelines – this strange game of wits and willpower. Dylan and the beast, head-to-head and nose-to-nose – their eyes locked in an unending battle of perseverance. Both seemed determined to win – the guardian, savagely ripping at the earth with its claws, and Dylan, remaining calm and composed in spite of its ferocity. For a second, Kit wondered what would become of them if Dylan lost. But his doubts were unwarranted.

Eventually, the creature's breathing slowed, and its muscles relaxed. Having proven herself worthy, the guardian halted its offensive grumblings. It finally broke eye contact and turned its head away from Dylan in deference.

"That's it," Dylan whispered, "That's a good boy." She smiled and held her hand out towards the creature, as one would to a beloved pet.

Kit's body immediately perked upon witnessing this. While Dylan may have succeeded in calming the beast, *surely this was too much*? He made a move to stop her, but was too slow. Holding his breath, he was forced to watch with foreboding, as the tips of Dylan's fingers finally met with the guardian's fur.

Fortunately, Kit's concerns proved fruitless yet again. Not only did the guardian allow Dylan's advances. But it seemed the creature was *actually* enjoying the interaction. Kit could hardly believe his eyes. In just a few minutes, the creature's manner had completely changed. The beast had lost all hostility towards them and turned completely mild... even welcoming. Kit watched, his mouth wide in disbelief, as he saw Dylan begin gently stroking the beast's head.

"Good boy," she repeated again softly, running her hand over the creature's smooth and enchanted pelt. Her skin met with the guardian's fur over and over, and simultaneously transmitted streaks of tan down the length of its body. With every touch, the two seemed to be growing more and more alike, as the beast slowly took on its new master's hue. Soon, the transformation was complete, and the creature's colour had turned completely to match Dylan's skin and outfit.

The scene was both strange and stunning at the same time. Dylan and the beast were like two veritable peas in a pod. The two seemed so happy to have found one another – a sort of odd, family reunion. Dylan was laughing and smiling widely, all the while, repeatedly pressing her palm against the guardian's giant forehead. The creature itself had its eyes shut tightly, and was gently nuzzling its face in close to Dylan's torso. Kit also thought he could hear purring sounds resounding from deep within the guardian's chest, as the hairs of its back ruffled with pleasure. The dodgy creature that had silently stalked them in the night was nowhere to be found now. Dylan had the giant cat practically eating out of the palm of her hand.

When she had had her fill of caressing the creature, Dylan gave it one last pat, and slowly rose back up to her feet.

"Well," she said, shrugging her shoulders at Kit, who now stared at her whimsically with eyebrows raised. "I guess that's that!" She smirked back at him. "Don't look so surprised, Kit. *I told you* I'd heard a monster in my dreams. I'd never been afraid of it before... I wasn't about to start now! Should we keep going?"

Kit was about to answer her, when the source's guardian interjected, making itself heard once more. It too, had gathered and poised itself, it seemed. It drew their attention by stamping its paws into the ground and spouting an odd whining sound. The sudden commotion caused both Kit and Dylan to turn automatically. They found the beast amidst the tall grasses to their left. Its fur had turned back to its original grassy blend. But they could still make out its head in the field, as it was turned backwards and facing them – eyes still glowing yellow in the dark.

"It wants us to follow it," Dylan said, somewhat distractedly. Her gaze appeared trapped in the creature's stare. It almost looked like the two were passing each other secret messages over the air, communicating covertly by exchange of glances. Kit felt distrustful of this bizarre new bond he observed between them. He bit his tongue, however, choosing instead to trust in his friend's instincts. This was Dylan's arena, after all. He was but a visitor to these parts.

And so, the three of them travelled together, single file through the field. The creature led the way, Dylan followed close behind, and Kit brought up the rear. Deeper and deeper into the tall grasses they went, the guardian ushering them farther and farther into its mystical meadow. The trail upon which it escorted them was erratic, always shifting from left to right, right to left – in a zigzag sort-of pattern. Soon, Kit, who'd desperately been trying to maintain his bearings, in spite of their guide's variableness, could no longer make sense of their route and lost all sense of direction.

"Are we sure this is right?"

He called ahead to his friend, all the while, slashing the tall blades of grass tickling his face out from in front of him. It seemed that the field was growing denser, the grasses thicker, with every step they took. Kit had to keep close on Dylan's heels, for he was afraid that if he lost sight of her for even a moment, he would most definitely be left behind.

"Where is this thing taking us?"

He tried calling to her once more through the heavy grasses obstructing him. But she did not answer.

Kit struggled against the vegetation blocking his path. He threw his arms out in every direction, knocking blades of grass out of his way, as he attempted to move forward through the field. Dylan and the beast were moving fast through the brush, and he was finding it difficult to keep up with them. It almost felt like the meadow was alive – that it was helping Dylan and her beast through its rampant vines, whilst using those *same* plants to impede his own movements – endeavouring to separate him from her.

Kit tried calling out to his companion again. "Dylan!" he cried, thrashing and wrestling against the grasses keeping him away from her. "Where are you?" But still, he received no answer. Dylan had disappeared in the thick tangle of grasses before him. He could no longer see her retreating profile ahead of him. It seemed the living meadow had achieved its aim in isolating him from her...

... but Kit was not so easily beaten. After all, he himself was *anything* but 'average'. He'd seen his share of odd and outlandish phenomenon in his time, survived through wars and rebellions, witch-hunts and coups. This measly field of twisted brambles was nothing compared to the countless dire odds he'd faced in his past.

Easily dealt with, he thought to himself with conviction, as he came to rest in the dark.

Taking a deep breath, Kit calmed himself. He closed his eyes and carefully focused upon the sounds around him. He heard the breeze gently sweeping through the grasses surrounding him, and the chirruping of crickets in the distance. He strained his ears even further, and heard the sound of his very own heart, beating deep within his chest. Concentrating, he managed to filter these sounds from his consciousness, leaving only the dead silence of the night streaming through his system. Patiently, he waited, until that silence was finally pierced.

The sound that roused him was quick and fleeting – a slight gasping sound, originating somewhere off to his right. It was gone as fast as it had come, but was all he'd needed to get back on track.

Lunging now, Kit gathered his strength and prepared himself to sprint. The gasp he had heard, only moments ago, had not been far. He estimated the distance separating him from it was less than twenty paces. *I can make it,* he thought, *if I run.* All Kit needed was a decent head start, a good first push to carry him through the mess of jumbled undergrowth blocking his path.

Gathering his strength, he drew in a sharp breath before thrusting himself forward through the barrier of towering grasses lying in his way. He did not hesitate, and tore through the raging field like it was nothing more than a cloud of upright tissue papers. The grassy blockade would hold him back no longer. He continued to charge forward, thundering through the brush as though nothing could stop him.

Panting, Kit finally emerged from the mess of wild vegetation. Like a raging bull, he escaped the confines of his cage and came barrelling through the final hurdle of twisted grasses – the edge of his tangled prison. The change in turf he experienced was sudden, and caused him to lose his balance. Kit fell headfirst out from the wild field, flailing his arms, and landed flat on his belly, face first into the ground. It took a second for him to collect himself after his tumble. But slowly, he pressed himself up from the ground, spitting out fresh morsels of earth and grass that had lodged themselves in his mouth. He wiped his lips with the back of his hand, rose to his feet, and finally lifted his head to face his surroundings.

Kit found himself standing within the borders of a large, circular clearing – a sort of glade within the meadow. The turf was flat and soft here – no more rampant vines, conspiring against him.

The glade, he estimated, was about fifty feet in diameter. It was grand, impressive and... somewhat unexpected – given the thick and turbulent underbrush growing at the edge of its borders. For the most part, the clearing was empty – just a large, hollowed out space in the field. There was, however, one object within it that stood out immediately: a sort of pedestal, jutting from the ground at its very center. Looking upon it, Kit couldn't help but feel that it looked a bit exposed, vulnerable.

As soon as he found the podium, however, he also found his missing friend. Dylan was standing at the foot of the ancient-looking altar. She wasn't moving. All of her attentions, it seemed, were turned upwards towards the stone pillar. So much so, that she didn't even hear Kit's footsteps as he drew nearer to her. The beast *also* appeared to have eyes *only* for the rock pedestal jutting from the glade. It stood loyally by Dylan's side, as if guarding her, but did not turn on Kit's approach.

When Kit had reached Dylan's side, he held his hand out and gently placed it upon her shoulder. Sensing his presence, she jumped, as if startled out of an intense daydream.

"There you are!" she exclaimed, resting her hand on her chest. "Where have you been?" she asked. Her manner seemed almost offended.

It was clear to Kit then, that Dylan hadn't faced the same difficulties as he in arriving there. The meadow did, in fact, have some sort of grudge against him, after all.

Not wanting to dwell on his struggles, he rolled his eyes and dismissed his companion's question. "Never mind that," he told Dylan brusquely. "What are we looking at?" He fixed his eyes upon the ancient stone pedestal, and finally saw for himself the thing that had Dylan so utterly enchanted.

Having come within arm's reach of the ancient pillar, Kit was finally able to grasp its purpose. The pillar, he realized, functioned as a sort of receptacle, a keeper of something incredibly precious. The stone column rose up and supported a moderately sized and thick stone slab. The slab, which was square-ish in shape, was tilted away from them. However, even from this angle, Kit could clearly see the gleam coming from the sparkling object encrusted at its core. Suddenly, the meadow's extensive security system (the guardian beast and all its pesky plant life) made perfect sense to him.

The jewel was incredibly bright. It protruded from the slab, and shed its white light all around them – like a brilliant star, shining in the night. It felt hot, too. Even at this distance, Kit could feel the jewel's radiance, gently warming the skin of his face. His eyes became trapped in the pull of the gem's brilliant light, and for a moment, he thought he would never again be able to look away. The ancient stone burned with a primordial energy – one older than even time itself. Its light seemed everlasting and Kit knew then, that they'd finally arrived at their goal.

The Aurora's source, he thought, *it's even more amazing than I could have imagined…*

With effort, Kit managed to tear his gaze away from the shining gem, in order to look back at Dylan. She was mumbling something under her breath.

"I'm not sure," she said, "I'm not sure what to do. My dreams, they never took me this far. What do I do now?"

"I think you're meant to touch it," Kit told her, encouragingly.

"The jewel is just a vessel. It's the energy *within* that you want. *That's* what you came all this way for. It's yours, Dylan, like it was your mother's before you. It's been here this whole time... waiting for you."

Dylan swallowed uneasily. She was nervous. Without even trying, Kit was able to hear the sound of her heart thumping loudly in her chest. After taking a deep breath, Dylan took her first step towards the stone pedestal. As she circled around it, she ran her fingers along its surface, as if feeling her way. There were two sets of stone steps circling the column, which led up to a higher platform. Dylan gazed upon it a moment, and then slowly made her way up the ancient structure.

Kit made a move to follow her, but was interrupted. The guardian, who until then had remained docile, suddenly shifted its gears towards him. After a short hiatus, it seemed the cat-like creature had decided to resume its caretaker duties – and with a vengeance, at that. Violently, it threw itself into Kit's path and let out a vicious roar, which put all of its previous aggressions to shame.

Startled by the unexpected resumption of the beast's hostilities, Kit took a few steps backwards. He held his arms out in surrender and called out to Dylan:

"I think I'll wait here," he yelled, still backing himself away from the snarling beast. "I get the feeling your friend, here, doesn't want me following you."

His voice trembled as he spoke. The beast had him literally shaking in his shoes. Without Dylan by his side to vouch for him, he feared the guardian viewed him as just another threat upon the Aurora's source. Thankfully, the creature was not completely beyond reason. As soon as Kit had backed away a few paces, it began to settle. When the distance between them had grown to about fifteen feet or so, the guardian ceased its growling and gently laid itself down in the grass at the foot of the podium. Its eyes, however, remained pinned on Kit, and it continued to watch him, all the while, licking its lips as if daring him to challenge it.

Satisfied that he was (for the moment) safely out of the guardian's reach, Kit laid eyes again upon the glade's podium. Dylan, he saw, was now standing upon the raised platform. He'd turned to find her at precisely the right moment. Her hand was extended, and she was moments away from making contact with the altar's glowing gem. Kit saw her fingers trembling in the jewel's light, and watched in awe as his companion finally placed her hand upon the glimmering stone.

A sort of warmth spread through him then. To witness the birth of a new Aurora was a privilege he'd never imagined would be bestowed upon him. In all his days, Kit struggled to recall a time when he'd beheld a more precious and rare sight.

Smiling, he watched as the light of the Aurora travelled out of its glimmering vessel, up through Dylan's arm and deep into her chest. He saw the startled look on Dylan's face, as she felt it nestle itself within her, as it came to rest in its new home – its rightful place. Dylan closed her eyes and reopened them suddenly as the light, still shining brightly from her flesh, finished its journey to her core.

The rite was over and the Aurora's glow was now dimming, fading, as it spread itself through the rest of Dylan's body. The brilliant light which previously had illuminated the glade was now gone, as was the guardian that had so diligently kept watch over it all these years.

Their mission a success, Dylan and Kit rejoiced. Their eyes met across the dark expanse which separated them, and they traded congratulatory nods in the night. Lost in their celebratory exchanges, neither of them foresaw the coming events.

Dylan, still standing upon the glade's ancient altar, was the first to see the mysterious man suddenly materializing in behind of her friend. And Kit, despite his rapid reflexes, was too slow to stop the blow that came at him from behind. He saw the frightened expression on Dylan's face, and before he could react, felt a sharp thud in the back of his skull. Everything went dark then, as he collapsed onto the ground.

-- CHAPTER THIRTY-FOUR --

ADVENT AURORA

Startled by the unexpected arrival of the dark figure, and of his unprovoked and unanticipated attack on her friend, Dylan did not move. She stood, frozen in place, her hands tightly gripping the edges of the ancient altar before her. Her palms felt clammy, and her eyes were filled with dread.

Luca.

She could only presume it was him. Who else would find cause for such despicable actions against them? Still, it was hard to believe this man could hate her so… her own family. What had happened between he and her mother, she wondered. What possible events could have led him down such a terrible path?

The man towering over Kit's now motionless body wore all black, which made him difficult to spot in the night. The glade had grown dark following Dylan's contact with the brilliant stone at its centre. The jewel encrusted in the stone slab before her no longer shone brightly in the night. Its radiance had gone, and with it, Dylan's spirited protector. The source's guardian, it seemed, had vanished the moment Dylan had laid hands upon the glowing gem.

With Kit out cold, this meant that Dylan was truly alone. She strained her eyes against the darkness, in an effort to better make out the figure standing ominously over her friend.

The man held what appeared to be a baseball bat, clenched tightly in his hand. That, or something similar… some other slender, solid, and elongated object. Dylan presumed this was the weapon he'd used in assaulting her companion from behind.

Kit.

He was lying unconscious at the man's feet. From this distance, Dylan couldn't tell how severe his injuries were, nor how hard he'd been hit. Kit had shown himself to be unusually resilient in the past, though. Dylan only hoped that his robustness also extended itself to head injuries, and that her companion would soon recover from the blow.

She flinched. The man had suddenly let fall his bludgeon in the grass. Having rid himself of his bulky weapon, he turned his face downwards, as if to admire his work. He was searching Kit's face, examining it more closely.

This is my chance, Dylan thought, *he's distracted. I should run. Now… while I still can.* But she was too slow.

"Dylan!" the man cried out to her over the glade. His voice was deep, icy, and sent chills down her spine. "You look more and more like your mother every time I see you," he said.

Those words, Dylan thought, spoken under different circumstances could potentially have been cordial, even friendly. But from *his* mouth… they were like poison – vile, full of hatred and contempt. To think her uncle had been watching her *all these years*, lurking in the shadows, waiting… It was enough to make her stomach lurch.

"You know," he told her, taking his first step in her direction. "I've been looking forward to this for *a very* long time." His tone was cold, empty, devoid of all compassion and empathy.

Dylan's body turned stiff as she listened. He laughed then – a disdainful, foul sort of laugh.

"And if it hadn't been for your friend here…" He made a gesture in Kit's direction. "It would have been *so much* longer! What a strange coincidence: the two of you, together like this. You'll be sure to thank him for me when he wakes up. That is, if you're still able to."

At this, Dylan saw Luca pull something from his belt. The dagger, which he now held out by his side, was smaller than Dylan had expected – about the length of a standard kitchen knife, only thicker and much sharper. Dylan saw it clearly, despite the darkness looming about them, for the blade seemed to be glowing – a strange bluish sort of glow. Dylan recognized the weapon as soon as she saw it.

The Extraction Blade, she thought – the cursed knife Kit had warned her about. Luca, she realized, was not wasting any time. He was coming for her… *now* – to take from her the gift she'd only just received minutes earlier. But Dylan would not give up her birthright so easily.

Not without a fight, she thought.

And so, she ran.

Jumping from the ancient podium's platform, Dylan landed on the ground and took off. She ran as fast as her legs would take her, towards the glade's edge and away from her pursuer. *If I can make it to the grass*, she thought, *maybe…* Being slenderer than he, Dylan imagined she would have an easier time navigating the thick grasses of the meadow. With a little luck, she may be able to slip away from him and disappear into the fields.

With her heart beating hard and fast in her chest, Dylan ran wildly through the dark. The edge of the glade was almost in her reach now. With every bound, she felt herself coming closer to it. *I'm going to make it*, she thought to herself hopefully. But as she neared the end of her sprint, something unthinkable occurred.

There, in front of her, suddenly standing in the shadow of the meadow's towering grasses, was Luca. He'd inexplicably reappeared directly in Dylan's path, and in the wake of some blurred distortion in the atmosphere. Dylan couldn't understand what had happened. One second, her uncle had been at least ten paces behind her, and the next, he'd magically materialized himself in her way and foiled her escape. The scene before her had gone all twisted and hazy, and when it had cleared, an addition had been made to the backdrop. Luca, standing with arms spread wide, ready to receive her.

Had her reflexes been slower, Dylan would surely have gone barrelling straight into her uncle's trap. As it was, however, she managed to stop herself in time. Throwing her legs out in front of her, she came to a screeching halt, but lost her balance in the process, crashing down into the ground with only her elbow breaking her fall.

Ignoring the dull throbbing in her arm, Dylan scrambled back up to her feet. Without hesitation, she turned herself about and high-tailed it in the opposite direction. Her mind was racing.

What was that? How was he able cut me off like that? Dylan remembered Kit's warnings to her. Her uncle had stolen something from him – one of his talents. *But what kind of skill lets someone be in two places at once? It can't be. It's impossible…*

Dylan desperately wracked her brain as she ran. *There has to be some sort of explanation…* And as she continued to contemplate her uncle's incredible feat, it recurred once more. Dylan's musings were interrupted then by the very distortion she'd been considering.

There, in front of her, was the same strange swirl in the atmosphere she'd observed before at the edge of the glade. It was happening again. Only this time, Dylan would be better placed to witness it.

She stopped herself in her tracks and stood staring at the blurry phenomenon in front of her. Eyes wide, Dylan held her breath – for the singularity before her was unlike anything she'd ever beheld before. It was almost as if reality was unfolding before her eyes, sinking or collapsing onto itself, making way for something new: some fresh element or person… a passenger.

Staring into the fleeting distortion, Dylan finally understood. *It's a portal*, she realized – a tear in the fabric of space, which allowed one to move from place to place instantaneously. *This* was how Luca had interfered with her escape. *This* was how he'd come to be in this very field, how he'd snuck up on them unnoticed.

Kit was right. It doesn't matter where or how fast I run... With this skill in his arsenal, he'll catch me. There's nowhere to go... nowhere to hide.

Dylan's heart sunk in her chest. The swirling phenomenon before her was now dissolving, and once more, depositing Luca in her path.

"You like?" he asked her, as he emerged from the hazy fissure in front of her. The space surrounding him returned to normal then, and Luca was left standing in its wake, a vile grin spread across his face.

"It's the most *amazing* thing," he told her, tilting his prized dagger into his field of vision and examining its bluish blade. "It's got to be one of the *best* skills I've collected yet. And to think, I never would have picked it up if it hadn't been for your friend over there. Did he tell you? I was actually hunting someone else at the time... but I sure am glad *he* came along. I mean... how *amazing* is this? I can just close my eyes, picture the place I want to go, and BANG! I'm there, in two seconds flat. It took a bit of practice. But, what can I say? I'm a quick study."

Luca brandished his knife in the air as he spoke. Dylan couldn't be certain, but it almost seemed as though he was enjoying himself. She didn't interrupt him. As long as he was talking, she had time... time to consider her options, maybe even come up with a plan. When Luca took one step forward, Dylan took one cautious step back, matching him move for move and simultaneously keeping her distance from him.

"This place..." said Luca, twisting his head around and examining the glade. "It brings back a lot of memories. Your grandmother, she brought us here, your mother and I... when we were kids. Right before she shipped us off with that American. I was young then, didn't really understand. But I knew it was special – even then. I watched her drag Lenora up to that *very* podium, and the next day, we were on a boat... sailing away from everything we'd ever known. It was Lenora's fault. She sold us because of *her*... because of her 'gifts'. I was just an afterthought, part of the packaged deal that was my *precious* little sister! I bet your mother never even told you about me. My *perfect* little sister went on to live her *perfect* little life, despite everything that happened to us! Like there was nothing wrong! She forgot *all* about it... she forgot all about *me*!"

At that moment, Luca rushed forward suddenly. With his free hand, he savagely shoved Dylan to the ground. Having taken her by surprise, Dylan was unprepared for his attack and only went tumbling down, landing roughly on her back. Luca went on with his vengeful speech.

"My sister never deserved her gifts!" he snarled through clenched teeth. "She was an ungrateful little brat, who never gave a damn about anyone but herself! You're just like her too – exactly the same..."

Having had his final word, he made his move in towards her. Dylan fought him, kicking her legs out instinctually and brandishing her arms. She felt her feet make contact with his shins, and for a moment, he recoiled. Luca flinched and Dylan rolled herself onto her stomach and attempted to slither out of his reach. She didn't get far, however, and a second later, felt his hand tightly gripping her ankle. Kicking and screaming, he dragged her body through the grass, pulling her back towards him, and collapsed on top of her.

"Hold still!" he yelled, now straddling her legs with his thighs and attempting to steady her hands, still flourishing wildly in the air.

Dylan wouldn't give up. Luca was clearly stronger than her, but she continued in her struggles against him, constantly twisting and wriggling from underneath him, trying desperately to fend off his attacks. Her efforts in the end, however, proved fruitless. Luca eventually caught her by the wrists and held her in place.

Having subdued her, he prepared himself for his final strike. Slowly, he raised the Extraction Blade into the air, and Dylan got her first real look into her uncle's face – his features now bathed in the bluish light of his prized weapon.

The feelings that came over Dylan in that moment were strange and unforeseen. Staring into her uncle's flashing eyes, she imagined she should have felt only fear, maybe even anger. But locked in his gaze, *something else* came over her. Those big black eyes, though filled with hostility and resentment, also felt *familiar* to her. The large scar running down his face was frightening, yes, but also told a story – one of pain and suffering.

In mere seconds, Luca's blade would come crashing down on her, and it was likely Dylan wouldn't survive. Regardless, her heart harboured him no bitterness then. *He* was as much a victim as she, she realized. Those eyes staring into hers were sad and tortured. Dylan couldn't help but feel pity for him then – her mother's brother, lost forever to hatred and despair.

Luca hesitated. Somehow, he'd recognized the compassion shining in her eyes, and faltered. All these years spent preparing for *this* moment, and not once, had he expected to be met with sympathy from her.

His split second's hesitation made all the difference, as Dylan suddenly felt her uncle's weight being ripped off of her. Luca had been tackled. Someone had intervened and gone tumbling onto the ground with Luca in tow. Dylan heard the two of them rolling around and wrestling each other in the grass. She knew in an instant the identity of her deliverer.

"Run!"

Kit's voice rang out clearly in the night. It was as Dylan had hoped. Her companion had regained consciousness just in the knick of time, and immediately came hurdling to her rescue.

Free from Luca's clutches, Dylan rose quickly to her feet. Kit and her uncle were only a few feet away from her. Though, it appeared the battle between them was not going her way. Kit, still bleeding from his forehead, was visibly dazed from his previous encounter. He was barely holding his own. His movements were sluggish and tired. He was losing the fight.

"Dylan, Run!"

Kit called out to her again, commanding her to save herself. But Dylan did not listen.

I won't abandon you, she thought. *We're in this together.*

There was little time. Even now, Dylan could hear Kit struggling against Luca in the grass. The two men were not holding anything back, throwing punches and hurling insults at each other as they clashed in the dark. Kit would not be able to hold out much longer… *not without help*. Her uncle was armed, after all. All he needed was *one* clear shot, one small opening – one mistake, and Kit would be finished.

Her heart thumping in her chest, Dylan was running again, across the grassy glade and past the stone podium at its center. Her eyes were locked upon the place where this mess had all began, where Luca had first revealed himself to her.

The bat. He had a bat with him…

Dylan remembered. Luca had assaulted Kit with it, when he'd first arrived. If she could find that bat…

It's our only chance, she thought.

Having arrived at her destination, Dylan hastily began searching the grounds for the missing weapon. She heard Kit's groans in the background and winced. Redoubling her efforts, she strained her eyes in an attempt to see more clearly. But it was too dark. In a last desperate attempt, Dylan fell to her knees and began blindly rifling through the grass with her hands. *Eureka!* Her fingers found the wooden handle, and moments later, she was sprinting back in the direction from whence she'd come – back to Kit's side.

With the wooden bludgeon in hand, Dylan felt her resolve return to her. She was closing in on Kit and Luca. She could see the outline of both their figures in the dark now, still having at each other in the grass.

But… something's wrong.

In her absence, it appeared Luca had gained the upper hand. Kit, it seemed, had lost much of his momentum. Somehow, Luca had found his way on top of him. He was holding him down and, as Dylan drew nearer, she realized:

I'm too late.

She'd arrived just in time to watch the bloody finale to their brawl. Dread poured into her soul and she watched, horrified, as her uncle raised his glowing knife into the air and plunged it deep into her friend's chest. She heard Kit cry out in pain, and felt her heart shatter, as tears welled up in her eyes and stung her. Time seemed to slow then, as it generally does in moments of terrible grief or loss, and Dylan only continued stumbling forwards in anguish.

"KIT!" she cried, tears running down her cheeks. "Noooo! Kit!" She rushed forward with the bat high in hand, as if freeing Kit from his attacker now would somehow have made a difference.

Kit must have heard her, though – for after receiving his fatal blow, he somehow rustled up the energy for one *final* move against Luca. With what could have been his last breath, Dylan saw her friend reach both his hands upwards and grab hold of Luca's wrists. His teeth clenched against unthinkable pain, Dylan watched, as Kit dug his fingers into her uncle's flesh. One by one, she saw him pull Luca's fingers from the deadly dagger's hilt and grip it tightly. Before she knew what was happening, Kit had taken hold of Luca's arm and the two men had gone toppling down into a torrential sea of twirling space. It was the *same* phenomenon Dylan had seen her uncle perform earlier – and it was tearing them away from this place.

There was a look of surprise on her uncle's face, as the two went tumbling into the swirling portal. That was how Dylan knew: *It was Kit.* Somehow, he'd activated his own power within the Extraction Blade, and used it to pull Luca along with him to somewhere out of reach. To somewhere far, far away from her.

Kit…

Her throat tight, Dylan watched with watery eyes as the twirling distortion before her swiftly came to a close. The meadow was quiet again – the sounds of her companion's struggles disappeared into that twirling abyss.

It's over, she realized, stepping shakily onto the very spot where, only moments ago, her friend had lain bleeding.

Part of her *couldn't* accept it – that he was gone. The scene before her felt… wrong somehow. This wasn't how their story was supposed to end.

Kit should be here, she thought. *We've won. He can't be gone…*

Dylan had finally found what she'd journeyed so far to get. As the Aurora, she would now be able to return home. Holly would be waiting for her… and sweet Dani. At long last, she would be able to set things right again. Everything she'd wished for would now come to pass. But without Kit, the victory felt… hollow.

With her head turned downwards, Dylan wept, as she circled the spot from which her friend had vanished, still dragging her wooden bat behind her. She saw Kit clearly in her mind – his sly smile, those dashing red locks and mysterious, maroon eyes. To think she would never again hold him in her arms… Warm tears rushed down her face and, sniffling, she brushed them away with the back of her hand.

He'd only been with her a short time – a month, maybe two. And yet, Kit had become such a big part of her life. The two of them had grown so close, so quickly. This *should* have been their beginning, not their end. How would she ever be able to let him go? He'd been taken from her so suddenly. It almost felt as though he was still here, calling her name.

Dylan.

She heard his voice again, whispering in her ear in that wonderfully soft, yet scratchy quality of his.

Dylan.

There it was again. Except this time, it hadn't sounded so pleasant. The voice Dylan heard sounded choked, as if it was obstructed in some way.

Her body turned stiff. Was her imagination playing tricks on her? Or had the voice come to her from behind? Swiftly, Dylan turned on her heels and felt her heart stop. Her eyes met with his, from across the glade.

"Dylan..."

It's Kit. He's alive!

Dropping her bat in the grass, Dylan rushed back towards her friend, who was slumped down on his knees on the far edge of the glade.

He's alive, she thought, *barely.*

As she came closer to him, Dylan glimpsed the pool of blood slowly expanding across her friend's chest. The red liquid ran down his arm and dripped from his fingers. It seemed that Kit had pulled Luca's weapon from his wound. He now held its hilt tightly in his hand. Dylan may have been mistaken. But it almost seemed that the Extraction Blade was glowing *even more* intensely now. Kit released his grip on the cursed weapon, as she drew nearer. The knife fell loosely from his hand, and he collapsed onto his back, just as she reached him.

Luca was nowhere in sight.

"You did it," Dylan cried, throwing herself onto her knees and hoisting her friend's head and shoulders up into her lap. "He's gone," she said smiling.

She looked down into Kit's face and immediately recognized how dire his condition was. The smile vanished from her lips. Kit was struggling to stay conscious. His gaze was wavering, eyelids fluttering somewhere between open and shut, and he was trying to say something.

"You…" he whispered. He coughed, and Dylan saw blood seeping from his mouth.

"Don't talk," she told him, as she struggled against his blood-soaked shirt, urgently searching for the source of his bleed. Without thinking, Dylan grabbed the Extraction Blade from the ground and began cutting through the red sopped fabric, thus exposing her friend's torso to the air.

Kit's blood was everywhere. Her hands were covered in it. It was warm and smelled of rust and metal. But Dylan wasn't sidetracked, not in the least. Her *only* thought was of helping him. Without hesitation, she ran her hands roughly along Kit's chest, clearing away his blood with her fingers and searching for his wound. She found it within seconds – a two-inch gash in his upper right pectoral.

Dylan applied pressure to the wound, pushing against the gushing injury with her hand. She felt Kit flinch under her weight, and heard him wince with pain, but refused to be shaken. The wound was still bleeding, and Dylan knew that at any moment, she could lose him again. This was her *last* chance.

There's no coming back from this, not even for him.

"You need a hospital!" Dylan cried. Her voice trembled, as she took the glowing Extraction Blade into her hand again and clumsily began shaking it about in the air. "How do I work this thing?! Kit! Wake up!" Swiftly, she pressed the hilt of the cursed weapon back into her friend's hand and closed his fingers around it. Tears welled in her eyes and she fought to hold them back. "I don't know how to use this stupid thing! *You* have to do it, Kit. You have to take us to a hospital. Kit, please! Please… you're dying!"

But Kit wasn't listening. He let the knife fall from his hand and weakly reached up to her face. Brushing his bloody fingers across her cheek, he stared into her tearful, green eyes and spoke to her once more.

"You," he told her, whispering between coughs and blood soaked chokes. "You can… Aurora…" Unable to speak anymore, he withdrew his hand from her face and found her hand instead, still resting over his chest wound. Squeezing it then, he nodded his head towards her, as though silently encouraging her to act.

"I don't understand," Dylan replied, her lips quivering. "What do you want me to do? I don't know how to fix this!"

But Kit didn't answer. Dylan watched in alarm, as her friend's eyes began rolling back into his head.

"No! Don't!" she wailed. "Kit, don't leave me!" Tightening her grip of his shoulders, she began shaking him violently. "You can't die! You can't!"

Her cries were interrupted then by the sounds of her heart, which began beating loudly in her ears.

Au.. ro.. ra..

Au… ro… ra…

The sound was deafening. It was pounding, thumping, and somehow, seemed to be slowing… the pause between each beat growing larger and longer.

Au…. ro…. ra….

Au….. ro….. ra…..

Her eyes grew wide, and her tears ceased. Dylan found herself staring at her blood stained hand, still pressing against Kit's chest.

That sound, she thought, *it's not my heart. It's his…*

Dylan was hearing the beating of Kit's dying heart. She could *feel* it… gradually decelerating, and with every last thump, felt his life slowly slipping away from her.

Au…… ro…… ra…...

Au……. ro……. ra…....

This was what Kit had been trying to tell her. *I'm different now,* she realized. Since entering the meadow, had Dylan not come into a powerful gift? Was she *not* the Aurora now? Did she not now possess the Aurora's incredible energy… that rejuvenating power that had once filled this field and its surrounding lands? Did it *not* now live inside of *her*?

> *They say that to be with Aurora*
> *is to never know illness or injury, to never feel pain…*
> *that she is life itself, eternal and… undying.*

Kit's words, spoken to her on that fated night, the night they'd first come together in the rain, now poured into Dylan's mind. And Maggie's words, upon reading her mother's journal:

> *Where there is life, even the most faint,*
> *the Aurora can preserve and protect it.*
> *And it will flourish under her care.*

If I'm the Aurora, Dylan thought, *then that means… I can do these things. I can save him. There's still time…*

With only her instincts to guide her, Dylan concentrated her mind upon the slowing heartbeat. The sound she heard grew louder, filling her ears and drowning out everything else around her. Taking a deep breath, Dylan closed her eyes and immediately was overtaken by her senses. Touch, taste, smell – they all came together now in a strange, new way. The beating of Kit's heart pounded in her ears, and Dylan followed it down to its source. She was transported then, deep into Kit's chest, and to his heart.

The dark tapestry before Dylan's eyes was suddenly replaced by vibrant images – pulsating shapes and wild colours. At first, the pictures were blurry, but they quickly improved, and Dylan soon saw how they all fit together.

It's his injury, she thought.

Dylan was seeing into Kit's wound, into the tear in his chest. His heart, deep red and throbbing, was right there in front of her. Had she wanted to, Dylan felt she could have reached out to it, right then, and grasped it in the palm of her hand. There was beauty in the way it moved, the very picture of life – the constant rhythm of it. Kit's heart itself appeared healthy… but one of its main arteries, she saw, had been severed. The blood flowing from the vein was spilling into his chest and lungs. Kit had suffered a broken rib too, which had perforated his right lung. The haemorrhaging had partially cut off his blood supply, and thus slowed the beating of his heart. For a moment, Dylan was overwhelmed in the face of the damage. But something changed then, and brought order to the mayhem surrounding her.

The severed artery slowly began to glow with a bright white light. It called to her, and looking upon it, Dylan finally understood what needed to be done. If Kit was to survive, she realized, *this* was the defect that needed her most urgent attention. And so, she allowed herself to become lost in the glow of the shattered vein. In her mind, Dylan visualized a pristine and healthy heart artery. And that vision soon came to pass. The artery began to mend. The fractured vein reconstituted itself, and like magic, restored flow to the dying heart. Kit's heartbeat immediately hastened, and Dylan turned her attentions to the other injuries before her. One by one, she addressed each and every wrong. The blood that had pooled itself in Kit's right lung evaporated, and the slit in his lung tissue was repaired. Air travelled back into the restored lung, and the cracked rib that had pierced it in the first place was also mended. Nerves, ligaments and muscles lining her friend's rib cage were restored, and soon, Dylan found herself slowly withdrawing from her elaborate expedition.

Opening her eyes, Dylan glimpsed her blood soaked hand, still resting over the site of her friend's chest wound. There was light streaming out from beneath her palm – the same light she'd observed deep within the jewel that had once held her family's legacy. The glow felt warm and soothing, and when it ended, Dylan knew she had finished. Smiling to herself, she withdrew her hand and saw that the large lesion beneath it had completely healed.

Just then, she felt Kit's body jump up in her arms. His eyes and mouth sprung open then, as he took a large gaping breath of fresh air. There was a look of alarm in his eyes at first, as though he'd just woken up from a bad dream. He looked around, and slowly began to settle again. His breathing slowed, and Dylan felt him suddenly take hold of her hand. He still lay in her arms, but was now alert and looking up at her.

"I knew you could do it," he told her gently.

Upon hearing his voice again, Dylan felt a surge of emotions within her. Words caught in her throat, but she managed to rustle up a smile in reply.

"It's over now," Kit told her. Slowly, he lifted his head from her lap and wrapped his arms around her trembling body. "It's Ok. We did it. You did it... Aurora."

CHAPTER THIRTY-FIVE

BACK TO THE BEGINNING

"I call it 'traveling'. And to me, it's as easy as breathing or walking. I've been *travelling* all my life, Dylan. It's how I get around. You drive cars, take trains or planes, and I... well, I *travel*. Ever since I was a child. That's really all there is to it."

Having fully recovered from his near-death experience, Kit was busy answering the many questions Dylan had about the strange, swirling portals she'd witnessed earlier. They hadn't yet left the glade. Dylan was still seated in the grass, and Kit was now standing in front of her. In his hand, he held the handle of the cursed dagger he'd stolen from Luca. He twisted and tilted the blade in his grip, staring at it intently with squinted eyes.

"Can you imagine what it would feel like, if someone could steal your ability to run? Or even to walk? Think about it, Dylan. That's how *I* felt, after your uncle stole my travelling from me. One moment, I had the world at my fingertips, and the next, I was grounded – *stranded.* It was like I'd been chained to the Earth, or imprisoned somehow. I couldn't move. I felt..."

"Trapped." Dylan cut in then and finished her friend's sentence. She'd been listening intently to Kit's tale, and finally felt she understood him – all of his hidden agendas and motives of the last few months, why he'd pursued Luca with such zest, why he'd infiltrated himself in her life and spied on her... She couldn't fault him for any of it, she realized – the lies, the deceit. Placed in his shoes, she may very well have done the same.

"It's like being a bird," she told him, "but not being able to fly."

"*Exactly*," said Kit, "like… my wings had been clipped or something."

Kit stared at her with wide eyes. He knelt down in the grass and took her hands in his. It was as if a weight had been lifted from his shoulders. At long last, no secrets existed between them.

Releasing her hands then, Kit reached down to his feet. Dylan watched him with curiosity, as he swiftly lifted the trim of his trousers and removed something concealed there, against his right ankle.

"What's that?" she asked, as he pulled the tiny object from his sock.

When he'd finished retrieving the item, Kit sat down and showed it to her. The object he held was a tiny glass vial containing what appeared to be a small amount of a faint red liquid.

"Just something Maggie cooked up for me," he told her, "before we left New York. Something she said would help me 'extract' from the Extraction Blade." Smiling, he added: "I guess I finally get to put it to the test."

Dylan didn't interrupt him. Instead, she watched in silence as Kit quickly unstoppered the little flask, and delicately poured the pale red fluid over the glowing blue blade. Careful not to let any of the liquid drip from the precious dagger, Kit wrapped his hand around the sharp surface and closed his fingers tightly around it, allowing it to cut into his flesh.

Dylan drew in a sharp breath then, as she watched the painful ritual. She opened her mouth, as if to speak, but before she could, heard Kit whisper something under his breath.

"*Mihi Reveni*," he said.

As the words left his lips, the glowing knife changed in colour. The blade, which had all this time been steadily radiating a bluish light, suddenly turned a devilish red. Blood began trickling down Kit's forearm, and… it was over, just as quickly as it had begun. The reddish glow coming from within Kit's grasp faded, and the Extraction Blade returned to its original state. Looking upon it now, Dylan thought the bluish glow of the blade somehow seemed a bit dimmer, less intense, than it had before.

"What just happened?" she asked.

Kit smiled in response. He handed her Luca's dagger and rose up to his feet. As he handed her the knife, Dylan saw that the skin of his hand had somehow remained intact, even in spite of the strange cutting ritual. The dagger, she saw, was covered in Kit's blood, and there were still a few drops running down his arm. His palm, however, was free of any wounds or gashes. The whole thing felt a bit eerie, but Dylan refrained from saying anything.

Kit stood before her now, with his back straight. He was stretching his neck and throwing his arms out in front of him, almost as if he was preparing himself for something.

"Moment of truth," he told her.

He took a deep breath then, and was gone, just like that.

Dylan watched in amazement as her friend vanished before her eyes. She thought she saw a thin fold materializing in the space before her as he left. But the phenomenon was *much less* pronounced this time around. In fact, it was barely noticeable – just a simple ripple in the air. Dylan didn't have much time to contemplate the deed, however, for a moment later, the *very same* faint distortion occurred again. Kit reappeared directly in front of her – in the exact spot he'd been standing in seconds earlier.

"Whoa!" Dylan exclaimed, jumping to her feet. "You did it! And without the dagger…"

Kit was laughing.

"It worked!" he cried. He patted himself down, as if checking that every part of his body, every limb, had made it back safely. "I can't believe it!" he said. "Maggie's potion worked! I'm back! I'm *me* again!"

Sighing, he held his hand out towards her.

"Are you ready?" he asked.

"Ready?" Dylan replied. "Ready for what?"

"Now that I'm back to my old self," Kit told her, "I can take you home."

"Take me home? You mean, you can take me…"

"Anywhere you want!"

"Is it safe?" she asked him. "It looked *different* that time – smaller… less obvious than before."

"Don't worry," Kit reassured her. "I know what I'm doing. I've had a lot more practice than your uncle, remember? Besides, if anything, the ride will be smoother with me than it was with the dagger. I think that thing *messed* with my powers a bit. I've got more control this way. Trust me."

He continued to hold his hand out, and smiled at her now, his palm open and inviting.

Dylan hesitated at first. But her desire to see her sister soon swayed her to accept his offer. Carefully, she placed her hand in his and told him: "Can you take me to the hospital, then? To Dani? I think I'm ready to see her now."

Smiling slyly, Kit pulled her in closer towards him. He took the Extraction Blade from her and tucked it away in his belt, before wrapping his arms tightly around her.

"Your wish is my command," he said. "You'll have to hold your breath. It's your first time, so… you might feel some *slight* discomfort on the way."

In hindsight, Dylan wished Kit had given her a fairer warning than this. In her opinion, the sensations that came over her next were *far worse* than 'a slight discomfort', as Kit put it. In fact, Dylan's first try at *travelling* made her seriously question whether she would ever submit herself to the experience again.

She was relaxed at first. Standing there in his arms, with her cheek pressed up to his chest, Dylan felt safe and warm. In a mere fraction of a second, however, everything changed. Suddenly, Dylan felt her body being moved across the landscape beneath her feet at lightning speeds. She felt her heart plummeting like a rocket deep into her chest, and she was bombarded with stimuli - everywhere. There was a clamour of high pitched sounds and burning, blinding lights all around her. Her senses were flooded, and her head throbbed, pounding like a hammer at her temples. And then, as though the pain were not already enough, Dylan couldn't breathe. The air had been sucked out from all around her, like a vacuum. And she was choking. She became light headed, dizzy and a wave of nausea washed over her. She was stumbling, losing her balance. The world around her was unstable, spinning and spiralling out of control. And then, she fell…

Dylan couldn't tell how long the fall had lasted. But at the time, it had felt like an eternity. When she finally came to, she was still standing in his arms, as if by some miracle. Shaking, she clung to him like a lifesaver in a tumultuous storm at sea. The ear-splitting tones she heard slowly dimmed themselves, only to be replaced by the cries of a familiar voice.

"Dylan?!"

It was a woman's voice, and Dylan recognized it immediately.

"Dylan?! How did you…?! What's happening!?"

Holly had been sitting quietly by Dani's bedside, taking part in her daily hospital visit, when her world had suddenly been turned upside down. She was standing now, gawking in Dylan and Kit's direction, for they'd suddenly appeared out of thin air at the foot of

Dani's hospital bed. The whole situation must have seemed impossible to her, but after a few staggered cries of astonishment, she grew quiet.

Holly stood there, shocked, speechless, and paralyzed with fright. Kit's appearance was not helping matters, either. He was dishevelled, to say the least. Bloodstains covered his clothing, and his shirt was ripped to shreds.

By this time, Dylan's perceptions were stabilizing. The ambient light seemed to be settling, and the room was no longer spinning around her. Carefully, she relaxed her grip around Kit's torso and very slowly disengaged herself from him. In turning, Dylan very nearly lost her balance. Her legs still felt a bit wobbly, but she caught herself on the metal railing of her sister's bed in time, and braced herself there.

"You alright?" Kit asked her.

His reflexes were as sharp as ever. He'd seen Dylan stumble, and threw his arms out automatically to catch her. Carefully, he now helped her back to her feet.

"Take a deep breath," he said. "It'll help. The feeling will pass. You just have to breathe through it."

"I'm fine," Dylan replied. "But for the record," she told him curtly, "that was more than just a *little* uncomfortable. I thought you said it'd be stable! You really need to work on your warnings, Kit, because *that* was awful. I feel like I've been in a train wreck…"

As she spoke, Dylan continued hobbling her way around her sister's bed. Kit muttered apologies to her as she moved, but Dylan wasn't listening anymore. She'd now caught Holly's gaze in hers and was smiling at her – the most brilliant smile she could manage, given the circumstances.

Her best friend, having had the time to shake her shock, rushed forward and took her roughly into her arms.

"Dylan! It is you! I've been so worried! I can't believe you're actually here."

Though overjoyed at seeing her friend, Holly seemed to recognize Dylan's shaken state and offered her her chair.

"Here," she said. "Sit down."

Grateful at the gesture, Dylan collapsed down into the seat and pulled herself in closer to her sister's bedside. Slowly, she reached her hands over and placed them upon Dani's forehead. She was about to close her eyes, when Kit interjected.

"Maybe you should wait a few minutes," he suggested in earnest. "Let yourself rest for a second? We just got back…"

Holly appeared confused. She stared at Kit, a look of utter bafflement in her face.

"What do you mean?" she asked him abruptly. She turned then to face Dylan, and asked her as well: "Dylan, what's he talking about?"

Her frustration seemed to be growing by the second, but no one paid her any attention. She turned again in Kit's direction, and asked in a more elevated tone this time: "Can someone *please* tell me what the *hell* is going on here?!"

Dylan ignored her friend's aggravated demands. She had neither the energy nor the will to launch into a lengthy explanation right then. And so, she chose instead to focus on Kit's concerns.

"I'm alright, Kit," she told him. "I can do this. *I want to*. Dani's waited long enough, and so have I. It's time."

Kit nodded his head in reply. Holly was still shooting both of them wild and befuddling looks of dismay. But Dylan ignored her. All of her attentions had turned to the slumbering girl in the hospital bed.

Moments later, Dylan was diving again, delving deep into Dani's head and leaving Holly, Kit, and everything else behind her. Like a magnet, she felt herself pulled towards the problem areas in her sister's skull – to the clusters of dead cells in the heart of her brain. She found them almost immediately. Tiny patches of lifeless matter at the core of Dani's head – dark and dim. It was like staring at a bundle of cavernous shadows, scattered across a sky of neon lights. The healthy cells surrounding the dead spots seemed alive with a sort of electricity – coursing with colourful currents of pink, white and yellow. The scene was stunning, and Dylan found herself in awe for a moment. She hadn't expected such a gorgeous spectacle – an orchestra of lights at the core of her sister's crown.

In staring at the sparkling scene, Dylan quickly came to recognize what work needed to be done. The lifeless patches scattered about the expanse of flashing lights needed to be restored – like holes in need of filling. Dylan took a deep breath and concentrated her mind upon them. When she exhaled, the clusters of dead cells slowly began to glow again. With but her breath, Dylan re-animated the lifeless tissues of her sister's brain. Life began anew in the neurons and synapses which for months, had lain useless and dead. The dark spots in Dani's head, once again, buzzed with energy. The damage was repaired, and soon, the tapestry was whole again – aglow with a million lights and electricity.

"What is she doing?"

Dylan could hear Holly's voice again, as she slowly retreated from her delicate operation and re-opened her eyes. In the time that she'd been gone, her friend appeared to have calmed herself. Holly merely looked curious now. She was staring over Dylan's shoulder and admiring the white glow that emanated from beneath her hands and which illuminated Dani's face.

"How is she doing that?" Holly asked, frowning.

But before Dylan or Kit could respond, they were interrupted.

Dani, the girl who for so long had lain comatose in her hospital bed, suddenly awoke. Her eyes sprung open and furiously began searching her surroundings. She looked scared at first, coughing and choking on the plastic tube, which still fed into her nose and down her throat. But then… she saw Dylan and Holly, her family, standing and watching over her, and a calmness spread through her. Tears welled in her eyes, and she smiled up at them warmly. She tried to speak, but the words caught in her still weak and obstructed throat.

The two girls standing over her bedside were overjoyed at seeing their little sister wake, at last. They were crowding her, squeezing her hand tightly and pushing themselves in closer to kiss and hug her repeatedly.

"It's a miracle," Holly exclaimed, as a single tear ran down her cheek. Her eyes spread wide and she turned then, to find Kit still standing at the foot of Dani's bed. He was smiling, watching in silence the beautiful reunion before him. He watched Dylan, especially, and Holly saw at once, the care and esteem that he held for her.

It was then that Holly finally saw what Dylan had seen in Kit, all those weeks ago. For so long, she had thought him to be the villain in their story – come to spread vile tales of fantasies and false hopes. But she'd been proven wrong. The evidence lay literally before her. Dani was awake. She was alive. *Whatever Kit was*, Holly thought, *he was good*. Her opinions of him thawed in that moment, and she realized she owed him a debt of gratitude.

"I don't know how you did it," she said to him then, "but thank you. Kit. I shouldn't ever have doubted you… I can't thank you enough, for what you've done for my family."

Her throat tightened with gratefulness, and she looked upon him with watery eyes.

Moved by her apology, Kit nodded his head then in a show of respect.

"I'll try to find a nurse or doctor," he told her. "She'll be wanting that tube out, I'm sure."

At this, he exited the room, and left the three girls to reacquaint and reconnect with one another – laughing and crying, overwhelmed with joy, and overflowing with bliss.

-- CHAPTER THIRTY-SIX --

THE CREPUSCULUM

The little Montreal apartment was alive with joy and laughter. In just a few days, the news of Danielle Dubois's recovery had spread, and Dylan and Holly had decided to throw their little sister a party, in honour of her waking. It was a strange sight. All of these people gathered in this tiny place to celebrate such an unusual event – almost like a reverse funeral or wake. Everyone their family had ever known had shown up to offer their well wishes, and to rejoice in Dani's unlikely return to life.

Dylan stood alone with her back pressed up to the kitchen counter. She was surveying the party from afar, watching their many guests happily bouncing around their little living room and mingling with one another.

Dani, herself, stood in the midst of this crowd, wearing a lovely, white dress and dangly earrings. She was the star attraction, after all, always surrounded by at least four or five people at any one time. The attention seemed to suit her though, for she was positively glowing.

Radiant, Dylan thought. Her sister, with her long locks of honey coloured curls, her deep pink cheeks and her million-dollar smile.

It was hard to believe that mere days ago, this dazzling beauty had been lost forever to an eternal sleep with zero chances of awakening. Looking at her now, she seemed no different than any of the other teenage girls at her side, giggling and whispering in each other's ears.

Dylan smiled. She was glad to see Dani so happy, surrounded by all of her friends. This was *all* Dylan had ever wanted for her little sister – to return to her the life that'd been so cruelly taken from her.

"You did good, Pickle."

Lost in thought, Dylan hadn't noticed Holly's approach. Her best friend had snuck up on her, and was now standing by her side. She was facing the kitchen counter, her back turned to the many festivities going on in the background. Looking upon her, Dylan thought she seemed a bit nervous. Holly's face was turned downwards, and she was fiddling with the leaves of a potted plant she'd removed from the living room. Her features too appeared a bit solemn.

"Is everything alright, Hol?" Dylan asked her.

Her friend didn't answer right away. She was still busying herself with the little plant in front of her, picking dead pieces from its stem and spraying it with water.

"I thought I told you that plant was a lost cause?" Dylan said, laughing. "I can't believe you're still nursing it."

Holly still didn't reply. She stopped then and looked upon Dylan with tearful eyes.

"I'm sorry," Dylan told her, feeling a bit guilty. "I was just kidding. Here." At this, she pressed a single finger against one of the plant's wilted leaves. There was a tiny flash of light, which emanated from her fingertip, and seconds later, the plant was rejuvenated – transformed into a gorgeous green shrub, complete with luscious, heart-shaped leaves and tiny white speckles.

Staring into the bright new foliage of her little bush, Holly couldn't help but smile. Her eyes dried, and she spoke at last.

"That's going to take some getting used to," she said with a small laugh, "But that's not it, Pickle." Her manner shifted, and she went on in a sadder tone: "It's just that… ever since you told me about your trip, I've been trying to find the right time… to tell you…"

Holly shrunk even further then. The party behind them was growing rowdier by the second, but the sounds of glee coming from the living room seemed to be hampering Holly's efforts at coming clean. There was a mixed look of shame and sorrow in her features. Her eyebrows were creased, and her eyes focused and intense.

"Whatever it is," Dylan told her, moving in closer towards her, "you can tell me. I promise… it'll be OK."

Holly seemed moved by her friend's sentiments. Tears fell from her eyes, as she launched into her confession, finally unburdening herself of her guilty secret:

"*I* was the one who called Luca, Dylan. *I* was the one who told him where you were going. You could have died, Pickle. And it would have been *my* fault… I thought I was helping you, but I couldn't have been more wrong. I should have *trusted* you, like you asked me to. I'm so sorry, Dyl. I wouldn't blame you, if you never spoke to me again! I've acted like such a fool these past weeks. And you were right all along. I should have listened."

In the face of Holly's revelation, however, Dylan did not flinch. Instead, she smiled, wrapped her arm around her best friend's shoulders, and pressed her forehead against hers.

"Don't be ridiculous," she told her. "I'm not angry with you. Not even a little bit. You did what you thought was right. You're always looking out for me, and I'm grateful for that. Besides, I'm sure Luca would have found me eventually, even *without* your help. So please, don't dwell on this a second longer, OK? Everything turned out alright in the end. I'm fine. Dani's fine. *Everything*… is fine. So please, go. Just enjoy the party, OK?"

Obviously relieved by her friend's response, Holly let out a sigh. She flashed Dylan a little smile, and turned then to re-join the crowd of visitors overflowing from the living room.

Dylan, on her side, resumed her surveillance of the party. She'd never been one for large gatherings, and much preferred observing such jubilance from afar.

Holly had now joined herself to a group of people gathered around a table of hors d'oeuvres. Amongst them, Dylan recognized Dr. Green and some of the hospital's staff, along with an out-of-uniform Michael with Cloud – his trusty, young pup – glued to his side. Nearby, Dylan saw her uncle Larry engaged in what appeared to be a lively conversation with their old neighbours, who'd all driven in from the countryside. Of course, all of Dani's dozens of school friends filled the remainder of the room. There was, however, *one* important individual who Dylan noticed was missing from the horde of gleeful guests.

Though unsurprised at Kit's decision to remove himself from all the commotion, Dylan set out then to locate her friend. Wandering through the mass of people, she made her way round the tiny apartment, peeking into both her own bedroom and Holly's. But Kit was nowhere to be found. At a loss, Dylan made her way to the apartment's front door.

Stepping out into the corridor, she immediately found her friendly fox, sitting by himself in the building's stairwell. His face was turned down in his lap, and he seemed absorbed by some small object, which he held in his hands. As Dylan drew nearer, she saw that the object was actually a cell phone, and that Kit was busy experimenting with its touch screen display.

"Is that my phone?" Dylan asked, as she stepped up in front of him.

Kit turned and looked at her. For a second, he seemed a bit stunned, as he looked her up and down with wide eyes.

"Yeah," he said. "Sorry. You seemed busy. So I borrowed it to call Mags."

"You're getting the hang of it, I see," Dylan teased. "I'm glad you're putting my lessons to good use!"

"Yeah," he answered, "*who knew* a phone call could *actually* be faster than travelling? I guess technology's finally caught up with me."

Dylan smiled at him, but Kit failed to return the sentiment. In fact, Dylan thought he seemed a bit troubled. She sat down next to him, but was interrupted before she could say anything.

"I never told you *why* I was in Vegas a few months ago," Kit told her. "The reason I crossed paths with your uncle, Dylan… I never told you… It was because we were chasing the *same* person – the same prize."

Dylan didn't say anything. She knew Kit well enough to know when *not* to interrupt him.

"As the Aurora," Kit said, "you have a very unique power, Dylan. One unlike *any* other in this World. It's special. I'm sure you know that now, but… what you *don't* know is that you're not the *only* one. There are *others*, like you… other families with… similarly grand gifts. They're different from yours, of course, but… passed in much the same way. *That's* who I was following that night, Dylan. The night I ran into your uncle. I was following… someone like you."

Dylan remained speechless in the face of Kit's curious tale.

"His name is 'Crepusculum'," Kit went on, "And in many ways, he's your opposite, Dylan. *Crepusculum* – it means 'dusk'. Aurora means 'dawn', if you remember? And so, we say that the Crepusculum is the Aurora's mirror, and vice versa. It's said that the Crepusculum wields the inorganic, just as the Aurora wields flesh and bone. Some say that he's the *ultimate* treasure, a source of… unending wealth and riches. In theory, he could manipulate matter into gold, much like a modern-day King Midas. And so, for ages, he's been *the* target for anyone who's anyone, looking to make a quick fortune. I'm ashamed to say that I myself… joined the hunt for him more than a few times in my life. In *our World*, hunting him has become a sport of sorts. People see the Crepusculum as a kind of, insurmountable mountain – an Everest to be conquered. But no one's *ever* been successful in tracking him down. Like the Aurora, the Crepusculum's family line has remained a secret for generations."

"Why are you telling me this?" Dylan asked brusquely. In listening to Kit's story, her manner had grown somewhat anxious.

"I'm telling you," Kit said, "because you *need* to know the dangers that are out there, Dylan. And because… I spoke to Maggie just now. She's returned from Vegas and, had some… *news*. I'm sorry to be the one to tell you, but… it looks like your uncle may have succeeded where so many others have failed. The man I was following that night, the one I suspected of being the new Crepusculum… He was murdered, not long after I was attacked. Maggie said the local authorities suspect the same man who assaulted me…"

"Luca," Dylan said, as she drew in a sharp breath.

"It's alright," Kit told her, inching himself closer towards her. "You're safe. Your family's safe. We have his dagger. He can't hurt anyone without it. We'll figure this out, Dylan. I promise."

Dylan nodded her head at him, somewhat absent-mindedly. The news had her understandably rattled, and so Kit attempted to comfort her. Gently, Dylan felt him press his lips against her forehead then and kiss her. It was the first time he'd ever been so forthright with his feelings for her, so Dylan was successfully roused from her fears.

Rising from the stairs, Kit held his hand out towards her and slowly helped her to her feet.

"You look… beautiful," he told her, "you know, in case… no one's told you yet."

Dylan looked down at her red cocktail dress and high heels. She blushed, before lifting her gaze again to find Kit still admiring her with his mysterious, maroon eyes. He smiled at her, before slowly leaning in to whisper something in her ear.

"I'll be right back," he said, gently stroking her cheek with his fingers. "Maggie wants me to go pick her up. Surprise, surprise – she loves parties!"

"OK," Dylan replied, never straying from his gaze. "Hurry back."

"Like a flash," Kit promised. And a moment later, he was gone – disappeared with nothing but a wrinkle left in the empty space before her.

The front door of the apartment opened then, and Dylan heard the sound of music emanating from within. A moment later, her sister's face popped out from behind the threshold.

"Dylan! There you are!" Dani exclaimed. "Come back inside. Come and dance with me!"

Dylan felt her heart swell unexpectedly, as she glimpsed her little sister – all smiles and sunshine – gazing at her from across the hall. Any worries she may have harboured, in that moment, evaporated on sight.

Kit's right, she thought. *We're fine. Whatever happens, we'll handle it. Together.*

And so, donning her happy face, Dylan re-joined the celebrations. Taking her little sister's hand in hers, she stepped back through her front door and into the party.

ACKNOWLEDGMENTS

When I first put pen to paper over ten years ago, I never imagined the thousands of hours of work that would eventually go into producing my first novel. *The Aurora Antidote* began as a few scribbles in a notebook, and grew into the 90,000-some words you see before you today. Needless to say, I couldn't have done it alone. I'd like to pay tribute now to those of you without whom it wouldn't have been possible.

First and foremost, I thank my parents and siblings. Mom, Dad, Sean and Stephanie. Without you, I would not have grown into the woman I am today. You helped fill my head with hopes and dreams, and nurtured the imagination that made this book possible. Mom, it is likely this novel would never have been written, but for our weekly visits to the Ottawa Public Library growing up. Thank you for imbuing me with your love of books. Dad, I doubt I would have had the perseverance to see this book through to the end, if not for you. You always pushed me to challenge myself, and never once, let me abandon my goals or commitments. Sean and Stephanie, I could not have asked for a better set of siblings than you. You have been my best friends and companions my entire life, supporting me through all of my endeavours. Thank you for suffering through dozens upon dozens of drafts, and for your insightful and helpful comments throughout this long and arduous process.

To my very first Beta Readers, Alexander Breeze and Emma Robinson. You'll never know how thrilled I was to hear your words of praise upon finishing my novel for the first time. It is encouragement like yours, which feeds me to continue on with this anthology.

A big thank you to my editor, Kim Graff, without whom my novel would have been much less succinct. The tools and advice you provided me with were instrumental in the final stages of editing, and made me a better writer.

I'd like to thank my friend, Mionah Larsen, for consulting with me early on, regarding the cover art for this edition of my novel.

A big thank you goes out to the talented Nikkie Stinchcombe, for helping me bring my characters to life through her gorgeous artwork.

To my kindred spirit and fellow author, Ryan Crawford. Thank you for all of your invaluable guidance and advice throughout the publishing process. I look forward to our continued collaboration, and have no doubt that our friendship will bear but better and brighter fruit down the road.

To my friend Nana Parry, who painstakingly read every first draft I ever wrote. Thank you for your always-unwavering support throughout these many years.

And finally, to my husband, Sebastian. You are my everything, my rock. Thank you for giving me the final push I needed to take the last plunge. Without your encouragement, it is likely this novel would have been left forever entombed in my laptop computer.

ABOUT THE AUTHOR

ELA HUGH is a Canadian author and lawyer. She was born and raised in Canada, to parents of French Canadian and Chinese Jamaican decent. From a young age, Ela was insatiably curious and longed to explore the world around her. Before she was ever able to travel, Ela satiated her thirst for adventure through a love of books. In her youth, she read every mystery she could lay her hands on, including every story ever written by Agatha Christie and Arthur Conan Doyle. Her love of mysteries is paralleled only by her passion for the fantastical. She is an avid Trekkie, devoted Marvel fan, and general supporter of all things 'magic' or 'make-believe'.

The Aurora Antidote first took shape in Ela's mind over ten years ago, following her second year of law school and a summer spent travelling in Japan, China and South East Asia. The tale and many of its characters have their roots in East Asian mythology.

www.elahugh.com

Follow Ela on and

@elahugh

Dylan and Kit will return in…

THE
CREPUSCULUM CURSE

COMING SOON